RENEGADE

"*Renegade* storms into the Susan May Warren universe with unending love and fierce protectiveness, and it doesn't get any better than this! *Renegade* is everything I want in the first book in a new series (and, let's be real, just in every book always): it introduces a great setting and the people who live there, complete with setting up controversy and conflict between both the people and that setting. When you add in the amazing lead characters, high stakes action, tender romantic moments, and lots of wise lessons, this is a book you won't be able to put down. Keep'em coming, please, Susan May Warren."

—AMY, GOODREADS

"What an amazing start to a new series. If you have read Chasing Fire: Montana and Chasing Fire: Alaska series, you would have noticed there were a group called The Trouble Boys. *Renegade* follows Rowen "Hammer" Wallace and Sierra Blackwell's story. Packed full of suspense, cattle rustling, and danger, Renegade is also about found family, family dynamics, secrets, and second chance romance."

—ALLYSON, GOODREADS

"I absolutely loved this book! I knew the moment I started reading that I was completely and totally hooked. If you like second chance romance stories with suspense, mystery, found family vibes, and even a redemptive arc, this is the book you need to be reading. And how fitting is it that it is book one in the series? I have a feeling this whole series is going to be a set of page turners!"

—JO|RUTH READS, GOODREADS

RENEGADE

HEROES OF RENEGADE

RENEGADE

HEROES OF
RENEGADE

RENEGADE

SUSAN MAY WARREN

SUNRISE
PUBLISHING

Renegade
Heroes of Renegade: Book 1 | The Brave

Copyright © 2026 Sunrise Media Group LLC
Print ISBN: 978-1-966463-74-0

This book is a work of fiction. Names, characters, places, and incidents are either products of the author's imagination or used fictitiously. Any similarity to actual people, organizations, and/or events is purely coincidental.

All Scripture quotations, unless otherwise indicated, are taken from the The ESV® Bible (The Holy Bible, English Standard Version®), © 2001 by Crossway, a publishing ministry of Good News Publishers. Used by permission. All rights reserved.

For more information about Susan May Warren please access the author's website at www.susanmaywarren.com

Published in the United States of America.
Cover Design: Sunrise Media Group LLC

Soli Deo Gloria

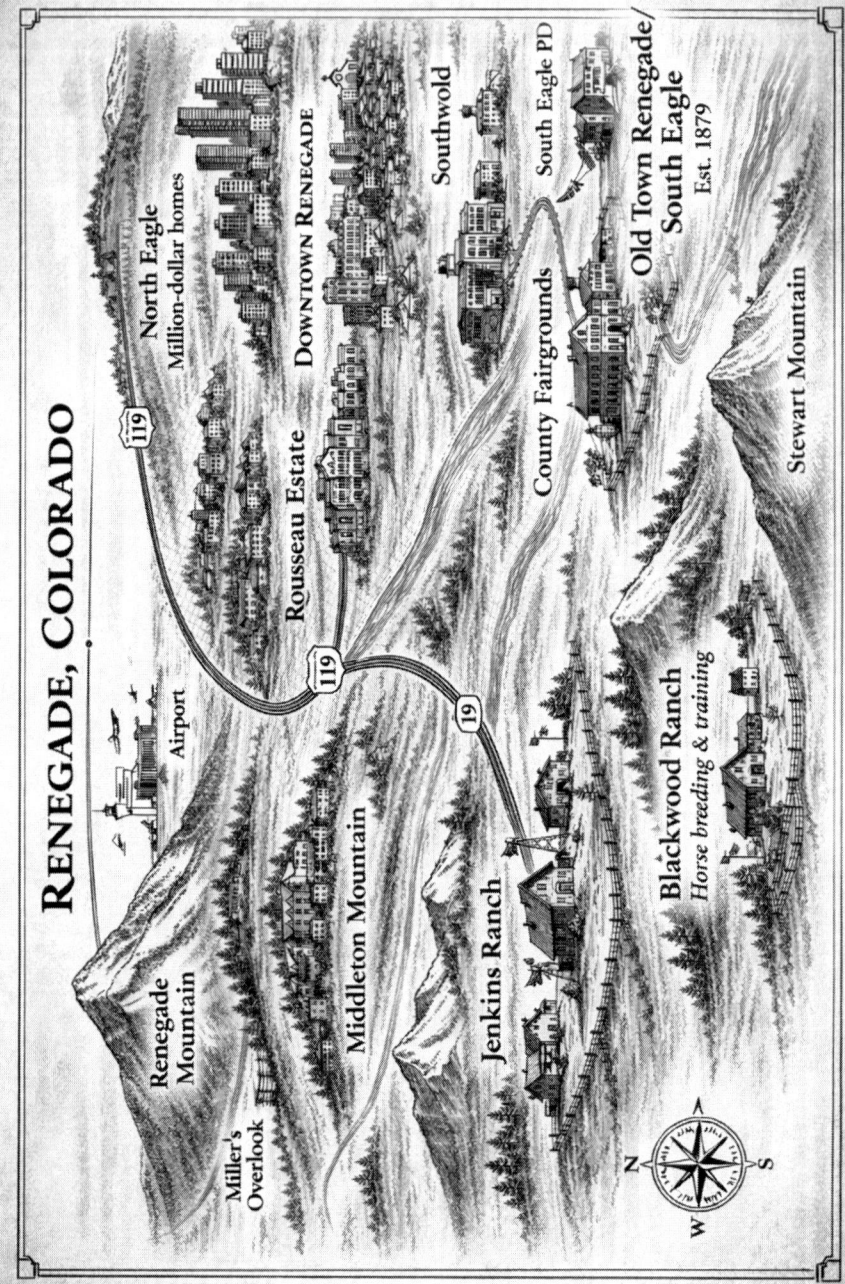

RENEGADE, COLORADO

119

119

19

Renegade Mountain

Miller's Overlook

Middleton Mountain

Jenkins Ranch

Blackwood Ranch
Horse breeding & training

Airport

North Eagle
Million-dollar homes

Rousseau Estate

DOWNTOWN RENEGADE

Southwold

County Fairgrounds

South Eagle PD

Old Town Renegade/
South Eagle
Est. 1879

Stewart Mountain

N W S E

Whom have I in heaven but you? And earth has nothing I desire besides you. My flesh and my heart may fail, but God is the strength of my heart and my portion forever.

PSALM 73:25-26 NIV

ONE

TROUBLE WAS STALKING HER. AND SIERRA WASN'T keen on being anyone's lunch. Especially not a one-hundred-and-fifty-pound mountain lion, with blood on its teeth.

Sierra Blackwood stood on the foothills trail, her breath forming white puffs in the October morning air. The tracks in the frost-covered pine needles told the story—massive paws four inches across, with claw marks extending beyond the toe pads. Fresh. Maybe thirty minutes ahead of them.

"Jackson, you see those prints?" Sierra's voice carried across the narrow trail, pitched low enough not to spook the cat but loud enough for her SAR team to hear.

Jackson Stewart materialized from behind a cluster of scrub oak, his military training evident in the way he moved—silent, controlled, eyes constantly scanning. His tactical gear was worn but functional, the kind of setup that screamed *former military.* "Yep. Big tom. Following the same trail as our missing hikers."

"We need to get moving if we want to find him first." She picked up her pace on the trail, already sweaty under her jacket.

The foothills rolled away toward the distant peaks covered in a mix of pine, aspen, and juniper. This terrain sat between the high country and the valley floor, where her ranch spread out in the distance. She could actually see the corner of her property from here—the old fence line that marked the boundary between Blackwood land and the national forest. The trail they followed wound through BLM land before connecting to the network of old mining roads that crisscrossed the area.

This was familiar country—harsh, but more forgiving than the high peaks. Every ridge held memories of childhood rides, every valley a lesson learned about reading the land. The terrain still demanded respect. One wrong step on these loose rocks could send a person tumbling down a thirty-foot drop into the creek bed below.

And out here, alone, that mistake could be your last. The vastness swallowed sound, swallowed hope. A person could scream until their voice gave out and never reach another soul.

She pressed forward, following the faint trail that wound between massive boulders and stands of pine.

Roland and Suzette Lopez, the couple from Denver, had been missing for eighteen hours now. City folks, probably wearing cotton sweatshirts and running shoes, definitely hypothermic by now if they'd survived the night. The temperature had dropped to twenty-eight degrees, and the wind chill made it worse.

"Kevin, Paige, you copy?" Sierra keyed her radio.

"Copy, Sierra." Kevin's voice crackled through the static. "We're about two hundred yards southeast of your position. Found some fabric caught on a deadfall."

"What color?"

"Blue. Looks like fleece."

Sierra closed her eyes briefly. Suzette Lopez had been wearing a blue fleece jacket when they'd started their "easy day hike" yesterday morning. Easy. Right. Nothing about the Renegade wilderness was easy, especially not in October, when the weather could turn lethal in minutes.

Their teenage children had called the Renegade Parks and Rec service when they hadn't returned home last night.

"Stay put. Don't approach until we clear the area. We've got a cat sighting up here."

"Mountain lion?" Paige's voice, pitched higher. She was newer to SAR, a substitute teacher who'd joined the team six months ago with her SAR K9. Good intentions, but she spooked easily.

"Affirmative. Jackson and I are tracking north along the ridge. You and Kevin work the lower trail system. Radio check every fifteen minutes."

Sierra clipped the radio back to her utility belt and pulled out her GPS unit. The coordinates put them at 6,800 feet elevation, still high enough that the air bit at her lungs with each breath, but low enough that the terrain was manageable. She'd been riding these hills since she was old enough to walk.

"Blood trail's getting heavier." Jackson pointed to dark spots on the granite slab ahead of them. "But it's not human."

Sierra moved closer, studying the crimson droplets that dotted the rock face. Too much blood for a small animal. Deer, maybe. Or elk. "He made a kill recently. That's good news and bad news."

"Good news—he might not be hunting. Bad news—he's territorial and won't want to share his territory with hikers."

"Or searchers." Sierra shouldered her pack and checked her bear spray. Fat lot of good it would do against a mountain lion, but protocol was protocol. "Stay twenty feet back. We don't want to corner him."

They moved along the ridge, following the intermittent blood trail and the deep gouges in the earth where something heavy had been dragged. If the hikers had stumbled across something that scared them, they might have panicked and run. Running was the worst thing you could do around a predator, but city folks didn't know that.

Her radio crackled. "Sierra, this is base. How's your progress?"

She keyed the mic. "Still tracking. Found evidence of a mountain lion kill in the area. Hikers may have encountered the cat."

"Copy that. South Eagle police are requesting an ETA."

Sierra bit back a word. The last thing she needed was pressure from law enforcement. "Tell them we'll have an update in thirty minutes."

The truth was, they might not find the Lopez couple at all. The wilderness had swallowed people before, leaving behind nothing but questions and grief.

Probably it was good to be out here. Kept her mind off the hole Grandpa Elway's death left in her life, the ranch's mounting bills, the rodeo in two weeks that gave her son a reason to go to school, maybe figure out how to work out his grief.

She sighed. Focus, Sierra. She'd deal with the dead after she saved the living.

She picked up the pace, following the blood trail as it curved around a massive boulder formation. The granite here was streaked with quartz veins that caught the morning sun and threw it back in brilliant flashes.

"Movement." Jackson's voice was barely a whisper.

Sierra froze, following his gaze to a cluster of pine trees about fifty yards ahead. A tawny shape moved between the trunks— fluid, powerful, built for killing. The mountain lion paused, massive head turning in their direction.

"Easy," Sierra whispered. "Back away slowly. No sudden movements."

The cat's ears flattened against its skull. Not good. That was aggressive posturing, the kind that preceded an attack. Sierra reached for her radio, no quick movements, everybody stay calm.

"Base, this is Sierra. We have visual contact with a mountain lion. Large tom, approximately one-fifty, showing aggressive behavior. Requesting immediate assistance from Fish and Wildlife."

"Copy, Sierra. ETA on Fish and Wildlife is forty-five minutes."

Forty-five minutes? They'd be cat food before then.

The mountain lion took a step toward them, yellow eyes fixed on Sierra with the kind of intensity that made her skin crawl. She'd encountered bears before, even aggressive bulls during breeding season, but nothing with the coiled lethal grace of a hunting cat.

"Jackson," she said softly. "You still have that sidearm?"

"Yeah, but—"

"Don't shoot unless he charges. Gunshots might spook him off, or they might bring him straight at us."

Jackson nodded, but slowly withdrew the gun.

The cat disappeared back into the trees, leaving nothing but the whisper of wind through pine needles.

"He's still out there," Jackson said.

"I know." Sierra studied the terrain ahead. The blood trail continued along the ridge, disappearing toward the old mining district that dotted this section of the foothills. If the hikers had gone that direction, they were in serious trouble. The area was a maze of abandoned shafts and unstable ground.

"Sierra!" Kevin's voice exploded from her radio. "We've got them! Both hikers, alive but in rough shape. We need immediate extraction."

She let out a coiled breath. Glanced at Jackson, who also nodded. "Copy, Kevin. What's your location?"

"About three hundred yards down the south face, near an old mining entrance. Sending you coordinates now."

"Medical status?"

"Male has a broken leg, possible concussion. Female is hypothermic but responsive. They're both scared out of their minds."

"Roger that. Jackson and I are en route. Have Paige prep the emergency shelter and warming packs."

They worked their way down the slope, Sierra checking occasionally for signs of the cat. The terrain here was riddled with old mining claims, most of them abandoned since the 1880s when silver played out. The park service had tried to seal the dangerous shafts, but there were too many scattered across the hillsides.

By the time they reached Kevin's position, Sierra could see why the hikers had taken refuge here. The old mining shaft was carved into the hillside, its entrance partially concealed by fallen timber and scrub brush. The wooden support beams, gray and weathered from decades of mountain storms, sagged at dangerous angles. Rusty cable and broken equipment littered the ground around the entrance, remnants of some long-abandoned silver claim.

Not a place she'd want to spend the night, but it had probably saved their lives.

Inside the mine entrance, two figures huddled together under emergency blankets. Suzette Lopez—late forties, wearing that bright blue jacket, albeit torn, that had helped them spot her—sat with her husband's head in her lap. Roland lay with one leg bent at an unnatural angle, his face pale with pain and cold.

"How long have they been like this?" Sierra knelt beside Roland, checking his pulse. Strong but rapid—shock, probably from the broken leg.

"Hard to say. Suzette's been pretty shaken up. Says they've been here since yesterday evening."

Sierra nodded, pulling out her medical kit. "What happened? How did you get hurt?"

Suzette's eyes focused on Sierra's face with obvious effort. "We were hiking. Following the trail toward the creek. Then we heard—" She shuddered. "A gunshot. Close. Really close."

"Where exactly?"

"Maybe a quarter mile from here? We were near that old ranch house when we heard it. Roland said we should go back, but then we saw someone in the trees. A man."

Sierra's blood turned to ice. "What did he look like?"

"I don't know. Like a hunter, maybe? He had a rifle. He was with another man. They were arguing and . . . then when he saw us, one of the men took off. And so did we."

"Why'd you run?"

"Too many movies?" Suzette made a face. "Instinct, maybe. When we heard the gunshot, Roland grabbed my hand and we took off through the trees. But the terrain was so rough, and it was getting dark. Roland tripped on a root and went down hard. I heard his leg snap." Suzette's voice broke. "I managed to get him here, but he's been in and out of consciousness all night."

Sierra processed this information while splinting Roland's leg.

"This man you saw," Jackson said. "Did he follow you?"

"I don't know. Maybe. I kept looking over my shoulder, but it was getting dark. Every shadow looked like someone watching us."

Sierra keyed her radio. "Base, this is Sierra. We need immediate helicopter extraction for one broken leg, possible concussion. Also requesting law enforcement support. Hikers report encountering armed individual in the area."

"Copy, Sierra. Sheriff's deputies are en route to your location."

They worked to stabilize Roland for transport.

"What house is she talking about?" Jackson asked.

"Oh, it's the old Wallace house," Sierra said. "It's on Jenkins land, but near the creek that forms the boundary between the Jenkins land and the national forest. And our land is right next door. Paige, help me get him on the stretcher," Sierra said. "We need to move before that weather hits."

Dark clouds were building over the western peaks, and the wind was picking up. They had maybe two hours before the storm arrived.

As they carried Roland down the mountainside, Suzette walking beside them, Sierra couldn't shake the feeling that they were being watched. The hair on the back of her neck prickled every time they passed through a stand of trees or around a bend in the trail.

"There." Suzette suddenly stopped, pointing to an opening in the pine trees. And through them, across the river, Sierra spotted the road that ran between her property and the Jenkins place. "That's where we saw him."

And the old Wallace place. The house commanded a clear view of the entire valley below, including the trail system and the distant ranch lands. The yellow single-story frame house sat in a clearing surrounded by towering cottonwoods and scrub oak, weathered but still solid after decades of mountain winters. A covered porch ran across the front, supported by simple wooden posts, while a lean-to addition stretched along one side. The metal roof showed patches of rust, and several windows were boarded up with plywood, but the structure looked sturdy enough.

The place had that abandoned look of a homestead where the family had simply walked away one day and never come back.

Really, they had, according to . . .

"Yeah, no one lives there now," she said, and made a mental note to ask Detective Martinelli to swing by. Not that trespassers mattered—no one was coming home to claim it.

The ambulance was waiting just ahead, in the trailhead parking lot. Jackson greeted his coworkers, then helped load Roland into the ambulance.

"You okay?" Jackson said as the ambulance drove away.

She'd been staring at the house, of course. She'd only visited once, and that had . . . that had gone badly.

"I'm fine. I need to get into town and pick up Huck."

Paige walked up with her German shepherd, Rex, at her side. The K-9 handler's radio crackled in her hand. "Police want to debrief you and your team. Can you come in?"

Sierra keyed the mic, her eyes still fixed on the hills above her ranch. "Copy, base. We're on our way."

She turned away from the house. The memories. The trauma. The sense that someone might be watching her—

Rex suddenly went rigid, his ears pricked forward. A low growl rumbled in his chest.

"What's he alerting on?" Jackson asked.

Paige studied her dog's body language. "Something's wrong. Rex, show me."

The German shepherd trotted toward a rocky outcrop behind them, about thirty yards from the old house, on the Blackwood side of the road, where another abandoned mine shaft cut into the hillside. This one was smaller than where they'd found the hikers, barely wide enough for a man to crawl through. Rex stopped at the edge of a shallow gully that ran alongside the mine entrance, his hackles raised.

"There." Paige pointed. "In the wash."

Sierra's heart hammered as she approached the depression. At first, she saw only rocks and scattered debris washed down from the hillside. Then her eyes focused on what didn't belong—a boot. Attached to a leg that wasn't moving.

"Oh no." Jackson scrambled down into the gully.

A man lay crumpled in the rocky bottom, his body twisted at an unnatural angle. He wore work clothes—jeans, flannel shirt, worn leather boots. His gray hair was matted with blood, and his face—

Sierra's knees nearly buckled. "Tom. Tom Hendrick. He owns the ranch two sections over from ours. His family's been ranching these hills as long as we have."

"Don't touch anything," Jackson said. He was already pulling out his phone.

Sierra stared at Tom's body, her mind racing. The position told a story—he'd been running when he went down, maybe trying to reach the cover of the mine shaft? Dark stains spread across his flannel shirt, and she could see the ragged hole where a bullet had torn through his chest.

Jackson hung up. "Police are sending a team. We need to secure the area and wait for them." He looked at Sierra. "We got this from here. Go get Huck."

"Thanks." She shoved her hands into her pockets, unable to shake the image of Tom's body crumpled in that rocky wash.

There was a killer in the hills. And it was dangerously close to her backyard.

Not for the first time, she wanted to stand, hands to the heavens, and scream.

And hope that somehow, she might be heard.

This was a bad idea. Rowan "Hammer" Wallace knew it in his gut. And his gut was never wrong.

He gripped the steering wheel of his Ford F-150 as the highway curved down from the mountain pass, revealing the Renegade valley spread out below him like a postcard from his past. The town had grown since he'd left—a lot. Sure, he'd kept to his side of town—the original core of Renegade, now called South Eagle, once a sleepy ranch community of thirty thousand, a forgotten corner just outside and to the southeast of larger Renegade. But now the city sprawled across the valley floor and beyond, even to the far ranchlands to the south.

The modest high-rise downtown rose from the center, but along the foothills to the north, new developments climbed the slopes in terraced subdivisions. Million-dollar homes dotted the mountainsides to the west, their glass facades catching the afternoon sun. To the south, the sprawling campus of what looked like a tech company, all modern glass and steel, gleamed in the afternoon sunlight. And what looked like a college area to the southwest.

"Look at that," Mack said from the passenger seat, pressing his face to the window. "It's nearly as big as Colorado Springs."

Luca Saxon leaned forward from the back seat. "Mountain towns always blow up like this. Rich folks from Denver discover them, property values skyrocket, and suddenly you've got Starbucks where the feed store used to be."

Some things were exactly as Hammer remembered though. The mountains still dominated the skyline, their granite peaks catching clouds that promised snow. The Redbank River still wound through the valley, though now it was lined with bike paths and pocket parks instead of cattle fencing.

Saxon wasn't wrong.

"We grew up on the outskirts—near the original settlement of Renegade." Hammer got off the highway and headed toward old Main Street. "It was all pickup trucks and ranch hands, a Western Mayberry. Sort of its own pocket community."

Thankfully, the bones of the old town were still here. The original Renegade community bank, the central brick schoolhouse, the street lanterns that lined a storybook street. The courthouse sat on its corner lot, red brick and white columns exactly as he remembered. The hardware store still bore the same hand-painted sign, though it now shared a block with a yoga studio and an organic coffee roaster.

"There." Mack pointed ahead. "At least some things haven't changed."

The Renegade Café occupied what had once upon a time been a soda fountain, complete with a long counter, round stools, and a jukebox in the corner. Red neon in the windows, hand-painted menu boards, and a sign that read *World Famous Chicken Fried Steak* in the same font Hammer remembered from twenty years ago.

Hammer pulled into a parking space directly in front, his truck looking out of place among the Subarus and BMWs that lined Main Street.

"You look like you're about to face a firing squad," Saxon said, cutting through Hammer's thoughts. "It's just lunch."

"In a town where everyone thinks I'm dead." Hammer's voice carried the controlled edge that made rookie firefighters step back and listen. "Where I've been dead for the better part of three years."

Mack shifted in his seat, still protecting the ribs that had been crushed in that bus rollover in Alaska six weeks ago. "Nobody's gonna recognize you. You were eighteen when you left. You're built different now."

Saxon snorted. "Built different. That's one way to put it."

Hammer ignored the comment. Two hundred pounds of muscle earned through Delta Force training and three years of wildland firefighting wasn't something you hid under civilian clothes. But Mack was right about one thing—the boy who'd run away after that final confrontation with his stepfather was gone. What sat in this truck was a man who'd survived things that would break most people.

"Besides," Mack continued, "we're not stayin' long. Just lunch, and then I want to drive out and see Dad."

Dad. Hammer let the word sit. Not *his* dad, of course. His dad was buried in a corner of land that time had forgotten. Next to his mother, but she'd come later, after he'd left Renegade.

But Mack's dad was still alive and probably terrorizing whatever woman was unfortunate enough to be in his orbit. Except now he was *Mayor* Alden Jenkins, with a title and so-called respectability that made Hammer's skin crawl.

But of course Mack wanted to see him. Because apparently Mack had a super-short memory. And a whole lot of forgiveness.

Not Hammer, thanks. "We're not going there, Mack."

"He's my father."

"He's a monster." The words came out flat, final. The same tone Hammer used when ordering a crew to evacuate a fire zone.

Mack's jaw tightened. "That's not how I remember it."

"Because you were eight when I left. And you don't remember the exciting parts. You remember the guy who taught you to throw a baseball and helped with homework. That's not the guy I knew."

He left out the rest, but it went something like, *not the jerk who'd beaten Hammer bloody every time he'd gotten mouthy*. Mack had been too young to understand why Hammer always had bruises, why he'd started spending so much time at the Blackwood ranch.

"Maybe he's sorry. At least, that's what he said to me."

Hammer just stared at him, the words gone.

"We eating or arguing?" Saxon opened his door, letting the October air sweep through the cab. "Because I'm starving, and that place smells like bacon."

South Eagle Police Station sat three buildings down, followed by the fire station, both modern brick structures that looked out of place among the weathered storefronts and carefully preserved historic buildings. An EMS truck was parked outside, rear doors open, paramedics unloading equipment. Hammer cataloged the scene automatically—serious call, not a routine transport. The kind of emergency that got everyone's attention.

"Looks like excitement," Saxon observed, following Hammer's gaze.

"Hope everyone's okay." Mack's voice carried genuine concern. He'd always been the one with the soft heart, even as a kid.

They pushed through the diner's front door, and Hammer was immediately transported back in time. The renovation had been done with care—the original bank's high ceilings and stone walls provided a dignified backdrop for the classic diner fixtures. Red vinyl booths lined the windows, chrome stools sat at a lunch counter that might have been salvaged from the 1950s, and the smell of coffee and grease filled the air.

"Sit anywhere you like, boys." The voice came from behind the counter, where a woman in her sixties was refilling salt shakers.

Gray hair pulled back in a practical bun, coffee-stained apron tied around a sturdy frame, hands that spoke of thirty years slinging hash and pouring coffee.

Hammer knew those hands. Knew that voice.

Dolores Simpson. Dolly to everyone who'd ever sat in one of her booths. She'd worked at the café when Hammer was in middle school, always ready with a sympathetic ear and an extra piece of pie for a kid whose home life was complicated.

"Back booth okay?" Saxon was already heading toward the corner, where they'd have a clear view of the street and multiple exits. Old habits.

Hammer followed, keeping his head down, hoping ten years and sixty pounds of additional muscle would be enough of a disguise. But when Dolly approached their table with a coffee pot and three mugs, her steps slowed.

"Heaven Almighty!" She nearly dropped the coffee pot on the table. "You've got to be kidding me!"

Nice. Now the entire world knew about the resurrection of Rowan Wallace.

"Rowan Wallace. I thought you were dead."

Yep, the diner went quiet. Conversations stopped mid-sentence, forks paused halfway to mouths, and every head in the place turned toward their booth.

Don't. Run. But yeah, his legs were itching. "Ma'am, I think you might have me confused with someone else." His voice stayed level, controlled, but Dolly's expression didn't change.

"Don't you 'ma'am' me, Rowan Sean Wallace. I changed your diapers when your mama brought you in here as a baby. And Mack—look how you've grown up." She grabbed a napkin and wiped the table where coffee had spilled.

She wiped her cheek with the back of her hand.

"It's okay, Dolly," Hammer said softly.

She looked up, met his eyes. "Oh, your mother would have

24

been overjoyed to know you came back." She looked up. "See, Maggie? I told you. He's not lost." She even winked as if she might be speaking through the unseen veil.

And now he couldn't move, his throat tightening. "Yeah." *Not lost.* That might be an overstatement.

"I'm sorry for the shock."

"Shock? Honey, *shock* doesn't begin to cover it." She wiped her hands on her apron, studying both their faces like she was memorizing every detail. "You both look good. Older, bigger, but good. Healthy."

"Thank you."

"Your mama would be so proud. God rest her soul." She turned to Mack. "And your daddy—well, he's gonna be beside himself when he hears you're back."

Hammer looked away.

"We're going to stop by the ranch later," Mack said, shooting a glance at Hammer.

"You should do that," Dolly said. "He's got an office in the town hall. Keeps regular hours, Monday through Friday." She paused. "Though I reckon he's gonna want to know about Rowan here. Last I heard, he was real torn up about losing him."

Hammer could be ill, right here. More likely the jerk was relieved that his biggest threat was out of the picture.

"Dolly, maybe we could keep this between us for now?" Hammer kept his voice casual. "We're just here for a day, and I'd hate to cause a stir."

"Course, honey. Though word's gonna get around anyway. You know how this part of town is. I'll get you some waters. Or do you want a root beer?" She winked.

He smiled. Nodded.

Saxon had picked up a menu. "What's good here?"

"Everything. But if you want my opinion, get the green chile cheeseburger. Best in three counties." She leaned in. "Never mind the chicken fried steak sign."

Saxon raised an eyebrow as she disappeared into the kitchen. "She's interesting."

"Yeah. Our mother's best friend," Hammer said. And shoot, he could hear his name being whispered, spreading through the diner like wildfire.

"Well," Saxon said, settling back in his seat, "so much for keeping a low profile."

"I was hoping for a little more time before everyone found out. By suppertime, half the county will know we're back."

"Wasn't that the point?" Mack said. "I mean—now that San-chez's father's been found, the charade is over. The Trouble Boys can come out of hiding. Wasn't that the point of coming back—to check on Sierra? To make sure she's okay after losing her grand-father?"

Saxon grunted. Set down the menu. "Not so easy not being dead anymore."

No duh. Because of course, Hammer's thoughts went immedi-ately to Sierra. How did a guy tell someone he'd abandoned that he'd been alive for three years while they thought he was dead? How did he explain that he'd let her grieve, knowingly?

A man approached a table next to theirs, lean and athletic with dark hair and a badge clipped to his belt. Detective, based on the shield design. Early thirties, with sharp eyes and the kind of confident bearing that came from military or law enforcement training. Clean-shaven, with an easy smile that didn't quite mask the watchful intelligence beneath.

He pulled up a chair and settled in with a weary sigh. "Hey, Dolly. Coffee when you get a chance?"

"Course, Mike." Dolly appeared with a fresh pot, filling his mug without being asked. "You look beat. Long day?"

"Getting longer by the minute." He took a grateful sip. "Thanks."

26

"That EMS truck outside earlier—everything okay?" Dolly's voice carried the kind of concern that came from thirty years of knowing everyone's business.

"Missing hikers. Search and rescue found them about an hour ago, both suffering from exposure. They'll be fine, but it was touch and go for a while." The man rubbed his forehead. "But that's not the worst of it. They found a body up there too. Near the Wallace place."

Hammer's coffee mug stopped halfway to his lips.

"A body?" Dolly's voice dropped to a whisper. "Who?"

"Tom Hendrick. Looks like he was shot."

"Oh no, not Tom." She covered her mouth.

"I know. The chief drove out personally to talk to his wife. Sierra Blackwood found him."

"That poor woman. Hasn't she been through enough?" Dolly shook her head. "You make sure you find the killer, Detective Martinelli." She walked away.

The name, the entire conversation, hit Hammer like a physical blow. He set down his mug carefully, keeping his expression neutral. But was Sierra in trouble?

"Shot?" Saxon leaned forward slightly. "Hunting accident?"

Detective Martinelli glanced over at their table, seeming to notice them for the first time. "Sorry, didn't mean to include you folks in police business. Just been a whopper of a day."

"No problem," Hammer said, his voice steady. "We couldn't help but overhear. You said this happened up by the Wallace place?"

"You know the area?"

"Used to," Hammer said, lifting a shoulder. "Haven't been back in years, but I remember that old house up there. Surprised anyone was out that way."

"Tom Hendrick was asking a lot of questions lately," Dolly said, refilling Detective Martinelli's coffee. "About mining rights and such."

Detective Martinelli shot her a look. "Dolly—"

"What? It's true." She gestured toward a corner booth with her coffee pot. "Tom and old Commissioner Elway used to sit right there every Thursday morning for years. Regular as clockwork. Last time they were in together—must have been two weeks before Elway died—Tom had worked himself into such a lather about those mining rights. Going on and on about mineral surveys and who was buying up water rights." Her voice softened. "Poor Elway just sat there listening, the way he always did. Never said much, but you could tell he was taking it all in. Man had the patience of a saint."

She paused, wiping her eyes with the corner of her apron. "Lord, I miss that man. Elway had a way of making everyone feel heard, you know? Never judged, never rushed anybody. Just listened."

"Commissioner Elway retired about three years ago, didn't he?" Detective Martinelli said gently.

"That's right. Turned in his badge and said he was going to spend his golden years fishing and working his ranch." Dolly's voice grew heavy. "Then that ATV accident took him just like that. Found him out on his back forty with that machine rolled over on top of him. They said it was a heart attack that caused the crash, but . . ."

She trailed off, glancing around the diner as if she'd said too much.

"But what?" Hammer asked quietly, but he could barely hear over the thunder of his heartbeat.

"But nothing. Just old-man talk. Tom took Elway's death real hard, that's all. Said he'd lost his best friend and the only person around here who understood what was really going on."

"What's going on?" Hammer felt Saxon's eyes on him, but kept his own gaze fixed on Detective Martinelli.

"And I'll take that coffee to go, Dolly." Martinelli stood up. Turned to Hammer. "You from around here?"

Sort of.

"Yes," Mack said. "I'm Mack Jenkins. And this is my brother." He held out his hand to the detective.

"Jenkins—"

"Yes," Hammer said. "That Jenkins."

Martinelli glanced at Rowan. "Then you're the dead older son."

Hammer raised an eyebrow.

Martinelli cocked his head. "Interesting. Well, welcome back, I guess. You still in the military?"

Oof, the man knew too much, maybe, but, "Nope."

"You knew Elway, then. Good man."

"I did." He met Martinelli's eyes, even as something cold settled in his chest. Elway Blackwood had been more than a good man—he'd been a lifeline. The steady presence who'd shown a trauma-tized ten-year-old what real strength looked like. Who'd taught him that power could be used to protect instead of terrorize.

"How's Sierra handling it?" The words slipped out before Hammer could stop them.

"Sierra? About like you'd expect. That woman's tough as nails, but losing her grandfather hit her hard. They were close, especially after her parents died when she was young." Martinelli studied Hammer's face. "You know the family?"

"We went to school together."

It was true, as far as it went. They'd also spent years as insepara-ble best friends, another two as teenage sweethearts, and one night as lovers before everything fell apart. But Detective Martinelli didn't need those details.

"She's been having some trouble lately," Martinelli continued. "Cattle rustling, equipment vandalism. Nothing too serious yet, but it's got her on edge."

"Any idea who's behind it?"

"Could be anyone. Hard times make people desperate, and there's been a lot of hard times around here lately. We're keeping an eye on things, but with the city expanding, the police force is thinning, and with only four detectives . . ." He shrugged. "We do what we can."

"Sounds like you need some help. Maybe in the area of private investigation?" Saxon said.

Martinelli raised an eyebrow.

Saxon grinned.

A radio crackled from Martinelli's belt. He unclipped it, listening to a burst of static and code numbers that meant nothing to Hammer but brought the detective to his feet. Dolly brought out his coffee.

"Got to run. Another call." He pulled a business card from his wallet. "Nice meeting you . . ."

"Rowan. Wallace."

Detective Martinelli raised an eyebrow. "Wallace."

"Mm-hmm." Hammer made no other comment.

"Okay. If you're planning to stick around, give me a call. We could use someone with your background."

"My background?"

"Military experience, leadership skills."

He headed for the door, leaving Hammer staring at the business card. Detective Michael Martinelli, South Eagle Police Station.

"Interesting," Saxon said. "Sounds like your girlfriend could use some help."

"She's not my *girlfriend*." Hammer slipped the card into his shirt pocket. "That was a long time ago."

"Uh-huh." Saxon's grin was all teeth. "Went to school together?"

Before Hammer could respond, Dolly appeared with fresh coffee and a plate of green chile cheeseburgers they hadn't ordered. The smell of grilled beef and roasted chiles filled the air.

"On the house," she said, refilling their mugs. "Consider it a welcome-home present."

"Dolly, you don't have to—"

"Hush. I've been feeding hungry boys for thirty years. I know one when I see one." She patted Hammer's shoulder. "Eat up. You look like you haven't had a decent meal in weeks."

Saxon bit into his burger with obvious appreciation. "This is incredible. What kind of chiles are these?"

"Hatch green chiles, straight from New Mexico. We get them roasted fresh every fall." Dolly beamed at the praise. "I've got apple pie too, if you boys have room."

A commotion outside caught Hammer's attention. Through the large front windows, he could see people gathering near the police station. The EMS truck was pulling away, lights flashing but no siren—a good sign. Whatever emergency they'd responded to was under control.

Then he saw it.

Parked in front of South Eagle Elementary School, an old beet-red 1968 vintage Ford F-100, with three on the tree and that white leather bench seat.

Time pinned him to the booth.

Especially when the driver's door opened and Sierra Blackwood stepped out.

Ten years collapsed into nothing. She was still small, maybe five foot five in her work boots, but she moved with the same confident grace that had captivated him as a teenager. Long dark hair caught the afternoon light as it fell in waves over her shoulders, framing a face that could have been carved from memory—every detail exactly as he'd carried it through a decade of trying to forget. The plaid blue flannel shirt she wore was rolled up to reveal slender forearms that spoke of ranch labor and mountain climbing, her jeans bearing the honest wear of someone who worked the land with her own hands.

Still breathtakingly beautiful in a way that hit him like a physical blow.

He might have even stopped breathing.

"Earth to Hammer." Saxon's voice seemed to come from a great distance. "You're staring."

"That's her." The words came out rough, barely audible. "That's Sierra."

"She's pretty," Saxon said.

Pretty didn't begin to cover it. Sierra had always been striking rather than traditionally beautiful—those high cheekbones, dark eyes that seemed to see straight through to a person's soul, full lips that could smile like sunshine or deliver a to-the-bone truth with equal effectiveness. But it was her presence that had always gotten to him, the way she commanded attention without trying, the quiet strength that radiated from her small frame like heat from a forge.

And oh, it just lit him on fire.

Her shoulders were set in that rigid line he knew too well—the posture that meant she was holding herself together through sheer willpower. Hammer had seen it before, usually right before she broke down crying in private, and the sight of it now made his chest tighten with the urge to fix whatever was hurting her.

"You gonna go talk to her?" Saxon asked.

"I don't know." Hammer watched as Sierra paused at the school's front steps, one hand resting on the railing.

"Seriously? Isn't that why you're here? So you can tell—"

"Maybe I should wait. Find the right time."

"When's the right time to tell someone you're back from the dead?"

Before Hammer could answer, the school's front door burst open and a boy came running out. Eight or nine years old, maybe, with sandy-brown hair and a backpack that looked too big for his small frame. He launched himself at Sierra with the kind of enthusiasm reserved for favorite people, and she caught him in a hug that spoke of overwhelming affection.

Her son.

The realization hit Hammer like a physical blow. Sierra had a *child*. Of course she did. Ten years was a long time—long enough to meet someone, fall in love, get married, start a family. Long enough to build a complete life that didn't include the guy who'd abandoned her without explanation.

"You okay?" Mack's voice was concerned. "You look like you've seen a ghost."

No, he'd just seen his future whisp away.

Because *he* was the ghost.

"I'm fine," he said, then looked at Mack. "Let's eat. And then let's move on. Our little visit into the past is over."

TWO

THE LAND WAS COUNTING ON HER. GRAMPS WAS counting on her. Drowning wasn't an option. But oh, Sierra was tired.

She stood at the kitchen sink, cold water running over her hands as she scrubbed dirt from beneath her fingernails. The granite dust from this morning's rescue still clung to her skin, along with the memory of Tom Hendrick's body sprawled among the rocks. She'd found two hypothermic hikers and one dead rancher. Not exactly the kind of day that made for easy dinner conversation with a ten-year-old.

The kitchen around her told the story of four generations of Blackwood women. She loved this kitchen. Honey-colored cabinets her great-grandfather had built by hand, countertops worn smooth by decades of meal preparation, and the massive farmhouse window that framed the ranch like a living photograph. Exposed beams stretched across the ceiling, darkened with age and smoke from the stone fireplace that dominated the great room beyond. This house had weathered a century of Colorado winters, raised children through the Depression, and sheltered her family through good times and lean.

Now it might not survive her.

Through the window above the sink, empty pasture stretched toward the foothills where granite outcroppings caught the late-afternoon light. The land rolled away in gentle swells covered with October grass, thick and green from recent rains—perfect feed for the thirty head of cattle that should have been grazing there. Instead, fresh tire tracks scarred the muddy ground near the far gate, and the silence felt wrong. Cattle made noise—lowing, shuffling, the sound of life. This quiet was the sound of money walking away in the night.

"Mom, you see me nail that loop on the fence post?" Huck's voice, bright with excitement, carried across the yard and into the window. "Morrie says I'm getting good enough to enter the junior competition."

Sierra turned off the water and dried her hands on a dish towel that had seen better decades. Through the window, her son stood in the corral that backed up to the house, coiling rope with the same focused intensity his father had shown at that age. The way Huck tilted his head when he concentrated, the particular way his left eyebrow quirked when he was pleased with himself—his father's expressions lived on in their son's face.

"I saw. That was a clean throw." She opened the refrigerator and pulled out ground beef, onions, and a can of tomatoes from the pantry. Spaghetti again. Simple, filling, and cheap. The kind of meal that stretched a grocery budget already pulled thin.

She'd spent her inheritance on the taxes to keep this place.

"Morrie says if I keep practicing, I might place at the Fall Festival Rodeo." Huck appeared in the kitchen doorway, his rope still in hand, cheeks red from the cool air. "Can we afford the entry fee?"

Twenty-five dollars. She had exactly eighteen dollars and thirty-seven cents in her checking account until her inherited annuity payment came in next week. But Huck's face held the kind of hope that made mothers move mountains.

"We'll figure it out."

"Is that mom-speak for no?"

Sierra started browning the beef in her grandmother's cast-iron skillet. Set another pan of water to boil. "It's mom-speak for 'we'll figure it out.'"

"Sweet." Huck dropped into a chair at the kitchen table, pushing aside a stack of bills she'd been reviewing. "Eli Martinez says his dad might sponsor some of the junior riders if they don't have the money. You know, pay their fees and stuff."

Her jaw tightened. She didn't need help, especially not from neighbors who were probably struggling just as much as she was. "We'll handle our own fees."

"But if people want to help—"

"We handle our own business, Huck."

Huck studied her face the way he did when he was trying to figure out if she was really okay or just pretending. Too smart for his own good, her stubborn, headstrong son. Determined to follow his own renegade heart. And break hers in the process.

Too much like his father in that regard.

"Go hang up that rope properly." She added onions to the skillet. "Grandpa Elway would have your hide if he saw good rope just lying around."

"Yes, ma'am." Huck disappeared toward the mudroom.

Sierra opened the can of tomatoes and dumped them into the pan, then walked over to the garbage and dropped it into the recycling.

Her gaze fell on the folded American flag sitting in its frame, hanging on the wall. Thirteen folds of red, white, and blue. Of course, the gloved officer hadn't handed it to her. But she'd ended up with it anyway.

That meant something, maybe.

She nearly reached up to touch it when the front door opened and boots stomped across the porch. Heavy work boots, not Huck's lighter step. "Sierra?"

Walt "Morrie" Morrison pushed through the kitchen door, his hat in his hands and concern written across his ruggedly handsome face. Early forties with steel-gray eyes and the kind of weathered good looks that came from a lifetime working outdoors, Morrie had worked for Gramps for fifteen years. These days, he worked for whatever Sierra could afford to pay him, which wasn't nearly enough. His dark hair was streaked with silver at the temples, and a well-groomed beard framed features that belonged in a Western magazine—all sharp cheekbones and strong jaw. But it was the genuine worry in his expression that made Sierra's chest tighten.

"Right here. How'd we do today?"

"Not good. Lost another dozen head from the north pasture. Found the fence cut clean through, tire tracks leading toward the county road."

Sierra's hand stilled on the wooden spoon. Twelve more head. At current market prices, that was another few thousand dollars gone. "Same spot as last time?"

"Different section, but same method. These boys know what they're doing. Professional job, not some kids looking for beer money."

"Any idea when?"

"Sometime after midnight, before dawn. I checked that pasture yesterday evening, and the cattle were all there." Morrie pulled out a chair and sat down heavily. "Sierra, we need to talk about hiring security. Or at least getting some cameras installed."

"With what money?" The question came out sharper than she intended. "Sorry. I'm just—it's been a long day."

"I heard about the SAR call. Tom Hendrick, right?" He shook his head. "That's a shame."

"Yeah." Sierra stirred the sauce, not trusting herself to say more.

Tom's death felt too close to Grandpa Elway's accident, too convenient for people who might want to pressure local ranchers into selling.

No. Her grandfather's death *had* been an accident. Oh, she wanted to believe that.

Because the other option could turn her cold, especially alone at night.

"There's something else." Morrie's voice carried the tone he used when delivering bad news. "Mayor Jenkins called this afternoon. Said he wanted to talk to you about some kind of opportunity."

Sierra's stomach dropped. Mayor Alden Jenkins—the man who'd been circling her ranch like a vulture since Grandpa Elway died.

"What kind of opportunity?"

"Didn't say. Just asked me to have you call him back." Morrie pulled a slip of paper from his shirt pocket. "Here's the number."

Sierra took the paper but didn't look at it. She knew Jenkins's number by heart—he'd been calling regularly since the funeral, always with some new offer to "help" her through her difficult time.

In fact, she'd gotten too much "help" from people who saw her as incapable, alone, and in over her head. Like Ralph Rousseau from Rocky Mountain Land Developers. His business card sat in the recycle bin, under the can of tomatoes.

The water on the stove had come to a boil. She dumped in spaghetti. "Morrie, you ever think about how convenient it is that all these cattle thefts started right after Grandpa Elway died?"

"What do you mean?"

"I mean the timing feels awfully coincidental. Grandpa Elway dies in a suspicious accident three months ago, Tom Hendrick turns up dead on the mountain, and suddenly every rancher in the county is losing livestock." Sierra turned down the heat under the sauce. "Makes you wonder if someone's trying to drive us all out."

Morrie was quiet for a long moment. "Jenkins has lost cattle too."

Oh. Maybe she shouldn't immediately jump to people trying to steal her home. "Maybe I should call him back."

Morrie got up. "Smells good. And yes, maybe. I'm heading home."

"You sure you don't want to stay for supper?"

He glanced at her, narrowed his eyes, and looked like he might nod when Huck slammed into the house. "I put Jasper in the horse barn. And coiled up the rope." His Jack Russell terrier puppy wiggled in past him, slipping on the wood floor.

"Jasper was out?" She glanced at Morrie.

"Huck was working on his cutaway roping."

Right. "I guess Jasper's the best choice."

"Until I win that prize!" Huck slid onto a chair at the table. "I'm getting myself a quarter horse."

Morrie smiled then. He bent and caught up the puppy. "Bandit, please learn not to scare the chickens." The dog licked him on the face and he made a noise. Set the dog down.

"Help me set the table?" she said to Huck. She glanced at Morrie. "And you're staying."

He smiled.

"Sure." Huck grabbed silverware from the drawer. "Hey, Morrie, you really think I'm ready for the junior competition?"

"I think you're getting close. Your loops are consistent, and your timing's improving." Morrie accepted a plate from Sierra. "But competition's different from practice. Lots of distractions, other kids watching."

"I'm not worried about other kids." Huck's chin came up with characteristic determination. "Grandpa Elway always said if you know you can do something, other people's opinions don't matter."

"Smart man, your great-grandfather." Morrie's gaze connected with hers, then back to Huck. "He'd be proud of how you're coming along."

Sierra blinked back tears as she drained the pasta water and
mixed the noodles with sauce. Simple food, but it filled the kitchen
with warmth and the illusion of normalcy. For a few minutes,
she could pretend they were just a regular family sitting down to
dinner, not a single mother trying to hold together a failing ranch.

The phone rang just as she was serving the pasta.

"Let it ring," Morrie said quietly.

But Sierra was already moving toward the phone, driven by
the same compulsion that made her check on cattle in the middle
of the night and balance the books until her eyes burned. You
couldn't solve problems by ignoring them.

"Blackwood Ranch."

"Sierra, honey, it's Mayor Jenkins. How are you holding up?"

Seriously.

Sierra gripped the phone tighter, her free hand resting on the
kitchen counter.

"I'm fine, Mayor. What can I do for you?"

"Well, I've been thinking about our conversation after Elway's
funeral. About the challenges you're facing with the ranch." A
pause that managed to sound both sympathetic and calculating.
"I heard you had more trouble with rustlers."

"Where'd you hear that?"

"We're neighbors, Sierra. Of course I'd know. And neighbors
need to look out for each other." Another pause. "That's actually
why I'm calling. I've got a proposal that might help with your
situation."

Sierra caught Morrie's eye across the kitchen table. He was
watching her carefully, his expression grim.

"What kind of proposal?"

"Well, I know you're struggling to keep up with the ranch payments, especially with the cattle thefts and all. Must be hard, trying to manage everything on your own." Jenkins's voice carried just enough pity to make her teeth clench. "I'd like to make you an offer on the property. Fair market value, cash deal, quick closing."

"The ranch isn't for sale."

"Now, I understand your attachment to the place. Elway raised you there, and it's got sentimental value. But sentiment doesn't pay bills or put food on the table." His tone shifted slightly, becoming more businesslike. "I'm prepared to offer you two hundred thousand, cash. That's more than enough to pay off your debts and get yourself established somewhere else. Maybe closer to the city, where Huck could have better opportunities."

Two hundred thousand dollars? As if. Add another zero and...

No, not even then. "Like I said, it's not for sale."

"I'm trying to help you here. These cattle thefts aren't going to stop, and you can't afford to keep losing livestock. Pretty soon, you won't have anything left to sell."

"Then do something about it. Find the rustlers. Morrie says you're losing cattle too."

"Well, we're looking into it, of course. Sheriff's department is investigating, but these things take time. Professional cattle thieves are smart, they know how to cover their tracks." A pause. "Hard to catch people when they know the area as well as the locals do."

Wait. *What?* "Do you think someone local is involved?"

She glanced at Morrie.

"I don't know. But the offer stands, Sierra. Think about what's best for you and that boy of yours. Elway wouldn't want you to sacrifice your future for a piece of land."

Was that a threat? She opened her mouth to retort, but the line went dead.

Sierra hung up the phone, trying not to shake.

"You okay?" Morrie asked.

She nodded and returned to the table, where Huck was spinning pasta around his fork.

"What did he want?" Huck asked around a mouthful of spaghetti.

"Just checking in." Sierra picked up her fork, though her appetite had disappeared. "Being neighborly."

"Mom, you know you get that line between your eyebrows when you're worried, right?" Huck pointed his fork at her face. "And it's showing right now."

"Eat your dinner."

"Is it about the missing cows? Because Gunnar St. Claire's dad says losing cattle is just part of ranching these days. Like coyotes or bad weather."

"Gunnar St. Claire's dad is a smart man." Sierra forced herself to take a bite. The pasta tasted like cardboard, but she chewed and swallowed anyway. "But our cattle aren't missing. They were stolen. There's a difference."

"What's the difference?"

"Missing means they wandered off or got through a broken fence. Stolen means someone took them on purpose." Sierra reached for her water glass. "And when someone steals from you on purpose, it could mean they're planning to do it again."

Morrie cleared his throat. "Maybe we *should* consider hiring some extra help. I know money's tight, but if we could get a couple of young guys to patrol the property at night—"

"With what payroll?" Sierra cut him off. "I can barely afford to pay you and the other two day hands what I owe."

"Then maybe it's time to consider other options."

"Like what?"

He put his fork down. "Like accepting help when it's offered. Just sell off a portion of the land. Your pride isn't worth losing the ranch."

Huck had stopped eating. Stared at them, his eyes wide.

Sierra took a breath, schooled her voice. "This ranch has been in my family since 1897. My great-great-grandfather built this house with his own hands, raised cattle through droughts and market crashes and two world wars." Her voice stayed steady, but her hands trembled slightly. "I was born in this house. My father was born in this house. And my son needs to live on the property of his family. This is our family legacy, and I'm not selling it to Alden Jenkins because I'm having a rough patch."

"Mom." Huck's voice was small, uncertain. "Are we going to lose the ranch?"

Sierra reached across the table and squeezed his hand. "No, baby. We're not going to lose anything."

"Promise?"

The word stuck in her throat. Somehow, "I promise we'll fight for it. Every day, as hard as we can."

It wasn't the promise he'd asked for, but it was the only one she could make.

Huck nodded, apparently satisfied. "Good. Because I want to raise my kids here, just like you raised me."

The words took her breath. But of course Huck saw his future on this land, the same way she always had. The same way Grandpa Elway had when he taught her to read cattle signs and fix fences and stand up for what mattered.

"Tell you what," she said, forcing brightness into her voice. "Let's finish dinner, and then you can help me check the horses. We need to make sure the barn's locked up tight tonight."

"Are you worried about horse thieves too?"

"I'm worried about being careful. There's a difference."

She avoided Morrie's dark look from across the table.

And tried to tell herself that she wasn't a fool.

But this land was all she had left. And she wasn't signing it over to anyone, no matter the cost.

The smart play was to drive away and never look back. But no, Hammer found himself knocking on the open doorway of the office of Detective Martinelli, of the South Eagle Police Station, watching the man sort through a stack of incident reports.

Mostly because he couldn't get the guy's words out of his head . . . *She's been having some trouble lately. Cattle rustling, equipment vandalism. Nothing too serious yet, but it's got her on edge.*

And there was the bit about Elway Blackwood dying under his ATV vehicle . . . *What?*

So yeah, there Hammer stood as the fluorescent lights buzzed overhead, casting harsh shadows across case files that probably told stories of desperation and bad choices. Same kind of desperation and choices that had driven him out of this place ten years ago.

"Mr. Wallace." Martinelli looked up from his desk, gesturing toward a chair. "Didn't expect to see you again so soon. Still thinking about that job offer?"

The detective's office was cramped but organized, with case files stacked neatly on metal shelving, and a coffee maker that looked like it had seen better decades.

"Maybe. Depends on what you can tell me about Elway Blackwood's death."

Martinelli frowned. "That's an odd question from someone who's just passing through."

Hammer settled into the chair. "Elway was good to me when I was a kid. Just want to make sure his death was really an accident."

Good to him? For cryin' out loud, the man had saved him. Old Elway had been the one constant source of stability during the worst years of his childhood, the neighboring rancher who'd shown him what real strength looked like, that a man's worth was measured by how he treated those who couldn't fight back.

And Sierra . . . No. He wasn't going there. Not yet. Maybe not ever.

"Any reason to think it wasn't?" Martinelli asked.

"Dunno. He was a big deal around here for many years. Made enemies. Was there an investigation?"

Martinelli pulled a file from his desk drawer and opened it. "ATV rollover on a steep section of pasture. Elway was out there alone. Machine flipped, pinned him underneath. The hired hand found him."

"Mechanical failure?"

"Ground was soft from recent rain, probably lost traction on the slope." Martinelli closed the file. "Coroner ruled it accidental death. No signs of foul play."

Hammer nodded, though something in his gut still felt unsettled. "What about this cattle rustling I heard about? Connected to anything bigger?"

"Doubtful. We're talking about small-time thefts, probably opportunistic. Cattle prices are high, security is low."

"Any pattern?"

"Smaller ranches, mostly. Places without full-time security or sophisticated alarm systems. For what it's worth, we're keeping an eye on things. Extra patrols, coordination with neighboring counties. These rustlers will slip up eventually."

"Any suspects?"

"Few possibilities, but nothing concrete. Could be local, could be outsiders who've scouted the area. Hard to say."

Hammer stood, extending his hand. "Appreciate the information, Detective."

Martinelli leaned back in his chair, studying Hammer with the kind of attention that made seasoned operators uncomfortable. "Why the interest?"

"Like I said, just . . . he was a friend."

"More than a friend." Martinelli's tone carried the weight of someone who'd done his homework. "Funny thing about South Eagle. This part of Renegade is like a small town—people remember things. And after you left the diner today, I made a few calls.

Rowan Wallace and Sierra Blackwood. High school sweethearts."
He raised an eyebrow.

Hammer kept his expression neutral. "I told you I knew Sierra
in high school. Natural to be concerned about old friends. And
I'm not sure why this is any of your business."

Martinelli held up a hand. "Just watching my backyard. People
care about Sierra and her son. Especially since Elway's passing. I
just . . . it's curious, you coming back from the dead now, of all
times."

Hammer blinked at him. "Why now?"

"Just . . . you know. Life isn't easy. She's lonely. And has a big
ranch—"

"I'm going to stop you right there, before someone gets hurt."
Hammer drew in a breath. But weirdly, something niggled inside
him. Wait—"Lonely?"

Martinelli drew in a breath. "Thanks for coming in. If you're
still interested in a job, I could set you up an interview."

One that would come with a background check, no doubt.

"Thanks. I'll keep that in mind."

Outside, he found Saxon leaning against the truck, studying a
colorful poster taped to a lamppost. "Check this out. Fall Festival
Rodeo, next weekend. Says here they've got junior competitions."

Hammer glanced at the poster, noting the prize categories and
entry fees. Twenty-five dollars for junior roping, fifty for adult
divisions. But there was decent prize money. "Five hundred dollars
for the overall junior champion. That's big dough for a kid."

"You should know," Mack said, appearing from around the corner, holding two cups of coffee from the diner. "Hammer was the
region roping champ for three years running."

"That was a long time ago."

"Not that long," Mack said. "Muscle memory doesn't disappear.
Bet you could still nail a calf in under fifteen seconds."

"Doubt it." Hammer took one of the coffee cups. "Skills like that need constant practice."

"Some things you never forget. Like riding a bike."

"Roping's not riding a bike, Mack."

"Maybe not. But you were good enough to earn scholarship offers. Remember? Colorado State wanted you for their rodeo team."

Hammer remembered. Full ride to study agricultural science and compete on the college circuit. A future that had evaporated the night he'd stood up to his stepfather and been forced to choose between that future and survival.

"That ship sailed a long time ago."

"Doesn't mean you can't appreciate good form when you see it." Saxon folded the poster and stuck it in his jacket pocket. "Who knows? Maybe we'll catch some of the competition while we're here."

"We're not staying for any rodeo," Hammer said. "But while Mack is out visiting his dad, I'm just going to nose around, see what I can find out about these cattle rustlers."

Mack made a triumphant fist.

"I don't know why you're so keen on visiting a guy who threw you out of the house when you were eighteen," said Saxon quietly.

Yeah, what he said.

Mack sighed. "It was a bad day. Dad and I got in a fight over Rowan's flag . . ." He shook his head. "He apologized. Told me to come back anytime."

"My flag?"

"Whatever. It's over."

Hammer's mouth tightened. "I'm only a phone call away."

"I can take care of myself." Mack shot him a look.

Hammer raised his hands in surrender.

"I'll help you nose around," Saxon said as they got into the pickup truck. "But I guess this means we'll also need a place to lay over for the night."

They stopped by the Mountain View Motel on their way out of South Eagle, and he and Saxon rented a couple rooms. "Maybe they'll air it out before we come back," Hammer said as they dropped their duffels off on the hard beds.

Dusk settled over the valley, headlights cutting through shadows.

The Jenkins ranch sat five miles west of the suburb of South Eagle, on prime bottomland that had been in the family for three generations. Although, back then, it hadn't been called Jenkins land, had it?

"Turn here." Mack pointed toward a gravel road marked by a wooden sign: *Jenkins Ranch - Est. 1952.*

Hammer stifled the growl in his chest. Whatever. He turned onto the drive, noting immediately how different this property looked from the struggling ranches they'd passed. New fencing stretched in perfect lines across manicured pastures where expensive quarter horses grazed on grass so green it looked artificially enhanced. Equipment sheds held tractors and implements that caught the last rays of fading sunlight, their red and silver surfaces gleaming in the golden hour.

The ranch house dominated the landscape like a monument to prosperity—a sprawling log construction with soaring gables and multiple dormers silhouetted against the deepening sky. Light spilled from the windows, casting rectangular pools of yellow onto the wraparound deck supported by massive timber posts. Professional landscaping surrounded the foundation with native stone planters and manicured shrubs that probably cost more than most ranchers made in a year.

The air here smelled different too—less like cattle and hay, more like money and ambition. Even the gravel driveway was perfectly graded, crunching under their tires with a sound that whispered expense. Wind chimes hung from the porch eaves, their sound eerily clear in the still evening air.

It felt more like a movie set than a working ranch—the kind of place built to impress visitors rather than raise livestock. The house lights made it look warm and inviting, but Hammer knew better.

"Looks like your father's done well for himself."

"Mayor's salary probably helps. Plus whatever he makes from the ranch operation." Mack was studying the house like he was memorizing details, his voice carrying a note of pride that made Hammer's stomach turn. "He always said hard work and smart decisions would pay off eventually."

Hard work. Hammer tasted bile at the back of his throat. This wasn't hard work. This was kickback and corruption, political connections and the kind of moral flexibility that let a man sleep at night despite his sins.

Hammer parked near the front porch, noting the security lights that flooded the yard with harsh white illumination. Motion sensors, probably. Multiple cameras mounted under the eaves. Either Mayor Jenkins had enemies, or he had something worth protecting.

"You coming in?" Mack asked as he opened his door.

"I'll wait here."

"He'd want to see you. I know things were complicated when we were kids, but—"

"Complicated?" He shook his head. "I'll wait here, Mack. Text me when you're ready to go."

"Listen. I get it. Just go. But I'm sticking around." Mack gave him a grim smile, understanding passing between them. Some wounds were too deep for time to heal, some relationships too broken for politics or politeness to repair.

Not that there was a relationship to be fixed.

Mack grabbed his duffel out of the back.

The front door opened before Mack reached the porch steps. Mayor Alden Jenkins stepped into the light—taller than Hammer remembered, broader through the shoulders, but carrying the same intimidating presence that had terrorized one young boy while charming everyone else. His dark hair was now streaked with silver, swept back from a face that had aged into the kind of gravitas voters mistakenly found reassuring. Deep lines etched around dark eyes that had learned to project sincerity on command, while his mouth held the practiced smile of a man who'd spent decades convincing people he was worthy of their trust.

The monster, in the flesh.

"Mack." Alden's voice carried syrupy pleasure. "Look at you. All grown up."

He hugged Mack, but Alden's gaze found Hammer through the truck's windshield.

Hammer bristled. "Let's go," he said as Mack went into the house.

"You okay?" Saxon. He looked over from the passenger seat.

"Yep."

Saxon sort of grunted, then looked out the window.

Of course, the drive back toward the motel, with a small detour, took him past the Blackwood ranch.

Whatever.

And sure, okay, he found himself slowing as the property came into view.

The contrast with the Jenkins spread was immediate and painful. Where Jenkins's ranch spoke of prosperity and careful management, the Blackwood place showed the strain of recent losses and deferred maintenance.

Fence posts leaned at odd angles along the gravel drive that led to a house that had once been magnificent. The two-story structure rose from a foundation of native stone, its cedar-shingle siding weathered to a soft gray that spoke of decades facing Colorado winters. Three distinctive gables crowned the roofline along with a welcoming, if saggy, front porch.

A few brave mums still bloomed in clay pots by the front steps,

Sierra's attempt to maintain some beauty despite everything else falling apart, maybe. The porch swing hung slightly crooked, and several of the cedar shingles curled at the edges, waiting for repairs that might never come.

Still, the house held dignity. Warm light spilled from the tall windows, and smoke drifted from the stone chimney, carrying the scent of burning wood and home-cooked meals. This wasn't a showplace like Jenkins's spread—it was a home where generations had been raised, where real work was done, where love lived in every weathered board and carefully tended detail.

At least, that was his memory.

His gaze went to the main barn. Classic red construction with white trim that had faded to cream, a peaked roof that still reached toward the stars with dignity. One of two barns—livestock in the other, newer barn away from the house. But in this one, they kept vehicles and tools and, well, Sierra's loft, built for her by her father.

The structure showed age in weathered boards and paint that needed touching up, but so many . . . many good memories. The kind of memories that could carry a man through . . . well, a decade.

Even death, and back.

Warmth stirred inside him.

Nope. Not going there.

Floodlights mounted on power poles turned the area around it into a stage, bright enough to practice by, warm enough to forget the October chill.

And there, in that circle of light, a boy was learning to rope.

Hammer pulled to the shoulder of the county road, turned off his headlights.

"Um, what are we—" Saxon started, cut off by Hammer's glance. "Hokay. We'll call this recon."

Hammer's mouth tightened. The boy stood in the corral beside the barn, coiling rope with focused intensity.

A man stood nearby, calling out instructions that carried across the night air. Early forties, solid build, the kind of broad shoulders and easy stance that spoke of a lifetime spent working cattle. A real cowboy, from his worn boots to the hat that sat naturally on his head.

"Keep your elbow up. Trust the weight of the rope. Don't force it."

Good advice. The kind Hammer had heard from Elway Blackwood twenty years ago.

The boy—Huck, that was his name—nodded and reset his position. He held the rope like he understood its potential, like the coiled hemp was an extension of his arm rather than a separate tool. When he threw, the loop sailed true and settled around one horn of the practice dummy.

"Better," the older man called. "But watch your follow-through. Keep that wrist straight."

Hammer found himself nodding in agreement. The kid had natural ability, but he was developing a bad habit that would cost him speed in competition. Someone needed to tell him to trust the motion, to let the rope do the work instead of trying to muscle it into position.

The boy reset and threw again. This time, the loop fell short, and Hammer saw him shake his head in frustration.

"Don't overthink it," Hammer murmured. "Feel the rhythm. Let it flow."

Saxon glanced at him. "Like riding a bike."

Hammer rolled his eyes. But, as if responding to his unspoken coaching, the boy took a deep breath and tried again. This throw was perfect—a smooth release, tight loop, clean capture. Even from fifty yards away, Hammer could see the satisfaction in the kid's posture.

The man . . . probably the boy's father, probably a good man who'd given Sierra the family she deserved . . . clapped his hands in approval. "That's it. You've got it now."

So much for her being *lonely*.

They practiced for another ten minutes before heading toward the house, their voices fading as they moved out of the light. The man's hand rested on the boy's shoulder. Huck laughed at something his father said.

A fist formed in Hammer's gut.

"You okay, Hammer?" Saxon had pulled out his phone, was scrolling.

The air carried the scent of hay and horses, of wood smoke and possibility. Stars blazed overhead in the clear mountain sky, and inside the home that he'd nearly called his, Sierra was probably putting her son to bed, reading him stories or listening to his plans for the junior rodeo competition.

And then she'd climb into bed with the man—

Wait. The man walked out of the house and got into his truck. Drove away.

Lonely.

Maybe they were separated.

Which meant he still didn't have a right to . . . Yeah, he should still keep driving. All the more reason not to get involved, to show up on her doorstep. *Surprise! I'm alive.*

Nope and double nope.

He sighed, staring at the empty corral and the memories it triggered. He'd stood in a similar circle of light twenty years ago, practicing the same skills with the same determination. Back when he'd been Rowan Wallace instead of Hammer, back when his biggest worry was whether he'd make the high school rodeo team.

Back when Sierra Blackwood had been the center of his universe.

The memory hit him without warning—their last night together, him battered and bleeding from his final confrontation with his stepfather, Sierra cleaning his wounds with gentle hands and fierce eyes.

"It's going to be okay," she'd whispered, pressing a cloth to the cut above his left eyebrow. "We'll figure something out. We always do."

"I chose the military," he said softly now.

Saxon looked up at him. "We all did."

He sighed. "I never regretted it until right now."

Silence next to him.

He put the truck into Drive.

Saxon put his phone away. "Let's stop and get some grub."

Hammer nodded, but the thought hit him that he should keep driving. Should collect Mack and head back to Missoula and the Jude County Smokejumpers training ground—the uncomplicated life of fighting fires and avoiding emotional entanglements.

He had no right to invade the happiness Sierra had built without him.

Clearly, Rowan Wallace needed to stay dead.

THREE

WHY ROWAN HAD WALKED INTO HER HEAD AND sat down last night, Sierra didn't know. But he spent the better part of the night there, alive and looking exactly like he had the day he'd promised to come back.

They'd been doing something silly—in the barn, him pushing her on the big swing. And oh, she'd leaned into it. Leaned into *him*.

So no wonder she woke just a little ragged, her soul battered. Grief, out for purchase again.

Now the morning air bit into her lungs, the sweet smell of sage grass and pine drifting down from the mountain, a haze hanging in the morning air, turning the world gray and quiet except for the steady sound of hoofbeats on pastureland and the creak of leather. She'd been on the back of her palomino, Honey, since dropping Huck off at school, needing to bring the cattle down for pregnancy checking before the weather turned. October in Colorado meant snow could hit any day, and pregnant cows needed different feed, different care, different everything.

"We're missing six more cows, Sierra." Jake Martin rode up beside her, his young face serious beneath the brim of his hat. Twenty-two years old and eager to prove himself, Jake had been working day labor for her since his high school graduation. Good kid, solid worker, reminded her of someone she didn't want to think about.

Six. Sierra's stomach dropped. These were her best breeding stock, the cows she'd been counting on to carry next year's calf crop. Without them, she wouldn't have enough calves to sell come spring. Without spring calf sales, she couldn't make the bank payment.

"Could be they drifted to the north pasture," called Tomás Ruiz from twenty yards away. Older than Jake, more experienced, Tomás had worked for Grandpa Elway before his death. "Grass is still good up there."

"Maybe." But Sierra's gut told her differently. Cattle didn't just disappear, especially not her best cows.

The dream flickered through her mind again, an old memory of Rowan, laughing, working with her grandfather, not unlike Tomás or Jake.

She could still see him perfectly—the way his sandy-brown hair caught the sunlight as it fell across his forehead, those impossibly blue eyes focused with quiet intensity as he worked with a difficult horse. He'd worn flannel shirts with the sleeves rolled up, revealing strong forearms that spoke of honest work, an interesting tattoo on his forearm that read, Trouble—that sounded right—and when he smiled . . . well, when he smiled, it transformed his whole face from serious to devastating. There had been something almost magnetic about the way he moved in the saddle, like he and the horse were extensions of each other, all fluid grace and controlled power.

Seeing him on a horse could simply undo her sad, pitiful teenage heart.

Stop.

What was her problem today? She hadn't thought about Rowan

for . . . okay, she often thought of Rowan. But she'd learned to live with the ache.

Maybe it was watching Huck mimic him so well with a rope last night.

"Sierra, you okay?" Jake, his gaze on her.

"I'm fine. Let's check the north pasture before we head back."

They rode to the high meadow, where Blackwood land bumped up against the national forest boundary. The pasture stretched out in a gentle bowl surrounded by aspen and pine, the grass still thick and green from October's rains. Beyond the far fence line, the terrain grew wilder—dense stands of timber climbing toward granite peaks, the same rugged country where she'd tracked those lost hikers yesterday. A dirt road wound along the edge of her property, toward the hiking area. Past Wallace—er, Jenkins land. And from here, she could see the approximate area where they'd found Tom Hendrick's body.

The thought sent a chill down her spine that had nothing to do with the mountain air.

A few scattered cattle grazed near the far fence line.

"All yearlings," Tomás said, riding back to her.

Sierra pulled out her phone and checked for cell service. One bar. "Jake, ride the fence line. Look for breaks, anything that doesn't belong."

"You think they got out?"

"I think six cows don't vanish into thin air."

She dismounted and studied the ground. Cattle tracks, horse tracks, the usual pattern of grazing animals moving across familiar territory. But there—near the fence line—something different. Boot prints. Recent ones, judging by the crisp edges and lack of weather wear.

"Sierra!" Jake's voice carried across the pasture, sharp with urgency. "Found your fence break!"

She swung back into the saddle and rode toward his position.

The fence section looked normal from a distance, but up close, the damage was obvious. Someone had cut the wire, then twisted it back together in a hasty repair job. Sloppy work, the kind done in darkness, maybe.

"This wasn't cattle pushing through," Tomás said, dismounting to examine the wire. "Clean cuts, deliberate spacing. Someone wanted our cows to walk right through here."

Sierra got off Honey and studied the ground beyond the fence. More boot prints, vehicle tracks, and the clear pattern of cattle being driven rather than wandering. Her chest tightened.

"They were stolen."

"Professional job too." Tomás pointed to the tire tracks pressed into the soft earth. "Look at these ruts. That's not a pickup truck. That's something heavy. Big trailer, commercial grade."

Sierra knelt beside the tracks, her SAR training kicking in as she analyzed the evidence. Dual rear wheels, wide spacing between axles, deep impressions that spoke of serious weight. Someone had backed a large stock trailer right up to her fence line and loaded her cattle like they were at a sale barn.

"Follow the trail," she said, mounting Honey again. "I want to see where they went."

The tracks ran a quarter mile, down through rough country, across a seasonal creek bed, and toward a dirt road that connected several ranch properties.

Sierra knew this road—it cut through what used to be Tom Hendrick's place, providing access to half a dozen spreads, including her own. Perfect for someone who wanted to move stolen cattle without using main highways.

"This is where they loaded them," Jake said, pointing to churned earth beside the road. "Lot of activity here. Multiple vehicles."

Sierra dismounted again, walking the perimeter of the loading area. More tire tracks, cigarette butts, boot prints from at least three different people. This wasn't some opportunistic theft by kids looking for quick money. This was organized, planned, professional.

The road stretched both directions, connecting ranches and providing access to county highways. But one direction led toward the spot where she'd found Tom Hendrick's body yesterday.

Sierra's blood turned cold. She looked up at Jake. "What if Tom Hendrick caught these people stealing cattle and they killed him for it?"

Jake frowned, and oops, she hadn't exactly shared the details with him.

And if that was true, who was the man who'd shot him?

She stood up. "Never mind." She pulled out her phone and started taking pictures of the tire tracks.

"What do you want me to do?"

"Grab the stragglers and push them to the rest of the herd. Then we'll move them all to the pasture by the house. And call Morrie and let him know."

She finished the pictures, then hiked back to Honey and helped with the roundup.

Back at the ranch, Sierra left Honey with Tomás and headed straight for her truck. The evidence wouldn't last long if weather moved in. The tire tracks would disappear with the first hard rain. She needed to get this information to Mike Martinelli before the trail went cold.

"Where you going?" Jake asked as she climbed into the cab.

"Police station. Stay close to the house until I get back. And Jake—keep your rifle handy."

"Want me to come with you? This could be dangerous."

Sierra looked at his young face, earnest and concerned. Sweet. "No. I need you here in case they come back."

"Sierra, do you think Hendrick was murdered?"

She looked at him. "Yes. I know he was. But now maybe we're closer to figuring out why."

"What if . . ." He looked down, slapped his gloves against his leg. "I just don't want you to end up like him." He gave her a wry smile.

"Listen. I have more than a little of my Grandpa Elway's justice gene in me. I can't sit on this, Jake. Keep an eye out. Morrie should be back from the store with parts for the bailer soon."

He nodded and stepped back from the truck. "Just feels like we're sticking our nose into another problem. And we're already up to our ears."

"Maybe. But my grandpa always said 'Just handle what comes at you, one problem at a time.'"

"This feels like a bushel."

"Maybe. But I can't just sit here and wait for them to take everything I've got left."

The words rooted inside her as she headed into South Eagle. She parked outside the South Eagle Police Station and sat in her truck for a moment, staring at the building where Detective Mike Martinelli worked.

Mike would listen. He would care. After all, they were still friends.

The door to the police station stood open, warm light spilling onto the sidewalk. Through the glass, she spotted Mike at his desk, coffee cup in hand, leaning back and chatting, nodding as if he were talking to someone.

Maybe she should have given him another chance. Although that felt so long ago, it seemed a silly thought.

Sierra took a deep breath and stepped inside. The receptionist looked up with a smile that faded when she saw Sierra's expression.

"I need to see Detective Martinelli," Sierra said. "It's about Tom Hendrick's death. And the recent cattle rustling. I think there's a connection."

"Go on back. He's with someone right now, but I don't think he'll mind."

She headed back, then knocked on the door frame. Mike looked up at her, and, for the briefest of moments, a look she couldn't place flashed across his face—surprise? Worry? Panic?

"Mike, I need to show you something. I think I found evidence that connects the cattle rustling to Tom Hendrick's death, and—"

The words died in her throat.

The man he'd been talking to, sitting in the chair across from Martinelli's desk, his back to the door, had turned.

Her world tilted off its axis.

Sandy-brown hair caught the office light, cut shorter than she remembered but still with that wayward strand that fell across his forehead. Those impossibly blue eyes—the same eyes that had looked at her with such love ten years ago, the same eyes she saw every day in her son's face—met hers with devastating recognition.

Rowan Wallace.

Alive. Real. Sitting three feet away from her in a green flannel shirt that stretched across shoulders broader than any eighteen-year-old boy had ever possessed.

This wasn't the lean teenager who'd kissed her goodbye. This was a man—weathered face and defined jaw covered with perfectly trimmed brown stubble, the kind of rugged masculinity that belonged on some *Rancher's Today* magazine cover. And yet, lines bracketed those stunning eyes now, his face etched by sun and wind and experiences she'd never know about. His hands—oh, his hands—rested on powerful thighs, and she could see the calluses, the scars, the evidence of a life lived hard and far from her.

He was staring at her with the same hollow-chested expression that she probably wore, his lips slightly parted as if words had died in his throat. The same mouth that had whispered promises against her skin, that had told her he'd come back, that had kissed her like she was his entire world.

Until she wasn't. Until he walked away and . . . died.

Died. She had his flag, for Pete's sake.

So clearly, *not dead.* Breathing. Devastatingly, impossibly real.

The sense of it all—the grief, the hopes, the . . . the *betrayal* crashed over her in a wave so violent it stole her breath.

And then the scream ripped from her throat before she could stop it.

———————

So, in truth, in all Rowan's imagined reunion moments, Sierra screaming had been dead last place on the list.

That and the way she looked at him—part horror, part betrayal, all in grief—

Yeah, tactical mistake, to show up here, at the police station. He blamed the lack of sleep at the Mountain View Motel. Rowan had managed maybe three hours, his mind churning with images of Sierra's ranch and the boy practicing roping under the floodlights.

"Place has all the charm of a fire camp," Saxon had said, pulling on his boots this morning. "At least in Afghanistan we knew the ground was supposed to be hard. I'm going to find coffee that doesn't taste like motor oil. You coming?"

"Go ahead. I need to check on Mack."

Rowan had pulled out his phone and sent a text.

_____ Rowan

How's the visit going? **You okay?**

The response had come back quickly.

Mack
_____

Good. Dad's showing me around the ranch. Lot of new equipment since I was a kid. Planning to stay through tomorrow if that's okay.

So, maybe he'd overreacted. Maybe the guy had changed. And Mack was hardly an eighteen-year-old kid. He knew how to handle himself.

When Saxon returned with coffee and local gossip, the news had been grim.

"Talked to some folks at the diner. Cattle rustling's been worse than Martinelli let on. Third ranch hit this week, always the same method. Professional operation, the cattle driven away in trucks."

"Which ranches?"

"Collins place lost twenty head on Tuesday. Hendrick's ranch got hit Thursday night. And this morning, someone cut Sierra Blackwood's fence and made off with her pregnant stock."

Rowan's blood had turned cold. "How many head?"

"Six. All breeding cows, all pregnant."

Oh no.

"The Blackwood ranch sits in the center of those ranches, with plenty of dirt backroads providing access routes that would let rustlers move stolen cattle without using main highways."

"Yep. You think Elway Blackwood would have noticed unusual activity?"

"He was police commissioner for a decade, so probably." And if Elway had gotten too close to the truth . . .

Rowan grabbed his keys.

"Where are you going?"

"I'm going to talk to that detective from yesterday."

Saxon picked up his coffee. "Good. It'll give me a chance to look into the legalities of getting a PI license."

This was what he got for thinking with his emotions instead of his brain. Because if Sierra had cattle stolen, of course she'd show up at the police station.

Now, Sierra's scream still echoed in his ears as she stared at him, her dark eyes wide, her hand over her mouth.

And all he could think was—oh, she looked good. Sure, he'd seen her yesterday, but today, up close . . . he couldn't breathe.

The years had transformed her from the beautiful girl he'd left behind into a full-bodied woman. Her dark hair fell in waves past her shoulders, catching the office light with subtle highlights that spoke of hours spent in mountain sun. Those eyes—the same warm brown that he'd held in his dreams—were deeper now, framed by long lashes and holding new depths, new layers.

She'd clearly lived a little life too.

She wore a plaid flannel shirt, the fabric hugging her curves, and a pair of jeans over cowboy boots that looked scuffed and work-worn. Of course.

"Oh my," she said softly.

Yep, Oh. My.

Ten years had only made her more stunning, more perfectly *herself*, and the realization that he'd lost all those years, all that time watching her become this incredible person, carved a knife into his chest.

He should have come home. Maybe never left.

"Sierra—" His voice emerged rough, unfamiliar. Ten years of being Hammer, and suddenly he was Rowan again, eighteen and desperate and completely undone by the girl next door.

"No." She shook her head. "No, this isn't happening. You're dead. You're supposed to be *dead*! I got the flag. I got the *flag*!"

The flag. Yes, right. He'd forgotten about the flag.

He should have told her then, that night his team had picked up Mack. That would have been the right thing to do.

Instead, she'd gotten the flag.

He deserved the betrayal in her eyes.

"Sierra, let me explain—"

"Three years!" The words seemed ripped from her throat. "I *buried* you, Rowan!"

Detective Martinelli had gotten up, morphed into a sort of—friend? Concern in his eyes. "Sierra, maybe you should sit down."

"Sit *down*?" She stared at him. Then her mouth opened. "Wait. You ... how long—did you ..." She glanced at Rowan, back to the detective. "How long have you known, Mike?"

Mike?

And the man seemed suddenly weirdly apologetic. "Just yesterday, but—it wasn't my news to tell—C'mon, Sierra, don't look at me like that . . ." He reached out for her.

No wonder the guy had given him the runaround. He had something going with her—or maybe wanted to.

Except, she wasn't in any place for complications, Bub, and he sort of wanted to step between her and *Mike*.

Rowan stood up.

She stepped back, as if . . . what? Was she afraid of him?

Maybe. Maybe not, because she drew in a steadying breath and her beautiful eyes hardened, and she shook her head. "You jerk."

Oh, well. He drew in a breath. "I am."

She glared at him, and his chest burned.

"Sierra, please. Let me—"

"Don't." The word came out fierce, final. "Don't you dare ask me to let you do *anything*. You lost that right when you let me believe you were *dead*."

She gasped as if at her own words.

It might hurt less if she put a knife in his chest than to see her eyes fill.

"I need to go." She turned for the door, but her legs seemed unsteady.

"Sierra, wait—"

She ignored him.

"Sierra," Detective—Mike—Martinelli said. "C'mon—"

She kept moving, down the hall. Stubborn as usual, and shoot, he couldn't *not* follow her.

"Sierra," he said. "I know about your missing cattle. That's why I'm here."

She stopped. Turned slowly, her face a mask of barely controlled fury. "What did you say?"

"Your cattle. The six pregnant cows that were stolen this morning. I know about them."

"How?"

Oh. "Um. A buddy of mine heard it at the Renegade Café. And I thought . . ."

She cocked her head at him.

"I'm worried you're a target."

She just shook her head. "What are you doing here? In Renegade?"

Oh. Um. He swallowed. "It's a long story."

"I'll bet." She held up a hand. "Save it. And I can take care of myself, thanks. I have for . . ." She glanced past him, and he guessed at Martinelli. "A long time."

Detective Martinelli cleared his throat. "Maybe we should all sit down and—"

"No." Sierra's attention returned to Rowan. "Listen. I don't know what happened, but three years of you being dead is just . . . well, there were seven before that where I stood waiting for you. And nothing—*nothing*, Rowan."

Oh, she was right, but still . . . "I was . . . Please let me explain."

"I don't want your help. I don't want anything from you."

"Sierra, these people are dangerous. What if they killed your grandfather?"

She blinked at him. Swallowed. "We had a funeral, you know. You might have come to that."

He might have, if he hadn't been fighting fires in Alaska and, well, still supposed to be dead.

She shook her head, turned away, kept walking.

"You can't handle this alone." Oh, he sounded desperate now.

"Watch me."

He caught up to her, now in the lobby. "I could talk to your husband, offer my services. Security consulting, ranch patrol. I still know how to cowboy."

She whirled around, and the look she gave him could have cut glass. "That won't be necessary."

Martinelli had followed too. "Sierra, maybe you should consider it. You're all alone out there, and if these rustlers are willing to kill—"

"Thanks a lot, *Detective*." She leveled the cutting look at Martinelli. "I appreciate the vote of confidence in my ability to protect my own property."

She headed for the door again.

And what was his problem that for three years—even ten total—he had managed to stay away from this woman, and yet now he couldn't let her out of his sight?

Rowan followed her through the front entrance onto Main Street. "Sierra, wait."

She whirled to face him on the sidewalk. She shook now, and oh, he wanted to reach out, to catch her arms.

To pull her to himself.

But, hello, Mr. Too Late. She was *taken*.

"Wait?" She laughed then, nothing of humor in it. "I've been waiting for *ten years*. I waited for letters that never came. I waited for phone calls. I waited for you to keep your promise to . . ." She swallowed, wrapped her arms around herself, looked away, and her voice dropped. ". . . to come back to me."

Oh. He had made that promise.

"It was complicated."

"Complicated." She spat out the word. "You know what's complicated? Running a ranch. Grieving. Raising a child alone."

He stared at her, and for some reason, the stupid words fell out of his mouth. "Sierra, I'm sure you and your husband can work it out."

Her mouth opened, and then again, a laugh. Only this time, thick with . . . what? Disbelief? Maybe because for sure he'd gone too far.

"I'm not married, thanks."

A beat. And then he just . . . just fell into it. "When I saw the boy with that man yesterday, I assumed he was your husband."

No. He did not say that. Leave. Leave *now*—

Her eyes widened. "You were watching my ranch."

He swallowed. "I was driving by. I saw him teaching the kid to rope, saw you both head inside. It looked like . . . family."

"It looked like a family because it *is* a family. Just not the kind you're thinking of." Sierra stepped closer—close enough that he could smell the scent of hay and horses that clung to her clothes. "That man is Walt Morrison. He works for me. Has worked for us since before Grandpa died. He's teaching my son to rope because there's *no one else to do it*."

The words hit him harder than they should have. No one else to do it. No father figure, no husband, no man in her life?

She'd been doing it all alone, just as she'd said.

"I can help."

She shook her head. "I don't need your help."

"Really?"

She stiffened, but he couldn't stop himself. "Six pregnant cows stolen, your grandfather dead under suspicious circumstances, and you don't need help?"

"Not from you."

He ignored the blow. "Why not?"

"Because you're ten years too late." Her voice broke on the last word, and her eyes filled. "I learned long ago how to handle things without you."

"I have promises to keep to Elway."

The words hung between them like smoke, and for a moment, Sierra's face went soft with something that might have been memory. Then her expression hardened again.

"Oh, you broke those long ago, cowboy."

Right.

He couldn't speak. Not, at least, until she turned away.

And again, he was the guy chasing her down the sidewalk. "Sierra—"

She glanced at him. "How long are you staying in town?"

The question caught him off guard. "I don't know."

"Figures." She shook her head, and for a second, just a flash, he saw something die in her eyes. "Same old Rowan. Never could commit to anything long enough to see it through."

Oh, that wasn't fair. But it benched him as she turned and walked toward her truck. Rowan stood frozen on the sidewalk, watching her go. This wasn't how their reunion was supposed to happen.

In his imagination, she'd been happy to see him. Shocked, maybe, confused about how he'd survived when everyone thought he was dead. But ultimately happy. She would have understood why he'd had to disappear, why staying dead had been the only way to keep her safe.

Go after her.

The voice of passion in his head. No. He'd done enough damage listening to his emotions today.

Sierra reached her truck and yanked open the door, then paused and looked back at him. For one heartbeat, he thought she might say something else. Something that would bridge the chasm that ten years had carved between them.

Instead, she climbed into the cab and started the engine.

Rowan watched her drive away, her taillights disappearing around the corner toward the county road that would take her back to the ranch. Back to the life that didn't include him. Back to the son she was raising alone and the dangers she was facing without backup.

"Well, at least she knows you're not dead."

Saxon's voice came from behind him. Rowan turned to find his friend standing in the doorway of the coffee shop, holding two cups and wearing the expression of someone who'd witnessed a train wreck.

"How much did you hear?"

"Enough to know that your woman is about as thrilled to see you as a tax auditor." Saxon handed him one of the cups. "Also enough to know she's in serious trouble and too stubborn to accept help from the one person who might be able to keep her alive."

Rowan stared down the empty street where Sierra's truck had disappeared. "She hates me."

"Can you blame her?"

"No."

"Good. That's the first step toward not being a complete idiot about this situation." Saxon took a sip of his coffee and made a face. "Though I have to say, for a dead man, you're remarkably bad at resurrection conversations."

"This isn't a joke, Saxon."

"I know it's not. That woman is in danger, and you're the best chance she's got of staying alive. Question is, what are you going to do about it?"

Rowan sighed. "I'm going to keep her safe," he said quietly. "Whether she wants me to or not."

"Even if she never forgives you?"

His chest tightened. "Even then."

Because some things mattered more than forgiveness. Some things mattered more than his own heart breaking into pieces on a sidewalk in Renegade, Colorado.

Keeping Sierra safe was one of those things.

Even if she spent the rest of her life hating him for it.

FOUR

SHE'D SPENT A DECADE TEACHING HUCK THAT honesty mattered most, but the biggest lie of his life was walking around Renegade with his same eyes.

Sierra sat in Bailey Sinclair's fourth-grade classroom, the kids having exited for the day, staring at the bulletin board covered with student artwork while her hands shook in her lap. Twenty-eight crayon drawings of "My Family" decorated the wall, and she could pick out Huck's immediately—a woman and a boy standing beside a red barn, two horses grazing in a green pasture. No father figure. Just the two of them against the world, exactly the way she'd raised him to see their life.

Except now his father was buying coffee at the Renegade Café and offering to help with cattle rustlers and asking about a husband who didn't exist. Because instead of telling her he was alive . . . he'd been spying on her.

Beautiful.

"Sierra?" Bailey looked up from the stack of math tests she was grading, her pen pausing mid-correction. Strawberry blonde hair cut in a practical bob framed her face, and concern wrinkled her forehead as she studied Sierra's expression. At twenty-eight, Bailey had the kind of wholesome prettiness that made parents trust her instantly with their children. "You look like you've seen a ghost."

"Maybe I have."

Bailey set down her pen and really looked at her—the way best friends did when they sensed disaster lurking beneath the surface. She pushed her chair back and moved to the supply cabinet, pulling out construction paper while keeping her attention on Sierra. "What happened? You were fine this morning when you dropped Huck off."

Fine. Right. Sierra stood and began helping Bailey sort the colored paper into neat stacks—red, orange, yellow, brown. October art projects, probably. Her hands needed something to do while her mind tried to process the impossible.

This morning she'd been a single mother running a struggling ranch and worrying about stolen cattle. Now she was a single mother who'd been lying to her son about his father being dead when he was apparently very much alive and sitting in the police station offering his services.

"Rowan's back."

The words hung in the classroom air between construction-paper pumpkins and a poster about proper comma usage. Bailey's hands stilled on the paper stack, several orange sheets fluttering to the floor.

"Rowan Wallace? *Your* Rowan?" Bailey's voice dropped to a whisper as she bent to collect the scattered papers.

Her Rowan. Yeah, she needed to stop thinking that way. "He's not my anything." Sierra bent to help her. "But yes. Rowan Wallace, who's supposed to be buried in the Renegade cemetery—and now I know why he wasn't buried at Arlington, thank you so much military who lied to me." She shook her head as she stood up, papers in hand. "I walked into Mike Martinelli's office this morning to report a connection between my missing cattle and maybe, I don't know . . . Tom Hendrick's death, and there he was . . . just—sitting there."

"Wait." Bailey stood up too. "You have more missing cattle?"

"Six head of pregnant cows stolen last night. Cut fence, tire tracks, professional job. But that's not—Bailey, Rowan said he knew about the rustling, said he could talk to *my husband* about providing security services." Sierra's voice cracked on the word *husband*. "He thought I was married."

"Oh, Sierra." Bailey took her hand, led her to a chair next to her deck. "Are you okay?"

Sierra sat. "No, I'm not okay. I screamed when I saw him. Literally screamed in Mike's office and then had a public argument with Mr. I'm Not Dead on Main Street."

Bailey reached for the water bottle on her desk and handed it to Sierra. "Drink something. You look like you're about to pass out."

Sierra took a sip, but it didn't help the spinning sensation in her chest. "He looks exactly the same. Older, bigger, but still . . ." She gestured helplessly. "Still him. Only better-looking, if that's possible."

"Yikes. What did you tell him?" Bailey raised an eyebrow. "Or what did he tell *you*?"

"He told me nothing. Nothing. And I said he was ten years too late. That I'd learned to handle things without him." Sierra's laugh came out bitter, hollow. "Then I told him he'd obliterated his promises to Grandpa Elway and walked away."

"Harsh." Bailey winced. "But accurate."

"He let me think he was dead, Bailey." Sierra's voice cracked on the words. "I got the *flag*. I mourned him."

Bailey was quiet for a moment, her mouth pressed into a thin line. "What are you going to tell Huck?"

The classroom fell silent. She had nothing.

Poor Huck.

"Does Rowan know?" Bailey's voice was barely audible.

"No." Sierra shook her head. "I don't think so. Although one good look at the kid . . ."

"Right?" Bailey shook her head. "Girl, that man's been a heart-throb since first grade. And your son Huck has his father's aura. Can't pry the girls away from him."

"Oh, I'm in trouble." She leaned back, her hands pressed to her face. "Huck thinks his father's dead—because, well, his father was *dead*. And he's turned the man into someone larger than life. We don't talk about him often, but sometimes he asks and . . ." She looked at Bailey. "Now what do I say? 'Your dad's alive, but he didn't care enough to tell us'?"

Bailey covered Sierra's hand with hers.

Sierra stood up and walked to the window overlooking the playground, where a few kids were still waiting for rides. "You don't understand. When I found out I was pregnant, Rowan had already broken his first promise. He told me not to write to him at boot camp, that he'd call when it was over. But he never called. And then I wrote to him, but the letter came back. I didn't know his rank, his address . . ." She lifted a shoulder. "And then . . . then Mack called and said Rowan had been deployed early, no leave."

"So you decided not to tell him about the baby."

"I decided not to tell him about the baby because his stepfather was a monster, and I didn't want Rowan coming home to that situation because of me. Because of a child he never planned to have." Sierra pressed her forehead against the cool glass. "I thought I was protecting him."

"And later? When you dated Mike?"

"I thought maybe Huck needed a father figure."

"Mike's a good man. What happened?"

She turned to Bailey. "What happened was that Mike wasn't Rowan, and I wasn't in love with Mike, and building a relationship

74

on that foundation was a disaster waiting to happen." Sierra turned back to Bailey. "It's possible that Huck isn't the only one who built up his father to superhero status."

"And then?"

"And then I was going to tell Rowan. Had actually convinced myself that he deserved to know, that Huck deserved to know his father. I even wrote the letter, explaining everything, asking him to come meet his son."

Bailey waited.

"Two days before I mailed it, Mack showed up on my doorstep with the notification that Rowan Wallace had been killed in action. Classified mission, body not recoverable, survived by his stepfather and half brother." Sierra's voice went flat. "So I went to the memorial and let Huck think his father was a hero who died serving his country. He was only seven, so it wasn't hard to make him believe that he'd left for war before he was born."

"That's not entirely a lie."

"It's not entirely the truth either. I even hung his flag on the wall, even though it wasn't officially mine."

"How'd you end up with the flag?"

She sighed. "I don't know. Mack showed up one day with it. He'd clearly been in a fight. He just handed it to me and walked away. And I . . . I kept it."

Bailey stood up and walked around her desk, leaning against it so she could face Sierra directly. "What are you going to do now?"

"I don't know."

"You have to tell them both."

"Do I? Huck's got a good life. He's happy, well-adjusted, smart, talented. Why blow that up because his supposedly dead father decided to come back to town?"

"Because that father is very much alive and has the right to know his child exists. And because that child has the right to know his father."

"What if Rowan doesn't want the responsibility?"

"What if he does?"

Sierra moved away from the window, pacing the small classroom space between desks sized for fourth graders. "You didn't see him this morning, Bailey. He's different. Harder. Ten years of whatever he's been doing have changed him."

"Of course they have. He was—maybe still is—a soldier. That has to have changed him. And you've changed too."

"Not that much."

"Really? The eighteen-year-old girl I knew couldn't run a ranch or lead search and rescue missions or raise a child alone."

Before Sierra could respond, the classroom door burst open and Huck bounded in with the energy of a boy who'd been sitting still too long.

"Mom! Miss Sinclair!" He dropped his backpack on a desk and grinned at both women. "Malcolm and Gunnar want to go practice roping at the arena. Can I go? Please? We want to work on our loops before the rodeo."

Sierra looked at her son—really looked at him—and saw Rowan in the tilt of his head, the way his left eyebrow quirked when he was excited, the unconscious confidence in his posture. And that was just his aura. He looked almost identical to his father at this age, from the slight build to the crazy notch in his ear that Bailey called his Spock ear. Yes, big, big trouble.

"Mom?" Huck's face scrunched with concern. "You okay? You look weird."

"I'm fine, baby. Just tired." Sierra forced a smile. "How long do you want to practice?"

"Couple hours? Mal's dad said he'd bring us all home by dinner time."

"Go ahead. Be careful."

"Yes!" Huck pumped his fist and grabbed his backpack. "Thanks,

Mom. You're the best." He disappeared into the hallway, his boots echoing on polished floors as he ran toward the exit.

Bailey waited until the sound faded before speaking. "He looks just like him."

"I know."

"The way he moves, the way he tilts his head when he's thinking. Even his laugh sounds like Rowan's."

"I know."

"Sierra, that man is walking around town, and it's not going to take much before someone puts it together. Huck has his eyes and his smile and probably his stubborn streak."

"Huck's stubborn streak comes from me."

"Does it? Or does it come from the man who stood up to his abusive stepfather and enlisted in the military rather than back down from a fight?"

Sierra sank into one of the student chairs, her knees suddenly unable to support her weight. "What do I do, Bailey?"

"You tell the truth. To both of them."

"What if it ruins everything?"

"What if keeping the secret ruins everything?"

They sat in silence for a moment, surrounded by motivational posters, reading charts, student artwork celebrating families.

"He offered to help with the cattle rustlers," Sierra said quietly. "And?"

"And I wanted to say yes. For about thirty seconds, I wanted to let someone else carry the weight of figuring out how to protect the ranch and keep us safe."

"But you didn't."

"But I didn't. Because accepting help from him means opening a door I've kept locked for ten years. I can't take the hurt of him betraying me again. He may have been the boy next door, but he was a renegade with my heart. Stole it, broke it into a thousand pieces, and the sad part is that now it's no good for anyone else." Her mouth pinched. "But I can't get hurt again. I just . . . can't."

"But Sierra. You're in over your head."

"Well, thanks for the vote of confidence."

"I'm serious. You're one of the strongest people I know, but everyone needs backup sometimes. Even you."

Sierra's phone buzzed with a text message. She pulled it out and read the screen, then frowned.

"What is it?"

"Mal's mom. Says her husband and she are running late to pick up the boys from roping practice. Wants to know if I can get them."

"Go. We can finish this conversation later."

Sierra gathered her things and headed for the door, then paused. "Bailey?"

"Yeah?"

"If you were in my position, what would you do?"

Bailey considered her. "I'd probably be terrified. And angry. But I'd also remember that God has a plan for everything—don't look at me that way. Even this, Sierra. He can take the impossible and our broken hearts and . . . well, I guess I'd trust Him. And eventually, I'd tell the truth. Because lies have a way of exploding at the worst possible moment, and you and Huck deserve better than that."

Sierra gave Bailey a hug before she left.

The drive to the rodeo arena took fifteen minutes through South Eagle and past the high school where she and Rowan had spent countless hours together. Sierra tried not to think about homecoming dances and football games and promises made. Tried not to remember the way he'd looked at her when he'd said he'd come back for her after boot camp.

Yeah. Renegade. Or more simply . . .

A liar.

The arena sat on the outskirts of the city, a collection of metal buildings and practice pens where local kids learned to rope and ride before graduating to bigger competitions. Sierra parked near the entrance and walked toward the sound of whooping and cheering.

She found the boys in the main practice pen, taking turns roping a mechanical calf that jerked and spun unpredictably. Huck was up, rope coiled in his left hand, concentration written across his features as he tracked the machine's movement.

The throw was perfect—smooth release, tight loop, clean capture. The kind of natural ability that couldn't be taught, only refined through practice.

"Nice one, Huck!" Mal called from the fence rail. "Bet you could place at state with throws like that."

"Maybe." Huck reset his rope, grinning with satisfaction. "My great-grandpa always said good roping was about patience and timing."

"What about your dad?" Jake asked. "Bet he was good at roping too."

Sierra's breath caught. It was an innocent question, the kind kids asked each other without thinking about the complexity of family situations.

"My dad died before I was born," Huck said matter-of-factly. "Military hero. Mom has his flag."

"That's cool. I mean, not cool that he died, but cool that he was a hero."

"Yeah. Mom says he would have been proud of me."

Sierra gripped the fence rail, her knuckles white. Would Rowan be proud? Would he see his son's talent and feel something other than obligation or resentment?

"Hey, Mom!" Huck spotted her and waved. "Did you see that throw?"

"I saw. It was beautiful, baby."

"Can we stay a little longer?"

79

"Actually, we need to head home. Mal's mom is running late, so I'm taking you boys home."

"Aw, come on. Just ten more minutes?"

"Huck."

"Fine." He coiled his rope with the exaggerated disappointment of a ten-year-old whose fun was being cut short. "But I'm practicing again tomorrow."

"We'll see."

The drive home was filled with the boys' chatter about roping techniques and the rodeo competition. Sierra half listened, her mind churning with Bailey's words.

And Rowan. Oh, she'd never pry the look of him, intense, those blue eyes on her, ripping through her world out of her mind.

She couldn't do it. Couldn't let him back in.

She dropped Mal and Gunnar at their respective houses, then headed toward the ranch as the sun began to set behind the mountains. October evenings came early, painting the sky in shades of orange and purple that made the landscape look like something from a postcard.

"Mom, can I ask you something?" Huck's voice was quieter now, more serious.

"Always."

"Do you think my dad would have taught me to rope?"

The question hit her in the chest. "Yes, baby. I think he would have loved teaching you all kinds of things."

"Do you miss him?"

Sierra's throat tightened. "Every day."

It wasn't a lie, exactly. She did miss Rowan every day—missed the boy she'd loved, the man she'd thought he might become, the father she'd imagined he would have been to their son.

"Do you think he would have liked me?"

Oh, no. "Huck, he would have loved you more than his own life."

That part was absolutely true. Whatever else Rowan had become, whatever choices he'd made about staying dead to the world, he would have loved his son with the fierce protectiveness that had always defined him.

But that was the Rowan she knew. This man . . . ? Oh, she didn't know.

They came to the final hill before the ranch, and Sierra saw the smoke before she saw the flames.

"Mom." Huck's voice was small, frightened. "Something's wrong."

Something *was* wrong.

The red barn was on fire.

Flames licked through the roof, sending sparks into the darkening sky. Smoke billowed across the pasture, and she could hear the sound of sirens in the distance—someone had already called the fire department.

Sierra floored the accelerator, her truck flying down the gravel driveway. No—nooo. The barn where her great-great-grandfather had stored his first harvest. The barn where Grandpa Elway had taught her to gentle horses and stack hay and understand what it meant to be responsible for something bigger than yourself.

The barn where she'd kissed Rowan Wallace for the first time when they were fifteen years old.

The barn where Huck was made.

Sierra pulled up to the house and saw Morrie running toward them from the direction of the fire, his face black with smoke and his eyes wide with something that might have been panic.

"Get to the house and stay there. Fire department's on the way, but this thing's burning fast."

Sierra climbed out of the truck on unsteady legs, pulling Huck close to her side as they watched four generations of Blackwood history disappear into smoke and flame.

And somewhere in the back of her mind, she heard Rowan's voice from this morning. *You can't handle this alone.*

He was going to haunt her forever. Because the stupid man just might be right.

How did he think he could just drive into Renegade and fix everything in a day?

Rowan stuffed his spare shirt into his duffel bag with more force than necessary, the fabric bunching against the worn canvas. The Mountain View Motel room looked exactly like what it was—a place where people stopped when they had nowhere else to go. Water stains decorated the ceiling, and the carpet held the accumulated odors of forty years of transient guests.

"Well, this has been educational." Saxon closed his laptop and stretched his arms over his head. "But I found us something better than this five-star establishment."

"Define *better*."

"Four walls, running water, and no one complaining about domestic disputes through paper-thin walls at three in the morning." Saxon gestured toward the laptop screen. "Furnished rental house on Aspen Street. Month-to-month lease, available immediately. Owner's a widow who moved to Phoenix and doesn't want the house sitting empty."

Rowan paused in his packing. "Us?"

"You didn't think I was going to let you handle this mess alone, did you?" Saxon's grin was all teeth. "Besides, I like drama. Very entertaining."

"This isn't entertainment, Saxon."

"No, it's a tactical situation requiring backup and intelligence gathering. Two things I happen to excel at." Saxon stood and moved to the window, pushing aside the faded curtain to peer out at the parking lot. "Plus, someone needs to keep you from making any more brilliant strategic decisions, like announcing your resurrection in the middle of Main Street."

"Technically, we were in the police station. And I'm not the only one who was dead."

"I didn't leave behind a girlfriend who was clearly waiting for me to return." Saxon quirked an eyebrow.

"Yeah, okay, that was . . . that's on me. But I was planning on returning." Rowan's jaw tightened. "That operation in Syria was supposed to be our last."

The memory of Sierra's scream hit Rowan in the chest again. The look on her face when she'd seen him—pure shock morphing into something that might have been betrayal. Or rage. Or both.

"She screamed when she saw me." His voice dropped to barely above a whisper.

"Oof. That's rough." Saxon's tone gentled slightly.

"She thought I was dead, so I get it."

"And now she knows you're not. Question is, what are you going to do about it?" Saxon turned from the window, his expression more serious.

"I told you. I'm staying."

"Even though she made it clear she doesn't want your help." It wasn't a question. Saxon knew him too well, had seen him make the same choice too many times in too many dangerous places.

"Those cattle rustlers are real." Rowan sighed. "And if they killed her grandfather and Tom Hendrick to protect their operation, they won't hesitate to kill her too."

"So you're staying." Saxon nodded like this was the answer he'd expected.

"I'm staying."

"Good. Because I already put a security deposit down on the house." Saxon's grin returned.

"You what?" Rowan's head snapped up.

"Relax. It's refundable if we change our minds in the next twenty-four hours. But something tells me we're not changing our minds." Saxon reopened his laptop and turned the screen toward Rowan. "Three bedrooms, two baths, furnished kitchen. Previous tenant was a teacher who kept the place immaculate."

The house looked normal. Ordinary. The kind of place where people lived regular lives and worried about regular problems like mortgage payments and lawn care.

"How much?"

"Less than we'd spend on hotel rooms if we stayed at anything decent. Plus, it gives us a base of operations if we're going to figure out who's behind this cattle-rustling operation."

"So you're really sticking around to play detective?"

"Yeah. This is the most interesting thing that's happened to me since we left Afghanistan. Besides, I checked into getting a license. I just have to pass an exam and get a background check."

Rowan cocked his head.

"My guess is that our friend Uncle Sam might have tidied that up for me. If not, maybe Jamie Winters can help."

"You think Jamie is going to flex her tech muscles to get you a job taking pictures of cheating husbands?"

Saxon's mouth opened. "And bail jumpers. C'mon." But he grinned.

"Seriously. You want to be a PI? You're just bored."

"I'm professionally unfulfilled. There's a difference."

"And you think investigating cattle rustling is going to fulfill you professionally?"

"I think investigating cattle rustling that's connected to multiple suspicious deaths might be exactly the kind of challenge I've been looking for." Saxon closed the laptop with a snap. "Besides, someone needs to watch your six while you figure out how to apologize to a woman for letting her think you were dead."

"I can't tell her why I had to stay dead."

Saxon was quiet for a moment, processing the implications. "Maybe just say *deep cover*?"

"I guess that works. Frankly, I don't think any explanation is going to cut it. But I can't live with myself if something happens to her and I could have prevented it."

Saxon stood and shouldered his own duffel bag. "Fair enough. Let's go look at the house, then you can decide what your next move is."

"I already know my next move. I need to talk to my stepfather."

"The mayor? Why?"

"Because he's in a position to know about local crime. And because something about the way Detective Martinelli described the cattle rustling didn't sit right with me."

"What do you mean?"

Rowan grabbed his jacket from the chair by the window. "I mean professional cattle rustlers don't usually operate in areas where the mayor is actively working with law enforcement to stop them. Unless the mayor isn't actually working to stop them."

"You think your stepfather is involved?"

"I think my stepfather is capable of anything if it benefits him. And I think it's worth asking some questions."

He took the highway out to the Jenkins ranch, not driving by the Blackwoods' and . . . fine, maybe he'd swing by on the way back.

The ranch looked even more impressive in the daylight. The honey-colored logs gleamed in the late-afternoon sun, and the professional landscaping was immaculate. Everything about the place screamed money and success.

He hated it.

"Impressive," Saxon said as they pulled up. "Your stepfather's done well for himself."

"My stepfather's always been good at taking things that don't belong to him. This place was built with corrupt money and kick-backs, even before he became mayor."

Mayor Alden Jenkins opened the front door before they reached the porch steps. "Rowan." His voice held just the right note of surprised pleasure, but his eyes remained cold. "Mack said you might stop by. It's good to see you, son."

Son. Whatever. This man had never been his father, had never earned the right to use that word. Rowan managed not to hit him.

"Alden." Rowan kept his voice neutral, professional. "This is my friend Luca Saxon. We're in town for a few days."

"Any friend of Rowan's is welcome here." Jenkins extended his hand to Saxon, who shook it with the easy confidence of someone accustomed to dealing with authority figures. "Come in, both of you. Mack's in the den."

A woman appeared behind Jenkins in the doorway—petite, blonde, probably mid-fifties, wearing an apron over a floral dress. Her smile was genuine, if nervous.

"This is my wife, Catherine," Jenkins said, his tone warming slightly. "Cat, this is my stepson Rowan and his friend."

"Oh my." Catherine's voice was soft with surprise. "Mack's told me so much about you. Please, come in. I just put on a fresh pot of coffee."

She didn't seem nervous, didn't look at Alden for permission. Almost like she wasn't afraid of him.

The interior of the house matched its exterior—Chesterfield leather sofas, a couple Robert Wogrin oil landscapes on the walls, and the kind of cleanliness that spoke of hired help. Family photos lined the mantelpiece, including several of Mack at various ages. Rowan noted the absence of any pictures that included him or his mother.

"Bro!" Mack appeared in the doorway between the living room and kitchen. "I didn't think you were coming by until later."

"Change of plans. Saxon found us a place to stay."

"You're sticking around?" Mack's expression shifted to

something that might have been relief. "I was worried you were going to disappear again."

"Not disappearing. Just need a base of operations for a few days."

Alden gestured toward the kitchen. "Coffee's ready. Why don't we sit down and catch up?"

It was like they were old friends or something. Rowan shot a look at Mack, who just lifted a shoulder.

Whatever. He was here for answers.

The kitchen had been remodeled—soaring ceilings with exposed timber beams, white custom cabinetry, and an island the size of most people's dining rooms topped with dark granite. A stone fireplace dominated one wall, because yeah, people cooked in an open hearth these days. Frankly, the entire place looked like it belonged in a European villa.

Alden poured coffee and sat in one of the leather barstools at the massive island. Catherine handed Rowan a mug.

"Sit," Alden said. His smile was all charm, political. "What brings my dead stepson back to Renegade after all these years? Must be something pretty important to drag you away from . . . what was it again? Firefighting?"

So, Mack had caught him up.

"Time was right," Rowan said simply, accepting the coffee but not drinking.

"Time was right." Jenkins chuckled, the sound carrying just enough condescension to set teeth on edge. "That's beautifully vague. You always were the mysterious type, weren't you, Rowan? Even as a boy. Secrets." He looked at Saxon, beside Rowan, and waggled his eyebrows, like Rowan might be a little crazy.

Crazy might not be too far from the truth if he spent too long here.

"Heard there's been some trouble around here lately," Rowan said. "Cattle rustling. Suspicious deaths."

Alden took a sip of coffee, his gray eyes on Rowan. "Suspicious deaths? Where exactly did you hear that?"

"Tom Hendrick was found by my dad's old place. Murdered."

Alden put his coffee down, frowned. "I didn't know that."

Please. Rowan didn't believe that for a Montana minute.

"People are saying it might be connected to the rustling," Saxon said.

"I'll have to talk to the police chief, find out what's going on." Then he leaned back with the confidence of a man who controlled the narrative. "You know how people like to gossip, especially when they're looking for someone to blame for their own poor decisions. Some folks just can't accept that hard times come from poor choices."

"Whose poor choices?"

A beat. "I suppose you've been talking with Sierra Blackwood." He met Rowan's gaze.

"I . . . not really."

"Then you don't know that she's about to lose her ranch. Barely holding on after Elway passed. Cattle rustling is an insurable loss, so . . ."

Rowan stilled. "You think she's *lying*?"

Alden lifted a shoulder.

"Detective Martinelli seemed to think the rustling was legitimate."

"Mike Martinelli's a good man, but he's got limited resources and a lot of territory to cover. Sometimes he has to take reports at face value even when there might be other explanations."

"Other explanations?"

"Cattle wander off, especially in this terrain. Gates get left open, fences get damaged in storms. It's easy to assume theft when the reality might be simple negligence."

Saxon leaned forward slightly, his voice carrying the tone of someone making polite conversation. "What about the deaths?

Tom Hendrick, Elway Blackwood. Those seem pretty cut and dried."

"I don't know about Hendrick's, but Elway's death was a tragic accident. Elway was getting on in years. Shouldn't have been out there alone." Jenkins sipped his coffee, his expression appropriately somber. "But that's ranch life. Dangerous work, especially for folks who don't take proper precautions."

"Elway Blackwood was one of the most careful men I ever knew," Rowan said quietly. "Taught me to check equipment twice and plan for problems before they happened."

"People change as they age. Reflexes slow, judgment gets cloudy. Elway might have been careful once, but even the best of us make mistakes eventually."

"The timing seems coincidental," Saxon said.

"Coincidences happen." Jenkins sighed. "Though I suppose it's natural for outsiders to see patterns where locals see random events."

Outsiders. The word carried just enough edge to make it clear that Rowan wasn't considered a local anymore, despite growing up here. That he'd forfeited his right to opinions about Renegade when he'd left for the military.

"Any theories about who might be behind the rustling?" Rowan asked. "Assuming it's actually happening."

"If it's happening—and that's a big if—it's probably someone from outside the area. We don't have those kinds of problems with local folks. This is a tight-knit community. People look out for each other."

"People like Sierra Blackwood."

"Sierra's had a hard time since her grandfather died. Running a ranch alone isn't easy, especially for a woman with a child to raise. Sometimes stress can make people see threats where none exist."

"Maybe the community should rally around her," Saxon suggested. "Help her through a difficult time."

"Oh, we've tried. I've made several offers to buy the ranch, give her enough money to start fresh somewhere else. But Sierra's always been stubborn. Refuses to accept help even when it's in her best interest."

Buy the ranch? Maybe. It was beautiful land.

If he were honest, once upon a time, he'd dreamed of running the Blackwood place.

"What would you do with the ranch if you bought it?" Mack asked.

Rowan looked at him, the words *Sierra would never sell* on his lips. But Alden answered first.

"Development, probably. That land has potential beyond cattle ranching. Tourism, recreation, maybe residential if the market supports it." Alden took another sip of coffee. "South Eagle needs economic diversification. We can't survive on ranching and mining forever."

"Sounds like you've given it a lot of thought."

"It's my job to think about the town's future. Sometimes that means making hard decisions about change."

He stared at him, and just couldn't . . . couldn't keep his mouth shut. "Change that would benefit people like you, who have the capital to invest in development projects? Change that would push out people like Sierra, who represent the old way of life, that stand in the way of progress?"

Silence filled the room. Mack frowned at him.

Catherine came over with a plate. "Cookies?"

"Sierra is in over her head. She needs to figure that out," Alden said tightly.

"No. This is about the fact you still haven't forgiven her."

Alden's eyes narrowed. And then he reached over and put a hand on Mack's wrist, possessive, as if claiming territory. "A man doesn't like to be accused of things he didn't do."

Rowan just stared at him. Then at Mack, whose mouth made a grim line.

"Seriously." But he wasn't about to unload there, in front of Saxon. Because he didn't need Saxon hearing about … well, about those times when he hadn't been Hammer Wallace. When he'd been small and weak and scared.

"Funny thing about being presumed dead," Alden said. "People move on. They forget you existed. You disappear." He made a gesture with his hand. "Poof."

Rowan stared at Alden, his throat tightening.

"So, this has been educational," Saxon said suddenly, standing and extending his hand to Rowan's stepfather. "Thanks for the coffee and the local perspective."

Alden somehow morphed, right then, into a politician, smiling, warm. "Anytime. You boys should come by for dinner while you're in town. I'd love to hear more about your adventures in Alaska."

"We'll see how our schedule works out." Again, Saxon, who now put a hand on Rowan's shoulders. Almost to hold him back? Right.

Rowan glanced at Mack. "You okay here?"

"He's fine," said Alden, and threw an arm around his shoulder.

Saxon cleared his throat.

"Text if you need anything," Rowan said and Mack nodded.

The drive back toward South Eagle was quiet at first, Saxon staring out the passenger window.

"You want to talk about it?"

"Nope."

Saxon grunted. "You're not the person you used to be. Don't listen to him."

Yeah, okay, Saxon got him. Probably better than he knew. Because, well, he'd been dead too.

"He married my mom two years after my dad died. I was ten.

91

Mack was born a few months later. Alden and I . . . we just . . . he didn't like me much."

Saxon nodded.

"Last time I saw him, he was, uh, bleeding from . . . well, let's just say that it was either leave town or go to jail, so . . ."

"And your mom?"

"She died about a year before that, so . . . it was just Mack."

"Which is why we went to get him."

"Things were getting tense. Mack reached out before the Syria trip. After the dust of the op cleared, I thought I'd stop in and see how he was . . . saw he'd been in a fight. Mack never told me why. I might have overreacted by grabbing him, but . . . I don't know. I'm okay never seeing that place again."

A beat, then, "And that story about Sierra? Him not forgiving her?"

He glanced at Saxon. "She, uh, told her grandfather that . . . well, maybe things weren't great at home. And he was the police commissioner then, so he sent a social worker around. Alden was good at making people believe his version of events. Especially people who wanted to believe the best about him."

"And he took it out on you."

"Let's not talk about—wait. Is that smoke?"

They crested the hill that overlooked the valley where Renegade sat nestled between mountain ranges. Black clouds of smoke billowed into the sky, visible even in the fading daylight.

"It's coming from the Blackwood ranch." Rowan floored the accelerator.

No, no—the red barn was consumed by flames that flared through the roof, sending tongues of orange and red flicking into the darkening sky. Smoke billowed in thick black clouds, carrying the acrid smell of burning hay and old timber. The fire had a voice—a crackling roar of destruction.

Not the barn!

Sierra stood near the house, a garden hose in her hands, directing a pathetic stream of water toward the inferno while another man worked frantically with a second hose from the other side. The barn's wooden siding glowed like heated copper in the firelight, paint blistering and peeling in long curls that drifted away on superheated air.

Sirens whined in the air.

Rowan skidded into the drive, nearly out of the truck before it fully stopped, running toward the scene.

The barn's structure was compromised but still standing, flames concentrated in the hayloft but spilling down the interior walls. The house remained untouched, fifty feet of gravel driveway providing a firebreak, but flying sparks sprayed dangerously close to the roof shingles.

"Saxon!" he shouted over the roar of the fire. "Get that hose over here! Wet down the house!"

He ran up to Sierra, who shot him a look even as she turned to the house.

"Are there any more hoses?"

"I don't—"

"Where's Huck?" The cowboy ran up to Sierra. "I lost him in the smoke!"

She stared at him, even as Rowan searched the yard.

"Inside the house—" She turned to it.

No. No, he wasn't. Because he spotted the kid—Huck—headed into the barn.

Rowan's blood turned to ice.

The barn's main door stood open, a rectangle of hellish orange light framing the entrance. Smoke poured from the opening, and the heat was already intense enough to feel from twenty feet away.

"Huck!" Sierra started running toward the barn.

Rowan caught her arm, spinning her around. "No! You'll get yourself killed!"

"He's my son!"

"I'll get him. Sax—keep her away!"

He took off running as Sierra screamed behind him.

The heat hit him like a physical wall as he reached the doorway, superheated air searing his lungs with each breath. He pulled his shirt up over his nose and mouth, squinting against the smoke that made his eyes stream.

The interior was a hellscape of shadows and leaping flames. Fire had consumed most of the hay stored in the loft above, raining burning debris down into the main aisle. The wooden support beams groaned ominously, stressed by heat and the weight of the collapsing structure above.

"Huck!" His voice was swallowed by the roar of flames.

A sound—crying, maybe, or a frightened animal—came from the middle of the barn. Rowan moved toward it, staying low, where the air was slightly cleaner, dodging falling embers that hissed and sparked when they hit the concrete floor.

He found the boy huddled in an empty horse stall, clutching a small Jack Russell terrier puppy against his chest. The kid's face was streaked with soot and tears, his school clothes singed and dirty.

"He ran into the barn. I couldn't leave him," Huck gasped when he saw Rowan.

"I know, buddy. But we need to go. Right now."

Rowan scooped up the boy, puppy and all, holding him tight against his chest as another section of hayloft collapsed behind them. The support beam nearest the door cracked with a sound like a gunshot, and the entire structure shuddered.

He ducked his head and ran.

He was back in Alaska, outrunning a wildfire, or maybe Montana, or even Syria, waiting to get ambushed.

Heat pressed down on them from above while flames reached out from both sides, turning the barn aisle into a corridor of hell.

Rowan's lungs burned with each breath, and sweat poured down his face despite the October evening air.

They burst through the doorway just as the main support beam gave way with a thunderous crash. Rowan stumbled and went down on one knee in the gravel, but kept his arms wrapped around Huck and the puppy.

He took the blow on his back, scuffed up, breathing hard, the kid alive against him.

"Huck!" Sierra ran over as they stumbled away from the fire, pulled her son from Rowan's arms and crushed him against her chest, sobbing.

Rowan sat up, heart thundering.

Sierra just held the kid, rocking him. "Don't you ever, ever do something like that again!"

Huck shuddered in her arms, still holding the puppy.

Brave little kid, for an eight-year-old. Stupid, but brave.

"Bandit was in there."

She pulled away, put her hands on his face. "Bandit's not worth your life. *Nothing* is worth your life."

Rowan pushed himself to his feet, coughing smoke from his lungs. His shirt was singed in several places, and he could feel the beginning sting of minor burns on his forearms, but he was alive. They were all alive.

And he intended to keep it that way.

FIVE

SIERRA HAD SPENT TEN YEARS TEACHING HER-self not to need Rowan Wallace.

And one night, one split second, had obliterated that lie.

The volunteer fire department had arrived with sirens wailing and lights flashing, but by then the barn was beyond saving. Captain Murphy and his crew had focused on containing the blaze and protecting the house.

Now, an hour later, the acrid smell of smoke still clung to everything—her clothes, her hair, the air itself.

Sierra stood on the back deck with Rowan and Samantha Williams, one of the firefighters, watching the barn's charred skeleton cool under the star-filled sky. Occasional sparks still glowed orange in the ruins where four generations of her family's history had turned to ash.

"Captain Murphy asked me to give you the preliminary findings," Sam said. Petite with shoulder-length blonde hair pulled back in a practical ponytail, she had the kind of no-nonsense demeanor that came from years of dealing with emergencies. She still wore her helmet, her turnout gear. "How do you think the fire started?"

"I don't know." Sierra shook her head. "I came home and it was in flames."

"Could've been faulty wiring," Rowan suggested. "Old barns, rodents chewing through insulation."

"Possible," Sam said, but her tone suggested she wasn't convinced. "Though the burn patterns are unusual. Fire seems to have started in multiple places, spread faster than it should have for natural causes."

"Unusual how?" Rowan stood with his arms crossed, his attention focused entirely on Sam's explanation.

And of course, Sierra's attention was focused on Rowan—the angry red burn marks across his forearms where embers had caught his skin, the soot streaked across his cheekbones, the way his flannel shirt was singed at the shoulders.

And oh—she couldn't stop seeing him the way he'd looked, a man practically on fire as he burst through those barn doors with flames licking at his back, Huck clutched against his chest.

Her entire life, packaged in the arms of the man she'd tried to forget.

Right.

And he'd had no idea—*zip*—that he was saving his own son.

"We found a burned patch in the back corner of the barn that doesn't match the rest of the fire pattern," Sam was saying. "Could be where accelerant was used, but we'll need to do a full investigation to be sure." Sam's mouth pressed into a thin line as she watched the crew finish the mop up, wind the hoses back into the truck. "I'll be back tomorrow with the state fire investigator to run some tests."

"But someone might have deliberately burned down my barn."

Sierra's voice sounded just angry enough to give her a little staying power. She wasn't going to curl into a ball and weep. Not yet.

"That's what we need to determine. Could be an electrical short, could be spontaneous combustion from hay, could be kids with matches, could be someone with a grudge." Sam shifted her weight from one foot to the other. "You have any enemies? Anyone who might want to hurt you?"

Sierra's jaw tightened. "More than I thought, apparently."

"Captain wants me to recommend you stay somewhere else tonight. Hotel, friends, family. Just until we know more."

"This is my home." Sierra's voice dropped to a dangerous quiet. "I'm not leaving."

"Then you shouldn't be alone. Anyone you can call?"

"She won't be alone," Rowan said quietly beside her. Except not quietly, because the words simply thundered through her, stripped away her words, her breath.

What?

Her mouth opened though, and maybe that was enough for him to round on her.

"I'm staying. Tonight, tomorrow, however long it takes to make sure you and Huck are safe."

She didn't ask how he'd learned his son's name—probably from her screaming it as he ran into the burning barn. "I didn't ask you to stay."

"You didn't ask me to pull your son out of a burning barn either, but I did it anyway." His eyes met hers in the porch light. "Some things don't require permission."

Sam cleared her throat. "So. I'll leave you folks to sort out the details. Need to get back and help Captain Murphy finish his report."

She headed down the deck steps toward her truck but paused and turned back. "Sierra? Be careful. If this was arson, whoever did it might not be finished."

Oh great. And there went any final scraps of argument to tell Superman to Stand. Down.

Apparently, she'd need to make up the guest room.

The truck's engine started and red taillights disappeared down the gravel driveway. Sierra crossed her arms over her chest. "I need to call my insurance agent tomorrow. Grandpa had coverage, but I don't know how much."

"We'll figure it out."

"We?" Hello. "There's no 'we' here, Rowan. You made that clear ten years ago."

"I . . . no, Sierra." He turned to her. "There are reasons I didn't come back—"

She held up her hand. "Save them."

"Really? You're not going to listen to anything I have to say?"

She'd headed off the porch to survey the damage. "I don't need to. You made your choice."

"I was in the military. We didn't have *choices*."

The barn stood like a blackened skeleton against the night sky, the wooden roof beams charred, the ribs of some massive fallen beast. The stone foundation remained intact, but everything above it had been consumed—century-old timber posts reduced to charcoal stumps, the hay loft nothing but empty air, and the smell of smoke that would linger for months.

Rowan stepped up behind her. "Okay, maybe I did make choices. But I'd call them mistakes. Terrible mistakes."

She closed her eyes. Sighed. "You can't just walk back into my life and fix everything, Row."

"Sierra. Someone tried to burn down your barn tonight, and I'm not leaving you and your son to face that alone."

Words, the terrible words that could dig through her, find root. Oh, she didn't want to need this man—

"Mom!" The kitchen door opened, and Huck appeared in the doorway, still clutching Bandit against his chest. The puppy had finally stopped trembling, but Huck's hair was damp from a quick bath and his face still showed streaks where tears had washed away soot. His pajamas stuck to his body, still wet in places.

"Mom? I'm hungry."

She shook her head. "Of course you are. There's leftover spaghetti—"

"I can get it."

She shot a look at Rowan. "I don't need another fire." She headed inside.

Rowan followed her.

Huck had filled a water bowl for the dog and now set it on the floor. The pup went over to drink, its whip tail wagging.

She took the container of spaghetti from the fridge, put it onto a plate to microwave.

"You did a dangerous thing, going after that dog," Rowan said softly behind her.

She glanced over her shoulder.

The man had gotten on the floor next to the dog. And Huck.

She turned away.

"Mom says I shouldn't have. Says I could've died."

"Your mom's right. But I understand why you did it."

She opened the microwave. Spotted Rowan patting the dog with his big hand. "Sometimes we take risks for the things we love. The trick is making sure the risk is worth it."

"Was Bandit worth it?"

"What do you think?"

Huck's forehead wrinkled in concentration. "I think maybe I should have asked for help instead of going alone."

Sierra braced her hands on the counter, her jaw tight. Don't cry. Don't—

"That's very wise. Asking for help isn't giving up. It's being smart."

Aw. Now he was talking to her. Jerk.

She glanced at him.

He smiled at her.

Jerk!

"Hey, what happened to your hand?" Rowan had noticed a cut on Huck's palm, partially hidden by the boy's pajama sleeve.

"Fell on a rake when I was running in. It's not bad."

"Let me take a look." Rowan examined it. "Yeah, it needs a Band-Aid." He got up, moved toward the cabinets. "First aid kit?"

"Above the sink."

He found the first aid kit and spread its contents on the table, then gently took Huck's hand in his. The cut was shallow but still seeping blood, the edges ragged from the rake's teeth.

"This might sting a little," Rowan warned, opening an alcohol wipe.

"I'm tough." Huck's chin came up.

"I can see that. But tough guys are allowed to say 'ouch' when something hurts. Being brave doesn't mean pretending things don't hurt."

And now she had to avert her eyes to the way Rowan so gently, terribly gently, doctored Huck's hand.

She remembered the touch, from years ago, and—

Nope. Nope. The barn was gone—it was a sign. Those days were gone with it.

"Are you a firefighter?" Huck asked.

Seemed like a logical question, and to her surprise, Rowan nodded. "I was. I was a hotshot. You know what that is?"

Huck shook his head.

"We fight wilderness fires. I worked in Montana, and then Alaska."

"Cool," Huck said.

She stared at him. "When was this?"

He glanced over at her. "The last . . . um, three years." He gave her a thin smile, then turned back to Huck.

Since he died?

"Do you have any scars?" This from Huck.

Rowan's hands paused for just a moment. "A few."

"Can I see them?"

"Huck," Sierra started, but Rowan was already rolling up his left sleeve to reveal a jagged scar that ran from his wrist halfway to his elbow.

"Whoa. How'd you get that?"

"This was when I was a soldier. Can't really talk about the details, but it involved some unfriendly people and a piece of metal that was sharper than it looked."

"Does it hurt?"

"Not anymore. Took a while to heal, but now it's just part of me." Rowan applied antibiotic ointment to Huck's cut. "My buddy Saxon says scars make you look tough. Girls think they're cool."

"Really?"

"Really. But the best part about scars is that they remind you that you survived something difficult. They're proof that you're stronger than whatever tried to hurt you."

Huck stared at his bandaged hand with new appreciation. "So this makes me tough?"

"This makes you a survivor. There's a difference."

Sierra's breath caught as she watched Rowan secure the bandage with medical tape, his dark head bent close to Huck's lighter one.

"All done." Rowan released Huck's hand and began cleaning up the first aid supplies. "Keep it dry for a day or two, and change the bandage tomorrow."

The microwave beeped and saved her from bursting into crazy tears.

She pulled the plate out and set it on the table. Grabbed a fork.

Huck took a chair and dug in. "My dad was a soldier."

She stilled.

Rowan sat in the chair opposite him. "Really."

"Yeah. He died though. Before I was born." Huck shoveled the noodles into his mouth, wearing much of the sauce on his chin. "Right, Mom?"

Oh. "Right." She met Rowan's eyes. "Good man."

Rowan drew in a breath. "I see."

She turned away. So maybe . . . oh, no, no. How was she supposed to do this?

A knock came at the door, and she looked over to see his friend come in. Dark hair, a military build. "I'm getting a ride to town with the fire crew. I'll find my own wheels. You coming?"

Rowan looked at Sierra, back to him. "I'm sticking around here."

The man glanced at Sierra, back to Rowan. "Alrighty then. Stay frosty." He shook his head and headed out.

"What does that mean?" Huck said.

"Oh, it's just a military term that means, you know, watch out for danger. Stay alert."

"Like be careful?"

Rowan glanced at Sierra. "Something like that."

She frowned, then walked over to Huck. He'd finished his food. "You need to get to bed. It's way past your bedtime."

"But I'm not tired." Huck's eyelids drooped as he said it.

"Nice try. Upstairs, teeth brushed, in bed in ten minutes."

"Can Rowan tell me a story?"

Sierra felt her carefully constructed walls beginning to crumble. "I don't think—"

"I'd be happy to," Rowan said quietly. "If it's okay with your mom."

Sierra looked at her son's hopeful face, then at Rowan's steady gaze. "One story. Then bed."

"Yes!" Huck pumped his good fist in the air. "Come on, Rowan. My room's upstairs."

Oh boy.

But she needed a hot minute here to gather her thoughts. She rinsed the plate, then put it in the dishwasher, then wiped the table and then . . . just stood at the window above the sink and stared out at the barn's remains.

How could it be that she got Rowan back the same day she nearly lost him?

She pressed the towel to her face, shaking.

The sound of Rowan's voice drifted down from upstairs, too quiet to make out words but carrying the cadence of someone spinning a tale. Huck's occasional laughter punctuated the narrative.

What was he doing here, in her house, tucking her son into bed like he belonged here? And every minute he stayed . . .

Except he *wasn't* staying, was he? His expression on the street when she'd asked him exactly that told her . . .

I don't know.

No, he wasn't planning on sticking around. Which meant she couldn't count on him. Not really.

Which of course, she knew. But how could she tell Huck about his father, only to have him break his little heart?

And yes, Rowan deserved to know. But not if he planned on walking away.

"He's asleep," Rowan said, coming down the stairs. "Kid was exhausted."

"What did you tell him?"

"Story about a soldier and his team who had to rescue some villagers from a flood. Nothing scary, just teamwork and problem-solving."

"He likes adventure stories."

"I figured. He's got good questions too. Smart kid."

Sierra's throat tightened. "He gets that from his father."

The words slipped out before she could stop them. Rowan went still.

"I'm sorry for your loss, Sierra." He stood at the bottom of the stairs. "He must have been a good man."

104

His gaze found hers. She just stared at him. *Really?* But, "He was." The truth felt heavy on her tongue. "Huck doesn't remember him, obviously. But I tell him stories."

"That's important. A boy should know about his father."

Sierra nodded. Instead of running. But in her head, she was sprinting. "I should make up the bed in the guest room," she said instead and started down the hall.

"Sierra."

Something in his voice made her turn. He was standing in the middle of her kitchen, hands at his sides.

"Thank you," he said finally. "For letting me stay. For letting me help with Huck. I know this isn't easy for you."

"You saved his life. It's the least I can do."

"It's more than that. You could have sent me to a hotel, could have kept your distance. Instead, you're letting me into your home."

She folded her arms. "Don't read too much into it. This is about safety, not sentiment."

"I know." He offered a smile. She looked away from its devastating power. "Still. Thank you."

Sierra nodded and grabbed fresh sheets from the linen closet.

The room was small but comfortable, across the hall from the den where she and Rowan had spent countless teenage evenings watching movies and gaming.

He came in and helped her make the bed, his corners sharp. She smoothed the cover over the bed. "I'll get you some towels."

He stepped back to let her pass. "I could use a shower."

And maybe first aid, but the last thing she wanted to do was put salve on his wounds. Yeah, that would only lead to trouble.

The man still had the power to turn her to rubble, maybe more so today.

"Me too. Help yourself to anything you want in the fridge. I'll be up early to check on the cattle." She pulled out a couple towels from the closet.

"I'll help."

"You don't have to—"

"S." He said her old nickname quietly, and she made the mistake of looking at him, her heart so loud he could probably hear it. "I'm here. Let me help."

Oh, heaven help her. She shoved the towels at him. "Morrie will be here at six. You can help him assess the damage, figure out what we can salvage."

"Sounds like a plan."

She turned to go, but his voice stopped her at the doorway.

"Sierra?"

"Yeah?"

"I know you don't trust me. I know I don't have the right to ask for anything from you. But I'm glad I was here tonight. Glad I could help."

She nodded without turning around. Because the truth was, she was glad too. Grateful and terrified and overwhelmed by how right it felt to have him here, helping with Huck, moving through her home like he'd never left.

But he *had* left. And he would leave again, eventually.

In fact, sooner would be better. Before either of them got too attached to this temporary arrangement. Before her son started thinking of Rowan as something more than a helpful stranger.

Before she started believing in dreams she'd buried ten years ago.

She made it to her bedroom and closed the door before the tears came. Silent tears for the barn and the sense of security that had burned away with the hay. Tears for the exhaustion that made her want to lean on someone else for just five minutes.

Tomorrow, she would probably have to start figuring out how to tell the truth. Tonight, she would just have to survive having him under her roof without finding herself tiptoeing back downstairs and watching him sleep, those dark lashes on his handsome face.

Rowan Wallace, the renegade who'd stolen her heart, wasn't dead.

And yet, it just might kill her.

———————————

He'd woken up in a lot of places over the past ten years— tents, safe houses, hotels that smelled like old socks. But none of them felt like home.

The sound of Sierra singing "Amazing Grace" in the kitchen drifted through the guest room door, and for one blessed moment, Rowan forgot he was supposed to be dead. Her voice carried the familiar melody with a sweetness that made his chest ache, soft and clear in the morning stillness.

For three heartbeats, he lay still in the double bed, eyes closed, letting himself believe he was eighteen again and this was just another Saturday morning in the life they'd planned together.

Then reality crashed back. The smell of smoke still clinging to his clothes. The charred skeleton of the barn visible through the guest room window. Ten years of separation stretching between him and the woman whose voice had once been his favorite sound in the world.

Rowan sat up, running a hand through his hair. The clock on the nightstand read 7:23 a.m. Early, even for ranch people, but the smell of bacon frying suggested Sierra had been up for a while.

He pulled on yesterday's shirt and padded barefoot toward the kitchen, following the scent of coffee.

She stood at the six-burner stove with her back to him, and for a moment, he could only stare.

Her dark hair fell in waves just past her shoulders, catching the morning light that streamed through the window. She wore a blue flannel shirt and worn jeans. At five foot five, she'd always been petite, but ranch work had kept her lean and strong, her movements graceful and economical as she worked at the stove. Even doing something as mundane as frying bacon, she projected the quiet competence that had always drawn him to her.

For a broken kid, a girl who believed in herself, in him, had magnetic power.

The kitchen island held evidence of her morning routine—coffee grounds scattered on the granite, a carton of eggs, strips of bacon laid out on a cutting board. Pendant lights hung over the island, casting warm pools of light that made the space feel intimate despite its size. Fresh flowers sat on the windowsill next to the sink, probably picked from the garden behind the house.

"Morning," he said quietly, not wanting to startle her.

She turned, spatula in hand, and smiled. The expression transformed her face, softening the high cheekbones that gave her such striking beauty and lighting up the dark-brown eyes that had always seemed to see straight through to his soul. "Coffee's fresh. Mugs are in the cabinet above the pot."

"Thanks." He moved to pour himself a cup.

The coffee maker sat tucked into a corner near the professional-grade stove, surrounded by the kind of well-organized chaos that spoke of a kitchen actually used for cooking rather than for show. Mason jars filled with utensils, a ceramic canister set that looked handmade, dish towels draped over the oven handle—all of it practical and lived-in.

"Sugar?"

"Yeah." His fingers brushed hers as she handed him the sugar bowl. The brief contact rippled through him.

Okay, sure. He could admit that the old desire had awoken inside him. But he wasn't here to woo her back.

Yet.

Aw, shoot. He needed to delete that from any mission parameters. It would only complicate things. Rock him off his game.

"Morrie called. He'll be a little late." She flipped the bacon.

"I need to bring Huck in for some rodeo training this morning. The Junior Buckaroos are having a practice today in prep for the rodeo next weekend."

"And Huck is in it?"

"Yeah."

He set down the mug and turned to face her fully, his hand gripping the counter edge. "I'd like to go. If that's okay."

Sierra's eyebrows rose, her spatula freezing mid-flip. "You sure? It's not exactly exciting. Just kids learning to rope."

"I'm sure." Rowan set down his coffee mug.

She narrowed her eyes a moment, then, "Okay."

Okay. He sort of wanted to pump his fist with a *hooah*. Except… "Although maybe I should stick around here. Make sure—"

"No one burns the house down?"

His mouth opened. "Um."

"I was sort of kidding, although I guess that's not funny." She sighed. "Morrie will be here."

Morrie. Yeah, the guy who *wasn't* her husband.

He quelled another fist pump. "So, what's Huck hoping to accomplish with the rodeo?"

"There's a grand prize of five hundred dollars for the junior division winner. He wants to use it to buy a horse." Sierra's voice carried a mix of pride and worry. "Been saving every penny he can get his hands on, but a good horse costs more than a kid can earn doing chores."

"He's got his eye on a particular animal?"

"Raol Martinez has a quarter horse gelding. Gentle enough for a kid but smart. Good bloodlines." She cracked eggs into the bacon grease, the whites sizzling and bubbling. "Huck's crazy in love with the horse."

"Sounds like he's got good taste."

"Gets that from his great-grandfather, I suppose. He loved

horses." She sighed and pain flickered across her features, quickly masked but unmistakable.

"I'm sorry," he said quietly.

She glanced at him. Frowned. Then, "Oh. Yeah. Me too." She stirred the eggs.

"Elway was a good man."

"The best." Sierra's voice caught slightly. "I still expect to see him coming up the driveway for Sunday breakfast. Still make too much coffee because he always drank three cups."

"I miss him too."

The simple words seemed to unlock something in Sierra's carefully controlled expression.

She turned away.

It was everything he could do not to cross the room, take her in his arms.

And *stop*.

"He would be proud of you, you know," Rowan said quietly, his voice rough with emotion. "Proud of how you've kept this place running, how you're raising Huck."

"How can you know that?" She slid two eggs onto a plate beside several strips of bacon and handed them to him.

He took the plate to the table. "Because I knew him. Because anyone with eyes can see what you've accomplished here."

Sierra considered him for a moment, then sighed. "Yeah, well, the inheritance he left barely covered the taxes on this place, and . . ." She leaned a hip against the counter. "I want Huck to grow up here."

"I talked to . . . Alden yesterday."

Her brow went up, and she reached for her coffee. "And no one was hospitalized?"

"Funny."

But she smiled, and it just lit something inside him. Those eyes in his.

She so knew him, even now.

"I still can't believe he got away with—"

He held up a hand. "It's over. And I'm a grown man. But yeah, I can admit that for a moment . . ." He made a face. "Anyway, he said he offered to buy your place?"

She made a sound. "Yeah. As if I would ever sell my property to that man."

He could kiss her, straight out, for that.

Instead, he dug into his eggs.

She cracked more eggs into the pan, and about then, Huck came downstairs. He wore pajama pants and a T-shirt, his hair sticking up in every direction.

Something about the way he smiled at his mom, walking over to steal a piece of bacon, just sort of jolted Rowan. Wow, he was a handsome kid.

"Morning, sleepyhead," Sierra said, kissing him on the head. "You're up early."

"Smelled bacon." Huck yawned and scratched his stomach. "Hey, Mr. R. You stayed."

He'd suggested the name last night during their little bedtime routine. Now he saw Sierra's mouth tweak up at it.

"Yep. I'll be around . . . for a bit."

Sierra glanced at him, but didn't deny it. Another *hooah*.

"Cool." Huck slumped into a chair at the table. "You going to practice with me today?"

"Yep."

Huck's eyes brightened immediately. "Awesome. Mal said he's been working on his backup loop all week. But I bet mine's still better."

"Confidence is good," Rowan said. "But practice is better."

"I practice every day. Well, except when it's raining. Or when Mom makes me do homework first."

"Homework always comes first," Sierra said firmly, setting a plate of eggs and bacon in front of her son.

"I know. But sometimes I think about how much better I'd be if I could practice *instead* of doing math problems."

"Math problems teach you to think logically. Problem-solving. That's useful for roping too," Rowan said.

Huck looked skeptical. "How?"

"Well, you've got a moving target, right? The calf is running, changing direction, trying to get away. You have to calculate speed, distance, timing. Figure out where the calf is going to be, not where it is right now."

"Huh." Huck chewed thoughtfully. "I never thought about it like that."

"Plus, if you win that five hundred dollars, you'll need to know how to manage money. Budget for feed, vet bills, equipment. Math becomes pretty important when you're handling your own finances."

"You think I can win?"

"I think you can do anything you set your mind to. But winning isn't just about talent. It's about preparation, practice, and staying calm under pressure."

"Did you ever compete?"

"Some. When I was about your age."

"Were you good?"

"Good enough."

Sierra snorted softly. "He was regional champion three years running. Don't let him be modest."

"Really?" Huck's eyes went wide. "That's so cool."

"How's the cut feeling this morning?" Rowan asked.

"Not bad. Kind of itchy."

"That means it's healing. We'll change the bandage after breakfast. Make it tight so it won't get ripped when you rope."

Sierra seemed to watch the easy interaction between them, her expression unreadable. Something flickered in her eyes—warmth, maybe, or pain. Or both.

"I should get in the shower," she said abruptly.

"I'll clean up the kitchen," Rowan said.

"You don't have to—"

"I want to."

She nodded and headed for the stairs but paused at the doorway. "Rowan?"

"Yeah?"

"I'm glad you came back."

He stilled.

She smiled. Then she disappeared up the stairs, leaving him alone with Huck and a terrible heat inside him.

"She likes you," Huck said matter-of-factly, scooping up the last of his eggs.

"What makes you say that?"

"She made you breakfast. She only makes breakfast for people she likes. Usually it's just cereal for me on school days."

"Maybe she was just being polite."

"Plus, she's singing again."

"She was singing when I woke up."

"She used to sing all the time when I was little. We'd turn on the radio and sing along. But she stopped a couple years ago. Now she only sings when she's really happy or really sad."

"Which one is this?"

Huck tilted his head, considering. "Happy, I think. She gets a line between her eyebrows when she's sad. Right here." He pointed to the spot between his own eyebrows. "She doesn't have the line this morning."

Smart kid. Observant. The kind of intelligence that would serve him well in life, whether he became a cowboy or something else entirely.

"Can I ask you something, Huck?"

"Sure."

"What do you want to be when you grow up? Besides a horse owner."

"Rancher. Like Mom and my great-grandpa. Maybe firefighter too, like you. Help people when they're in trouble."

"Those are both good goals."

"What did you want to be when you were my age?"

"Happy," Rowan said without thinking.

The honesty of the answer surprised him. Wow. But yeah. Happy, and most of that had centered around Sierra.

Until life sort of exploded. But if he were honest . . . maybe that was what drove him back here.

Huck studied him. "Are you happy now?"

He lifted a shoulder. "Getting there."

"Good. Mom deserves to be around happy people. She works too hard to have to deal with grumpy grown-ups all the time."

"You have grumpy grown-ups around?"

"Sometimes Mom and Morrie argue."

"You like Morrie?"

"He's great. Teaches me to rope. And he gives me books."

"What kind of books?"

"Adventure stories mostly. Stories about people who go on quests and save other people and have to be brave even when they're scared."

"Really."

"He doesn't have any kids. Says reading is good preparation for life."

So maybe he didn't hate this Morrie guy quite so much. "True," Rowan said.

"Yeah. Plus, heroes always get the girl in the end."

Rowan coughed, trying to cover his reaction.

"You okay?" Huck asked.

"Fine. Just went down the wrong way."

"Mom says that happens when you try to drink and think at the same time."

"Your mom is a smart woman."

"The smartest. And she's pretty too. Don't you think she's pretty?"

"Very pretty."

"Good." He smiled.

Before Rowan could figure out how to respond to that, Sierra's voice drifted down from upstairs.

"Huck! Come get ready! We need to leave for the arena soon!"

"Coming!" Huck slid off his chair and headed for the stairs, then turned back. "Mr. R?"

"Yeah?"

"I don't know what my mom meant, but I'm glad you came back too."

The boy disappeared up the stairs, leaving Rowan alone in the kitchen with the morning sunlight and the lingering scent of bacon and the sound of Sierra moving around in the room above his head.

Yeah, yeah, him too.

SIX

SHE SHOULD HAVE KNOWN THAT SAYING YES TO Rowan's request to join them would only drag up the past.

Sierra sat on the bleachers of the Renegade Community Arena, her travel mug of coffee growing cold in her hands as she watched the practice session. The morning sun slanted across the dusty arena floor, where a dozen kids worked on their roping techniques under a couple volunteer cowboys' patient instruction. Parents dotted the stands around her, some chatting quietly while others called out encouragement to their children below.

Rowan had sat beside her for the first twenty minutes, making polite conversation about the weather and the upcoming Fall Festival Rodeo. But she'd seen the way his eyes kept drifting to the arena, the way his hands unconsciously mimicked the movements of the kids practicing their throws. When one of the instructors had called out a correction about wrist position that was completely wrong, Rowan had shifted restlessly in his seat.

"You should go down there," Sierra had finally said.

"I don't want to interfere—"

"Rowan." She'd given him the look that had worked when they were teenagers, the one that said she could see right through his protests. "Go help."

But it wasn't just the past she was worried about. It was how normal this morning had felt when she'd come down from taking a shower and found him in her kitchen, another pot of coffee brewing, a snack for Huck half packed on the counter. He'd moved through her space like he belonged there, reaching for mugs in the right cabinet without asking, and for a hot, dangerous minute, she'd let herself imagine this was her life—waking up to find Rowan making breakfast, their son chattering about his plans for the day, the three of them moving around each other with the easy familiarity of an actual family.

That was the real danger. Not the past, but how effortlessly, just like that, he fit into her present. How right it felt to have him here, how much she wanted to keep him.

She was already in so much trouble.

And it had only gotten worse. Now she watched him move between the young ropers like he'd been teaching children his whole life, his voice carrying clear across the arena as he demonstrated techniques that most of these kids had never seen before. The parents around her had started whispering, asking who the newcomer was, commenting on how naturally he worked with their children.

And Huck—her heart squeezed as she watched her son hanging on Rowan's every word, his face bright with the kind of hero worship she'd never seen him direct at anyone before.

"Keep your wrist loose," Rowan was saying, his voice patient. "The rope needs to flow, not fight you."

Huck nodded seriously, his small hands working to position the coils correctly. "Like this?"

"Better. Now, remember what I said about your stance. You want to be balanced, ready to move with your target."

Sierra's breath caught as memories crashed over her—Rowan at sixteen, cocky and confident, showing off with his lasso at the county fair. He'd roped her then, literally, pulling her close with a grin that had made her teenage heart stutter.

"Caught myself something pretty," he'd said, his voice low and teasing.

"Let me go, Rowan Wallace," she'd said, but of course she hadn't meant it.

"Not a chance."

The memory was so vivid she could almost feel his hands on her waist again, could almost taste the cotton candy and excitement in the air. They'd been so young, so sure they had forever stretching ahead of them.

"Mom, watch!" Huck's voice snapped her back to the present.

Her son threw the lasso with surprising precision, the loop sailing toward the practice dummy and settling neatly around one of its horns. Huck whooped and turned to Rowan with shining eyes.

"I did it!"

"You sure did." Rowan's smile was pure pride. "Natural talent."

Natural talent. Sierra's heart squeezed.

"Try it again," Rowan said.

As Huck reset his position, Rowan glanced over at Sierra. "He's good. Really good for his age."

"He's been practicing since he was six." The words came out steady, but Sierra's pulse hammered. "My grandfather taught him the basics."

"Your grandfather was a good teacher." Rowan's voice held history. "He taught me a lot too."

For a second, Rowan's eyes searched hers, and Sierra felt like he could see straight through to her soul. All the secrets, all the years of silence, all the guilt she'd carried.

Tell him. The conviction hit her like a hammer. *Tell him now.*

"Got it!" Huck's shout interrupted her. The rope had indeed caught the dummy's horns, and Huck was doing a victory dance that involved a lot of arm pumping.

Rowan walked over to the fence, laughing. "That's some celebration."

"Yeah, well, he never does anything halfway." She glanced at Rowan.

He looked pure cowboy in the light of the arena, a little dusty, his shirt rolled up over his strong forearms, a little whisker grizzle on his skin.

Oh boy. She looked away.

"You okay? You seem . . ." Rowan's gaze lingered on her face.

"I'm fine." The lie tasted bitter. She wasn't fine. She was terrified and hopeful and guilt-ridden and . . . oh, shoot—maybe still painfully in love with Mr. Not Sticking Around.

What was she doing letting him into her *house*? Her life? "Just thinking about things."

"What kind of things?"

The question hung in the air between them.

"We're breaking for lunch." Huck jogged back over, rope coiled in his hands. "Can we come back for the afternoon session?"

The moment shattered. Sierra closed her mouth, the words swallowed back down.

"Sure," Rowan said.

Huck climbed over the fence. "You ever done any breakaway roping, or tie-down?"

"Some," Rowan said, with a smile tugging up his face.

Huck looked at his rope, back out to the arena. "But I bet I could learn pretty fast if I had the right teacher."

He looked hopefully at Rowan, and Sierra's heart clenched at the naked adoration in her son's eyes. Sure, Morrie had filled in, tried to be a sort of father figure. And then there was Mike, for a little while. But really, it had been Great-Grandpa who'd filled that role.

Now, watching Huck and Rowan together felt like watching pieces of a puzzle finally click into place.

"I bet you could," Rowan agreed. "Tell you what—let's work on your form a bit more, then maybe we can set up some different targets."

"We're going to do horseback work after lunch," Huck said.

"That's when it'll get fun." Rowan glanced at Sierra. "Kowalski's deli still open?"

They bought thick roast beef sandwiches and Sierra's favorite potato salad and ate lunch at a picnic table outside the Renegade Community Arena, watching other families enjoying the crisp October afternoon. The arena buzzed with activity—kids practicing for next week's youth rodeo, parents offering encouragement from the sidelines, the familiar sounds of horses nickering and people laughing mixing with autumn air.

Sierra unwrapped her sandwich, stealing glances at Rowan as he ate. Even something as simple as lunch felt different with him here, more complete somehow. Huck chattered between bites, pointing out friends and explaining the arena's layout like a tour guide.

"That's where they'll have barrel racing," Huck said, gesturing with his sandwich. "And over there's the roping ring. Mr. R, can you help me practice? Please?"

"Rowan, you don't—"

"Sure," Rowan said. He got up and walked over to the roping ring, where a weathered cowboy was helping a group of kids with their technique.

"Go ahead," Sierra mumbled to herself. "We'll finish eating."

And of course, instead of just observing, Rowan walked straight into the ring. Sierra watched him approach the instructor—Buck Gilmore, one of the area's best ropers. Buck's weathered face broke into a grin as Rowan extended his hand, and Sierra could see them talking, Buck nodding with obvious respect.

"Who's that man talking to Mr. Gilmore?" asked a young girl at the next table.

"That's Mr. R, my mom's friend," Huck said proudly. "He's teaching me to rope."

Within minutes, Rowan had borrowed a lasso and was demonstrating a technique Sierra had never seen before. The kids gathered around him like he was the Pied Piper, their faces bright with attention. He showed them a complicated wrist movement, his voice carrying clear instructions across the arena.

"Keep your elbow steady," Rowan called to a boy about Huck's age. "The power comes from your core, not your arm."

Sierra found herself remembering another moment—Rowan at seventeen, pulling her into the kitchen after one of her grandpa's barbecues. The party had been winding down, most of the guests heading home, but Rowan had lingered. He'd always lingered.

"Dance with me," he'd said, even though there was no music.

"Here? In the kitchen?"

"Especially here."

He'd pulled her close, swaying to some rhythm only he could hear. Sierra had melted against him, her head on his shoulder, breathing in the scent of soap and hay and something uniquely Rowan. For those few minutes, she'd felt completely safe, completely loved, completely sure that they were meant to be together forever.

Now, watching him with all these kids—patient, encouraging, completely natural—that same sweeping longing crashed over her. This was what she'd dreamed of during all those lonely nights— Rowan here, their family finally complete.

"Mom, can I go practice too?" Huck had finished his sandwich and was practically vibrating with excitement.

"Go ahead," Sierra said, and Huck ran out into the ring. Rowan, of course, turned and smiled at him, and her heart nearly exploded.

Tell him. The words simply flamed inside her. *He deserves to know. They both deserve to know.*

Yes. Yes, he did.

They brought out horses, and for the next hour, Sierra watched her son learn alongside other kids while Rowan moved between them like he'd been teaching children his whole life. Huck's natural talent was obvious—he picked up techniques faster than kids who'd been practicing for months. Several parents commented on his skill, and Sierra's heart squeezed with pride and guilt in equal measure.

"I think that's enough for today," Buck Gilmore finally called out. "Don't want to tire out these horses before next week's competition."

The kids groaned but began gathering their gear. Rowan walked back over, coiling his borrowed rope with practiced ease.

"Thanks for letting me help," he said to Sierra. "That was fun."

"You're a natural teacher," she said softly. "Those kids loved you."

"They're good kids. Huck especially." Rowan's gaze found her son, who was saying goodbye to his friends.

"We need to get back." Sierra stood, suddenly needing movement. "I want to check on the cattle before evening chores."

"I need to stop by the hardware store and pick up some supplies," Rowan said. "I'd like to set up some security around the house."

And weirdly, just like that, the dream shattered. Right. He was here because he thought she needed his protection. She couldn't take care of herself.

Not because . . . well, not because they might be a family or something crazy like that. Clearly the sunshine had gone to her head.

"Sure," she said and dumped the picnic wrappers into the garbage.

They stopped at the hardware store, and Rowan picked up most of his supplies. Then they drove home, the sun sliding down to the backside of the day.

Huck stared out the window, humming. She hadn't heard him do that in ages. So maybe it wasn't such a terrible thing to have Rowan around. Even if it might not be permanent, he could be good for Huck.

As they turned up the gravel drive, Sierra's peaceful mood evaporated. Two official vehicles sat parked near the barn's charred remains—Detective Martinelli's unmarked sedan and a white SUV with *Colorado State Fire Investigation* emblazoned on the side.

"What's all this?" Rowan asked, his voice immediately alert.

"I don't know," Sierra said, pulling up beside Martinelli's car.

Mike Martinelli approached as they climbed out of the truck, his expression professionally neutral. Beside him walked a woman in her mid-thirties, wearing khakis and a polo shirt with the state fire marshal's badge.

"Sierra, sorry to show up unannounced," Martinelli said. "This is fire investigator Robbie Swenson. She wanted to take a look at the barn while the scene was still fresh."

"We can't confirm it was arson," Swenson said quickly, apparently reading the worry on Sierra's face. "But we're running some tests on the burn patterns, just to be thorough. Insurance companies like documentation."

Sierra's shoulders sagged with relief. "So someone didn't deliberately—"

"The damage pattern does suggest accelerant, but it might simply be flammable material that caught fire—paint cans in the rubble. But it could be an electrical origin, faulty wiring in the back corner. Old barns, rodent damage to insulation—it's more common than people think."

"We already talked to your hands," Martinelli added. "Tomás and Jake said they left around five, didn't see anything unusual. Morrie was out in the north pasture working on the hay bailer until after dark, didn't notice the fire until he came back and saw the flames."

"That's a relief," Sierra said, and meant it. The thought that someone had deliberately tried to destroy her family's legacy . . .

Well, that sort of meant that maybe Rowan didn't need to stick around, didn't it?

"I don't know," Rowan said. "Her grandfather updated that wiring about ten years ago. I helped him." He shook his head. "How long before the results come back?"

"Lab results take a few days," Swenson said. "But based on what I'm seeing here, I really think you're looking at an electrical fire. Probably been smoldering in the walls for hours before it finally caught."

Rowan nodded, gave a grunt, not of agreement.

And suddenly, painfully, Sierra realized that . . . shoot, she didn't want Rowan to leave. And maybe that showed on her face, because Rowan glanced at her, his voice low.

"You okay?"

"I guess so. I was so afraid someone had done this on purpose."

"No matter how it happened," Rowan said quietly, "you wouldn't be facing it alone."

Oh. *Oh.* And she didn't know why she drank up his words, why she nearly turned to him to throw her arms around him.

But standing there beside the ruins of her barn, watching her son chase fireflies in the gathering dusk while investigators documented the end of one chapter of her family's story, Sierra realized something had shifted. For the first time in ten years, she didn't feel like she was carrying the weight of the world by herself.

Maybe that was worth risking everything, even her secrets, to keep.

If Sierra wasn't in danger, he didn't have to stay, right?

The silence stretched between them as they walked back into the house, Huck racing ahead to wash his hands.

Rowan automatically cataloged potential threats—sight lines from the driveway, cover positions, escape routes. Old habits from a decade of dangerous work, but useful when someone might be targeting the woman he loved.

Because that's what this was about, wasn't it? Not wanting to find reasons to stay, but needing reasons to keep Sierra safe.

Needing reasons to stay.

Because he was painfully and forever in love with the girl—*woman*—next door.

He simply hadn't left the kid who wanted her to be impressed with him behind—that much he'd figured out after spending the day showing off his old skills. Her smile lit a sort of fire in him and did nothing to douse the old memories.

Caught myself something pretty.

Yeah, he was in trouble.

They went inside, and he set the bag of security equipment on the kitchen table. Maybe this was overkill.

"You're doing it again," Sierra said, pulling ground beef from the refrigerator.

"Doing what?"

"You used to get really quiet when you were thinking about something. Sort of pulled into yourself."

He glanced over at her. Shoot, she remembered him that well? Maybe he'd been the one who'd forgotten who he was. In fact, he'd felt more like himself today, with a rope in his hand, teaching Huck and the others rope tricks, than he had in a while. Or maybe a different side of himself, one he'd tucked away for too long.

She set the meat on the counter. "The fire investigator said it wasn't arson."

"She said inconclusive and *probably* not arson. There's a difference." Rowan moved to the kitchen window.

The barn's charred skeleton cast long shadows across the yard, a reminder of how quickly things could turn dangerous.

"You think I'm in danger." It wasn't a question.

Rowan turned from the window, meeting her dark eyes. "I think someone wants you gone. The methods don't matter as much as the results."

Sierra's hands stilled on the package of meat. "You're scaring me."

He met her eyes. "Good. Scared keeps you alive."

The words seemed harsh, but fear was a tool he understood. Fear made people careful, made them check locks and avoid dark corners and call for help when they needed it.

"Mom, can I watch TV?" Huck appeared in the doorway, his face clean but his hair still bearing traces of arena dust.

"After dinner," Sierra said. "Go get cleaned up properly. We have church tomorrow—so scrub."

"But—"

"Go." Sierra's voice carried enough authority to send Huck trudging toward the stairs, muttering about unfair parental tyranny.

Rowan's mouth quirked upward. "Some things never change."

"What do you mean?"

"You still get that look when you're not having any arguments. Same expression you used to give me when you tried to talk me out of doing something dangerous."

"I was usually right." Sierra began browning the meat.

"You were always right. Drove me crazy." Rowan leaned against the counter, breathing in the scents of home cooking and Sierra's shampoo. This—this *ordinary* moment of watching her cook dinner—this was what he'd been missing without even knowing it. "What are you making?"

"Goulash." She kept her eyes on the skillet. "Not exactly gourmet, but it's what we can afford."

The slight defensiveness in her voice made his jaw clench. She shouldn't have to worry about grocery budgets, shouldn't have to stretch meals to make ends meet. Not when he had money sitting in accounts he'd barely touched.

"I could—"

"No." The word came out sharper than necessary. "I mean, thank you, but we're fine."

Rowan studied her profile, reading the stubborn pride that had always been part of her appeal. Sierra Blackwood didn't accept charity, never had. But this wasn't charity—this was him . . . well, finally stepping into a life he'd thought would be his.

Maybe still could?

He moved to the sink and began washing dishes that had been sitting in the basin since morning.

"You don't have to do that."

"I know." He rinsed a plate and set it in the drainer. "But my mother raised me right."

The casual mention of his mother sent familiar grief through his chest.

"I was so sad for you when she died."

"I was OCONUS, so I didn't hear about it until after the funeral. Felt too little too late to come home, so . . ." He lifted a shoulder.

She looked at him, her brow creased. "You never said goodbye?"

Rowan's hands stilled in the soapy water, the words a rock in his chest. "I left straight from your house, went to Denver, joined up. So, yeah. Not really."

She nodded. Glanced upstairs as if looking for Huck, back to him. "She was . . . she was an amazing, strong woman. And very . . .

well, very kind to me. Especially after . . ." She trailed off, catching her lower lip.

"After I abandoned you." The words emerged soft, mostly because he hated hearing them aloud. "I'm . . ." He swallowed. "I'm sorry I didn't come back."

"I know." She gave him a small smile, then added onions to the pan, the sizzle loud in the sudden quiet. "You had your reasons. Besides, it's in the past."

It felt too easy to dismiss.

In the past. What they'd had didn't feel finished, didn't feel relegated to memory. Watching her move through her kitchen, seeing how she'd raised Huck, being here in this house that felt more like home than anywhere he'd been in a decade—none of that felt past tense.

"What time's church tomorrow?" The question surprised him as much as it seemed to surprise her. Where had that come from?

Sierra's spatula froze mid-stir. "You want to go to church?"

No. Yes. Maybe. "If that's okay."

She turned to study his face, clearly looking for the joke. "You do remember you weren't exactly a believer before, right? Used to say church was for people who were afraid to think for themselves."

Rowan winced and set a pan to dry on the rack. Grabbed a towel. Those words sounded even worse coming from her mouth than they had from his eighteen-year-old arrogance. "I said a lot of stupid things when I was eighteen."

"So what changed?"

He leaned against the counter, considering how much to reveal. "Being dead makes you think about, well, *being dead.* And over the past couple years, Saxon and I and a couple other buddies have been in some big scrapes. Wildfires that should have killed us, situations where we had about a one percent chance of survival."

"But you survived." Her voice came out softer than before.

"We survived. And after the third or fourth time that happened,

I started thinking maybe someone upstairs was looking out for us." He poured himself the last of the morning coffee and put it in the microwave. "Hard to explain unless you've been there."

The truth was more complicated than that. He'd started questioning his lack of faith the night they'd survived a firestorm in Montana. And then his buddy Kane had looked at him and said, *Someone's got to be keeping score, brother. Otherwise, none of this makes sense.*

But Sierra didn't need the full theological crisis that had followed. Just, "There were a few Christians on our team, and they believed that God was looking out for us. Sort of rubbed off, I guess. So maybe it's worth a look."

Sierra studied his face with those dark eyes that had always seen too much. "Well. This should be interesting. Half the congregation thinks you're dead."

The microwave beeped. He rescued his coffee and added sugar. Turned to her. "Are you ready for the questions?" The thought of facing a church full of people who'd known him as a boy, who'd attended his memorial service, made his stomach clench. But if he was going to build a life here, it had to start somewhere.

For a second, that thought gripped him, sank in. Build a *life* here.

And then . . . yes. *Yes.*

"Are *you* ready for the questions?" She tilted her head up to meet his gaze, challenge sparking in her expression.

"It has to happen sometime if I'm going to stick around."

And just like that, Sierra's breath caught.

Something—hope? Worry? Panic?—flickered in in her eyes before she shuttered it away. Huh. He didn't know where to land with his response.

"Redeemer Community, nine-thirty service," she managed. "Unless you'd rather stay here and guard the place."

"No, I'd like to go. If that's okay."

"It's okay." The way she said it suggested it was more than okay, and something warm unfurled in his chest. Maybe he'd misread the look in her eyes.

Huck thundered back down the stairs, his hair damp from actual washing. "Can I help cook?"

"You can set the table," Sierra said. "And no complaining about the placemats."

"The placemats are stupid. Who needs flowers on their eating space?"

Rowan grinned and helped him set the table.

The goulash was simple but fed his bones. Huck peppered him with questions about firefighting, military life, and whether he'd ever met any famous people.

"I met a movie star last summer. A guy named Spenser Storm."

"Oh, I know him. He was in a TV series my mom likes to watch." He glanced at her. "*Trek of the Osprey*."

"Can't help that Quillen Cleveland is still my favorite leading man." She winked.

Oh, she was cute.

"Can we watch a movie?" Huck asked as Sierra cleared the dishes.

"Homework first."

"I don't have any homework. It's Saturday."

"Reading, then."

"Mom." Huck's voice carried a whine.

"What if we compromise?" Rowan said. "An educational movie."

"Define *educational*," Sierra said, but her tone suggested she was willing to negotiate.

"I was thinking maybe something from when we were kids. Show Huck what movies used to look like before everything was computer-generated."

"Please, Mom?" Huck bounced in his chair. "I promise I'll read extra tomorrow."

Sierra's mouth made a grim line as she looked between her son and Rowan.

And he didn't know why, suddenly, he cared. Why he longed to sit in the old den with her, sharing popcorn, his arm stretched out over the top of the sofa so she could snuggle against him.

The thought, however, seeped in and took possession. *Please?*

"Fine. One movie," Sierra said. "And I'll even let you pick the popcorn flavor."

"Yes!" Huck pumped his fist in victory, and Rowan had to hide his own smile. *Yes!*

Twenty minutes later, they were settled in the den with a bowl of buttered popcorn between them. Sierra had chosen *The Princess Bride*, and a jolt of memory hit Rowan so strong it nearly stole his breath. They'd watched this movie together in high school, curled up on this same couch while rain drummed against the windows. *As you wish, Sierra.*

Rowan claimed the far end of the couch, his spot. Huck sat in the middle, Sierra across from them. So, no snuggling, and hello, he probably needed to shut down that kind of thinking.

She hadn't exactly made any moves to suggest rekindling the past.

But she hadn't kicked him out either.

"This is old," Huck announced as the opening credits rolled.

"This is *classic*," Sierra said.

"Same thing."

"Watch and learn, kid," Rowan said. "This movie has everything. Sword fights, pirates, true love, revenge—"

"Rodents of unusual size," Sierra added, glancing at him. The easy way she fell into their old banter made his chest tight.

"I don't believe they exist," Rowan quoted automatically,

earning Sierra's laugh, the sound pure and bright and exactly as he remembered.

As the movie progressed, Rowan found himself watching Sierra more than the screen. She looked relaxed for the first time since he'd been back, some of the constant tension finally easing from her shoulders. When Westley revealed his identity to Buttercup, she mouthed along with the dialogue.

"As you wish," Rowan murmured, remembering another night, another version of themselves who'd thought they had forever.

Sierra's eyes flicked to his. She remembered too. The knowledge passed between them like an electric current, dangerous and impossible to ignore.

"Mom, can I have more popcorn?" Huck's voice cut through the moment.

"There's plenty in the bowl."

"It's all the way over there." Huck gestured dramatically toward the coffee table like it was miles away instead of three feet.

"Then get up and get it."

"But I'm comfortable."

"Tragedy," Sierra said dryly, and Rowan bit back a grin. Some things never changed.

Huck sighed heavily and hauled himself off the sofa with theatrical suffering. He grabbed the bowl of popcorn and settled back on the sofa.

In doing so, he leaned against Rowan.

Oh. He looked at the kid, feeling the weight, the warmth, and something shifted inside. He couldn't move.

"This is actually pretty good," Huck said as Inigo Montoya began his sword fight with the Man in Black.

"Told you," Rowan said, but his voice emerged funny.

Calm down. It didn't mean anything.

By the time the credits rolled, Huck was fighting sleep despite his insistence that he wasn't tired. His eyes had gone heavy, and he was curled against his mother.

"Bedtime," Sierra announced.

"Can't I stay up a little longer? It's Saturday."

"It's after nine, and we have church in the morning."

"Five more minutes?"

"Now."

Huck sighed, a little dramatically, but he got up. "Night, Mr. R," he said.

"Night, big Huck," Rowan said and held out his fist. Huck banged it and then trudged upstairs with all the enthusiasm of a condemned man.

"He's a good kid," Rowan said.

"He is." Sierra began gathering empty popcorn bowls and glasses. "Gets that from his father."

The words hit Rowan like a slap. Aw, shoot.

Sierra had a child with another man, had built a life with someone else. And while the logical part of his mind had accepted this reality days ago, hearing her mention Huck's father so casually made it real in a way that left him breathless.

"Sierra—"

"I should clean up." She stood quickly, clearly needing distance.

But Rowan caught her wrist. Gently. "Wait."

She looked down at him, her pulse visible in the hollow of her throat.

"Talk to me. Please."

Sierra sank back onto the couch. "What do you want to know?"

"Everything. These past ten years, what happened to you, how you ended up . . ." He gestured vaguely toward the stairs where Huck had disappeared, then stopped. He had no right to ask about her relationships, no claim on her past.

"How I ended up with a son?" Her voice came out steadier than her expression suggested.

"That's not what I meant."

"Isn't it?" She pulled her wrist free and tucked her hands in her lap. "I got pregnant without meaning to, but he's my entire world."

Each word felt like a knife between his ribs. She'd gotten involved with someone else pretty quickly after he left, it seemed, had been pregnant while he was stumbling through advanced training.

Maybe even during his first deployment.

"What happened to his dad?"

Sierra's breath caught. "I told you. Died serving his country."

The irony was brutal. Another soldier, another man who'd chosen duty over family. At least Rowan had reasons—anger, and then forces beyond his control.

"I'm sorry. That must have been hard."

"We managed."

"You shouldn't have had to manage alone." The words came out rough, probably weighted with his own guilt and regret.

"We weren't alone. We had Grandpa."

"But not his father."

"No." The word carried hurt. "Not his father."

Rowan wanted to reach for her hand again, but a gulf had opened between them. "For what it's worth, he would be proud of the son you raised. He's amazing, Sierra."

"Thanks." Sierra's eyes shimmered with unshed tears. She swallowed. "What about you?" Sierra asked, her voice thick with emotion. "What happened after you left? Really happened?"

Yeah. Maybe it was easier to talk about his own failures than to sit with the knowledge that she'd loved someone else, had created a child with another man.

"I went through basic training, went through advanced training, became a Delta Force operator. Became someone new, someone I thought I wanted."

She nodded. "And then?"

"Then I deployed. When it came time to re-up, I did it without looking back." He sighed, met her eyes, holding her gaze. "I never thought I'd end up dead. At least, officially."

"What does that mean?"

This was the part that mattered, the explanation he owed her for ten years of silence.

"We were on a rescue mission. A woman—a valuable asset—had been taken by some very bad people. My team and I went in to get her out."

"And?" Sierra had gone completely still.

"Someone on our team betrayed us. Set us up to be ambushed. By the time we fought our way out and got the woman to safety, officially, we didn't exist anymore." His jaw clenched at the memory—gunfire in a warehouse, Kane kidnapped and held, a woman who'd been used as bait in a trap designed to kill them.

It had taken them three years, all the way up until this summer, to unravel it all and find justice.

"Why were you betrayed?" Her voice barely rose above a whisper.

"Because the person who betrayed us had connections. High-level connections, and we weren't sure what we might be walking into. It was safer for everyone if Rowan Wallace and Luca Saxon and the rest of the team died on that mission."

And then he couldn't stop himself. He reached out and took her hand. Held it. Then he met her eyes. "I never stopped thinking of you."

"You could have told me." Her voice cracked.

"I wanted to. But . . ." He sighed. "It got complicated."

"You came to get Mack though. So he knew."

"Mack was in trouble. He'd gotten into a fight with his dad a few months before, when he told him he wanted to enlist. I was worried it would go south, so after the dust settled, I circled back and grabbed him. He's been traveling with us ever since."

"Were you ever going to tell me?"

He nodded. "Yes."

"When?" The single word held years of hurt and waiting.

"Today." His eyes met hers, willing her to understand. "I came back to Renegade to tell you I was alive. To see if there was any chance—"

He stopped, the words too big, too dangerous to speak aloud. "Any chance of what?"

"Of us. Of finding our way back to what we had."

Sierra's breath caught. "Rowan—"

"I know it's been ten years. I know you've built a life here, that you have Huck to think about. But seeing you again, being here with you—" He lifted their joined hands, pressing a kiss to her knuckles. And here went nothing—"I never stopped loving you, Sierra."

The words hung between them. She swallowed, her eyes wide. Then she tore her hand away. "Oh, no . . ." She stood up.

"Sierra?"

She rounded on him, her eyes glazed. "You can't just show up and say that." Sierra's voice shook.

"Why not? It's true."

"Because you left." Ten years of hurt poured into those three words. "You promised you'd come back, and you left."

"I had to leave. After what happened with my stepfather—"

"You could have taken me with you."

The accusation hit harder than a physical blow. "You were eighteen years old with a full scholarship to Colorado State. I wasn't going to ask you to give that up for a boy with no future and a lot of anger."

"That should have been my choice."

"Maybe. But I was eighteen too, and scared, and I thought I was protecting you."

Sierra paced to the window, stared out into the blackness.

"Sierra—"

"I waited for you." She turned to face him, eyes hot. "For two years, I waited. I kept thinking you'd come home on leave, or call, or write. *Something.*"

Her words could knock him over. She'd *waited?* What about Huck?

That didn't feel like waiting.

She wiped her face. "And now you're back, expecting what? That I'll just pick up where we left off like nothing happened?"

"I'm not expecting anything." He stood slowly, reading the pain and anger radiating from her small frame. "I'm hoping. There's a difference."

Sierra wrapped her arms around herself, suddenly looking fragile and young. "You're going to break my heart again. I just know it, and this time . . ." She swallowed. Shook her head. "I can't do this."

"Can't do what?"

"This. Us. Whatever this is." She gestured between them with sharp, frustrated movements. "I have Huck to think about."

Rowan took a step toward her, then stopped when she flinched. "What if we take it slow?"

A pause. "How slow?"

"As slow as you need. I'm not going anywhere, Sierra. Not this time."

The promise felt like an oath, binding and absolute. He'd spent ten years running from this feeling, from the knowledge that he'd left the best part of himself in this house with this woman. He wouldn't make that mistake again.

"You said you didn't know. That you weren't staying . . ."

"The only thing that could make me leave is if you asked me to."

Sierra stared at him, searching his eyes, as if testing his words. He let her look, let her see the decade of regret and longing he'd carried.

"I should get some sleep," she said finally. "Church comes early."

Oh. Sure. What did he think—that's she'd leap into his arms?

Shoot. Maybe. He nodded. "Of course."

She started down the hallway, then stopped. "Rowan?"

"Yeah?"

"I'm glad you came back. Even if this is complicated, even if I don't know what comes next—I'm glad you're alive."

"Me too," he whispered.

Sierra climbed the stairs, her footsteps soft on the worn wood. Rowan stood in the middle of her living room, surrounded by the debris of their evening—empty popcorn bowls, coffee mugs, the lingering scent of her shampoo.

He moved through the kitchen methodically, turning off lights and checking locks. But his mind wasn't on potential threats. It was on the woman upstairs, on the son she'd raised alone, on the life she'd built from the ashes of his abandonment.

Tomorrow would bring church and questions and the slow, careful work of rebuilding trust. Tonight, he just wanted to hold on to the feeling of being home, of belonging somewhere that mattered.

It was more than he'd had in a very long time.

And if he was very careful, very patient, it might be enough to build a future on.

SEVEN

SIERRA PRESSED HER BIBLE AGAINST HER RIBS and studied the disaster unfolding on the church lawn. Rowan crouched beside Huck near the old oak tree, his large hands patient as he demonstrated some kind of finger game. October sunshine filtered through the cottonwood leaves, casting dancing shadows across their matching expressions of concentration.

They already loved each other.

Pastor Williams's voice still rang in her ears, the familiar verses from Psalm 73 hitting different today. *Surely God is good to Israel, to those who are pure in heart. But as for me, my feet had almost slipped; I had nearly lost my foothold.*

Her feet had almost slipped, all right. Last night, Rowan had completely undone her. *I never stopped loving you, Sierra.*

She certainly hadn't been pure in heart at that moment.

Then he'd told her how he'd been betrayed by someone he trusted. His story wasn't lost on her—or the hurt in his eyes and . . .

And in that moment, she'd been selfish. So selfish. Because

having him in her home felt easy and right, and the minute she told him about her own betrayal . . .

She saw it all slipping away.

So no, not pure in heart on many fronts.

And now, Rowan and Huck were laughing like father and son, and oh, what a mess she'd brewed up.

"You okay, Sierra?" Bailey appeared at Sierra's elbow, coffee cup steaming in the crisp air. Her floral sundress and denim jacket looked perfectly put together, her dark hair in a loose braid down her back.

"The sermon hit close to home." Sierra tucked a strand of hair behind her ear. "I've been feeling a little . . . well, like I'm in over my head."

Bailey's eyebrows shot up. "What brought this confession on?"

"Maybe I've been holding on too tight to things that were never mine to control anyway."

Bailey followed her gaze to where Rowan was now teaching Huck some elaborate handshake. "Oh, I see. Mr. Incredible out there, playing with—"

"Don't say it."

"Huck."

She glanced over at her.

Bailey sipped her coffee, the picture of innocence. "Look at those two."

Sierra couldn't look away if she tried. Huck's tongue poked out in concentration as he tried to mirror Rowan's movements. When he finally got the sequence right, Rowan's face split into a grin that transformed his entire expression from controlled to boyish. The resemblance was becoming impossible to ignore—the same stubborn cowlick, the same way they both tilted their heads when thinking through a problem.

"They look good together," Bailey said quietly.

Devastatingly good. Sierra's chest tightened. "Last night he told me he still loved me."

Bailey looked at her. "Girl—what?"

Sierra glanced at her.

"Aw, what is that face?" Bailey took another sip of coffee.

"I haven't told him yet."

"Sierra—"

"I know! I've had the conversation a thousand times in my head, but . . . what if . . . what if he's angry? What if he walks out on us? On Huck. What if—"

"Please." Bailey glanced again at Huck and Rowan. "The fact he hasn't figured it out already is . . . well, the man must be blind."

"I keep sort of alluding to the fact that maybe . . . it was someone else."

"Why?"

Sierra sighed. "I just—"

"You're tired of people leaving you."

Sierra drew in a breath.

"You do know that when people die, they aren't leaving you on purpose."

"I know. But Rowan did die, on purpose. And didn't tell me. On purpose."

Bailey's mouth made a grim line. "I get that. But he's here now. And he still loves you. And you, Miss Do It Yourself, have loved Rowan Wallace since the fourth grade."

Sierra's throat tightened. "I just don't . . . He was betrayed before. By a friend. And I could see the hurt in his eyes and . . ."

"You don't want him to hate you."

"I don't want him to leave."

"Look at that man. He's crazy about your kid. Tell him. It's time."

"Sierra Blackwood?"

A dark-skinned woman in pressed khakis and a professional

polo shirt approached, her graying hair pulled back in a neat bun. Cecily Simmons from Vanguard Insurance. The woman had that particular look of someone bearing news that wasn't entirely good.

"Hi, Cecily." Sierra forced a smile.

Cecily's smile was warm, but her eyes held concern. "I was hoping to catch you. Save myself a trip out to the ranch."

"Is there a problem with the claim?"

"Not exactly a problem." Cecily glanced around, lowering her voice. "But the grapevine's been talking, and . . . well, is there any hint that the barn fire could have been arson?"

Sierra frowned. "They came out last night, told us it was electrical."

"Well, our investigator says that they marked it as still under investigation."

"Will that slow the claim?"

"It gets tricky. And it'll be delayed until the investigation is finished. I'll be by tomorrow to go over some details."

Delayed. "I need to clear the land and start rebuilding."

"I understand." Cecily patted Sierra's arm. "Try not to worry too much. These things have a way of working out."

Sierra nodded as Cecily walked away.

"What was that about?" Bailey moved closer.

"Insurance issues. The rumor is someone set the fire."

Bailey's coffee cup paused halfway to her lips. "Are you serious?"

Before Sierra could answer, Huck's voice carried across the lawn. "Mom! Come see what Mr. R taught me!"

"Mr. R?" Bailey said.

"Don't," Sierra growled and looked up to find both males watching her.

"Coming," she called back, pasting on a smile.

She and Bailey crossed the lawn, their heels sinking slightly into the soft grass. Huck bounced on his toes, his church shirt already half untucked and his dress pants grass-stained at the knees.

"Watch this!" Huck launched into an elaborate handshake with Rowan, his face scrunched in concentration. "It's called the Delta Snake. Mr. R learned it in the Army."

"Very impressive." Sierra ruffled his hair, warmth spreading through her chest despite everything.

Rowan walked over to them. "Bailey Sinclair?"

"Rowan Wallace, as I live and breathe."

He grinned at Bailey, who stepped back to assess him. "Still got that crazy Spock ear."

His mouth opened. Closed. "Clearly you're still my biggest fan."

She rolled her eyes. "Just trying to keep my girl out of trouble." She put an arm around Sierra. "You know what they say—Mama, don't let your babies fall in love with a cowboy."

"I'm not sure those are the right words."

"Oh, they're the right words." But she grinned and he grinned back, and Sierra laughed. "Okay, you two. The happy reunion is over. I'm starved."

"I could eat," Rowan said.

Bailey finished her coffee. "And I have papers to grade. Stay out of trouble, you two. Huck, see you tomorrow."

"Bye, Miss Sinclair." Huck took off for the truck.

Rowan fell in beside Sierra as they walked out to the parking lot. "So maybe coming back from the dead wasn't such a big deal."

She glanced at him and shook her head.

He frowned, but she ignored it and climbed into his truck.

Huck slid into the back seat. "Can we have roping practice today?" He leaned over the seat.

"Buckle up, Huck," said Sierra.

"Sure," Rowan said.

"I should check the cattle in the south pasture," Sierra said as they pulled out into the highway. "Make sure they have enough water."

"Want company?" Rowan asked.

The simple offer made her chest warm. "I'd like that."

Huck spent the rest of the drive talking about the upcoming festival and the other contestants and peppering Rowan with questions about his own rodeo wins.

Rowan had the patience of . . . well, she supposed a guy who spent hours hidden under a bush or something, watching for bad guys through a rifle scope. And that was her extent of Delta Force knowledge.

But the fact that he'd been some kind of special-ops soldier sort of hit her, watching him drive, sitting there with so much . . . well, strength. He'd grown into a big, solid, strong, beautiful man.

I never stopped loving you, Sierra.

Okay, so maybe Bailey was right. Time to tell him.

The house came into view, the cedar-shingled home with its soaring gables and wraparound porch looking like something from a *Mountain Living* magazine. Oh, she loved this house.

Seemed like it was time it had a family again.

They pulled up and she got out, Huck sliding out of the back seat.

Rowan came around the car. "Huck! Stop!"

Huck practically skidded to a stop in front of the step.

"Sierra." Rowan's voice had changed, gone sharp and alert. "Is your front door usually open?"

Sierra followed his gaze. The front door stood ajar, just a few inches. She would have missed it.

"No." Cold flooded her veins. "I locked it before we left for church."

Rowan's entire demeanor shifted in an instant. The relaxed man who'd been teaching her son fancy handshakes vanished, replaced by someone harder, more focused. "Stay here, both of you."

His voice turned her still. She reached for Huck and pulled him against herself.

Rowan's eyes scanned the house, the yard, the tree line beyond. "Someone's been here."

"What's wrong?" Huck said.

"Probably nothing, buddy," Rowan said, his voice softening, just a little. "Just . . . stay with your mom."

The door frame showed scratches around the lock. He stepped up the porch stairs, then eased the door open with his boot.

"Stay here," Rowan said. "Do not come inside until I say it's clear."

"Rowan—"

"Sierra." He turned to face her, and she saw something she'd never seen before—the soldier he'd become, the warrior who'd survived things she couldn't imagine. "Trust me on this. Please."

The word *trust* hit her like a physical blow. She nodded, pulling Huck closer.

Rowan disappeared into the house, moving with a silence that was somehow more frightening than noise would have been. Sierra strained to hear something—footsteps, voices, anything—but only silence echoed back.

Huck fidgeted beside her, and Sierra fought the urge to follow Rowan inside.

"Clear," Rowan's voice finally called from inside. "But you're not going to like what you see."

Sierra stepped through her front door and gasped. The living room looked like a tornado had hit it—couch cushions thrown across the floor, the drawers to her grandmother's china cabinet opened, books off the case, scattered everywhere.

"They were looking for something," Rowan said grimly. "Question is, what?"

Sierra moved through her violated home, cataloging the damage with a tightening fist in her gut. The kitchen had been ransacked—drawers pulled out, cabinets emptied, even the flour and sugar canisters dumped across the counters.

"Mom?" Huck's voice was small. "Why would someone do this?"

Sierra knelt beside her son, pulling him into a hug. "I don't know, baby. But we're going to figure it out."

Huck pushed away. "I'm going to check on my room." He scampered up the stairs, and she nearly followed him when Rowan called from down the hall—

"The worst damage is in here!"

Sierra followed his voice to her grandfather's office at the end of the hall—the room that had been his sanctuary, his command center for running the ranch. Ransacked. Every drawer had been yanked out, papers scattered across the floor. The old filing cabinets stood empty, their contents strewn everywhere. Even the picture frames had been removed from the walls, the photos dumped carelessly on the desk.

"They spent the most time here," Rowan said, crouching beside the overturned desk chair. "This wasn't random. They knew what they were looking for."

Sierra picked up a photograph from the floor—her grandfather with a prize bull from five years ago. The glass was cracked, spider-webbing across his proud smile.

"But what could Grandpa have had that someone would want badly enough to break in for?"

"Good question." Rowan straightened. "What kind of records did he keep? Financial stuff? Ranch business?"

"Everything." Sierra's voice came out hollow. "He was meticulous about documentation. Breeding records, financial statements, correspondence with other ranchers, veterinary reports, land surveys . . . It was the detective in him."

And then . . . wait. "The land surveys."

"What about them?"

"He had a tube, over here in the corner. Land surveys that he'd gotten a few months before he . . . a few months ago."

"Why?"

"There've been rumors lately about mineral rights in this area. Development companies sniffing around, asking questions about property lines and water rights." Sierra's pulse quickened. "What if someone was looking for documentation about our land boundaries?"

Rowan's expression darkened. "That would make sense. Especially if someone was planning to challenge your ownership or make you an offer you couldn't refuse."

She blinked at him. "Was that a Godfather reference?"

He sighed. "I'm just saying . . . remember Alden offered to buy your place, so—"

Right. She'd forgotten that he'd gone to his stepfather to ask about the rustling. And it hit her afresh. He'd done that . . . for *her*.

And maybe it was the destruction around her, maybe the softness of his voice, maybe just the fact that Rowan was here, standing in the middle of her messy life, but . . . tears burned her eyes. She put her hand over her mouth, turned away. *Don't cry. Don't—*

"Hey." Rowan's voice gentled, and suddenly he was there, his hands on her shoulders. "We're going to figure this out."

She turned then, and he pulled her against himself.

And oh, just like that, memory crashed over her. His strong arms around her, the rugged, manly smell of him, the sense that he had her.

Rowan and Sierra, with a big heart around it, forever and ever.

She just wanted to hang on. Never let go. Don't lean in, don't— aw. She was a goner against the hard planes of his body, the manly aftershave smell of him, the way his heart thumped against her ear. The man could still turn her to liquid.

He finally eased his hold on her, tipped up her chin, a question in his eyes. "You okay?"

Not even a little. "Yeah." She stepped away. "What are we going to do?"

147

He stood in the room, hands on his hips, and Sierra could nearly see the tactical wheels turning in his mind. Finally, "We're going to need help," Rowan said quietly. "This is bigger than we thought."

━━━━━━━━━━━

Rowan's hands stilled on the security camera as his blood still simmered beneath his controlled exterior. Whoever had violated Sierra's sanctuary had made a deadly mistake.

After they called the police, and after they'd taken photographs and dusted for prints, they spent the rest of the afternoon putting her house back together.

Then he'd started installing the security system, phase one.

He planned on having the entire perimeter locked down within a week. Phase two.

The front door sensor beeped as he tested the connection for the third time. Perfect. He moved to the kitchen window, adjusting the angle on the exterior camera until it captured the full approach to the house. His phone buzzed with the live feed—clear picture, night vision enabled.

He wouldn't get caught off guard again.

The sound of truck tires on gravel pulled his attention to the window. Saxon's newly acquired Ford pickup—something that looked like it had seen better decades but ran clean—rumbled up the drive with Mack riding shotgun. Both men climbed out, Saxon looking decidedly uncomfortable in his attempt at ranch wear. Phase three.

"Nice truck," Rowan called from the porch, not bothering to hide his amusement.

"Don't start." Saxon wore a flannel shirt, jeans, and aviator sunglasses, which he took off to survey the scattered security equipment. "Dolly at the diner said it belonged to her late husband. Seemed I might blend in."

Rowan shook his head. "Dolly? You're on a first-name basis with the locals already?"

"Information gathering requires building relationships," Saxon said, then grinned. "Not only does she make excellent pie, but she knows everyone's business for three counties."

"You just like pie." Rowan grinned, the first genuine smile he'd felt since discovering the break-in.

Okay, maybe there might have been smiling on the inside when Sierra had clung to him earlier. Like she might need him.

"What did you find out about the mineral rights?"

"Still working on it. Property records require a delicate touch. But I'm making friends, earning my PI credentials one slice of apple pie at a time." Saxon nodded toward the security equipment. "How's the fortress coming?"

"Almost finished." Rowan held up his phone, showing the camera feeds. "Motion sensors on all windows and doors, exterior cameras covering approach routes and the barn area. Everything feeds directly to my phone."

Mack whistled low. "Impressive. Think it's enough?"

The question hit the center of Rowan's chest. Was anything enough when it came to protecting the people he loved? His mind kept circling back to the image of Sierra and Huck walking into their ransacked house, the stripped look on Sierra's face.

"It's a start," he said finally.

"Do you think they found what they were looking for?"

"I don't know."

"Hammer." Saxon's voice carried the weight of experience. "You know whoever did this will escalate if they don't find what they're looking for."

"I know." Rowan's jaw tightened. "That's why we're going to find them first."

The screen door creaked, and Huck bounced onto the porch,

wearing work gloves that swallowed his small hands. "Mr. R! Mom said I could help with the wiring."

Looking at the kid's eager face, Rowan felt something shift in his chest. What a great kid. Once upon a time, he'd dreamed of having a son.

Wow, that came out of nowhere. "Want to learn how security systems work?"

"Yeah!" Huck practically vibrated with excitement.

"Mack, Saxon—meet Huck." Rowan gestured to the boy. "Sierra's son."

Mack crouched to Huck's level, extending his hand with a grin. "Nice to meet you, Huck. I'm Mack, Rowan's brother."

"You don't look like brothers," Huck said, shaking hands solemnly.

"Half brothers," Mack explained. "Different mothers, same questionable taste in dangerous careers."

Saxon nodded at the boy with professional courtesy. "Pleasure to meet you."

"Are you a cowboy too?" Huck asked.

"Private investigator," Saxon replied. "Think of me as a detective who works for regular people instead of the police." He turned to Rowan, however, and cocked his head. "See? I blend."

Rowan rolled his eyes.

"Cool!" Huck turned back to Rowan. "Can we start with the hard stuff?"

"Absolutely." Rowan handed him a small screwdriver. "First rule of security installation—measure twice, drill once."

For the next hour, Rowan worked with Huck to install the remaining sensors while Saxon and Mack helped organize equipment. The boy proved surprisingly adept with tools, his small fingers perfect for threading wires through tight spaces.

"Like this?" Huck asked, carefully connecting red wire to red terminal.

"Perfect. You've got natural instincts for this kind of work."

"My dad was good with his hands too." Huck's voice carried casual pride. "Mom says he could fix anything."

The words hit Rowan harder than they should have. Every kid deserved a father to teach them things, to show them how to be a man.

"I'm sorry you lost your dad," Rowan said quietly. "Losing a parent is hard."

"Did your dad die too?"

The question caught Rowan off guard. "Yeah. I was just a little older than you when it happened."

"How?"

"Horse kicked him in the head." He sighed. "It was an accident. He was trying to break a wild stallion, the animal got out of hand."

He left out the part where his dad had died saving Rowan's life. Stepping in front of the horse and taking the kick meant for him.

Huck's eyes went wide. "That's scary."

"It was." Rowan set down his tools, giving the boy his full attention. "After that happened, I spent a lot of time here at your mom's ranch. Your great-grandfather was . . . he was kind to me when I needed it most."

"Grandpa Elway was the best." Huck's face lit up. "He taught me everything about horses and roping and being strong when things get hard."

"He taught me those things too."

Huck grinned.

They worked in comfortable silence for a few minutes, Huck's small hands steady as he helped position the final sensor. Something about the boy's focus, his determination to get everything exactly right, struck Rowan as familiar.

"There." Huck stepped back to admire their work. "Think that'll keep the bad guys out?"

"I think it'll give us fair warning when they try." Rowan tested the connection on his phone. "Nice work, partner." He held out his hand, and he and Huck did the Delta Snake handshake.

"I can't believe you taught him that, Hammer," said Saxon. "Now he's an official Trouble Boy."

"Why does he call you Hammer?" Huck asked.

Saxon answered for him. "It's a nickname from the military. When you focus on a problem and don't give up until it's solved, they say you're like a hammer hitting a nail. That's our man here."

"That's so cool!" Huck's eyes lit up. "Can I have a nickname too?"

"What would you want to be called?" Rowan asked.

"Something tough. Like . . . Lightning. Or maybe Storm."

"I think you need to earn a nickname," Saxon said with mock seriousness. "Has to come from something you're really good at."

"I'm good at roping," Huck said hopefully.

"Then maybe we'll see," Rowan said. "Nicknames take time."

A pickup drove into the driveway, and Huck left the porch. "Morrie!"

"Who's that?" Saxon said, walking over to Rowan.

"Sierra's ranch foreman." He stood, watching the man get out of the car.

Saxon stood next to him. "Any reason to suspect him?"

"Don't think so."

Saxon grunted.

Yeah, what he said.

He walked out to the yard to meet Morrie, who was surveying the barn damage. "Howdy."

The late-afternoon sun cast long shadows across the blackened timber and twisted metal. The smell of smoke still lingered in the autumn air, mixing with the scent of hay and horses from the intact buildings nearby.

Morrie glanced at him, his weathered face grim as he approached.

"Afternoon," Morrie said. "Heard you boys were installing some security measures."

"Basic precautions," Rowan replied, noting the territorial edge in the foreman's voice.

"Good thinking." Morrie's gaze lingered on Rowan with obvious assessment. "Sierra's been through enough trouble lately."

"That's the plan—to make sure she doesn't go through any more."

"See that you do." Morrie sighed then and lowered his voice. Huck had picked up a rope, started twirling it in loop circles.

"Sierra's been carrying this place on her shoulders since Elway died. She doesn't need anyone making her life harder than it already is."

Rowan glanced at him, tried to tamp down a crazy spark of irritation. "I'm not here to make her life harder."

"Maybe not intentionally." Morrie's eyes narrowed. "But sometimes folks bring trouble without meaning to. Sierra's got enough to worry about without adding heartbreak to the list."

Heartbreak? The word carried weight that suggested Morrie's concern went beyond professional duty to his boss.

"Understood," Rowan said evenly, though his jaw tightened.

"Good." Morrie straightened, his voice returning to normal volume. "Now, about this barn. Gonna need heavy equipment to clear the debris before we can start rebuilding."

"What kind of timeline are we looking at?" Saxon asked. He'd said nothing at Morrie's warning.

"Depends on the insurance payout and whether we hire contractors or lean on neighbors for help." Morrie glanced at Rowan. "Community around here tends to take care of its own."

Mack had come out to join them from where he'd been installing motion detectors on the back of the house. "Neighbors helping with the rebuild? I'm sure my dad will help."

Yeah, whatever.

"It's an old tradition. Barn raising, they used to call it. Though I suppose now it's more like barn clearing and rebuilding." Morrie's expression softened slightly. "Elway helped build half the barns in this county over the years. Folks remember that kind of thing."

"When would something like that happen?" Rowan asked.

"As soon as the insurance agent is done. Maybe this weekend if the weather holds." Morrie studied Rowan's face. "You planning to stick around for it?"

"As long as Sierra needs me here."

"Hmm." Morrie's grunt was noncommittal, but his eyes held calculation. "Well, if you're gonna be here, might as well make yourself useful. We have roundup in the morning—going out to the western pasture. You ever done any ranch work?"

"I think I can handle myself."

Morrie made a grunt. "Okay then."

Rowan turned to Huck. "Huck, want to help me check the perimeter before dinner?"

"Can Bandit come?"

As if summoned by his name, the Jack Russell terrier bounded around the corner of the house, tail wagging furiously. The pup had clearly been digging, his nose caked in dirt.

Huck handed him a doggie treat.

"Sure."

"We're taking off," Saxon said and extended his hand. "Call if you need anything."

Mack too. "Nice to see you and Dad bonding."

He wasn't bonding with Alden Jenkins, thank you.

Mack and Saxon pulled out while Rowan walked the fence, Huck chattering about school and friends while Bandit investigated every interesting scent. When they reached the front porch again, Rowan called the dog over.

"Sit," he commanded.

Bandit looked at him with intelligent brown eyes but remained standing.

"Sit." Rowan demonstrated, placing his hand on the dog's hindquarters and gently pushing down while repeating the command. "Got any more of those treats, Huck?"

He handed him a fistful.

After a few tries, Bandit finally settled into a sitting position.

"Good boy!" Rowan pulled out one of the treats. "I used to try and teach my dog how to do this."

He balanced the treat on Bandit's nose, the dog's eyes crossing comically as he tried to focus on the prize just inches away.

"Stay," Rowan commanded, holding his hand up in a stop gesture.

Bandit trembled with the effort of not moving, his whole body vibrating with restraint. After a second, he shook his head. The biscuit fell off and Bandit gobbled it up.

"Shoot."

"My dad used to do this with our old dog, Bernie." The memory surfaced, swift, with a tiny punch to his heart. "He said patience and consistency were the keys to training anything—dogs, horses, kids."

"Your dad sounds like he was really smart."

"He was." Rowan handed Huck a biscuit. "Want to try?"

For the next twenty minutes, they worked with Bandit on the trick. Huck proved to be a natural trainer, his young voice carrying the perfect tone of authority mixed with affection. What a great kid. He hadn't been lying to Sierra.

"I think he's getting it!" Huck exclaimed as Bandit successfully sat long enough for the biscuit to balance.

"You're a good teacher. You understand animals."

"Thanks. Mom says I get that from my dad." Huck beamed with pride.

The kid mentioned his dad a lot, it seemed. Maybe because Sierra did? "Does your mom talk about your dad often?"

"Sometimes. When I ask questions." Huck shrugged, tossing another biscuit for Bandit. "Mostly she just says he was a good man who would've loved me very much."

"I'm sure he would have."

They headed back toward the house as the sun began to sink toward the mountains, painting the sky in shades of orange and gold. The security lights Rowan had installed flickered on automatically, casting pools of brightness across the yard.

"Those are so wicked," Huck said. "It's like having robot guards."

"Something like that." Rowan chuckled. "Though hopefully we won't need them."

"Do you think the bad guys will come back?"

The question was asked with such innocent curiosity that Rowan's chest tightened. How did you explain to a kid that some people were willing to hurt others for money or power?

"I think they might try," he said. "But if they do, we'll be ready."

"Good," Huck said. "Mom's been worried. She tries to hide it, but I can tell."

Oh, and that just made his heart hurt.

As they approached the porch, the screen door opened and Sierra stepped out wearing an apron over her jeans. The sight of her—hair escaping from its ponytail, flour dusting her hands, domestic and beautiful in the golden evening light—hit Rowan harder than it should have.

"Perfect timing," she called. "Dinner's almost ready."

"It smells incredible," Rowan said, breathing in the rich aroma of pot roast and herbs wafting from the kitchen.

"Mom makes the best pot roast in Colorado," Huck declared.

Bandit picked right then to dart off the porch, barking.

Huck lit out after him.

"Where are Saxon and Mack?"

"They headed back to town," Rowan said. "Saxon is probably heading in for more of Dolly's pie."

Sierra laughed. "Saxon's going to be the talk of the diner if he keeps that up. Dolly's got the best information network I know."

"Maybe he'll find out everything we need to know."

"Maybe he will." Sierra's smile was warm, and Rowan just about reached out, touched his hand to her face, the urge to curl his hand around the back of her neck, maybe pull her close sweeping over him.

And right then, he didn't care if she'd loved another man. He was the man here, in front of her.

And he wanted her back.

Huck bounded up the porch steps and paused to remove his cowboy hat, running his fingers through hair that stuck up at odd angles. As he turned his head to address his mother, the evening light caught his profile, and Rowan's breath stopped.

There, just visible above the curve of Huck's ear, was a small bump in the cartilage structure—the same distinctive hitch that Rowan saw in the mirror every morning.

His Spock ear.

The same genetic quirk that his own father had carried.

The same one that had made Rowan self-conscious as a teenager until Sierra had kissed him right there and told him it was perfectly imperfect, just like the rest of him.

His vision tunneled. Everything else—the sound of Sierra and Huck talking, the evening breeze, the distant lowing of cattle— faded into background noise as his mind raced through calculations.

That night—their last night together. He'd been wounded, broken.

And she'd comforted him.

And then, then they'd lost themselves, maybe, in the emotion of the moment, and . . .

What?

He forced himself to breathe, to think, but he couldn't tear his gaze away from Huck.

How could he have been so terribly blind? The stubborn cowlick. The way he tilted his head when concentrating. The natural ability with tools and animals. The natural talent with a rope.

His stubbornness and eagerness and . . .

"Earth to Rowan." Sierra's voice broke through his spiraling thoughts. "You okay?"

"I'm fine," he managed, though his voice sounded strange in his own ears. "Just tired."

"Well, come on inside. Food always helps with tired."

Sierra headed back into the house, and Huck started to follow, but Rowan caught his arm gently.

"Huck? Can I ask you something?"

"Sure."

"How old are you exactly? When's your birthday?"

"I'm ten. My birthday's June fifteenth."

June fifteenth.

Rowan's mind immediately calculated backward. Nine months before June would put conception around . . . September.

He'd left Renegade in early September, eleven years ago.

The math worked.

His legs wobbled. This boy—this bright, brave, patient, stubborn boy—was his son.

His *son*.

Sierra had been pregnant, and she'd never told him. She'd let him disappear from their lives, let him miss ten years of birthdays and Christmas mornings and first days of school and scraped knees and bedtime stories.

She'd let him miss *everything*.

The betrayal hit him like a physical blow, and he nearly stumbled. Caught the door frame. Then, the swell of it all swept through him and hollowed him out. Ten years of his son's life, gone forever. Ten years of being a father . . .

"Mr. R?"

Huck's voice snapped him back to the present. The boy was studying him, and Rowan realized he was staring.

"Sorry, buddy. Just thinking."

"About what?"

About how your mother stole ten years of my life. About how I have a son and never knew it. About how everything I thought I understood about the past has just been turned upside down.

"Nothing important."

They went inside, where Sierra had set the table for three. The kitchen smelled of rich gravy, tender meat, fresh bread—but as they ate, he tasted nothing.

Every time he looked at Huck, the resemblance seemed to shout at him. Every time he caught Sierra's eye, he had to look away.

He needed answers. The questions simply coiled inside him, swelling.

But how did you ask a question like that? How did you say *Did you keep my son from me for ten years?*

Huck told his mother about the security installation and Bandit's training progress, and Sierra asked about homework and chores.

This should have been his life. These dinners, these conversations, this family.

"Huck, go wash up and get ready for bed," Sierra said finally, pressing a kiss to the top of her son's head as she gathered up the plates. "School tomorrow."

"Aw, Mom. Can't I stay up a little longer? Mr. R was going to show me how the security cameras work."

Mr. R. Not *Dad.* He desperately needed to put his fist through something.

"Tomorrow," Sierra said firmly.

Huck sighed dramatically but hugged both his mother and Rowan good night before heading upstairs. As his footsteps faded, silence settled over the kitchen.

Sierra began washing dishes. Rowan watched her work, studying her profile, looking for signs of guilt or deception. But all he saw was the same Sierra he'd always known—strong, capable, beautiful.

A woman who'd apparently been lying to him for a decade.

"Sierra."

She looked up from the sink, soap bubbles clinging to her hands. "Yes?"

The moment stretched between them, loaded with everything he wanted to say and couldn't figure out how to voice. But the question had been building in his chest all evening, growing heavier with each passing moment until he couldn't see past it, breathe, even, with the weight of it.

"Is there something you need to tell me?"

EIGHT

SIERRA'S HEART STOPPED AS THE QUESTION hung in the kitchen air. Her hands stilled on the dish towel, her mind scrambling. The careful way he was watching her, the controlled tension in his posture—it all clicked into place with sickening clarity.

Oh no. He knew. Or suspected.

"What do you mean?" Way to dodge, Sierra. But . . .

She wasn't ready. Her pulse hammered in her throat.

Rowan stepped closer, his blue eyes never leaving her face. "You know what I mean."

Sierra's throat went dry. She turned off the water. Turned to him. Took a breath, her hands still wet.

"Night, Mom! Night, Mr. R!" Huck's voice called down from upstairs, followed by the sound of his bedroom door closing.

The interruption shattered the charged moment between them. Sierra seized on it like a lifeline. "I should check on him," she said, not meeting Rowan's eyes. "Make sure he's settled."

She practically sprinted from the kitchen, felt his gaze burning into her back as she took the stairs two at a time. Her hands shook as she quietly opened Huck's door to find him already burrowed under his covers.

Huck's bedroom was every ten-year-old boy's dream—navy blue walls lined with string lights that cast a warm glow across framed rodeo stars. His ancient bed—the same one she'd slept in as a child—was covered in a denim comforter.

"Mom?" Huck's voice was drowsy as she pulled his covers up. "Mr. R's really smart about security stuff."

"He is."

"'Cause he was a soldier, like Dad was."

She couldn't breathe. So much lying, and her world was sand between her fingers. "Yes."

"I'm glad he's here." Huck's eyes drifted closed. "It feels . . . safer. I like him."

And how was she supposed to hold it together now? Sierra kissed his forehead, her throat tight with unshed tears. "Sweet dreams, baby."

For a second she stood at the top of the stairs, painfully aware that Rowan stood at the bottom.

And then, like a coward, she fled to her own room.

Tomorrow. She'd figure it out tomorrow, in the light of day.

After Huck had gone to school. And after coffee.

Maybe after a night of rehearsing the conversation, again, in her head.

Her bedroom was a sanctuary with its white shiplap walls and exposed wooden beams that her grandfather had restored himself. The antique iron bed frame held layers of soft white linens and a faded green quilt that had belonged to her grandmother. Simple botanical prints in weathered frames hung on the walls, and a small reading chair sat beside the window with its cream curtains drawn back to let in moonlight.

Maybe she could lock herself in, never leave.

She went through the motions of her nightly routine. Brushing her teeth, washing her face, changing into soft pajama pants and an old T-shirt. All the while, her mind churned.

Do you have something to tell me?

No, no—yes! Oh . . .

What would Rowan do when he found out? Would he hate her for keeping Huck from him? Would he try to take her son away? Would he disappear again, unable to handle the responsibility?

Or worse—would he stay out of duty but resent them both for "trapping" him?

Sierra pulled back her covers and slipped into bed, but sleep laughed at her. She stared at the exposed beams overhead, moonlight painting silver rectangles across the hardwood floor through her bedroom windows. The house creaked around her, settling into night sounds, but her mind refused to quiet.

Ten years of secrets. Ten years of lying by omission. Ten years of watching Huck grow up without his father because she'd been too proud and too scared to tell Rowan the truth.

But I was protecting him, she told her ceiling fan. *He had dreams. He wanted to serve his country, see the world, be something bigger than the life he was living. A baby would have ruined everything.*

Yeah, the words just felt hollow tonight. Especially after watching Rowan with Huck. They were two peas.

Maybe she'd been protecting herself more than anyone else.

Exhaustion finally claimed her somewhere around midnight, dragging her into restless dreams.

She was eighteen again, standing at her kitchen sink, when she heard the truck pull up outside . . .

Through the window, she watched Rowan climb out, moving stiffly, his shirt torn and bloody. Even in the twilight, she could see the bruises on his face.

Her heart lurched, then, guessing. She flew to the door, yanking it open before he could knock.

163

"Rowan! What happened?"

"He doesn't get to . . . he doesn't . . ." His jaw tightened and he shrugged away from her when she touched him, his voice hoarse. Blood trickled from a split lip, and his left eye was already swelling shut. "He's going to call the cops."

"We need to get you cleaned up. Come on."

She led him through the dark house to the barn, not wanting to wake her grandfather. Oh, he'd be furious. Maybe even get in his truck and drive over to the Jenkins household and have it out with Alden.

And maybe get hurt too.

No, it needed to be an official visit, with Rowan the one filing charges.

In the tack room, she found the first aid kit they kept for horse injuries and guided Rowan to sit on a hay bale.

"This might sting." She dabbed antiseptic on the cut above his eyebrow, her touch as gentle as possible.

"Doesn't matter." Rowan winced but didn't pull away. "Nothing matters anymore. He's going to press charges, and I'll go to jail."

"Don't say that. We'll fight him—"

"He'll win. What I say won't matter." He looked away, so much wreckage on his face.

"You matter, Row. To me, you matter."

He looked up at her then, eyes holding pain that went deeper than physical wounds. "Sierra . . ."

"I love you." The words spilled out before she could stop them. "I've loved you since we were kids, and I can't stand seeing you hurt like this."

Something broke in his expression. He reached for her with shaking hands, pulling her down until she straddled his lap on the hay bale. "I love you too. Wow, Sierra, I love you so much it terrifies me."

When he kissed her, she tasted blood and desperation and so much longing, it just spilled into her.

She lost herself, her hold on the right now. On anything but him.

Rowan's hands tangled in her hair, and she poured everything into that kiss—all her love, all her faith that they could build something beautiful together despite the ugliness that he had to live with.

"I have to leave," he whispered against her mouth. "After what happened tonight, I can't stay in Renegade anymore."

"Then take me with you." She met his eyes, held his gaze. "I don't want to be without you."

He pulled back to study her face in the dim barn light. "Are you sure?"

"I've never been more sure of anything."

And at the moment, that night, she was. Sure of her choices, sure of the way she loved him, let him love her.

Rowan seemed as scared as she was, or maybe that was simply the trauma of the night shaking out of him, but he turned his attention to her in a way she'd never felt before. Spoke her name in whispers that embedded her soul.

He made her feel precious and powerful and completely loved. And gave her promises in the hay-scented darkness. Forever promises. Family promises.

"I'll come back for you," he said the next morning, right before he drove away.

Sierra jerked awake to the sound of crying. Her heart pounded as she oriented herself—her bedroom, not the barn. Present day, not ten years ago.

And not her tears.

The crying sounded from down the hall.

"Huck?" She leaped out of bed, down the hall to her son's room.

He was thrashing in his sheets, trapped in a nightmare. His sandy-brown hair stuck up at odd angles, damp with sweat, and his face was flushed. Tears streamed down his cheeks as he fought invisible demons.

"No, no, no!" he sobbed. "Bandit! *Bandit!*"

"Huck, baby, wake up." Sierra sat on the edge of his bed, gathering him into her arms. "It's just a dream. You're safe."

His eyes flew open, wild and unfocused. "Mom?"

"I'm here. You're okay."

"The fire," he gasped, clinging to her, choking on sudden, hot tears. "I was falling, and Bandit was so scared, and I couldn't get to him. The smoke was so thick, and I could hear him crying, but I couldn't . . ." He clung to her and wept.

Sierra's heart shattered. She'd known the fire had traumatized him, but she hadn't realized how deeply the images had burned into his mind.

"Shh, it's over. Bandit is fine. See?" Indeed, the dog had put his head into Huck's lap. "You saved him."

"But I didn't . . . I didn't save him."

"Hey." Sierra cupped his face in her hands, making him look at her. "You know what I think?"

Huck shook his head, still hiccuping.

"I think God was there that night. And when you needed help, He sent Rowan. Mr. R." Sierra smoothed his hair back from his sweaty forehead. "You didn't have to save Bandit by yourself. Sometimes God sends people to help us when we can't do it alone."

His big blue eyes fixed on hers. "You really think so?"

"I know so. Rowan was exactly where you needed him to be, exactly when you needed him."

Some of the tension left Huck's small body. "He's pretty cool."

"He was. He is." Sierra's voice caught. "Do you think you can try to sleep now? I could get you some warm milk."

"Don't go."

Sierra settled beside him on the narrow bed, humming softly until his breathing evened out and his grip on her hand relaxed. When she was sure he was deeply asleep, she whispered out of the bed and tiptoed toward the door.

A shadow in the hallway made her jump.

Rowan stood there in rumpled jeans and a T-shirt, his dark-blond hair mussed from sleep—or lack thereof. Even disheveled at two in the morning, he was devastatingly handsome. The stubble along his strong jaw had darkened, and his eyes held concern and something else she couldn't name. The dim hallway light caught the planes of his face, emphasizing the masculine beauty that had captured her heart in fourth grade and never let go.

"Is he okay?" he whispered.

"Nightmare about the fire. He'll be okay." Sierra pulled Huck's door mostly closed, leaving it cracked in case he called out again.

"Poor kid. That kind of trauma . . ." Rowan ran a hand through his hair. "Is there anything I can do?"

The question, asked with such genuine care, made Sierra's chest tight. Here was a man who'd known Huck for all of three days, and he was already thinking like a father.

Because, well . . .

"Are you okay?"

She looked away, her arms wrapped around herself.

"Can we talk?" he said.

"Now?"

"I'm not sleeping. Are you?"

She sighed. Shook her head.

"Please talk to me."

And that was just it. No anger. No fury. Just . . . oh, her eyes filled.

He frowned a moment, then took her hand. They moved quietly down the stairs together, Sierra painfully aware of his presence beside her in the darkness.

Yeah, no way around it, this was going to hurt.

"Can I heat up some hot cocoa for you?"

She spotted the pot already on the stove.

He walked over to it. "Figured if I was going to be awake, might as well make something useful."

The gesture hit her harder than it should have. He remembered. After all these years, he remembered that hot cocoa was her comfort drink of choice.

"You don't have to take care of me."

"Maybe I want to." He poured the steaming chocolate into two mugs, adding marshmallows without asking. Because he knew.

Sierra accepted the mug with shaking hands, wrapping her fingers around the ceramic for warmth. They stood on opposite sides of the kitchen island, the silence heavy.

Rowan's eyes searched her face in the soft overhead light. "Sierra . . ."

"Yes." The word came out barely above a whisper.

Rowan went very still. "Yes what?"

Sierra lifted her chin, meeting his gaze directly for the first time all evening. Her heart hammered against her ribs. "Yes, he's yours."

Silence. Rowan's face went through a dozen expressions in the space of a heartbeat—shock, hurt, anger, wonder, grief. All of it flickering across his features before he locked it down behind his careful control.

For a long moment then, he just stared at her. Sierra held her breath, waiting for the explosion, the accusations, the demands for explanations.

Instead, Rowan set his mug down with deliberate precision, turned without a word, and walked out of the kitchen.

Sierra stood alone in the soft light, listening to his footsteps retreat down the hall and the quiet click of his bedroom door closing.

The truth was finally out.

And he'd just . . . walked away?

He had a *son*. A ten-year-old son who didn't know he existed, who'd been growing up without him.

Ten years of birthdays, first days of school, scraped knees, bedtime stories—gone. All of it gone.

Rowan's hands shook as he sank onto the edge of the bed, his chest tightening until each breath felt like swallowing glass. The moonlight streaming through the window painted everything silver and cold.

And yes, he'd suspected it, but . . .

Oh, he hadn't expected the simple yes to shut him down, stop his breath, take out his heart. Or for the heat—the fury, really—to rush into the cold, open space.

He shouldn't have left her there. But he didn't know just what might come out of his mouth.

He hung his head, spots dancing at the edges as his heart hammered against his ribs.

Breathe. Count. Control.

The Delta Force training kicked in automatically. Four counts in, hold for four, out for four. Again. The shaking in his hands slowed, then stopped.

But the heat remained, coiled in his chest like a living thing. Hot and sharp and demanding action. His jaw clenched until his teeth ached, and his hands curled into fists against his thighs.

She'd kept his son from him. For ten years, she'd let him believe he had nothing, no one, no reason to come home. While he'd been bleeding for strangers in foreign deserts, his boy had been here. Learning to ride horses, practicing roping, growing up thinking his father was dead.

Unfair. The word echoed in his mind, sharp and bitter. *So unfair.*

Kane's voice drifted through his memory then, spoken over a campfire in Alaska last summer. *God has a plan, Hammer. And it's a good one. Trust Him.*

Trust. Kane knew what he was talking about—the man had nearly lost the woman he loved last summer. If anyone understood the cost of love and the weight of second chances, it was Kane.

But the sermon from this morning surfaced too, Pastor Williams's voice carrying weight across the hours. *Surely God is good to Israel, to those who are pure in heart.*

Pure in heart. Rowan almost laughed, but the sound would have been too bitter, too broken. He was about as far from pure as a man could get. Blood on his hands, scars on his soul.

The betrayal by his teammate had put a special kind of darkness in his soul.

And this felt just as black.

He stared out at the moonlit ranch, the same view he'd gazed upon as a broken teenager seeking refuge from his stepfather's fists. Sierra's grandfather had offered sanctuary then, no questions asked, just quiet acceptance and the kind of steady love Rowan had never known existed.

And then, she'd betrayed him.

How was he supposed to process this?

A soft knock at his door made him freeze.

"Rowan?" Sierra's voice, barely above a whisper.

He didn't trust himself to answer. Didn't trust his hands not to shake again if he unclenched them.

"I'm so sorry." The words cracked in the middle, and he could picture her standing there in her pajamas and robe, face streaked with tears, looking as broken as he felt.

Silence stretched between them, cracked only by the old house settling around them.

"I'll . . . I'll leave you alone." Her footsteps retreated, soft on the hardwood.

No. *Wait.*

He was on his feet and pulling open the door before conscious thought could stop him.

Sierra stood halfway down the hall, her back to him, shoulders shaking with silent sobs. Moonlight from the hallway window caught the copper highlights in her dark hair, and she looked so small, so fragile, that his anger cracked down the middle.

"Sierra."

She turned, and the devastation on her face gutted him. Her eyes were red-rimmed, cheeks wet with tears, and she held her robe closed as if it were armor that wasn't quite strong enough to protect her.

"I'm sorry," she whispered again. "I know you hate me. I know you—"

He closed the distance between them in three strides. For a heartbeat, Sierra went rigid, her eyes wide and uncertain, as if she expected him to walk past her or turn away. Then her face crumpled, and he pulled her against his chest before she could finish the sentence. She melted into him, her arms wrapping around his waist.

And she sobbed.

"I don't hate you," he said into her hair, breathing in the familiar scent of her shampoo. "I could never hate you."

Her body shook against his, and he held her tighter, the fury from moments before sliding away. His chest tightened with her sobs, the sound cutting through him, laying open his heart. And shoot, but she fit against him exactly the way she always had, like they'd been designed for each other.

They had, once upon a night. And if he were honest, that night had stayed with him, meant more to him than it should.

He shouldn't have let it get that far. But that was then, and this was now. And it was time to reckon with it. He set her away from him.

"Come on." He guided her toward the family room, needing space and light and somewhere that didn't feel quite so much like the edge of a cliff. "We need to talk."

Rowan turned on a single lamp, casting everything in soft gold.

Sierra perched on the edge of the cognac leather sofa, still clutching her robe. Rowan took the chair across from her, needing distance to think clearly.

"He's perfect, Sierra." He said, his voice husky. "Huck is perfect."

Fresh tears spilled down her cheeks. She searched his face, as if looking for anger, for condemnation, for the judgment she clearly expected to find. "I wanted to tell you. So many times, I wanted to—"

"Why didn't you?" He couldn't keep the hurt from bleeding through. Not anger—he was trying so hard not to be angry—but the raw ache of everything he'd missed. "Why keep him from me?"

Sierra wrapped her arms around herself, looking young and vulnerable and exactly as she had when she'd stolen his heart, first in a childhood crush, and then forever at eighteen.

"You were so angry, so broken, and you had dreams. You wanted to serve your country, see the world." She took a shaky breath. "A baby would have ruined everything."

"That wasn't your choice to make."

Her own accusation about him leaving echoed in his ears. No—this was different. He'd been trying to *protect* her.

"I know," she said softly. "I know that now. But I was eighteen and scared, and you'd left me for your big dreams. I thought . . . I thought I was protecting you."

Oh.

And then the heat just twisted out of his chest. He could see it—young Sierra, pregnant and alone, trying to figure out how to tell a boy who'd just gone through boot camp, about to train for special forces, that he was about to become a father.

"Then you deployed, and I did write a letter, but it was returned to me. And when I asked Mack, he said he didn't know where you were."

And that was on him, wasn't it? The thought burned through him. He closed his eyes, looked away. Sighed. "I'm sorry."

At her silence, he turned back to her.

"I was going to try again," Sierra continued, her voice gaining strength. "Tell you about Huck, maybe send pictures. But then . . ." She swallowed hard. "By the time I found the courage to write again, Mack showed up and said you were killed in action."

"No wonder you told him his father died."

"Well . . ." She lifted a shoulder. "He did."

The words hit him with unexpected force. Of course. So she'd grieved him, raised their son alone, thinking he was gone forever.

"How hard that must have been for you." The realization crashed over him, washing away the last of his anger. "Raising him alone, thinking I was dead."

"He saved me," Sierra said quietly. "After I lost you, Huck was all I had left. He kept me going when I wanted to give up."

Aw, he couldn't help it. He moved to the sofa, sat beside her, close enough to touch but not quite ready to bridge that gap.

"I shouldn't have slept with you that night." The confession tore out of him as if it were bleeding. "I was angry and broken, and I . . . I let my emotions lead."

Her gaze turned soft, almost comforting. "And I said yes. There were two of us there. And Huck is the best thing that ever happened to me. He's all I had of you for ten years, Rowan." She touched his hand. "You were the love of my life."

The love of my life. The words hit him in the chest, stealing his breath. But, past tense. Hello . . . *were* the love of her life.

Still. "You kept me alive," he said, his voice barely above a whisper. "During the worst missions, the darkest moments, thinking about you was what got me through. You were my safe place in a storm, Sierra. But I . . . I couldn't come back. I dove into my life, my missions because . . . well . . . it was the only way to protect you."

"From Alden?"

He stared at her, his throat thickening. "From *me*."

She stilled. "What? Why?" Tears tracked down her cheeks again. "Why did you think you had to protect me from yourself?"

"Because . . . Sierra. I was raised in violence and anger and hurt, and all I knew was to punch back. And the military let me do that. But I was terrified of that version of myself, that . . . anger. I needed to get it out of my system, maybe, and then walk away from it until I could get it under control."

She stared at him. "You were never that way . . . not with me."

Oh. "No. But . . . there are sides to me that you don't know. And yes, the military taught me how to stay in control, to think past my emotions. But sometimes . . ." He let out a shaky breath.

"You listen to me, Rowan Wallace. You're nothing like Alden Jenkins. But you are *everything* like Sean Wallace. Gentle and kind and brave—" She put her hand to his chest. "I know your heart." Sierra reached for his hand again, her fingers warm against his skin. "I've always known your heart."

The touch undid something in his chest.

"I don't deserve you," he said, his voice rough with emotion.

"Yeah, you do."

The space between them disappeared. He cupped her face in his hands, memorizing the feel of her skin, the way her eyes fluttered closed as he leaned in.

And then he kissed her. Oh, he kissed her. Ten years of waiting, of missing her, of remembering how she felt in his arms. She tasted like tears and hope and everything he'd dreamed about during starless nights.

Sierra.

Her hands fisted in his T-shirt, pulling him closer, and he put his arms around her, pulling her to himself, and deepened the kiss, pouring everything he couldn't say into the connection between them.

She was warmth and home and forgiveness he *didn't* deserve, but oh, how he wanted. His hands tangled in her hair, and she made a soft sound against his mouth that sent heat through his veins.

He just might lose himself again, and nearly pushed her back into the sofa cushions, when he broke away, breathing hard, meeting her eyes.

"There you are," she said softly. But her eyes were dark with desire.

"I feel like Gramps is going to walk in any second," Rowan said, his voice rough.

Sierra laughed, the sound bright and real in the quiet room. "He's certainly watching."

"That's comforting. Sheesh."

She laughed. "He loved you, Rowan."

A beat, and then . . . oh. "He knew. About Huck. He *knew*."

"Of course he did."

He blew out a breath and sat up, put his face in his hands. "He must have hated me."

Her hand was warm on his shoulder. "No. He saw you in Huck. Knew how much I loved you. He was a man of justice, but he knew mercy too. His faith was . . ." Sierra paused, as if searching for words. "It was his foundation. When my parents died, when I thought my world was ending, his faith kept me together. He prayed every night at dinner, and you were always part of those prayers."

Rowan went still. "What?"

"Every single night. He prayed for your safety, for your peace, for your heart to find its way home." Sierra's voice was soft with memory. "And he grieved for you when you died. He loved you like you were his own grandson."

The words hit Rowan dead center, a sternum hit that shuddered through him. For ten years, while he'd been convinced he was alone in the world, a good man had been lifting his name to heaven every night.

"I don't understand," he said, his voice thick.

"What?"

"How a man like him could see something worth saving in someone like me."

"Because love sees potential, not just present circumstances." Sierra traced patterns on his chest with her finger. "Gramps always said that God's specialty was taking broken things and making them beautiful. We just have to let Him."

God is good to those who are pure in heart. The verse echoed in his mind, but for the first time, it didn't feel like condemnation. Maybe purity wasn't about perfection. Maybe it was about being willing to let the broken places heal.

Not holding on so hard to the wounds, but leaning into the healing.

Sierra lifted her head to look at him, a cloud darkening her eyes. "Please don't break my heart, Rowan. I can handle losing the ranch, losing everything else. But I can't handle losing you again."

He cupped her face in his hands, thumb brushing away a tear that had escaped. "I'm not going anywhere, Sierra. Not ever again."

"Promise?"

"I promise."

And he kissed her again. Softly this time, holding back his urgency.

Because, you know, Gramps might be watching.

He finally pulled away, and she met his gaze with a smile. "Now we have another problem," she said.

He frowned.

"How do we tell Huck?"

Rowan's chest tightened. "I don't know. But we'll figure it out. Together." He pressed a kiss to the top of her head. "We're going to build something beautiful here. The three of us. I promise."

And this time he meant to keep it.

NINE

HOW WAS SHE SUPPOSED TO TELL HUCK THAT the man he'd been hero-worshipping was actually his father?

"Mom, watch this!" Huck demonstrated the wrist motion Rowan had taught him, his small hands working through the complex movement while sitting in the passenger seat of her truck. "Mr. R says the rope has to flow, not fight you. And you have to be balanced and ready to move with your target."

Sierra's chest tightened at the pure admiration in her son's voice. "You've really taken to his teaching."

"He's so cool. And patient. Like, when I mess up, he doesn't get mad or anything. He just shows me again." Huck's eyes lit up with excitement. "It's amazing how fast we became friends, you know? Like we've known each other forever."

Of course. Blood calling to blood, father and son recognizing each other on some instinctive level.

"The rodeo's only a few days away," Huck continued, practicing his rope movements. "Think I'll be ready?"

"I think you'll be amazing," Sierra said, her voice thick with emotion.

Last night had changed everything. Seeing Rowan in the moonlight, feeling his arms around her, knowing that he loved her and wanted to be here—it was like waking up from a ten-year dream.

But now came the hard part.

She pulled up to the Renegade Elementary School, the old brick building standing proud against the morning sky, with its white trim and classic early-1900s architecture. The two-story structure looked exactly as it had when she'd attended classes here twenty years ago.

"Have a good day, kiddo." Sierra leaned over to kiss Huck's forehead. "I'll pick you up after school."

"Thanks, Mom!" Huck bounded out of the truck, backpack slung over one shoulder, already calling out to friends gathering near the front steps.

Sierra watched him disappear through the heavy wooden doors, her heart swelling. As she pulled away from the school, she tried out conversations.

Huck, I have something important to tell you about Rowan . . .

No, that sounded too ominous.

You know how much you admire Rowan? Well, there's a reason for that . . .

Too cryptic.

Remember how I told you your father died? Well, I wasn't exactly telling the truth . . .

Oh, that was a good one. That would shatter his trust in her completely.

The drive back to the ranch gave her too much time to think, too much space for doubt to creep in. Could she really believe Rowan was staying? He'd made promises before—not to her directly, but to himself, to his future, to the dreams that had pulled him away from Renegade ten years ago.

But then she thought about the way he'd held her last night, the conviction in his voice when he'd said he wasn't going anywhere. And this morning, he'd ridden out with the hands as if he belonged here.

So why wouldn't he stay? He had a son now. A family. A place where he was needed and wanted.

The ranch came into view, and Sierra's heart swelled watching Rowan work alongside Morrie on the fence line near the south pasture. Even from a distance, she could see how naturally he moved.

He was a born cowboy. His flannel shirt stretched across his shoulders as he lifted a fence post, tool belt hanging low on his hips, cowboy hat shading his face from the morning sun.

She couldn't tell from here whether this was routine maintenance or something more concerning.

Sierra pulled her truck into the yard, gravel crunching under the tires as autumn sunshine streamed through the windshield. She was getting out when another vehicle pulled into the yard—a silver sedan that looked distinctly out of place among the ranch trucks.

Cecily Simmons emerged from the driver's seat, digital camera in one hand and clipboard in the other. She wore pressed khakis and a polo shirt, her dark hair pulled back in a neat bun.

"Morning, Sierra," Cecily called out, her voice warm despite the early hour. "Hope you don't mind me coming by unannounced. Figured we should get this assessment started so we can move forward with your claim."

Sierra walked over to her, the loamy scent of the morning mixing with the pastureland and the lingering smell of creosote.

"Of course." Sierra gestured toward the blackened remains. "Though I have to warn you, it's not pretty."

Cecily's expression softened with sympathy. "But that's what we're here for—to help you rebuild."

They walked toward the barn ruins together, Cecily already raising her camera to capture the extent of the damage. The morning light made everything look stark and final—twisted metal beams reaching toward the sky, charred timber scattered across the concrete foundation, the acrid smell of destruction still clinging to the air.

"Tell me about the barn," Cecily said, adjusting her camera settings. "What was the original structure?"

"Built in 1952 by my great-grandfather," Sierra said, her voice catching slightly. "Forty-eight hundred square feet, twelve stalls, hay loft storage for about three hundred bales." She paused, watching Cecily document the damage. "For a long time, it was the heart of our operation."

Cecily snapped several photos from different angles. "What did you primarily use it for?"

"Horse boarding, training, and more recently, tool and vehicle storage. But honestly?" Sierra's voice grew wistful. "It was more than that. It was . . . home."

Cecily lowered her camera, studying Sierra's face.

Sierra walked closer to the ruins, careful of the debris scattered across the ground. "When I was little, maybe seven or eight, my dad built me a fort in the hay loft. Nothing fancy—just cleared out a space, draped blankets between the support beams, added an old braided rug. It was my special place."

"Sounds perfect for a little girl."

"It was. Especially after . . ." Sierra's voice trailed off, memories surfacing that she rarely allowed herself to examine. "My mom lost a baby when I was eight. A little brother. I barely remember the details, but I remember how sad the house felt afterward. How quiet."

Cecily's expression grew gentle. "I'm sorry, honey. That's a hard loss for any family."

"My dad knew I was struggling. The fort became my escape, you know? I'd climb up there with books and snacks, and he'd let me stay until dinner. Sometimes he'd even bring me hot chocolate and sit with me while I read." Sierra's eyes misted at the memory. "He said every girl needed a castle, even if it was built from old horse blankets."

"My husband Art always said the same thing. He and your dad worked together in the volunteer fire department for years. Art felt so bad when your mama lost that baby. And of course, when you lost your parents." She gave her a sad smile. "You were so young, but so strong."

Oh. She'd almost forgotten that Cecily's husband would have known her parents.

She sighed. "I don't feel strong."

Cecily stopped photographing and turned to face Sierra directly. "Honey, can I speak plainly?"

Sierra nodded.

"I've been in this business for fifteen years, and I've seen a lot of folks face this kind of loss. You've had more than your share—parents, grandfather, now this barn. That's an awful lot for one person to carry."

"It is."

"But here's what I've learned. When life gets this hard, you've got two choices. Give up, or believe that something bigger than yourself is going to carry you through it." Cecily's brown eyes met hers. "Psalm 73 talks about having no one in heaven but the Lord, no one on earth besides Him. That's not about being alone—it's about knowing who's really in control when everything else falls apart."

Sierra's breath caught.

"Art and I lost our first baby. Miscarriage at six months." Cecily's voice remained steady, but Sierra could see the old pain in her eyes. "Thought my world was ending. But sometimes the Lord has to strip everything away before He can show us what He's really building."

Tears burned Sierra's eyes. "How do you keep believing when it feels like you're losing everything?"

"Because losing everything teaches you that the things you can't lose are the only ones that really matter." Cecily gave her a soft smile. "Family, faith, love. Those are the foundations that don't burn, honey."

We're going to build something beautiful here. The three of us. I promise.

Yes. Yes, they were.

"You know what I think?" Cecily said, taking more pictures. "I think your daddy built you that fort for times exactly like this. Sometimes we all need a safe place to figure out our next move."

"Even when the fort burns down?"

"Especially then. Because that's when you learn that the real castle was never the boards and blankets anyway. It was the love that built it."

Sierra's throat tightened with emotion. "I want to rebuild. I want to believe this place has a future."

"Then that's what we'll make happen." Cecily made notes on her clipboard. "I'll have the preliminary report filed by tomorrow, and we'll get a check issued."

"Just like that?"

"Honey, I've been watching you handle this crisis with more grace than most people manage on their best days. You've got ranch hands who respect you, a son who adores you, and unless I'm much mistaken, a good man working on your fences who looks at you like you hung the moon." Cecily smiled. "That's Rowan Wallace, isn't it?"

"You recognize him?"

"I recognize the boy in the man I saw. He looked at you that same way even back then. Except, I thought he died."

"It's complicated."

"It looks pretty simple to me." She winked.

Heat crept up Sierra's neck. "Is it that obvious?"

"Only to someone who's been married for twenty-three years." Cecily chuckled. "The way he kept glancing over here? As if to make sure you were okay? Either he's very dedicated to his job, or very dedicated to you."

Sierra looked toward the fence line where Rowan and Morrie had been working. They'd finished and were nowhere to be seen. They'd probably gone to join the other hands.

Cecily finished her assessment, and they were walking back toward their vehicles when the sound of hoofbeats caught Sierra's attention. She turned to see Rowan riding hard toward them, his horse's hooves throwing up clouds of dust as they approached at a pace that made Sierra's pulse spike.

Something was wrong.

Rowan pulled up short, the horse dancing beneath him as he swung down from the saddle as if he'd been born in it. His face was grim, jaw set in a way that made Sierra's stomach clench with dread.

"Sierra." He glanced at Cecily, his voice low. "I need you to come with me."

"Why? What's wrong? More cattle missing?"

Rowan's eyes met hers, and she saw something there that made her blood run cold.

"No," he said quietly. "Worse. We have half a dozen head of cattle in the southwest pasture. And they're all sick or dying. Whoever is stealing your cattle has escalated to simply killing them."

Someone was winning the war on the woman he loved.

The cow's labored breathing filled the South Eagle Veterinary Clinic as Rowan watched the vet examine Sierra's sick Hereford.

"When did you first notice the symptoms?" Dr. Chen pulled on latex gloves, her movements efficient as she approached the examination table where they'd managed to get the sick heifer positioned. She was younger than Rowan had expected, maybe early thirties, with long black hair pulled back in a practical ponytail and intelligent dark eyes that missed nothing. Her white lab coat was pristine over navy scrubs, and everything about her demeanor spoke of competence.

The clinic was a far cry from the old-fashioned country practice most people expected. Dr. Sarah Chen had built a state-of-the-art facility that could handle everything from routine checkups to emergency surgery. Stainless-steel examination tables dominated the main treatment area, surrounded by gleaming cabinets filled with medical equipment. The sterile white walls were broken by digital monitors displaying vital signs and X-ray-viewing boxes that cast blue light across the polished concrete floors.

The fluorescent lights overhead cast everything in harsh white, making the animal's distress more apparent. The heifer's flanks heaved with each difficult breath, foam collecting at the corners of her mouth.

"This morning." Rowan's jaw tightened as he watched the cow struggle. "Found her and five others down by the pond, all showing the same signs. Excessive salivation, lying on the ground. Three were already dead."

"Mm-hmm." Dr. Chen ran her hands along the cow's neck, checking lymph nodes with practiced efficiency. "And they were all near your water source?"

"The stock pond, yeah. Fed by the creek that runs through our—through Sierra's south pasture."

"Did you bring water samples like I asked?" Dr. Chen straightened, pulling off her gloves and reaching for fresh ones.

Rowan held up a small cooler. "Three different collection points along the creek, plus one from the pond itself."

"Good thinking." Dr. Chen accepted the cooler, immediately pulling out the labeled vials. She arranged them on the testing station. "This isn't the first case I've seen like this in the past month."

"What do you mean?"

"Tom Hendrick's cattle up north of town had similar symptoms three weeks ago. Lost two head before we figured out it was their water source." Dr. Chen moved to her testing station, a sophisticated setup that looked more like a hospital lab than anything Rowan had seen in a rural vet clinic. "Took the water to Denver for analysis. Results came back showing elevated lithium levels."

"Lithium?" Rowan stood back, arms folded. He hated standing here without anything to do. "Is that a problem around here?"

"Shouldn't be, no." Dr. Chen began preparing samples. "But with all the mineral exploration happening lately, sometimes things get stirred up underground."

"Or someone's stirring them up deliberately."

Dr. Chen paused in her work, studying his face with those sharp dark eyes. "You think someone's contaminating water sources on purpose?"

"I think someone's been targeting specific ranches for the past few months, and now they've escalated from rustling to poisoning livestock." Rowan's hands clenched into fists at his sides. "How long does it take for the poison to work?"

"If it's lithium toxicity, the animals showing symptoms now have maybe twelve to twenty-four hours before organ failure sets in. The ones still mobile need to be moved away from the contaminated source immediately."

Rowan pulled out his phone, dialing Morrie's number. The foreman picked up on the second ring.

"How's the cow?" Morrie said, his voice gravelly.

"Poisoned. Lithium in the water." Rowan kept his voice level despite the storm building in his chest. "I think we need to move the entire herd away from the south pasture. Get them to the north section, away from any creek water."

"Already on it. Jake and Tomás are helping me move them now."

"Good. I'll be back shortly."

Rowan ended the call and turned back to Dr. Chen, who was running tests on the water samples. Her equipment hummed quietly, digital readouts flickering as the analysis progressed.

"How definitive will these results be?" he asked.

"If there's lithium contamination, I'll know within the hour," Dr. Chen said. "But based on what I'm seeing with your cow and what happened to Tom Hendrick's herd, I'd bet money we're going to find elevated levels."

And Rowan didn't say it, but what if the man had discovered just who had poisoned his cattle and went after them?

And ended up dead in a creek bed.

"The Hendricks' ranch is near Sierra's. Anyone else been affected?"

"Not that I know of, but I only treat livestock. Could be other vets have seen cases."

Rowan's phone buzzed with a text from Saxon.

Saxon
_____

Meet me at police station. Have
information re: Elway **Blackwood**.

"Dr. Chen, I need to step out for a bit. Can you call me the moment you have results?"

"Of course. And Mr. Wallace?" She looked up from her testing station, her expression grim. "If someone is deliberately contaminating water sources, they're not just killing cattle. They're destroying livelihoods. People's entire way of life."

"I know." Rowan's voice carried quiet menace. "That's exactly what I intend to stop."

He texted Sierra as he walked back to the truck.

_____
Rowan

Where **are** you?

No answer. He pocketed his phone.

Saxon's truck was already parked outside the South Eagle Police Station. Rowan spotted him through the glass doors, talking with someone in uniform. Saxon looked more polished than usual in dark jeans and a button-down shirt under his leather jacket, his dark hair freshly cut, and his beard neatly trimmed. Everything about him projected competence and authority—so look who really was diving into the PI world. Interesting.

Detective Michael Martinelli looked like he'd aged five years since Rowan had seen him yesterday after coming out to survey the destruction of Sierra's house. His white shirt was wrinkled, tie loosened, and dark circles shadowed his eyes as he gestured toward a stack of files on his desk.

"Wallace." Martinelli stood when Rowan entered, extending a hand. "Saxon here's been filling me in on what you've discovered."

"And I've been learning some interesting things myself." Saxon nodded toward a chair, his expression grim. "Sit down. This is bigger than we thought."

Rowan remained standing, too wired to relax. The fluorescent lights overhead cast harsh shadows, and the smell of old coffee and paper filled the air. "The vet thinks it's lithium poisoning. She was able to save our cow, but she thinks it's deliberate. Says there was another case north of here three weeks ago."

"Tom Hendrick's place," Martinelli said, consulting his notes. "We investigated but couldn't find evidence of deliberate contamination. Figured it was environmental. But now, I'm not so sure."

"What changed your mind?" Saxon asked, leaning forward in his chair.

"You asking questions about mineral rights and land acquisitions." Martinelli rubbed his forehead, exhaustion evident in every line of his face. "I started looking at patterns. Sierra's place, the Hendricks' spread. Tom's death. He also had a suspicious fire last month. And all of them have been approached by the same real-estate company in the past six months."

Saxon leaned forward. "What company?"

"Rocky Mountain Land Development. But that's where it gets interesting." Martinelli pulled out a manila folder, spreading documents across his desk. "When I ran the incorporation papers, the company traces back to one corporate umbrella."

"Which is?"

"Meridian Holdings. It's a conglomerate. Land. Biotech. Even commercial properties."

"How many ranchers have they approached?" Saxon asked.

"At least eight that I can confirm. Maybe more." Martinelli's expression darkened. "And here's the kicker—every ranch that's been hit with 'accidents' refused to sell."

Rowan's hands clenched into fists. "This is organized corporate terrorism."

"That's what I'm starting to think." Martinelli gestured toward another stack of files. "Problem is, I'm stretched thin right now. Had two teenagers OD this weekend, both in critical condition at Renegade Mercy General Hospital. Parents are demanding answers, and the DEA's breathing down my neck about drug trafficking."

Saxon and Rowan exchanged glances. "Any connection between the overdoses and this land grab?" Saxon asked.

"No. It's just a growing problem. A new drug we can't identify." Martinelli's jaw tightened.

Saxon had pulled out his phone to consult his notes. "Ever heard of a guy named Ralph Rousseau? He's at the helm of Rocky Mountain Land Development."

"I think we need to have a chat with Ralph Rousseau," Rowan said.

Martinelli gave him a look. "You need to step back, Wallace. You're not deputized."

"I could be."

The detective held up a hand. "Just, take a breath."

"You said you were short-staffed."

"Okay. Listen. I'll talk to him. And I'll keep in touch. I will let you know if . . . if we need to involve you."

"I'm already involved," he said with a growl.

Martinelli's mouth turned into a grim line.

Rowan turned to Saxon. "What did you find out about Sierra's grandfather?"

"Talked to Police Chief Bruce Balluff this morning. He said Elway Blackwood was old-school law enforcement, used to be a detective before he became police commissioner. Balluff mentioned that Elway had been investigating something on the side before he died."

"Investigating what?"

"Land deals. Water rights. Balluff said Elway was also suspicious about the number of ranchers being pressured to sell, especially given the recent mineral surveys in the area."

"And then he conveniently dies in an ATV accident."

"That's what I'm thinking too," Saxon said quietly. "But thinking and proving are two different things."

"What kind of minerals are we talking about?" Martinelli asked.

"I got these from the county office." Saxon pulled out a geological survey report, spreading it across the desk next to Martinelli's files. "Lithium-beryllium deposits. Significant ones, according to this. With the electric-vehicle boom and tech-industry demand, lithium mining has become incredibly lucrative."

"Lucrative enough to kill for?" Rowan said.

"Potentially. Lithium extraction is a multibillion-dollar industry. If someone identified a major deposit under local ranch land, they'd need to acquire the mineral rights to access it."

"And if the ranchers won't sell willingly . . ."

"You make their lives miserable until they do." Saxon's voice was grim. "Fires, livestock poisoning, probably escalating pressure until they give up and leave."

Martinelli leaned back in his chair, which creaked under the movement. "This is all speculation unless we can prove deliberate contamination."

Rowan's phone rang. Dr. Chen's name appeared on the screen.

"Dr. Chen. What did you find?"

"Lithium levels three times what's considered safe for livestock consumption." Her voice was tight with concern. "This isn't environmental, Mr. Wallace. Someone introduced concentrated lithium into your water source."

"How concentrated?"

"Enough to kill every head of cattle that drinks from that pond within forty-eight hours."

Rowan went a little cold. "Thank you, Doctor. Please document everything for a police report."

"Already doing it. And Mr. Wallace? I'm calling the other ranchers to compare notes. If this is happening to multiple ranchers, we need to establish a pattern."

Rowan ended the call and looked at Saxon and Martinelli. "Confirmed. Deliberate lithium poisoning."

"That's attempted destruction of property, at minimum." Martinelli stood, reaching for his jacket. "Could be attempted murder if anyone had consumed that water."

Rowan stilled. "Sierra and Huck use well water for the house, but they could have easily been exposed. I need to call her."

"Make the call," Saxon said. "But Rowan? We need to be smart about this. If Meridian is behind this, they have serious money and resources. They won't hesitate to escalate if they feel threatened."

Rowan stepped outside to make the call, needing air and space to control his anger before talking to Sierra. The afternoon sun felt too bright after the fluorescent lighting of the police station, and Main Street bustled with normal small-town activity that felt surreal, given what he'd just learned.

She answered on the second ring.

"Rowan? How's the cow?"

He'd loaded the heifer into the cattle truck, but Sierra had taken her truck to pick up Huck from school.

Now the worry in her voice made his chest tight. "The cattle poisoning could be deliberate. Lithium contamination in the water."

"Deliberate?" Sierra's voice rose, and he could hear the truck door slam in the background. "Someone poisoned our livestock on purpose?"

"That's what it looks like. Where are you now? Did you get my text?"

"Yes. I just dropped Huck at home. He's working on homework. I'm heading back to help Morrie with the cattle."

"Don't go to the south pasture. Stay away from the creek."

"Rowan, if someone's willing to poison our cattle . . ."

"They might be willing to do worse. I know." He stared out at the mountain in the distance, the clouds gathering. "Listen. Stay alert. I'm with Detective Martinelli and Saxon at the police station. I'll be home soon."

He refused to hear how normal that sounded. *Home. Soon.*

"Rowan?"

"Yeah?"

"Be careful."

"They won't get the chance to hurt anything else I love." He blew out a breath. "I'll call you as soon as I know more."

Rowan ended the call and rejoined Saxon and Martinelli.

"What's our next move?" Rowan asked.

"I contact the state police and request support for a major investigation," Martinelli said. "This crosses county lines now, which gives us more resources."

"And I keep digging into Meridian and Rocky Mountain Land

Development," Saxon added. "Follow the money, find the connections."

"What about Sierra and Huck?" Rowan glanced again at his phone. Protective instincts were screaming at him to get them somewhere safe immediately.

"They need to be careful," Martinelli said. "Escalation to human targets isn't unthinkable."

"I'll handle their security," Rowan said. "But I want to track these guys down before they can escalate further." He looked at Martinelli as he headed out, stopping at the door. "And to be clear, I won't be stopping in for a badge to take down someone who might be trying to kill"—he looked at Saxon, and back to Martinelli—"my family."

Detective Martinelli raised an eyebrow.

Rowan didn't care. And he didn't look back.

Line drawn.

TEN

SIERRA CARRIED COFFEE TO THE MAN WHO'D turned her ranch into a fortress, wondering when she'd stopped being afraid of needing someone.

Four days of living under Rowan's protection had transformed the Blackwood ranch into something her grandfather never would have recognized. Security cameras perched on fence posts throughout the property, their red lights blinking steadily in the late-afternoon sun. Motion sensors lined the perimeter, and she'd grown accustomed to the subtle crackle of radio communication from the earpiece Rowan wore constantly. Even now, as he sat on the porch steps watching Huck practice, his posture spoke of a man ready to move at the first sign of trouble.

The changes should have felt oppressive. Instead, Sierra felt safer than she had in months.

Maybe years.

"Thought you might need this," she said, offering him the steaming mug.

Rowan looked up from where he'd been observing Huck's practice session, and wrapped his strong hand around the mug. "Thanks. Saxon's due back from his perimeter check in twenty minutes, but I wanted to watch Huck."

She smiled at that and followed his gaze to where Huck was practicing in the makeshift arena they'd set up away from the barn ruins. Her son sat astride Jasper, her grandfather's old quarter horse, working through tie-down roping drills with the focused intensity of someone twice his age. The horse was twenty-three now, steady and patient, the same mount that had carried Huck safely since he was three years old.

"He's getting good," Rowan said, genuine admiration in his voice. "Really good."

"Of course." Sierra settled beside him on the steps, close enough to catch the familiar scent of his soap mixed with autumn air. "Natural talent." She smiled up at him.

He smiled back, something warm in his eyes. So, apparently he'd forgiven her.

Now, they still struggled with how to tell Huck.

They watched in silence as Huck guided Jasper into position, rope coiled and ready. The boy's technique was flawless—quick release, perfect loop, clean dismount to tie the calf. Even the imaginary calf he was practicing on would have been secured in record time.

"That horse moves like molasses," Rowan said.

"Jasper keeps him safe," Sierra said. "That's what matters."

"Poor kid."

"He's ten years old, Rowan."

"He's a *Wallace*." Rowan's blue eyes held hers. "Danger's in his blood."

The words hung between them, loaded with meaning neither was quite ready to address. Sierra's chest tightened as she looked from Rowan to Huck, seeing the resemblance that became more obvious every day.

"We need to tell him," she said quietly.

"I know." Rowan's hands tightened around the coffee cup. "I just . . ."

"What?" Sierra studied his profile, noting the tension in his jaw.

"I don't want to mess this up. He's got the rodeo on Saturday, and he's been working so hard." Rowan sighed. "What if knowing changes everything for him?"

"What if *not* knowing is worse?"

Rowan was quiet for a long moment, watching Huck reset for another practice run. "You're right. But Sierra?" He turned to face her fully. "He's built up his dead father in his head to a sort of superhero status." He swallowed. "What if I'm not what he wants?"

The rawness in his tone wrecked her. "Seriously."

"I don't want to disappoint him."

Oh, Rowan. She put her hand on his. "He will probably be shocked, no doubt. But . . . he's also going to be over the moon. He thinks you're Superman."

Rowan didn't seem convinced. "He'll know I lied to him. To you both."

She nodded.

He turned away then and swallowed.

"That's not all, is it?"

This time his sigh was deeper. He set down his coffee and ran a hand through his hair. "What if I'm not good at this family thing? I remember what I'm capable of. What I did to Alden."

Sierra's breath caught. They'd never talked about that night in detail, not really.

"He tried to press charges," she said softly. "After you left."

"What?" Rowan's head snapped up. "Aw, I knew he would."

"Alden came to see Grandpa the next day. Said you'd attacked him without provocation, that you were dangerous." Sierra's voice grew stronger as she remembered her grandfather's response. "Grandpa told him that if he pressed charges, it would interfere with your enlistment. Said the military was probably the best thing for you at that point. I think he might have mentioned, too, that he would testify on your behalf. And perhaps he added other threats, I dunno. But no charges were filed in the end."

His eyes widened. "Your grandfather saved me from jail."

"My grandfather saved you from a stepfather who deserved what you gave him and more," Sierra snapped. "But Rowan, you have to stop thinking that protecting yourself makes you like Alden."

"You don't understand." Rowan's voice roughened with old pain. "When I hit him, when I felt that power, that ability to hurt someone . . ." He shook his head. "I scared myself, Sierra. I wanted to *keep* hitting him."

"Because he'd been hurting you for years. Because you were eighteen and finally strong enough to fight back." Sierra reached for his hand, lacing their fingers together. "That doesn't make you him."

"How can you be sure?"

"Because you're like your *dad*." The words came out with quiet certainty. "You run toward trouble to protect people, not away from it."

Rowan looked away then, something broken on his face. "My dad died because of me."

Sierra stared at him. "What? No, he didn't, Rowan. It was an accident."

"He was working with a new horse in the corral, trying to train him. Green broke, but still skittish." Rowan's voice grew distant, lost in memory. "I was chasing our barn cat. Stupid cat had gotten into the feed room, and I was trying to catch him before he made a mess."

Sierra waited, sensing the weight of whatever was coming.

"I ran right into the corral without thinking. The horse spooked, reared up. Dad saw what was happening and threw himself between

SUSAN MAY WARREN

me and those hooves." Rowan's voice cracked. "Took the kick that should have been mine."

"Rowan . . ."

"If I hadn't been chasing that stupid cat. If I'd just paid attention, looked where I was going . . ." He shook his head. "My mom was right. If I'd just controlled myself, controlled my emotions, he'd still be alive."

Tears pricked Sierra's eyes. "You were eight years old. Children chase cats. Children run without looking. That's what children do."

"Children get people killed."

"Fathers protect their children. That's what *fathers* do." Sierra found his gaze with hers. "Your dad didn't die because you were reckless. He died because he loved you enough to put himself in harm's way."

Rowan was quiet for a long moment, staring at their joined hands.

"What if I can't be that kind of father?" he asked finally.

"You already are." Sierra gestured toward where Huck was practicing. "You've been here six days, and you've already turned this place into the safest spot in three counties. You watch him practice and your whole face lights up. You worry about his confidence and his technique and whether telling him the truth will mess up his focus." She squeezed his hand. "Trust me, you're already that kind of father."

He swallowed, but nodded, something raw and hopeful on his face.

They watched Huck dismount and check his imaginary time, then pump his fist in celebration.

Oh, her heart just swelled with the overwhelming desire to protect this moment forever.

"We should probably head inside soon," Sierra said, though she made no move to stand. "I need to start dinner, and you should check in with Saxon."

"In a minute." Rowan's eyes were fixed on the barn ruins visible beyond the practice area. "What are you planning to do about that?"

Sierra followed his gaze to the twisted wreckage. The skeletal remains of the structure seemed to burrow further into her soul every day.

"I don't know," she said. "The insurance adjuster said we'd need a bulldozer to clear the debris, but we haven't gotten the insurance money yet . . ." She shrugged, trying to project a confidence she didn't feel. "I guess I'll figure something out."

"Leave it to me."

The simple statement carried such quiet authority that Sierra felt her chest tighten. "Rowan, you don't have to—"

"Yes, I do." He turned to face her, his blue eyes serious. "This is our home now. Our life. Let me handle the barn."

Our home. Our life. The words sent warmth spreading through her chest, followed immediately by a terrible, familiar fear that tightened her throat.

"What if you change your mind?" The question slipped out before she could stop it.

"About what?"

"About this. About us. About staying." Sierra's voice grew smaller, more vulnerable than she intended. "What if you decide this is too complicated and you just . . . leave?"

Rowan studied her face with those penetrating blue eyes. "Why would you think that?"

"I don't know. Learned behavior, I guess." Sierra wrapped her arms around herself. "I've always been the one people leave. My parents, then you. Mike."

"Mike? Detective Martinelli? What does he . . . oh . . . Oh." He drew in a breath. "Now I get why he was so protective."

She made a face. "Yeah, we dated. When Huck was about five years old. Just for a few months, but . . . it didn't work."

198

"Why not?"

"He wasn't you. And he knew it, and I knew it. So, yeah . . . And he was pretty hurt. Said I had impossibly high standards and that I'd never be happy because I didn't know how to let anyone help me."

"Now I'm going to have to kill him."

He didn't look like he might be kidding. And his next question came out soft, a little broken. "Did you love him?"

Oh, Rowan.

"No." The answer came easy. "I tried to. I wanted to give Huck a father, wanted to build something normal and stable. But like I said, Mike wasn't . . . he wasn't you."

"Sierra . . ."

"I do have high expectations," she continued, the words tumbling out in a rush. "For myself, for my son, for anyone who wants to be part of our lives. And maybe I am too self-reliant. Maybe I don't know how to depend on other people. It's just . . . it's weird, you know? Depending on someone else. I've been taking care of myself and Huck for so long that letting someone else help feels . . ."

"Dangerous," Rowan finished.

"Terrifying. Because what if I get used to it? What if I let myself believe in this, in us, and then you realize I'm not worth the trouble?"

Rowan set down his coffee and turned to face her fully, his hands framing her face with infinite gentleness. "Are you kidding me right now? Sierra Blackwood, you listen to me. You've raised an incredible son, you've kept this ranch running despite every obstacle thrown at you, and you've somehow managed to forgive me for leaving when you needed me most."

His thumbs brushed away tears she didn't realize had fallen.

"You wanna hear something crazy?" He grinned. "I was even

jealous of Morrie," he admitted, his voice rough. "The way he protects you, looks out for you. I thought maybe you two . . ."

"Morrie's got his own wife," Sierra said, a smile tugging at her lips. "He's just protective because Grandpa asked him to look out for us before he died."

"You want to know the truth?" Sierra's voice grew stronger, more certain. "You're the one, Row. You always have been. Even when I was eighteen and scared and pregnant, even when I thought you were dead, even when I tried to move on with Mike—it was always you."

Something shifted in Rowan's expression, a wall coming down that she hadn't even realized was there.

"Sierra . . ." His voice was rough with emotion.

"I love you," she said softly, but the words broke out, felt like freedom. "I loved you when we were kids, I loved you when you left, and I love you now. Whatever comes next, whatever happens with the ranch or the threats or telling Huck—I love you."

Rowan's response was to put his hand behind her neck, pull her to himself, and kiss her, soft and sure and full of ten years of longing. Sierra melted into him, her hands fisting in his shirt as she kissed him back with everything she had.

It wasn't a possessive kiss, like the one nights before, on the sofa, but one of reassurance and depth, one of knowing and being known and maybe even belonging.

Perfect. And right. And—

"What are you doing?"

He froze, and she did too. Then she turned.

Huck stood there in the sunshine, staring at them. "Why are you kissing my mom!"

Oh. Rowan held up his hands. "I—" Then he looked at Sierra, almost panic in his eyes.

"You shouldn't kiss her. You're not—" He marched right up to Rowan. "You're not my dad!"

Oh.

Sierra glanced at Rowan, whose jaw tightened.

"Huck," he started.

"I know he's dead. But . . . but you can't just . . . just show up and . . . I want you to leave. Right *now*!"

He stared at Rowan, breathing hard.

Rowan had found his feet. "Huck, calm down."

"You stay away from her!"

Rowan held up his hands, like he might for a skittish horse. "Son, we need to talk to you—"

Huck started to back away.

"Huck, honey, come sit down," Sierra said. She glanced at Rowan, but what choice did they have? "We need to talk to you about something important."

"About what?" Huck's voice pitched high, the way it got when he was scared or upset.

Sierra looked at Rowan, who nodded almost imperceptibly. There was no going back now.

"About your father," Sierra said quietly.

Huck went very still. "My father's dead!"

"No, honey. He's not." Sierra's voice broke slightly. "Your father is very much alive."

He just looked at her. Frowned, his breaths coming fast.

Then he looked at Rowan and stilled.

And right then, the entire world seemed to pause, as if finding its feet, the very air still and unbroken.

Huck's gaze darted between Sierra and Rowan, and then he took a long breath, and his mouth opened.

"Yes," she said softly. "Rowan is your father, Huck. I should have told you sooner, should have—"

"No. No—my father is dead. He's . . . he's . . . ." He stared at Rowan.

Then Huck simply rounded and ran.

"Huck!" Sierra started after him, but Rowan grabbed her arm.

"Huck!" Rowan boomed.

But Huck wasn't listening anymore. He sprinted toward Jasper. The paint horse stood ground-tied where Huck had left him, reins dragging in the dirt.

"Huck, no!" Sierra shouted, but her son was already there. In one fluid motion, born of years in the saddle, Huck grabbed the saddle horn and swung himself up onto Jasper's back. The horse sidestepped once, sensing the tension radiating from his young rider, but Huck was already gathering the reins with hands that shook with hurt and fury.

"Huck, wait!" Rowan called out, moving toward them, but it was too late.

Huck dug his heels into Jasper's sides, and the paint horse exploded into motion. They shot across the pasture like a bullet, Huck leaning low over the horse's neck as they headed straight for the fence line at a dead gallop. Sierra's heart stopped—there was no gate in that direction, just barbed wire and—

But Huck knew this ranch better than anyone. At the last possible second, he wheeled Jasper toward the creek crossing, the place where the fence dipped low enough to clear. Jasper took the jump without hesitation, sailing over the wire with room to spare before disappearing into the thick stand of cottonwoods beyond.

"Sheesh." Rowan was already vaulting the corral fence, moving toward one of the other horses with grim determination. "Stay here. I got this."

Rowan didn't waste time with a saddle. He slipped a bridle over Thunder's head and swung up bareback, the old cowboy in him turning his movements sure.

"Rowan, be careful," Sierra called as he turned the quarter horse out of the corral.

"I'll find him," Rowan said. Looked at her. "I'll bring him home."

Then he took off, his mount stretching into a gallop across the pasture.

Sierra watched him, the drumbeat of hooves fading until all she could hear was the wind in the grass and her own ragged breathing.

———————————

What if his horse threw him and Rowan lost his son before he even got to be his father?

The thought hammered through Rowan as he watched Huck disappear across the fields. Sierra's confession still echoed in his ears—*You're the one, Row. You always have been*—but that overwhelming declaration would have to wait. Right now, his ten-year-old was riding pell-mell across dangerous terrain, rutted with prairie dog holes and cattle hoofprints, clearly emotionally out of control.

Like father, like son, maybe.

Aw, he'd handled that badly. Shoot.

Huck was a quarter mile ahead now, coming up fast to the creek that cut through the south pasture.

Please don't fall—please don't fall!

But Jasper picked his way down the rocky slope into the ravine, as if the old horse could read Rowan's mind.

They reached the bottom.

Huck's scream cut through the evening air like a blade.

Rowan's blood turned to ice as he watched Jasper rear up, front hooves pawing the air while Huck fought to stay in the saddle. Even from this distance, Rowan could see the way Huck's hands grabbed for the saddle horn.

He missed and tumbled off and landed in the creek bed.

And in that second, Rowan was again eight years old, watching his father throw himself between those deadly hooves and the little boy who'd been chasing a barn cat. The sickening thud of impact. The way his dad had crumpled to the ground and never gotten up.

Not again. Not his son.

Rowan drove his horse down the slope, stones scattering under its hooves as they plunged toward the creek bed, and spotted what had spooked Jasper—a coiled rattlesnake sunning itself on a flat rock near the water's edge.

Now it had coiled tight, as if to strike, its rattle sizzling in the air. Jasper reared again, just above Huck.

Without thinking, Rowan launched from the horse's back, caught Huck around the waist, and pulled him clear just as Jasper's hooves crashed down where the boy's head had been seconds before.

Rowan hit the ground hard, cushioning Huck's fall with his own body as they rolled away from the terrified horse. Pain shot through Rowan's shoulder, but he barely felt it.

He bounced to his feet and pulled Huck up, pushed him behind him. Then he put his hand out toward Jasper.

"Easy, boy, easy." Rowan kept his voice calm and soothing as he slowly reached for his sidearm. The snake was still coiled, still rattling its warning.

The gunshot echoed off the ravine walls. The rattlesnake's head disappeared in a spray of blood and rock fragments, its body writhing briefly before going still.

Jasper jerked and bolted, but Rowan grabbed its trailing rein a second before it could escape. The horse's momentum pulled him along the dry creek, and again the horse reared.

Rowan stepped back, kept his hand up, let the horse land, shake it out. "You're okay, buddy."

Jasper snorted and he pawed, but his eyes found Rowan's.

Rowan waited a moment, then took a step. "You're okay."

The old horse snorted again and shook his head.

Rowan holstered his Glock, then put a hand on Jasper's soft nose.

The animal bowed his head and then stepped up to him, bumping him.

"Yeah. Sorry for the ruckus," he said, moving his hand over the horse's neck. He then turned and looked for Huck.

The kid was sitting on the creek bank with his knees drawn up to his chest.

"You hurt?"

"No." The word came out small and shaky.

"It's okay to be scared. Rattlesnakes are serious business." Rowan settled beside Huck on the rocky ground, close enough to touch but not quite. "Jasper was just protecting you both. Smart horse."

Huck ran a hand across his eyes, his snotty nose.

Yeah, him too. Maybe they just needed a minute.

"Can we talk about it?"

Huck looked away, his head in his folded arms.

"I love your mom."

Huck sighed.

"And you."

The kid didn't move.

Okay, so maybe—

"Are you really my dad?" His voice emerged soft, almost broken.

Rowan's seemed to match it. "Yeah, buddy. I really am."

More silence. Then, "Why didn't you come back before? Didn't you want me?"

And now he got it. Why Huck had insisted he was dead.

Because dead didn't mean rejected. Dead didn't mean his father had chosen not to come home. And maybe Huck was only ten and didn't truly understand his snarled emotions.

He just knew it hurt.

"Huck. I didn't know about you," Rowan said quietly. "I swear on my life, I didn't know you existed until a few days ago."

More silence.

"But Mom said my dad was dead. And she wouldn't lie to me."

What a good kid. "She didn't lie. She *thought* I was dead. For a long time, everyone thought I was dead. It was . . . complicated." He searched for words that would make sense to a ten-year-old. "Because of my job, I had to disappear for a while. Your mom had no way of knowing I was still alive."

Huck drew in a breath and looked at him then, those blue eyes bright with tears. "What kind of job?"

"Soldier. I was a soldier. Just like I told you. Just like your mom told you."

Huck swallowed. "Why did you come back?"

"Well, my mission—the one that kept me dead—ended. And the first thing I thought of was . . . well, seeing your mom. I needed to tell her I *wasn't* dead. And then I heard about your great-grandpa dying and . . . he was important to me, so I thought I'd stay and help and . . ." He put his hand on Huck's shoulder. "And then I met you."

Huck just kept staring at him. "Did you know I was . . . who I was?"

"No. Not until a couple days ago."

"Then why did you stay?"

"Because . . . like I said, I love your mom. And I love you."

"You don't even know me."

"I know you're brave. I know you ride like you were born in the saddle. I know you practice roping until your hands blister because you want to be the best." Rowan's voice roughened with emotion. "I know you take care of your mom and help around the ranch and that you've got the biggest heart of any kid I've ever met."

"Mom told you that stuff."

"No, she didn't. I mean, she would, probably. But I can see it for myself." He turned to him, and now his chest simply cracked and his throat tightened and, shoot, he could barely speak the words. "I know you're the best thing I never knew I had."

Huck's composure broke at that. The tears he'd been holding back spilled over, and suddenly he was sobbing—great, wrenching sobs that spoke of ten years of questions and loneliness and the desperate desire for a father.

And Rowan, shoot, he just reached out and pulled the kid to himself.

Pulled his son to himself.

Because he was his *father*.

"I wanted you to come back," Huck choked out between sobs. "Every birthday, every Christmas, every time kids at school talked about their dads. I wanted you to not be dead so bad."

Rowan's own eyes burned, filled. He closed them. "I'm sorry, buddy. I'm so sorry I wasn't here."

And then Huck put his arms around him and held on.

Rowan had never felt more undone in his life. "Listen. I'm here now, and I'm not going anywhere. Not ever."

Huck finally leaned up. "Promise?"

"I promise." Rowan met his son's eyes and wiped tears from Huck's face with gentle thumbs. "I've got ten years of birthdays to make up for. Ten years of bedtime stories and homework help and teaching you everything I know about being a man. If you'll let me."

Huck studied his face with serious eyes. "Will you teach me to shoot? Like you just did with the snake?"

Of course he would ask that, and Rowan laughed. "When you're older. Much older." A smile tugged at Rowan's lips. "But I'll teach you to fix engines and change oil and all the things my dad taught me before . . ."

"Before he died?"

"Yeah." Rowan's voice grew quiet. "Before he died saving me from a horse that was spooked, just like Jasper was today."

"Is that why you were so scared? When Jasper reared up?"

"Terrified," Rowan said. "I couldn't lose you, Huck. Not when I just found you."

"I'm sorry I ran away."

"Yeah. That wasn't smart. You have every right to be upset. But you need to figure out how to keep your cool when your emotions feel too big, okay?"

The sound of hoofbeats made them both look up. Sierra appeared at the top of the ravine, mounted on her palomino mare. Even from this distance, Rowan could see the tension in her shoulders, the fear and anger warring in her expression.

"Huck Elway Blackwood!" Sierra's voice carried down to them clearly as she guided her horse carefully down the slope. "What in the world were you thinking, riding off like that? You could have been killed!"

"Sorry, Mom." Huck swiped at his eyes, trying to erase evidence of his tears.

Sierra dismounted and was across the creek bed in three strides, pulling Huck into a fierce hug. "Don't you ever scare me like that again. Do you hear me?"

"I hear you."

Sierra's eyes found Rowan's over Huck's head, and he saw the moment she registered his emotional state. His eyes were still damp, and she clearly saw it. But instead of saying anything, she simply smiled—a soft, understanding smile that made him ache.

Oh, he loved her.

"What happened to the snake?" she asked, noticing the scattered remains on the rock.

"Mr. R shot it," Huck said, pulling back from his mother's embrace. "It was huge, Mom. And Jasper got scared and reared up, but Mr. R caught me before I fell."

"Did he now?" Sierra's eyes held Rowan's, and he saw gratitude there, mixed with something deeper.

"Just doing my job," Rowan said quietly, standing and brushing dirt from his jeans.

"What job is that?"

"Being his dad."

The simple statement hung in the air between them, and Rowan watched Sierra's expression soften further.

"Good job."

They were gathering the horses and preparing to head back when Sierra suddenly went still.

"What is it?" Rowan asked, immediately alert.

"Look." Sierra pointed toward the ridge above them, where a lone horse was picking its way down the slope toward the ranch buildings. A riderless bay gelding.

Rowan's blood chilled. "That's Morrie's horse."

"Where's Morrie?" Sierra's face went pale.

The horse appeared calm but tired, his reins trailing and his saddle slightly askew. No signs of violence, but no sign of his rider either.

"I'll get the horse, then we should head back, see if we can raise Morrie on the walkie."

Sierra met his gaze, her eyes dark.

"I'll find him," Rowan said quietly. "I'll find him."

ELEVEN

MORRIE HAD BEEN MISSING FOR HOURS IN THIS weather. If he was hurt, if he was lying out there in the rain, he could die of exposure

The thought hammered through Rowan's mind as he guided the ATV through another sweep of the south pasture, headlights cutting through the relentless downpour. He shouldn't have left the ranch, shouldn't have let Sierra and Huck out of his sight, but Sierra knew how to handle a gun, and Morrie wasn't answering his walkie. If Rowan had to tear apart every acre of this land to find him, that's what he'd do.

Three hours of searching in the downpour had soaked Rowan through to the bone. What had started as a light evening drizzle when he'd left the ranch had turned into a relentless Colorado cloudburst that turned every dirt road into a muddy trap and reduced visibility to mere feet beyond the ATV's headlights. His radio crackled with static as Saxon's voice cut through the storm.

"Anything on the south section?" Saxon's words were barely audible through the interference.

"Negative." Rowan had to shout over the rain hammering against his helmet. "Moving toward the junction now."

The junction. The place where three ranch properties met—Blackwood land, Jenkins land, and Tom Hendrick's spread. It was rough country, cut by ravines and dotted with stands of pine that could hide a dozen men. If someone wanted to ambush a lone rider, it would be the perfect spot.

Rowan guided the ATV down a steep slope, the machine's tires fighting for traction in the gloopy mud. His headlights swept across the landscape in arcs, picking out details that disappeared as quickly as they appeared—a flash of fence wire, the gleam of standing water, the ghostly shapes of cattle huddled under sparse trees.

Then he saw it.

A splash of color that didn't belong in the monochrome world of rain and shadow. Rowan killed the engine and climbed off the ATV, his boots squelching in the mud as he approached what looked like a heap of old clothes in a drainage ditch.

It wasn't clothes.

Morrie lay crumpled on his side, his weathered face pale and slack, his hat off, tossed away, rain streaming down his face. Blood had soaked through his denim jacket, spreading across his abdomen in a dark stain. His breathing seemed shallow and labored, each breath a visible struggle.

"Morrie!" Rowan dropped to his knees beside the unconscious man, his hands automatically checking for a pulse. Weak but steady. He grabbed his walkie. "Saxon, I found him. He's injured."

Static answered him, then Saxon's voice, tense with concern. "How bad?"

"Gunshot wound to the abdomen. Unconscious, lots of blood loss." Rowan was already assessing their options. The nearest hospital was forty minutes away in good weather. In this storm, it might as well be on the moon. "I need to get him somewhere warm and dry. Call 911, tell them to meet us at the Jenkins place."

"The Jenkins place? Rowan—"

"It's the closest shelter." He refused to think about what going to his stepfather's house would mean, couldn't let childhood trauma interfere with saving a man's life. "Just make the call."

Rowan gathered Morrie in his arms, surprised by how light the wiry foreman felt. The older man had always seemed so solid, so permanent, but injury had made him almost fragile. Rowan settled him as gently as possible in the passenger seat, buckling him in.

The Jenkins ranch house sat on a rise about half a mile away, its windows glowing yellow against the storm. He fixed his eyes on those lights and drove toward them through the driving rain.

The ATV made it halfway up the sloped dirt road before the mud claimed it.

Aw. Of course. The wheels spun, kicking up mud, but no purchase, the engine whining as the machine settled deeper into the saturated earth. He tried reverse, tried rocking it forward and back, but it only wedged the ATV deeper into the muck.

"Sorry, Morrie," he muttered, gathering the unconscious man in his arms. He carried him fireman style, arm and leg secured over his shoulder. He didn't want to think of what he might be doing to his injury.

The guy was heavier, suddenly, than before.

The Jenkins house loomed larger as Rowan climbed the hill. Green metal roofing gleamed wet in the porch lights, and smoke rose from the stone chimney despite the rain.

Please be home.

He climbed the wooden steps, his boots echoing on the covered porch.

Rowan raised his fist and pounded on the heavy wooden door.

Catherine answered. She wore her hair pulled back in a neat

bun, and her eyes widened when she saw him standing there with an unconscious man draped across his shoulders.

"Oh my goodness! Come in, come in!" She stepped back. "What happened?"

"Gunshot wound. He needs immediate medical attention." Rowan stepped into the warmth of the house, water dripping from his clothes onto the hardwood floor. "I called for an ambulance to come here."

"Good." Catherine was already moving toward the back of the house. "Mack! Alden! We need help!"

Rowan carried Morrie toward the large sectional sofa near the fireplace, trying not to look at the familiar details that triggered unwelcome memories. The kitchen doorway where he'd stood listening to his mother and stepfather argue. The staircase where he'd learned to make himself invisible. The corner where he'd once hidden after Alden's fist had split his lip.

He doused them and tucked them away for now.

"Rowan?" Mack appeared from the den. "What happened?"

"Found Morrie shot at the junction. Lost a lot of blood." Rowan eased the foreman onto the floor. No need to get blood on the sofa.

Catherine appeared with towels and a first aid kit. "Maybe we should drive him to the hospital?"

"Renegade Mercy is forty-five minutes, minimum. And in this weather . . ." Mack shook his head.

"Saxon is calling it in. Help is on its way."

Rowan stripped off his wet jacket and knelt, checking Morrie's pulse again. Still weak, still thready. The older man's weathered face was gray and pale in the lamplight, his beard matted with rain and blood. Even unconscious, Morrie looked tough. Still, even the hardiest of men could succumb to this kind of injury. *Please don't die.* Sierra couldn't lose someone else.

"Apply pressure here." Rowan guided Catherine's hands to the wound. "Keep it steady but don't press too hard."

"Is he going to be okay?"

"He seems tough. If anyone can pull through this, it's a tough cowboy Morrie." Rowan hoped he sounded more confident than he felt.

Heavy footsteps on the staircase. Alden. Rowan tensed, muscle memory from childhood.

"Rowan," Alden said. "What's this?"

Rowan didn't look at him. "Morrie's been shot. Saxon called 911. They're on the way."

"How long ago did this happen?" Catherine asked, still maintaining pressure on Morrie's wound.

"Not sure. He's been missing for about four hours, but the wound looks relatively fresh."

The sound of vehicles approaching made everyone look toward the windows. Headlights cut through the rain-streaked glass—multiple vehicles moving fast up the long driveway.

"That was quick," Mack said, moving toward the door.

A man came through the open door, lean, late twenties with sandy-brown hair and intelligent blue eyes. He carried a medical bag and moved with the confidence of someone accustomed to emergency situations.

"Jackson Stewart, Renegade Ambulance One. What's happening?" His voice carried easy authority as he surveyed the scene.

"Gunshot wound to the abdomen. Exposure. He's lost a lot of blood."

Two more EMTs came in behind Jackson, who knelt beside Morrie. "Pulse is thready, blood pressure's low. Let's get an IV started." Jackson started checking Morrie's wound. "We'll get a pressure bandage on this."

And that's when Saxon appeared in the doorway, shaking rain from his dark hair. "Got here as fast as I could. Where'd you find him?"

"Drainage ditch about half a mile south of here. Just lying there in the rain." Rowan's voice was grim. "Single gunshot wound to the abdomen. Professional or lucky amateur, hard to say."

"Wait." Jackson looked at him. "You said the junction of the three properties?"

"Yeah. Why?"

"That's the same area where Sierra found Tom Hendrick last week."

Rowan stared at him. "You think there's a connection?"

"Two bodies in the same general area?" Saxon said. "Could be coincidence, but . . ." He shrugged. "I don't believe in coincidences anymore."

Jackson addressed his other EMTs, now carrying in a backboard. "He's stable enough for transport, but we need to move fast." He stood up as they worked to move him onto the backboard.

"Will he make it?" Rowan asked.

The others strapped him in as Jackson turned to Rowan. "He's lost a lot of blood, but if the bullet missed the major organs and if we can get him to surgery in the next hour, I'd say his chances are good."

"I've notified the police." This from Alden, who'd disappeared into the kitchen earlier. "They'll meet you at the hospital."

The EMTs carried Morrie from the house. Rowan made to follow, but Alden put a hand on his arm.

He stiffened. Turned.

Alden's mouth had made a grim line. "When this is over, when Morrie is out of the woods, maybe we could talk. There are things I need to say."

"I don't think—"

"Listen. I know we got off to a rough start a few days ago, but . . . I'm not the same man I was when you left." Alden's voice softened, almost . . . apologetic? "I know you have no reason to believe that, but it's true. I . . . I carried a lot of anger back then. It was hard to live up to Sean Wallace."

Rowan stared at him, his mouth opening, closing. Words left him. But Mack's voice was in his head.

He told me he was sorry.

Alden met his eyes. "I can't take back the past, but I'm not that man anymore. I'd like a fresh start."

Before Rowan could respond, the sound of sirens filled the air. The ambulance pulling out. "I gotta go."

He turned, but as he did, his gaze landed on the table by the door. On the business card that lay on the wooden top.

Ralph Rousseau, Rocky Mountain Land Development.

Rowan picked up the card. A handwritten message was scrawled on the back.

It's time.

"Man's been persistent, I'll give him that," Alden said, clearly seeing his actions.

Rowan turned to him. "How long has he been trying to buy your place?"

"Six months, maybe more. Started friendly enough, but lately . . ." Alden shook his head. "Yesterday he came by in person. Said I was being foolish, that accidents happen to people who don't know when to take a good deal."

"And you told him?"

"Same thing I've told him every time. This land isn't for sale." He met Rowan's eyes. "It's been in your family for three generations."

Yes, yes, it had. "Have you had any problems? Cattle getting sick, equipment failing, fires?"

"You asked me that before. Some cattle went missing, but no trouble like the neighbors. But then, I've got good security."

Rowan pocketed the business card and followed them out.

"Rowan." Alden stepped out onto the porch beside him. "For what it's worth, I'm proud of the man you've become."

He just stared at the man. Then he nodded curtly and headed toward his truck. He had bigger problems than his stepfather's belated attempt at redemption.

Saxon stood by his truck, holding his phone.

"I should go with him," Rowan said, glancing at the retreating ambulance.

"No need. I'll follow in my truck." Saxon's expression turned serious. "I'll drop you back at the house. You should get back to Sierra and Huck. This could be a distraction while someone hits the ranch."

And he just stilled. Wanted to bang his head on something. "You think—"

"I think we're dealing with people who plan ahead. Go home. I'll handle things at the hospital." Saxon pocketed his phone. "I called Detective Martinelli. He'll meet us at the scene tomorrow morning. We need to process that area properly."

"What time?"

"Early. Seven a.m. That'll give you time to get back for the rodeo."

The rodeo. Yes. He couldn't miss that. Thankfully, Sierra's monthly annuity check had come in, and she'd paid Huck's entrance fee on Monday.

The drive home took fifteen minutes through muddy back roads. By the time he pulled into the Blackwood ranch yard, his gut was a coiled knot.

"Call me with updates," he said to Saxon as he got out.

The house was dark except for a single light in the living room window.

Rowan eased the door open. "Sierra?"

A shotgun barrel appeared in the doorway, followed by Sierra's pale face. Her hair was disheveled, a fierceness in her eyes. She wore pajama pants and an oversized flannel shirt, and her bare feet.

Her posture suggested she'd been sitting in the dark for hours.

"Well, hello there, Annie Oakley," Rowan said.

Recognition dawned in her eyes. Her rigid posture softened slightly, but the gun remained steady.

"Maybe let me do the shooting," he said as he gently moved the barrel away from him, then eased the weapon from her grip.

"How is he?" she whispered.

Rowan set the shotgun aside and pulled her into his arms. "He's stable, on his way to the hospital."

"Who would shoot Morrie?" Sierra's voice was muffled against his chest.

"Same people who've been targeting your ranch. Same people who want your land." Rowan held her tighter, breathing in the familiar scent of her hair. "But they made a mistake tonight."

She lifted her head. "What kind of mistake?"

"They showed me exactly how far they're willing to go." Rowan's hands framed her face. "And now I know how far I'm willing to go to stop them."

***

Be brave.

Sierra took a deep breath, standing in the doorway of her grandfather's office, morning sunlight streaming through the windows and illuminating dust motes that danced in the golden air. The rich wood paneling seemed to glow in the early light, and everything looked exactly as he'd left it. His reading glasses still sat on the massive oak desk beside a half-finished crossword puzzle. His coffee mug—the one that read *World's Best Grandpa*—sat empty beside a stack of unopened mail that had been accumulating for months.

The familiar scent of leather and Old Spice aftershave hung in the air, making her chest tight with loss.

Yes, she should have done this days ago when they were putting the house back together, but every time Sierra walked into this room, she could still see him sitting at that desk.

Huck was so excited about the rodeo today, and she needed to focus on that, but these papers needed to be sorted, and maybe if she started with the easy stuff—old bills, ranch records—she could work up to the personal things. Rowan would be back soon, and then they could be, well, a normal family, right? Just going to watch their son compete.

Rowan's words hung in her mind. *I'm meeting Saxon and Detective Martinelli at the scene. I'll be back in time for Huck's competition, I promise.*

She'd called the hospital this morning and gotten an update on Morrie from his wife. He'd survived the night, was out of ICU, the tough dog that he was.

Just start with something easy. She moved to the desk and picked up the stack of mail, sorting through bills and advertisements. Electric company, feed store, ranch equipment catalogs—all the mundane business of running a cattle ranch that had continued arriving long after the man who'd built it was gone.

"Mom!" Huck's voice carried down the hallway, followed by the thunder of his boots on the hardwood floors. "Where's my good belt? The one with the silver buckle."

"Hanging in your closet behind your church shirt," Sierra called back, not looking up from the papers.

A few moments later, "Found it! How long until Mr. R gets back? I want to show him my rope work before we leave."

He still hadn't called Rowan *Dad*, but she wasn't pushing. It would come. Maybe. Hopefully.

Sierra glanced at the clock on the mantel. Eight thirty. Rowan had been gone for over an hour, and the rodeo started at noon. "He should be back soon, baby. Keep getting ready."

She tackled the filing cabinet next, sorting through years of ranch records and tax documents. It was easier to focus on the numbers, the practical details of hay purchases and veterinary bills, than to think about the personal items that would come later.

An hour passed before she worked up the courage to approach the bookshelf where he'd kept his personal correspondence. Her fingers traced the spines of his favorite novels—Louis L'Amour westerns and Tom Clancy thrillers—before reaching for the ornate wooden box where he'd kept important family documents.

Inside, she found pictures of her parents, their marriage certificate, her birth certificate, report cards from elementary school that he'd saved. At the bottom of the box was a framed photograph that made her breath catch.

She was thirteen in the picture, wearing cowboy boots and a fringed vest, her hair in two braids that hung past her shoulders. Her grandfather stood beside her, his arm around her shoulders, both of them grinning at the camera. She remembered that day—her first time competing in barrel racing, nervous and excited and desperate to make him proud.

"I miss you so much, Grandpa." The words came out as a whisper, her throat tight with unshed tears. "I don't know how to do this without you. How to keep the ranch going, how to protect Huck, how to be half the person you raised me to be."

She traced his face in the photograph with one finger, remembering the sound of his laugh. "But I have something amazing to tell you. Rowan came back." A smile tugged at her lips despite the tears. "Remember how you always said he was a good kid who just needed a chance to grow up? Well, he grew up, and he came back, and Grandpa . . . he's incredible. He's patient with Huck, and strong, and protective. He looks at me the way Dad used to look at Mom. Like I'm his whole world."

Her voice grew stronger as she spoke. "He's teaching Huck things you would have loved to see. Roping, and how to be brave, and what it means to be a good man. And he loves us—really loves us, not just because we need him but because we're his family now. You'd be so proud of the man he became."

She wiped away a tear with the back of her hand. "I just wish you were here to see it. To see Huck with his father, to see us finally being the family you always wanted for us."

The photograph showed them both so happy, so sure of their place in the world. Sierra had never imagined that day that she'd be sitting in his office alone, sorting through the pieces of a life cut short.

She went to put it back, but it didn't sit flat on the bottom, so she picked it up. Huh. She turned it over and found a small latch hidden behind the backing. When she pressed it, the back of the frame popped open to reveal a small brass key taped to the inside.

What? Sierra stared at the key. She'd been through every drawer in this desk, every cabinet in this office. Where was there a lock she hadn't found?

She stood up, looking around the room with new eyes. The filing cabinets used regular keys. The desk drawers weren't locked. But there, hanging on the wall behind his desk, was her parents' wedding portrait in an ornate silver frame.

No. That felt too easy. But when Sierra lifted the heavy frame from its hook—what in the world?—she found a small safe built into the wall, its door flush with the wood paneling and painted to match, with a small keyhole.

The brass key fit perfectly.

An envelope folder sat inside the safe, the manila folder inside thick with documents. Her hands shook as she pulled it out and returned to the desk, spreading the contents across the surface under the morning light.

The first item was a newspaper clipping from the Idaho Falls *Post Register*, dated six months ago. The headline read: "Mysterious Deaths Rock Mining Community." The article detailed the suspicious deaths of two environmental activists who'd been investigating lithium mining operations in southern Idaho. Both men had been found shot in remote areas after raising concerns about water contamination and illegal mining practices.

Sierra's blood ran cold as she read the details. The pattern was identical to what had been happening in Renegade—intimidation, environmental sabotage, and ultimately, murder for those who refused to be silenced.

The next item was a hand-drawn map of the local area, with ranch properties marked in different colors. Her own ranch was marked in red, along with the Hendrick place, the Jenkins spread, and three others. A note in her grandfather's scrawl read:

All have water rights and mineral access.

Beneath the map were geological surveys showing lithium deposits throughout the area, with the highest concentrations centered around the ranch properties marked on his map.

"Mining operations," Sierra breathed, understanding flooding through her. "It was never about the land. It was about what's underneath it."

Her grandfather's notes were meticulous, documenting months of research into Ralph Rousseau's business dealings. Shell companies, out-of-state investors, equipment purchases that didn't match his claimed business activities. And on a Post-it Note, the words *Shadow Syndicate*.

The final document in the folder was a draft letter addressed to the Colorado Bureau of Investigation. Sierra's hands trembled as she read her grandfather's words, hearing his voice.

I am writing to report my suspicions regarding a criminal conspiracy operating in and around Renegade,

Colorado. Local businessman Ralph
Rousseau has been systematically
targeting ranch properties with
significant lithium deposits, using
intimidation, sabotage, and, I believe,
the killing of cattle to force property
owners to sell.

I have documented evidence of
environmental contamination, equipment
sabotage, and threatening behavior
directed at multiple ranchers in our
area. Two men who I believe were
attempting to expose similar operations
in Idaho were found dead under
suspicious circumstances.

I fear that this operation is part
of a larger criminal enterprise with
connections beyond our local area. I
urge immediate investigation before
more lives are lost.

I have attempted to warn my fellow
ranchers, but not all believe the threat
is real. I spoke with Mayor Alden
Jenkins yesterday to alert him of
this threat and am copying him on
this letter.

Although I no longer hold the office to compel a further investigation, I request a response to my suspicions and an investigation into this matter.

His signature was scrawled on the bottom.

Sierra's heart pounded as she processed what she was reading.

What if her grandfather hadn't died in an accident? What if he'd been murdered because he was getting too close to the truth about Ralph Rousseau and his criminal actions? And why hadn't he sent the letter?

A phone number was circled on one of his notes, with *Call Mayor* written beside it in urgent handwriting. The date next to it was two weeks before his death.

"He tried to warn Mayor Jenkins," Sierra whispered.

She grabbed her phone and tried calling Rowan, but it went straight to voicemail.

"Mom?" Huck appeared in the doorway, dressed in his competition clothes and practically vibrating with excitement. "Is Mr. R back yet?"

"Not yet." Sierra stood up, forced a smile. "But he'll be here. He promised."

"Okay!" Huck bounced on his toes. "I can't wait! This is going to be the best day ever!"

Sierra managed a smile for her son, but her mind was racing. The evidence in front of her painted a terrifying picture—a criminal organization willing to kill to get what they wanted, and her family was standing directly in their path.

She tried calling Rowan again. This time, he answered on the fourth ring.

"Sierra? Is everything okay?"

SUSAN MAY WARREN

"Rowan, I found something. In Grandpa's office. He was investigating Ralph Rousseau, and—"

"Slow down. What did you find?"

"Evidence. Documents, maps, newspaper clippings. Grandpa wasn't just suspicious about Ralph—he had *proof*. Mining operations, shell companies, connections to murders in Idaho. He wrote a letter to the CBI two weeks before he died. But he never sent it."

Silence on the other end of the line.

"Rowan? Are you there?"

"I'm here, Sierra." His voice sounded pinched.

"There's more. He tried to warn Mayor Jenkins a couple weeks before he died."

Silence. Then, his voice turned hard. "Listen to me carefully. Take Huck and go to the rodeo. Stay in public, stay visible, and don't go anywhere alone. I'm going to be late, but I'll meet you there as soon as I can."

She sank down into her grandfather's desk chair. "Should I be scared?"

"No. Okay, maybe enough to keep you alert. But Sierra? We're going to figure this out."

She nodded, even if he couldn't see her. "Hurry."

"I'll be there."

They hung up and Sierra repackaged all the documents and locked them back in the safe. The frame went back on the wall, and the key went back into the picture frame. To anyone looking, the office appeared exactly as it had before.

But everything had changed.

Maybe she had a little of the old police commissioner in her genes. The war that had taken her grandfather's life was far from over.

And she was ready to fight.

TWELVE

ROWAN HAD PROMISES TO KEEP. IN OTHER WORDS, he needed to wrap this up and get back to the ranch.

He crouched beside the drainage ditch where they'd found Morrie twelve hours ago, dawn mist rising from the rain-soaked earth around him. The storm had passed, leaving behind a world washed clean and gleaming. Water pooled in tire ruts that scarred the muddy ground, and crime-scene tape fluttered in the morning breeze. The air smelled of wet pine and disturbed earth, tinged with the metallic scent of violence that still lingered despite the rain's best efforts.

His tactical training kicked into overdrive as he studied the bloodstained rocks where Morrie had fallen.

Rowan stood, mud squelching under his boots as he surveyed the junction where three ranch properties met. The natural ravine carved a deep channel between rocky outcroppings, scattered with pine trees that provided perfect cover for an ambush. "This isn't exactly on his way home from anywhere."

"Nope." Detective Martinelli took pictures as he walked the site. His rumpled suit jacket hung loose over rain gear, and coffee stained his white shirt despite the early hour. "Question is, what was Morrie doing out here in the first place?"

Saxon emerged from behind a cluster of boulders, a new Nikon hanging around his neck and a professional-grade metal detector in his hands. His dark clothing was soaked through, and red-clay mud caked his boots to the ankles. "I found the shell casings."

Rowan's chest tightened as he joined Saxon, who pointed to three brass shell casings that lay scattered in the mud nearby, their copper gleam catching the weak sunlight filtering through storm clouds.

"Bottleneck casings. From a .308."

"Could be a hunting rifle," said Saxon.

Rowan sighed.

"Everything okay?" Saxon said.

"Sierra called. She thinks her grandfather was murdered."

"That's not news," said Saxon.

"Yeah, but she says she found a file of evidence that Elway tucked away. She'll meet me at the rodeo and I'll get the details."

Saxon set his metal detector on high and continued to scan the area.

"You're really committing to this PI thing, aren't you? Next you'll be carrying a magnifying glass and wearing a deerstalker hat."

"Mock me all you want, but this equipment is top-notch." Saxon hefted the metal detector and grinned. "And it's already paying dividends."

"Please tell me you actually know how to use that thing and aren't just waving it around hoping for the best."

"I'll have you know I watched three YouTube videos before we got here." Saxon's grin stretched wider. "Plus, I read the manual."

"On audiobook?"

"Funny, Hammer." He moved away down the ravine as Martinelli walked over with plastic bags. A crime-scene technician followed him.

"Any word from the hospital?" Rowan said to Martinelli.

And he definitely didn't let himself think about the fact that Martinelli had dated Sierra. Kissed Sierra.

Nope, he needed to let that go.

"Morrie made it through surgery. Still unconscious, but the docs think he'll pull through."

"Hey, guys! I found something!" Saxon shouted. "Looks like someone was conducting water analysis out there."

"Water analysis?" Rowan followed Martinelli down the ravine, toward Saxon.

The equipment Saxon had discovered was sophisticated and expensive—portable testing units, sample collection containers, and what looked like a chemical analysis station partially concealed behind a fallen log. Everything was scattered as if someone had abandoned it in a hurry, leaving behind thousands of dollars' worth of scientific equipment.

"This isn't ranching test gear." Martinelli pulled on latex gloves to examine one of the testing units. "This is laboratory-grade stuff."

The crime-scene technician had followed, carrying the shell casings. "Water contamination testing, from the looks of it. Probably checking for mineral content, maybe pollutants."

"Or maybe checking to see if their pollution was working," Rowan said, his jaw muscles bunching. "Testing to make sure the lithium levels were high enough to kill livestock."

Saxon's metal detector began beeping insistently near a stand of pine trees. He moved toward the sound, sweeping the device in careful arcs across the wet ground.

"Got something here," he called out, his voice tightening. "Something metallic, fairly large."

"Probably just a beer can," Rowan said, but his boots were

already carrying him toward Saxon's position. "Or maybe the crown jewels. Hard to tell with your advanced detection methods."

"Mock me after I find the smoking gun." Saxon knelt and began carefully brushing mud and pine needles away from whatever had triggered his detector. "Besides, I've been taking this seriously. Read two books on criminal investigation, watched every episode of CSI."

"Well, that makes you practically an expert." Rowan crouched beside him, his amusement draining away as Saxon's digging revealed a metal briefcase. "On second thought, maybe you should stick to the detection part and let the professionals handle the excavation."

Martinelli approached with the crime-scene tech. "Step back, boys."

The briefcase that emerged from the mud was expensive and waterproof, designed to protect sensitive equipment. When the tech opened it, they found what looked like a mobile laboratory—testing strips, chemical reagents, digital pH meters, and documentation that made Rowan's hands clench into fists.

"Water contamination protocols," the tech read from a laminated instruction sheet. "Lithium introduction methods, dosage calculations for livestock toxicity levels." She looked up, her face pale. "This is roughly a how-to manual for poisoning water sources."

Martinelli's voice dropped to a growl. "This equipment proves they're not just buying land—they're actively contaminating it to force sales."

Rowan stood up, cast a look toward the Jenkins ranch house.

The business card was still in his pocket. He pulled it out and read the note.

"So what's our play?" Saxon asked, probably reading the change in his expression.

"We go talk to Ralph Rousseau," Rowan said. "Find out what he knows about this operation."

"Hold on." Martinelli raised a hand. "We don't have enough for a warrant yet. This is all circumstantial until we can connect him directly to the crimes."

"How much do we need?" Rowan's thumb flicked the card.

"More than we've got. But we can certainly ask him some questions, see if he's willing to cooperate."

Saxon glanced at his watch. "What time does the rodeo start?"

"Noon. Huck's event is at two." Rowan did the time math. "If we move fast, we can have a conversation with Rousseau and I can still get there in time to watch him compete."

"Or," Saxon said carefully, "you could head to the rodeo now and let Martinelli and me handle the questioning."

"Not happening." Rowan's jaw set. "If Ralph Rousseau killed Sierra's grandfather and shot Morrie, I want to look him in the eye when we ask him about it."

The crime-scene tech looked up from packaging evidence. "Detective, this equipment alone suggests a major operation."

Martinelli nodded. "I'll call my office and see if we can get backup when we go see Rousseau." He got on the phone and walked away.

Rowan studied the abandoned equipment scattered across the crime scene. "Professional operation, expensive gear, sophisticated planning. This isn't the work of some local real-estate developer. This is on a scale that requires serious money and resources."

Saxon nodded.

Martinelli came back. "Okay. I have the address for his office. We'll start there."

"Listen," Rowan said. "We find Rousseau, we ask our questions, and then I get to the rodeo. Simple." Rowan turned toward his truck. "Saxon, you and I will coordinate the approach. Martinelli can handle—"

"Whoa there." Martinelli stepped forward, his badge catching the morning light. "This is my jurisdiction, my case, my call. You're along as a consultant."

Rowan's mouth opened, then closed. Military habits died hard, but this wasn't the Trouble Boys, and he wasn't the team lead. This was Colorado, and Detective Michael Martinelli was running point.

"Right. Your show, Detective."

"Glad we understand each other." Martinelli's voice carried no malice, just the quiet authority of someone who knew his job. "Rowan, you ride with me."

"Don't trust me, Detective?"

Martinelli's eyes narrowed, just a little, then he shook his head. "I just don't want this to go south, get messy. You listen to me, do this by the book, and we'll get Rousseau and have a nice chat."

"And if he lawyers up?" Saxon asked.

"Then we back off and build a better case." Martinelli's expression hardened. "But maybe he'll feel like talking once he sees what we found here."

Rowan was already moving toward Martinelli's vehicle.

"Keep me updated," Saxon called after them. "And Hammer?"

"Yeah?"

"Try not to strangle him before we get answers."

"Now you're the funny man."

Martinelli's engine turned over with a rough cough, and they pulled away from the crime scene. The morning sun climbed higher, burning off the mist and revealing the full scope of the abandoned equipment scattered across the ravine.

The terror targeting his family would end today.

This just might be the best day of Sierra's life. Second best, because of course, the day Huck was born landed number one. But it felt like a rebirth of sorts, the birth of her family, the culmination of her wildest dreams.

Except Rowan was late.

The October afternoon spread across the county fairgrounds like a picture postcard, the kind of Colorado day that made Sierra grateful to call this place home. Brilliant blue sky stretched endless overhead, painted with wispy white clouds that drifted past snowcapped peaks rising majestically in the distance.

Autumn aspens dotted the mountainsides like scattered coins, their leaves shimmering gold against the dark green of pine forests.

Perfect weather for a fall rodeo. Perfect weather for watching her son compete while his father cheered from the stands.

So why did she feel like she should be looking over her shoulder, waiting for life to scurry up and take it all away from her?

Sierra guided the horse trailer into the back parking area of the fairgrounds, gravel crunching under her tires as she navigated between rows of gleaming aluminum trailers and pickup trucks. The staging area buzzed with controlled chaos—kids practicing their runs, parents offering last-minute advice, horses snorting and stamping in the crisp air.

The distant sound of the announcer's voice carried across the lot, welcoming families to the Renegade County Fall Festival Rodeo.

"Easy, boy." Sierra patted Jasper's neck as she backed him out of the trailer. The old paint horse stepped down carefully. At twenty-three, Jasper had seen plenty of rodeos, but his ears swiveled attentively as he cataloged the familiar sounds of competition day.

"Mom, I can handle him." Huck appeared at her elbow, his competition number pinned to his shirt and his chaps buckled to perfection. His hat sat at exactly the right angle, and his boots gleamed from the polish he'd applied that morning. Everything about him radiated preparation and confidence, though Sierra

SUSAN MAY WARREN

caught the nervous energy in the way his hands moved—adjusting his rope, checking his gloves, straightening his number.

"I know you can." Sierra handed him Jasper's lead rope, her chest warming with pride at how natural he looked with the horse. "Just remember what Rowan taught you about staying relaxed. Jasper picks up on your energy."

Huck's face lit up at the mention of Rowan's name. "Do you think Mr. R will really make it? I mean, I know he said he would, but . . ."

"He'll be here," Sierra said, trying to believe her words. *Please, Rowan, don't let us down.* "Wild horses couldn't keep him away from watching you compete."

"I . . . um . . ." Huck started, then stopped, color creeping up his neck.

"What?"

"I was thinking . . . maybe can I . . . can I call him Dad?"

Oh. *Oh.*

She knelt in front of him. "Do you want to?"

He nodded, but his eyes filled.

She reached out to adjust his hat, using the gesture to buy herself a moment. "You can call him whatever feels right to you. But yes, he's your dad, and I think he'd love to hear you say it."

He looked away, then back to her, his blue eyes earnest in hers. "What if I mess up my run? What if I'm not as good as he was?"

Clearly Huck was all about breaking her heart today. She stood. "You want to know a secret about your dad?" Sierra guided Jasper toward the warm-up area, Huck walking beside her. "He wasn't just county champion three years running. He was state champion twice. And you know what? He told me you're already better at ten than he was."

Huck's eyes went wide. "Really?"

"Really. He said you've got natural talent and good instincts.

233

The rest is just practice and confidence." Sierra squeezed his shoulder. "And you've got plenty of both."

He grinned, and her heart simply split wide apart. She pulled him close. "I'm so proud of you."

He wiggled away. "I gotta warm up, Mom."

She laughed. "Yep." They spent the next twenty minutes working Jasper through his paces, letting the old horse remember his job while Huck settled into the rhythm of competition preparation. Other kids moved through similar routines around them, the air filled with encouraging words from parents and the occasional whicker from horses recognizing friends.

"Riders for the ten-and-under tie-down roping should start heading to the staging area." The announcer's voice crackled across the parking lot. "We'll begin competition in approximately thirty minutes."

Huck dismounted to lead Jasper into the staging area.

Sierra pulled out her phone, checking for messages from Rowan. Nothing since his text two hours ago saying he'd be there soon. She typed quickly.

Sierra

Huck's asking for you.
Competition starts in 30.
Where are you?

"Mom, I think I'm ready." Huck looked up at her with the kind of determination that reminded her so much of Rowan it made her chest tight. "I got this."

"You absolutely do." Sierra gave him a quick hug, breathing in the scent of sunshine and confidence that clung to her son. "Go show them what a Blackwood can do."

"A Blackwood-Wallace," Huck corrected with a grin.

"Even better."

She watched him lead Jasper toward the staging area, her heart swelling. How she'd survive this day, she didn't know. Too much joy, really, for a woman who'd lost everyone.

And yet still found her happy ending.

Sierra made her way toward the arena, weaving between families claiming spots on the metal bleachers. The afternoon sun caught the dust kicked up by horses in the arena, creating golden clouds in the air. Vendors hawked popcorn and cotton candy, their calls mixing with the sounds of excited children and neighing horses.

She spotted Bailey Sinclair halfway up the bleachers, waving like a crazy person. "Sierra!"

Sierra climbed toward her best friend, dodging families with coolers and bleacher chairs, apologizing for stepping on toes and squeezing past knees.

"Finally." Bailey shifted over to make room. "I thought you'd never get here. How's our boy doing?"

"Confident. Nervous. Ready." Sierra settled beside Bailey, scanning the arena where younger kids were finishing their events. "And asking if he can call Rowan 'Dad.'"

"Oh my gosh." Bailey clutched Sierra's arm. "Wait. Rowan *knows*?"

"Yep."

"How did that go?"

Sierra heated despite the afternoon breeze. "Better than I ever dared hope. He was shocked, of course, and maybe a little angry, but . . . Oh, Bailey, the way he looks at Huck . . ." She shook her head. "It's like he's been waiting his whole life to be a father."

"And Huck knows."

"Yeah. He found out last night. It was . . . well, let's say dramatic. But yeah, he knows."

"That's huge. How are you handling it?"

"Honestly? I'm thrilled. Terrified, but thrilled." Sierra pulled out her phone again, checking for new messages. Still nothing. "It feels like everything's finally falling into place."

"Speaking of falling into place"—Bailey's voice dropped to a conspiratorial whisper—"how are things between you two? Please tell me you're not just coparenting."

"We're figuring it out." Sierra's smile grew wider despite her attempt to stay casual. "But no, we're definitely not just coparenting."

"Sierra Blackwood, are you blushing?"

"Maybe."

"Oh, this is so good!" Bailey grinned. "After everything you've been through, you deserve this."

"It feels too good to be true sometimes," Sierra said, checking her phone again. "Like I'm waiting for the other shoe to drop."

"Stop that right now. Some people get their happy endings, and you're one of them," Bailey said. "Rowan came back, he wants to be a father, and he clearly adores you. Accept the blessing and stop looking for problems."

The announcer's voice boomed across the arena. "Ladies and gentlemen, we're ready to begin our ten-and-under tie-down roping competition. These young cowboys have been practicing all year, and they're excited to show you what they can do."

Sierra's attention shifted to the staging area, looking for Huck. She didn't see him, but the place was cluttered with animals and contestants.

"Oh, I meant to ask," Bailey said, leaning closer to be heard over the crowd noise. "I heard something at the grocery store about Morrie getting hurt. What happened?"

Sierra's stomach dropped. She'd been so focused on the rodeo and Rowan's investigation that she hadn't thought about how quickly news traveled here.

"He had an accident yesterday," she said, cutting her voice low. "He's in the hospital, but the doctors think he'll be okay."

"That's terrible. What happened?"

"I don't know all the details." Okay, sort of a lie, but the last thing she wanted was to stir up fear. "Rowan and Mike are looking into it."

Sierra typed another text to Rowan.

Sierra

Seriously, where are you? Huck's event is **starting**.

"First up, we have contestant number twenty-three, Gunnar St. Claire, riding Thor . . ."

Sierra watched as a boy about Huck's age guided his horse into the arena. The crowd quieted as Gunnar positioned himself, rope ready, concentration written across his young face. When the calf was released, Gunnar's throw was clean and fast, his dismount smooth, his tie efficient.

"Nice run, Gunnar!" the announcer called as the boy waved to the crowd. "That's going to be hard to beat."

Three more contestants followed, each with varying degrees of success. Sierra found herself analyzing their techniques, noting things Huck did better, places where he could improve. She checked her phone for an answer.

None.

"Next up, contestant number thirty-five, Eli Martinez, riding Cisco . . ."

Sierra's attention was divided between the arena and her phone.

Sierra

Are **you** okay?

She tucked the phone away.

"And now, contestant number forty-one, Sarah Beth Collins, riding Buttercup . . ."

The girl's run was flawless, her tiny frame handling the large calf with impressive skill. The crowd erupted in applause, and Sierra found herself clapping along while her eyes stayed glued to her phone.

Nothing.

"Our next contestant is number forty-seven, Huck Blackwood, riding Jasper . . ."

Sierra's head snapped up, her heart leaping. She scanned the arena entrance, waiting for Huck and Jasper to appear.

The entrance stayed empty.

"Number forty-seven, Huck Blackwood," the announcer repeated.

Sierra stood up, craning her neck to see the staging area. Where was he? Had he gotten nervous? Backed out at the last minute?

"We'll give number forty-seven another moment," the announcer said. "Sometimes these young cowboys need a minute to get ready."

But the entrance remained empty.

"All right, we'll move on to our next contestant. Number fifty-two, David Harrison, riding Blaze . . ."

Sierra's blood turned cold. They'd skipped Huck.

"Bailey, I have to go check on Huck," Sierra said, her voice tight.

"I'm sure he's fine. Probably just got nervous."

"No, you don't understand. Huck was so excited." Sierra was already moving, pushing past knees and muttering apologies as she worked her way down the bleachers. Bailey followed her. "Something's wrong."

She half walked, half ran to the staging area. Maybe Jasper had gone lame, maybe Huck had gotten sick, maybe, yes, he'd just lost his nerve at the last moment.

"Has anyone seen Huck Blackwood?" she called to the group of parents and officials clustered near the entrance of the staging area.

"He was here fifteen minutes ago," one of the officials replied. "Seemed ready to go. Then when we called his name, nobody could find him."

Sierra's chest tightened. "What about his horse?"

"That's the strange thing. The horse is gone too."

She turned to Bailey. "Keep looking."

Then she pushed through the crowd toward the back parking area, her boots crunching on gravel as she moved between trailers and trucks. Maybe Huck had taken Jasper back here for some reason. Maybe he'd needed more warm-up time, or maybe Jasper had spooked and he'd had to calm him down.

But as she rounded the corner toward where she'd parked her trailer, her blood turned cold.

Jasper stood near a cluster of trucks, his reins trailing in the dirt, saddle still on but his rider nowhere to be seen. The old horse looked confused, his muscles rippling, and he nickered when he saw Sierra approach.

"Huck?" Sierra called, her voice echoing off the aluminum trailers. "Huck, where are you?"

No answer.

She grabbed Jasper's reins, her hands shaking as she checked him over. No signs of injury, no indication that he'd thrown his rider. He just stood there, patient and confused, waiting for someone to tell him what to do next.

"Huck!" Sierra's voice rose, carrying across the parking lot. "This isn't funny! Where are you?"

But only the wind answered, carrying the distant sounds of the rodeo.

That's when she saw it.

Huck's hat lay in the dirt beside her truck, its perfect shape crushed and dusty, the chin strap broken as if it had been yanked off his head.

She stared at the hat, her mind struggling to process what she was seeing. Huck would never leave his hat. Would never abandon Jasper. Would never miss his competition unless . . .

Unless someone had made him.

She snatched up the phone, her hands shaking so badly she could barely dial Rowan's number.

"Come on, come on, pick up," she whispered, pressing the phone to her ear.

It rang once. Twice. Three times.

Voicemail.

"Rowan, something's wrong," she said, her voice breaking. "Huck's missing. His horse is loose and . . . please call me back. Please."

She ended the call and tried again, panic rising in her throat like bile.

The sound of a vehicle approaching made her look up. A white van was pulling into the parking area, driving slowly between the rows of trailers. Sierra barely registered it as she hit redial on her phone.

Still no answer.

The van pulled up beside her truck and stopped. The side door slid open.

"Mom?"

The voice was weak, scared, but unmistakably Huck's.

Sierra pocketed the phone and spun toward the van, running. "Huck? What—"

Strong hands grabbed her arms, and a man yanked her toward the open van door. She fought, kicking and clawing, but another man appeared, dragging her into the vehicle's dark interior.

A hood dropped over her head, cutting off her vision and muffling her screams.

"Mom?!" Huck screamed. "Mom!"

The van door slammed shut, and the engine roared to life.

And all she could think, as the van drove away, was that she'd been right to worry about the other shoe dropping.

She just hadn't imagined it would land quite this hard.

THIRTEEN

THIS SHOULD BE STRAIGHTFORWARD. FIND RALPH, question him about the conspiracy, get the evidence they needed to shut down this operation. Maybe he'd lawyer up, maybe he'd try to run, but either way they'd get their answers. Then Rowan could get to the rodeo and watch Huck compete. Simple plan, clean execution, family time afterward, happy ending loaded up for mission success.

The drive to Rousseau's office took twenty minutes through the winding roads that connected the rural crime scene to downtown Renegade.

Rowan's fingers drummed against the passenger door handle while Detective Martinelli navigated the curves, plotting their entrance.

Two-man entry through the front, Saxon covering the rear exit. Check for vehicles in the parking area, assess security measures, identify escape routes. Standard building clearance protocols. Simple interrogation setup with Martinelli taking lead, Saxon documenting, himself reading body language and microexpressions.

Aw. He needed to step back, because clearly this wasn't Martinelli's plan as he pulled up to the front of the office complex. All modern glass and steel, with manicured landscaping, the building spoke of corporate money and legitimate business interests—so not the look of an evil lair.

Except it made it the perfect cover for criminal activity, right?

Martinelli's radio crackled with updates from the surveillance team. "Subject's residence appears empty."

"Copy." Martinelli keyed his mic. "Maintain position and report any movement."

Saxon pulled up beside them in his truck.

They approached the main entrance together and found the door unlocked. Their boots scuffed against polished concrete as they crossed the lobby. The receptionist's desk was unmanned and the office shut down for a Saturday.

"Hello?" Rowan called out, his voice carrying in the empty space. "Anyone here?"

A door opened down a hallway, and a young woman emerged. Her hair was pulled back in a neat bun, and she clutched a stack of papers against her chest. Her eyes darted between the three men. "Can I help you?"

"We're looking for Ralph Rousseau," Martinelli said, displaying his badge. "Official police business."

"Mr. Rousseau isn't here." She frowned. "He didn't come in this morning."

"When did you last see him?" Martinelli asked.

"Yesterday afternoon. He left around four and told me to cancel all his appointments for today. I came in to finish up the paperwork on a couple upcoming closings."

"Did he say where he was going?" Rowan said, refusing to glance at his watch. But he still had time.

"No, but..." The woman hesitated, her voice dropping to barely above a whisper. "There were some men here yesterday. They didn't look like clients."

"What did they look like?" Saxon said.

"Professional, but sort of scary. They wore expensive suits, but like tough guys. They went into Mr. Rousseau's office and closed the door. When they left, Mr. Rousseau seemed rattled. He left shortly after that."

Rowan glanced at Martinelli, who said, "Rattled how?"

"Like . . . I don't know. Maybe like someone had just threatened him?"

Saxon and Rowan exchanged glances.

"Ma'am," Martinelli said, "we're going to need you to come with us to make a formal statement. And we'll need access to Mr. Rousseau's office."

"Is he in trouble?" Her voice fell, quavered.

"We're trying to figure that out," Martinelli said.

They followed her down the hall to another office. When she opened the door, she gasped.

"This his office?" Rowan asked.

She nodded, her hand to her mouth.

Desk drawers hung open, papers were scattered across the floor, and a wall safe stood empty with its door ajar. The chaos said *panic*.

"Looks like he was gathering documents," Martinelli said, walking into the room. "Don't touch anything."

He said it to Rowan, maybe, but he wasn't an idiot.

Or maybe he said it to Saxon, because he'd picked up a business card from the floor, studying it. "This is interesting. TerraCorps Mining Solutions."

"They're one of our clients," the woman said.

His phone buzzed with a text. He glanced at the screen, expecting an update from the surveillance team. Instead, he saw Sierra's number.

Sierra
_____
Huck's asking for you.
Competition starts in 30.
Where are you?

Shoot. He needed to go. But they still didn't have Rousseau in custody.

"Problem?" Saxon asked.

"Time's running out. Huck's competition starts soon." Rowan pocketed his phone. "We need to find Rousseau fast."

Martinelli's radio came to life. "Detective, we have a situation at the Rousseau residence. Neighbors reported hearing gunshots earlier this morning."

"Copy that. En route." Martinelli was already moving toward the door.

The drive to Rousseau's house took a thousand hours, a.k.a. fifteen minutes. "If Rousseau's been killed or kidnapped," Rowan said, "we're not dealing with a local businessman gone bad."

"You're thinking organized crime?" Martinelli asked, taking a corner that required Rowan to brace himself.

"Maybe." He looked out the window. He should have gone to the rodeo. But he couldn't leave with this knot in his gut.

Tall pines flanked the entrance to the Rousseau estate, the driveway winding nearly half a mile through manicured landscaping before the house came into view. The home rose four stories, with balconies on the upper floors overlooking lawns so perfectly groomed they could have graced the cover of a landscaping magazine. Police vehicles lined the drive, their red and blue lights slashing across the massive stone structure like a scene from a crime drama.

A uniformed officer approached as they climbed out of their vehicles. "Detectives? We've got a problem."

"What's the situation?" Martinelli asked, already pulling on latex gloves.

"House is empty, but there are clear signs of a struggle. Blood on the kitchen floor, overturned furniture, back door standing open." The officer consulted his notes. "Neighbors heard gunshots around six thirty this morning. Nobody called it in though."

"Any sign of Rousseau?" Saxon had pulled up behind them and now stalked up.

"Negative," said the officer. "But we found his wallet in a bedroom drawer. If he left willingly, he didn't take much with him."

Rowan studied the house. "Security system?"

"Disabled from the inside. Maybe he knew his attackers."

Rowan turned to Martinelli. "Think about it. We get evidence pointing to Rousseau, we come looking for him, and conveniently he's been taken."

"What are you thinking?" Saxon asked.

"I don't know. Maybe he knows something they don't want us to find out."

"Or maybe he crossed them," Saxon said. "The real architects of the conspiracy eliminated their local operative before he could be arrested and questioned." He pulled out his phone. "I wish we had those GPS tracking rings we used during firefighting operations. Would make finding people a lot easier."

"Wait," Rowan said. "You could call Jamie Winters. See if she can track Rousseau's GPS through his phone."

"She helped us thwart the bio-bomb conspiracy last summer. If anyone can locate a missing person through technology, it's Jamie." Saxon was already dialing, stepping away.

Martinelli just stood there, frowning.

"What?" Rowan said.

"What if they're using him as bait?"

Rowan stilled. "What?"

"Any reason to think they'd want our attention elsewhere?"

Rowan frowned. "Where?"

"I don't know. Just that the Blackwoods' place has been targeted a lot. I keep thinking about Rousseau's office. Looks a lot like the damage left at Sierra's place."

Rowan stilled. "Huck and Sierra. They're at the rodeo."

"They're probably fine, right? All those people. Still, I think we get a unit out to her house." Martinelli picked up his walkie.

Rowan grabbed his phone. Another text had come in.

Sierra _____
Seriously, where are you? Huck's
event is starting.

And then another, about ten minutes later.

Sierra _____
Are you okay?

And then three missed calls. Oh, he was in trouble. He pocketed the phone. Better to show up, pronto, and explain face-to-face.

Saxon was jogging back from his vehicle.

"Got him." Saxon's voice cut through his brooding. "Jamie tracked his phone to an industrial area about twenty minutes from here. Looks like a food-processing plant."

"Food processing?"

"Alpine Fresh Foods. They make frozen pizzas." Saxon consulted his phone. "Jamie says his GPS signal has been stationary there for the past three hours."

Martinelli approached. "What's the plan?"

"We go get him," Rowan said. "Three of us, quick entry, fast extraction."

"Hold on." Martinelli raised a hand. "We don't know what we're walking into. Could be a trap, could be a hostage situation. Protocol says we call for backup."

"How long will that take?"

"Hour, maybe two."

"We don't have time for protocol," Rowan said. "Every minute we wait is another minute they have to eliminate Rousseau or move him to a different location."

"And every minute we rush in unprepared is another chance we get ourselves killed." Martinelli's gaze fixed on Rowan's.

Saxon stepped between them. "What if we compromise? Fast reconnaissance, assess the situation, then decide if we need backup?"

Martinelli considered this, then, "Reconnaissance only. We see what we're dealing with before making any moves."

Rowan got in the truck with Saxon, not needing any of Martinelli's ire.

The drive to Alpine Fresh Foods took twenty minutes through industrial sections of the city. He stared out the passenger window at warehouses and processing plants, his hands clenched in his lap.

"I hate this," he said finally.

"Hate what?" Saxon said.

"Being helpless. Not seeing the entire picture. I'm walking in blind." Rowan's jaw tightened. "And not just now, but with Sierra, and Huck and . . ." He blew out a breath. "Last night, Huck nearly got killed." He actually put a hand to his chest.

Saxon glanced at him in the rearview mirror. "Well, look who's human."

"I gotta figure out how to get past this—"

"Past loving someone? Rowan."

"Past letting emotions rule my life instead of logic and training."

"That what you're worried about? Feeling too much? C'mon."

"My stepfather was ruled by his emotions. Anger, jealousy, the need to control everything around him." Rowan's hands clenched tighter. "I swore I'd never be like that. Never let feelings make me hurt the people I was supposed to protect."

"But your real dad was different, right?"

Rowan looked at him. "My dad died stepping in front of a horse to save me. Pure emotion, no tactical thinking, just panic." Rowan's voice cracked slightly. "Got himself killed because he acted on his emotion instead of thought."

Saxon was quiet for a moment, then spoke carefully. "That was love, Hammer. We're all affected by our emotions, but living by our emotions and letting love lead are two different things."

"How so?"

"You can feel something—anger, fear, whatever—but love is combined with truth. Love sees the bigger picture." Saxon took a corner, heading deeper into the industrial district. "Love says, I will do the hard thing, say the hard thing because it's right. Emotion simply reacts to panic and fear and hate. God has emotion—He feels jealous. And angry. But everything He does is out of love. That's the plumb line, the thing that keeps us moving in the right direction. And keeps us from going off the deep end."

He glanced at Rowan. "And as far as helplessness, the truth is that God is on our side, at least according to Kane, right?"

Kane. His Delta Force buddy who'd nearly lost the woman he loved last summer, who'd trusted God even when everything looked hopeless.

"Kane trusted God when Sanchez was taken," Rowan said quietly. "Said that God was bigger than his worst fears."

Rowan looked out the window, at the industrial landscape, concrete and steel, loading docks and chain-link fences. But beyond it all, the Rocky Mountains rose against the afternoon sky, their granite faces catching the golden sunlight and throwing it back in displays of purple and rose.

Whom have I in heaven but you? The psalm drifted through his mind, words from Sunday's sermon that suddenly felt desperately personal. *And earth has nothing I desire besides you.*

God. I want to trust You. Help me to trust You.

The Alpine Fresh Foods complex appeared ahead of them. Everything about it looked legitimate, from the company sign to the employee parking area.

"Looks normal," Saxon said as they pulled into the visitor parking area.

"Too normal. If you wanted to hold someone, this would be perfect. Soundproof buildings, legitimate cover, easy access for vehicles."

They got out, and Martinelli joined them. "Stay behind me," he said as he approached the main entrance.

Fine. But Saxon and Rowan flanked him.

The front door was locked.

"Around back," Martinelli said.

Rowan nodded, and they edged along the building to the loading area.

The giant garage door was closed, but they tried the side door. Unlocked.

"Backup is twenty minutes out," Martinelli whispered. "We could wait."

"Or we could end this now." Rowan pulled out his Glock. So did Saxon.

"For the love. Listen, on me, and this doesn't get messy. No shooting."

Inside, darkness and shadow blanketed the area, a couple trucks parked in the space. Light streamed through the grimy window of a back office.

Rowan scrambled up to it, pressed against the wall, and Saxon took the other side. Rowan peeked in.

Ralph Rousseau sat tied to a chair in the center of the room, wearing a T-shirt and pajamas. A gash across his forehead had dried into a dark scab, and his left eye was swollen shut.

Three men sat inside, smoking cigarettes.

Rowan glanced at Saxon.

"Guys," Martinelli said. "Me first."

Rowan's jaw tightened, even as Rousseau's voice lifted.

"Please. I did everything you asked. I threatened the ranchers, made them sell their properties, I kept quiet about the Shadow Syndicate."

The Shadow Syndicate. Rowan *knew* it. This wasn't just about local land deals. This was part of something much larger.

"Plans change," one of the men replied, pulling out a pistol. "Nothing personal."

Go, *go!*

Martinelli read his mind. He nodded as Saxon moved out and kicked open the door. Then the detective burst in, his weapon trained on the gunman. "Police! Drop your weapons!"

Rowan rolled in, sighted the man who'd raised his pistol.

He wasn't sure whose shot took him out. The shooter crumpled where he stood. The other man dove behind the desk. The third took off, running, shooting.

Rowan threw himself sideways, ducking behind a filing cabinet as bullets splintered the wood paneling where his head had been seconds before.

Saxon had jerked back out of the room. Martinelli pulled Rousseau to his feet.

And then it just . . . happened.

The armed thug rose from behind the table, swinging his pistol toward Martinelli. Rowan stepped out, his weapon already trained center mass. Two quick shots. The gunman's chest exploded in crimson.

And then another shot, outside the room.

Rowan glanced at Saxon, but he'd taken off, footsteps echoing down the garage.

Martinelli moved to check the downed gunmen, his weapon still drawn. "Clear," he called, kicking the fallen pistol away.

Rowan took off, out of the office, after Saxon. He found him standing in the driveway, breathing hard.

"Lost him. He had a vehicle waiting." He turned. "Should I go after him?"

"Let's get Rousseau."

They ran back inside.

Rousseau lay on the floor, his breathing labored. A gunshot leaked blood from his abdomen, which Martinelli tried to staunch. "I need to call this in."

They traded places and Martinelli got up, stepped away.

Saxon knelt next to Rowan. "He doesn't look so good."

"You think?" Rowan rolled him over, cutting the ropes with his tactical knife. "We're the good guys. You're safe now."

Rousseau met his eyes. "I never meant it to get this far." Blood trickled from the corner of the man's mouth. His voice came out thick and slurred.

Martinelli approached, holstering his weapon. "Medical's on the way. How is he?"

"Alive, but barely," Rowan said, noting the man's dilated pupils and shallow breathing.

"The ranchers," Rousseau whispered. "They're going after the families now. The Blackwoods, the Hendricks, anyone who won't sell."

Rowan stared at him. "What do you mean, going after the families?"

"Leverage. Kidnapping. Whatever it takes to force the sales." Ralph's gaze struggled to focus.

Martinelli's phone rang, cutting through the warehouse silence. He glanced at the screen, frowning.

"Detective Martinelli," he answered, his voice tense.

"Who's doing this—" Rowan started.

"Hammer." Saxon gestured to Martinelli with his head.

Something wasn't right. Martinelli was looking at him, eyes dark, jaw tight.

Rowan stood up.

"Agent Kim, I'm putting you on speaker," Martinelli said grimly. "Please repeat what you just said."

A woman's voice filled the room, crisp and professional with an undercurrent of urgency. "This is FBI Agent Quinn Morley. I'm at the county fairgrounds. We have a kidnapping situation."

Rowan met eyes with Saxon. No, *no*—

"Two victims, a woman and a child, taken from the rodeo grounds approximately thirty minutes ago. Witnesses report a white van, professional operation."

"Description of the victims?" Martinelli said.

"Woman, late twenties, dark hair, about five foot four. Child, male, approximately ten years old. They were taken from the competitor staging area."

Sierra and Huck.

And he was thirty minutes away.

"Rowan!" Martinelli's voice.

But he and Saxon had already started to sprint.

———————————

Stay calm.

Mostly because Huck was scared, looking to her to fix this, his eyes wide with terror in the dim van.

Her too, but along with it—rage. Her ten-year-old son sat with his competition chaps torn at the knee, his cowboy hat missing. A purple bruise bloomed across his left cheek.

Someone had hit her son. So yeah, not so much fear as white-hot rage.

Sierra could see through the hood—a man the size of a tank, which she dubbed him, sat in the back of the van with them. Dark pants, dark shirt. Armed. Like they might be criminals or something.

"I'm right here, Huck." She didn't sound like herself, really. "Everything's going to be okay."

Except, why would it? Because she'd hurt herself kicking at her captors, and Tank had grabbed her foot and twisted it—she wasn't sure it was broken, but her ligaments burned. So yeah, the lie tasted bitter on her tongue.

Still, it had to be okay. Because she refused to consider anything else.

"Where are you taking us?"

Tank looked over at her. "You'll find out soon enough, lady."

The zip ties around her wrists had cut off circulation twenty minutes ago, but she kept flexing her fingers anyway. Oh, if she only thought like Rowan, then she could assess threats, look for weapons, find escape routes. Figure out what they wanted so she could give it to them and get Huck out safely.

But no, all she could think was . . . *Please, God, save us.*

She guessed it might be over a half hour since they'd grabbed them from the barn. Three left turns, two rights, one cattle guard, approximately southwest based on the sun's position filtering through the van's grimy windows. Tank kept checking his phone, the device dwarfed in his massive hands. The nervous younger one—Twitchy, she decided, based on his constant fidgeting—was sweating despite the October cold seeping through the van's metal walls.

Twitchy's toothpick paused mid-chew. "Maybe she should shut up."

Sierra stilled, digging deep into her fury instead of fear.

Please, God.

"Billy," Tank growled. "Focus."

Focus? On what?

She swallowed, fought tears.

Rowan might be at the rodeo by now, would have figured out they were missing. And she refused—okay, not well—to be angry at him.

He should have been there. He should have kept his promise. Then Huck would be safe and—

Nope. She didn't want to blame him, but . . . but the fact was, she should have known better. He'd broken promises before. And sure, maybe he was trying to protect her, but . . .

But his idea of protection and hers seemed miles apart.

Now her eyes did burn, did fill. But see, this was what happened when she let down her guard.

Fine. She'd been taking care of herself and Huck for ten years, and she could do it again. She just needed to be smart, be strong, and keep Huck safe until she could get them out of this.

The zip ties around her wrists had some give. Billy—so Twitchy had a name—kept looking away when Huck sniffled, his conscience apparently not completely dead.

Details. Gather details. Stay ready.

Tank's gun rode on his right side in a shoulder holster, the leather worn smooth from use. The van smelled like motor oil and stale cigarettes, overlaid with the metallic tang of fear.

Please, God.

The van slowed, tires crunching on gravel.

They stopped in front of a house, and through the gauzy black, it looked familiar . . .

Oh no.

Peeling yellow paint clung to weathered siding in patches. The front porch sagged under the weight of neglect, and windows stared back at them like dead eyes.

The old Wallace place.

"No." The word escaped before she could stop it.

Tank's grin revealed teeth stained yellow from tobacco. "Recognize it, do you? Guess the boss was right about you knowing the family history."

Sierra's mind raced. Boss? Family history? Ice formed in her veins as the pieces clicked into place. This wasn't random. This wasn't about cattle rustling or land grabs.

This was personal.

The van door slid open with a metallic screech, and cold mountain air rushed in. Billy grabbed Huck's arm, hauling him toward the opening.

"Don't touch him!" Sierra lunged forward despite her restraints, her injured ankle sending fire up her leg. Tank caught her easily, his grip bruising her shoulders.

"Easy there, wildcat. You'll see your boy soon enough." Tank yanked the hood off her. His breath reeked of chewing tobacco and whiskey. "Boss wants to have a chat with you first."

They dragged her from the van, her boots hitting the gravel with jarring impact. Her ankle nearly buckled, forcing her to lean against Tank for support—a humiliation that burned worse than the physical pain, and shoot, she cried out.

Billy hauled Huck toward the back door, the boy's boots dragging in the gravel. "Mom!"

"It's okay, baby. Be brave." Sierra's voice broke despite her efforts to keep it steady.

The back door opened before they reached it.

Sierra froze.

Alden Jenkins stepped into the doorway. He wore pressed khakis and a polo shirt and looked every inch the politician.

A murdering politician.

"Sierra Blackwood." His voice carried the same cultured tone she remembered from town council meetings, but underneath lurked something darker. Something that had always made her skin crawl.

Evil, probably.

"Alden." Sierra straightened despite Tank's grip on her arm. "You know Rowan will find you. This won't end well."

The man smiled, just a hitch up the side of his mouth. "Here's hoping."

She swallowed bile.

Alden stepped aside as Tank muscled her through the doorway.

The house's interior smelled of neglect. Dust motes swam in the late-afternoon sunlight streaming through grimy windows. The living room furniture sat covered in sheets, ghostly shapes that spoke of abandonment. The stone fireplace dominated one wall, its hearth cold and dark. Built-in bookshelves flanked the mantel, their shelves empty except for cobwebs.

This was where Rowan had hidden when his stepfather's rages grew too violent. Where he'd nursed bruises while planning his escape.

She'd found him here once, furious, breaking things. So maybe there was truth to his fear of his anger spiraling out of control. He'd scared her, for a moment, even as her heart broke for him.

It still did.

"I know he came here. Hid here." Alden followed her gaze around the room. "I should have burned this place long ago."

"What's going on, Alden? Why am I here? Why is Huck here?"

Tank shoved her toward a straight-backed chair positioned in the center of the room. More zip ties waited on the seat, along with a manila folder thick with documents.

"Sit." Tank's command brooked no argument.

Sierra's ankle gave out as he pushed her down, pain shooting up her leg like liquid fire. She bit back a cry.

Billy dragged Huck to a matching chair beside her, the boy's face pale with terror. "What do you want with us?"

"Smart boy. Gets right to the point." Alden picked up the folder. "Just like his father."

Sierra stared at him.

"I know exactly who fathered your son," Alden said. "I've known it since the day I saw you pregnant. And the resemblance is rather obvious once you know what to look for." He opened the folder. "It does make this messier than I'd wanted, however."

Huck's blue eyes—Rowan's eyes—widened with confusion. "Mom? What's he talking about?"

"Your father is my stepson, boy. The same man who abandoned you both without a backward glance." Alden's voice carried false sympathy that made Sierra's skin crawl. "The same man who's probably miles away right now, completely unaware that his family is in danger. He doesn't care about you—he'd rather be where the action is. Mr. Hammer. Tough as nails. Living for danger."

"You're lying. He loves us." But Huck's voice wavered.

"Am I?" Alden pulled out legal documents covered in dense text. "Let's discuss why you're here, shall we?"

Sierra forced herself to focus on the papers rather than the hurt in her son's eyes. The heading made her gasp. *Quit Claim Deed Transfer.*

"I'm not signing that." Her voice came out steady despite the heat filling her throat. "You're not getting my land."

"Ranching is dangerous work. Accidents happen all the time on ranches. Fires, for instance. Very tragic when they claim whole families."

What?

"I'd hate for your ranch to fall into probate. Could take years to claim the rights." Alden's tone turned businesslike, as if they were discussing weather instead of murder. "You're going to sign over your ranch to me, along with all mineral rights and water access. Upon your death, of course."

"Upon my—" *What?* And then, "You won't get away with this, Alden. You can't just . . ." Her voice dropped. "I have a son."

"I know." He folded his arms. "That's the problem. That was *always* the problem. Sean Wallace had a son. And I thought maybe I'd taken care of that by making him run from Renegade—especially when he was killed overseas. Never thought he'd come back from the dead."

She tried to unravel his words—"Wait. The land. It doesn't belong to you. It belongs to Rowan. As Sean Wallace's son. You stole it from him—"

"Rowan was gone when his mom died," he said. "And Mack wasn't old enough to inherit."

"Rowan doesn't know the land is his."

Jenkins raised a shoulder.

"And now that . . ." She looked at Huck. "The land belongs to *Huck*."

"It's a big spread, once you combine the Blackwood place," he said quietly. Then he nodded at the men behind her.

But she kept her gaze on him. "This is about *land*?"

"Oh, honey. It's much more than land." He got up. "I'm going to need you to sign these documents."

Sierra's heart hammered against her ribs. "And if I refuse?"

Alden nodded to Billy, who pulled a knife from his belt. The blade whispered against Huck's throat, drawing a thin line of blood.

"Then your son dies. Slowly. While you watch."

"Stop!" Sierra lunged forward, but Tank's hand on her shoulder slammed her back into the chair. "He's just a child!"

"He's his father's son." Alden's voice carried no emotion. "And you're going to sign those papers, or he's going to learn . . . well, like father, like son."

And she saw it then, Rowan, hiding his bruises, Rowan, scared, angry, vowing to fight back someday. Rowan, driven from his legacy because of what this man had done to him and made him do.

"Rowan will kill you."

He smiled. "I'm counting on him trying."

Jenkins would kill him. Or maybe Rowan would win—and end up in prison for the rest of his life.

The threat hung in the air like poison gas. Sierra stared at the documents. Sign, and they died anyway. Refuse, and Huck suffered before they died.

"The pen is right there." Alden gestured to a ballpoint pen lying beside the folder. "Sign, and I promise his death will be quick. Painless."

"Mom, don't." Huck's voice came out smaller than she'd ever heard it. "Don't do what he says."

"Brave boy." Alden's approval made Sierra's stomach turn. "Just like his father at that age. Right before I broke him."

Sierra exploded toward him, everything inside her on fire. "You touch one hair on his head, and I swear—"

Tank caught her around the waist and threw her back into the chair.

Slapped her.

The world spun and Huck screamed.

"That's enough," Alden said. He stepped up to her, even as she blinked past the blinding pain.

"What are you going to do?" Alden's laugh cut through her fury. "Call for help? Your boyfriend doesn't even know you're missing. Face reality, Sierra. No one is coming to save you. You're *alone*."

She stilled, tears streaking down her face. Then, quietly, yes . . . She lifted her chin. "If I sign this, you let him go." Sierra's voice came out steady and hard. "He walks out of here unharmed."

"I'm afraid that's not possible. It doesn't solve any of my problems." His voice softened. "But I promise his end will be swift."

"Then I don't sign."

Billy pressed the knife deeper, and Huck whimpered. A fresh line of blood welled against the blade. But, oh, her son was brave.

"Last chance. Or he dies in front of you."

She bit her lip and nodded.

And somehow, the words from Sunday swept into her, through her. *Whom have I in heaven but you? . . . My flesh and my heart may fail, but God is the strength of my heart and my portion forever.*

I am not alone.

Tears burned down her face. Sierra reached for the pen with shaking fingers. Around her, the house seemed to echo with the ghosts of Rowan's childhood—all the times he'd been powerless, all the times he'd been forced to choose between bad and worse.

Now she understood why he'd run.

And he should keep running.

Her signature flowed across the bottom of the document, each letter a small betrayal of everything her grandfather had built. The ranch. The legacy. The future she'd planned for Huck.

Gone in a few strokes of ink.

"Excellent." Alden gathered the papers with obvious satisfaction. "That wasn't so difficult, was it?"

"Please, Alden. Let him go." She hated how small her voice felt, how broken.

"I told you, that's not possible. But don't worry—you'll be together."

The slosh of liquid was audible in the sudden silence. The sharp smell of gasoline filled the air, overlaying the dust and decay with something far more sinister.

"Gasoline?" Sierra's heart rate spiked as understanding dawned. "You're going to burn us alive?"

"Accidents happen." Alden's voice held no emotion. "Old houses. Faulty wiring. Very tragic."

Billy began dousing the room, the gasoline darkening the hardwood floors in spreading pools. The fumes made Sierra's eyes water.

"Please, Alden. Don't—"

Tank tied her ankles to the chair legs, then secured Huck the same way. The boy had gone silent, probably shock setting in as his young mind tried to process their situation.

She looked at him. "Huck. I'm here. I'm right here."

Alden pulled a silver lighter from his pocket, the metal gleaming in the late-afternoon light. "Don't worry. The smoke will kill you before the flames do."

Her mouth opened. "You really are the devil."

Alden flicked the lighter open. "Only to some."

The flame caught on the first try, a tiny orange tongue.

"Don't—Alden!"

He dropped the lighter.

Fire raced across the gasoline-soaked floor like liquid lightning, reaching the walls in seconds.

"Mom!" Huck screamed.

Alden fled through the kitchen door.

"Tip your chair over, Huck! We need to get low!"

Huck was crying but obeying, rocking his chair to turn it over.

Then she heard it—footsteps. Voices shouting over the roar of flames.

"Sierra! Huck!" Rowan's voice cut through the chaos.

"Here!" Sierra screamed back. "We're here!"

The front door exploded inward. Rowan burst through, his expression fierce, fury in his eyes. He charged into the room, spotted Sierra, but Tank and Billy spun toward the door, weapons raised.

Two shots. Billy dropped, shouting, clutching his shoulder as blood seeped between his fingers. He scrambled into the kitchen.

Tank had found cover behind a sofa.

Shots from the kitchen pinned Saxon down behind an entry wall.

Rowan advanced on Tank, no armor, just fury on his face. "Drop it."

Tank fired at him.

A shot tore at his shoulder, and Rowan barely flinched. He barraged the sofa with shots and then rolled behind a chair.

"Sax! Get Huck!"

Billy got up, fired at Saxon, then took off.

Saxon turned to Huck.

Another shot—maybe from Billy, but just like that, Saxon was down.

"Mom!" Huck screamed.

Sierra fought against the zip ties, ignoring the pain as they cut deeper into her wrists.

Smoke filled the room, thick and acrid. Sierra's eyes streamed tears, but she kept working at her restraints. The chair rocked with her efforts, but the ties held.

The fire reached the ceiling now, hungry flames racing across old wood with terrifying speed.

She struggled in her chair even as Rowan charged for them.

Nope. Tank leaped at him with surprising speed for such a large man.

They collided with bone-jarring force. Tank's momentum drove them both into the doorframe, which cracked under the impact. Rowan twisted, breaking free, then landed a devastating uppercut that snapped Tank's head back.

Tank swung wild, his fist whistling past Rowan's ear. Rowan countered with a precise strike to the throat, followed by a knee to the solar plexus. Tank doubled over, gasping.

Saxon rolled to his knees, apparently down but not out. Blood dripped onto the floor.

"Get Huck!" Rowan roared just as Tank made one last desperate lunge at him, pulling a knife from his boot. The blade flashed in the firelight, slashing toward Rowan's ribs. Rowan caught Tank's wrist, twisted hard. The knife clattered away across the burning floor.

A final elbow to Tank's temple dropped him. The big man hit the floorboards and didn't move.

"This place is coming down!" Saxon shouted as he moved toward Huck.

But his knee crumpled, and he landed on all fours.

"I got him!" Rowan's knife sliced through Huck's restraints in seconds. The boy fell into his father's arms with a sob, and for just a moment, the fierce warrior crumpled.

"I've got you." His voice broke on the words. "I've got you, buddy."

"Go!" Sierra fought against her own restraints, desperation giving her strength. "Get him out of here!"

Saxon fought his way over, and his knife sliced through her bonds. She grabbed the knife out of his hands, went to work on her ankle restraints. "Go! Go! I'm right behind you!"

Rowan looked between her and Huck. Then he grabbed Saxon by the back of his shirt, Huck on his hip. "Move!"

Saxon half stumbled, half crawled toward the door.

Then they were gone, swallowed by smoke and darkness.

Sierra sawed at her restraints. C'mon, *c'mon!*

The zip ties finally gave way as a burning beam crashed down over Tank.

She rolled away, her injured ankle screaming in protest.

The ceiling groaned ominously overhead.

She got to her knees, crawling hard for the kitchen door.

The ceiling fell, a beam flaming right in front of her. She jerked back, scrambling down the hallway.

Trapped.

Through the smoke and flames, she heard Rowan's voice screaming her name. But the fire was too hot now, the smoke too thick. Even he couldn't reach her through the inferno.

She pressed her hands over her mouth. And yet, even as the house burned around her, an odd sense of peace washed over her.

Who do I have in heaven but You?

Huck was safe.

That had to be enough.

FOURTEEN

NO.

No.

Sierra did not die today.

Huck's scream shook Rowan free of watching the front of his house collapse, the woman he loved inside.

"Hammer—you can't go back in there."

He rounded on Saxon with such a look that Saxon held up his hands. "It's a death trap!" Blood gushed down his leg, but Saxon had wound a belt around the wound and was even finding his feet.

So, maybe not life-threatening.

Rowan had set Huck down on solid ground fifty feet or so from the burning house, his hands trembling as he released his son. The boy had felt weightless during the sprint through the front door, but now Rowan's arms shook.

Huck clung to his shirt, fists twisted in the fabric. "Don't go back in there!"

"I have to." Rowan pried his son's fingers loose. "Stay with Saxon."

"Daddy, please!"

The word punched through him. Hollowed him out and shook through his body.

Daddy.

Behind him, the fire raged.

He didn't have time, but he turned, took a breath, and put his hand on Huck's shoulder. "I'm getting your mom. Stay here and be brave."

Then he turned toward the house.

Saxon stood between him and the house. "Front entry's blocked. Whole roof section came down."

"Kitchen door?" His voice came out steady now.

"Fully engulfed. You'd never make it through."

Rowan turned back toward the house, his mind cataloging options. The structure was nearly engulfed, walls of flame, and inside—collapsing supports, air so superheated it would sear his lungs.

But Sierra was in there. His Sierra.

"East bedroom window." He was already moving, stripping off his jacket as he ran. "Same way I used to sneak in and out as a kid."

Paint bubbled and peeled from the siding in long strips that curled away from the boards. The smell hit him—burning wood, melting plastic, and underneath it all, the sharp chemical tang of accelerant.

Someone had wanted this place to burn fast and hot.

The bedroom window sat six feet off the ground, its glass already spider-webbed from the heat. Rowan wrapped his jacket around his fist and punched through, clearing the shards before hauling himself up and through the opening.

The interior stole his breath. Flames raced across the ceiling in waves, fed by decades of dry wood and whatever accelerant the arsonists had used.

Smoke cut visibility to almost nothing. Rowan dropped to his hands and knees, where the air was cleaner, and crawled toward where he hoped the living room would be.

"Sierra!" The shout came out as a croak, his throat already raw.

A crash echoed through the house as something heavy collapsed in the kitchen. The whole structure shuddered, and Rowan felt the floor vibrate under his palms. They had minutes, maybe less, before the entire place came down.

"Here!" Sierra's voice, muffled but strong, came from his right.

The bathroom. The woman had made it to the bathroom, had climbed into the tub.

He shut the door behind him, muffling the fire.

"Huck!"

"Already out. Safe with Saxon." He reached for the window. It didn't move, too many layers of paint sealing it shut.

And frankly, it was too small for his shoulders anyway.

She was struggling to stand.

He turned to her. "Can you walk?"

"I think so." But she stood with one leg favored.

A support beam groaned overhead.

And that was just it. He swooped her up into his arms, pulled her tight against him.

"Close your eyes. Put your head against my chest." Somehow, he'd put away his emotion, found the part of him who'd extracted civilians from war zones. "Don't look up, don't breathe deep, and trust me."

Sierra pressed her face into his shirt. "Let's get out of here." Her body trembled against him.

The hallway to the bedroom had become a tunnel of fire. Flames licked down from the ceiling and reached up from the floor, leaving a narrow corridor of furnace air in between. Rowan kicked aside burning debris and plunged through.

The fire licked across the ceiling, and the walls had begun to char.

But the window was clear.

Rowan boosted Sierra through the opening first, lowering her as far as he could before letting her drop to the ground outside. She landed hard, with a cry, but crawled away from the house, putting distance between herself and the flames.

A thunderous crack split the air as the main support beam started to give way. The entire back half of the house groaned.

Rowan dove through the window as the bedroom ceiling started to sag.

He hit the ground and rolled.

By the time he came up, the rest of the house had folded. Where the structure had stood moments before, nothing remained but a pile of burning timber reaching toward the darkening sky.

"Mom!" Huck's voice cut through the roar of flames. The boy was running toward them, Saxon limping hard close behind, both their faces streaked with soot.

Even Saxon's face twisted, as if he might cry.

Sierra struggled to sit up, favoring her injured ankle. "I'm okay, baby. I'm okay."

Huck threw himself into her arms. She rocked him as he sobbed.

And over their son's head, her eyes found Rowan's.

"Thank you," she rasped.

Rowan nodded, not trusting his voice. The tactical calm was cracking, and his hands started to shake even as he moved everyone far from the fire—enough to breathe clean air and not feel the heat.

Then he simply collapsed in the dirt and grass beside them, breathing hard.

Saxon disappeared, hobbling away, and then, after a bit,

reappeared with a first aid kit. He handed it over to Rowan. "Emergency services are en route. Should be here in a minute."

"How'd you find us?" Sierra had turned to Saxon, who now loosened the belt over his wound. Tore open his pants leg.

"We tracked your phone," Saxon said. "We have a friend."

Rowan stood now, staring at the house. "Who were they, Sierra?"

She leaned back, stared at him, her eyes wide.

Something about the way she looked at him . . . "What?"

"It was Alden."

A beat, then . . . wait. "*What?*"

"Alden Jenkins took us. Got me to sign over the ranch to him."

He sat in the grass, the house behind him an inferno. "What are you—"

Saxon's phone rang. He dug it out of his leg pocket. "Martinelli." He put him on speaker.

"We heard the sirens," Martinelli said without preamble. "What's your status?"

"Everyone's alive."

Sierra leaned over to the phone. "We're at the old Wallace place. It's on fire."

Seemed like a too simple thing to say, really. Rowan's hand clenched.

"Who took you, Sierra—did you see them?"

"Yeah," Rowan growled, cutting her off. "Alden Jenkins. My stepfather."

"You sure?"

Rowan grabbed the phone. "Yeah, we're sure, Mike. So put out a BOLO for the guy—"

"Rowan, don't—"

"Do not tell me don't." He hung up. Handed the phone to Saxon, his entire body shaking. He met Sierra's eyes.

Sirens wailed in the distance, growing louder as fire trucks and ambulances raced toward the scene. Red and blue lights flickered through the smoke, promising help that was still minutes away.

"Rowan." Sierra's voice was soft but steady. "Look at me."

He knelt beside her, noting the way she held her ankle and the bruises forming on her wrists from the zip ties. But her eyes were clear, focused, alive.

"He wanted me to sign papers," she said. "Land transfer documents. Said they'd kill Huck if I didn't."

"Did you sign?"

"Yes." Her voice cracked. "Of course I did. I signed everything."

Of course she did. Rowan's hand found hers, their fingers intertwining. Then he leaned forward, pressed his forehead to hers. "I would have too. You are the bravest person I know."

She huffed out a breath. Looked at Huck. "I was terrified."

Emergency vehicles were already arriving—fire trucks with their lights strobing red and blue against the smoke, ambulances with EMTs moving toward them with equipment.

Fire personnel got out, started unwinding hoses, probably to keep the fire from catching on the dry grass and starting a wildfire.

"Sierra!" Jackson Stewart jogged over with an oxygen mask and medical kit. "You okay?"

"She could use air," Rowan said and got up. Huck refused to move from where he sat beside his mom.

Jackson fitted the mask over her face, then began checking her vitals. Sierra leaned into the oxygen, her color already improving as the clean air replaced the smoke in her lungs.

"Rowan!" Detective Martinelli's voice cut through the noise as he approached at a near run, his face grim. "I put out the BOLO." He stopped, crouched in front of Sierra, and Rowan would forgive him for the look of tenderness. "You okay?"

She nodded.

Martinelli turned to Rowan. "I don't understand. Why would—"

"Because this land belongs to Rowan," Sierra said. "All of it. But with Rowan dead, Alden grabbed it. Or thought he had hold of it, and then, of course, Rowan came back, and it got complicated."

"But what about the lithium and the land rights?"

"He's the mayor. Of course he knows how valuable the mineral rights are," Saxon said. "My guess is that when Sierra and the others didn't give in, well, this was his last best hope."

Rowan stood there, and all of it just boiled inside him. The man who'd terrorized his childhood, who'd broken his mother's spirit, who'd driven him from his home. The man who'd been playing the reformed mayor while orchestrating a campaign of terror against his own community.

The man who'd just tried to burn his family alive.

"We'll find him," Saxon said quietly, lethally.

A black pickup pulled up, past the fire trucks.

Mack got out, running hard toward Rowan, his face pale as he took in the burning ruins and emergency vehicles. "I saw the smoke from the house and—" He stopped, his gaze on Sierra and Huck. "What happened?"

"Your father just tried to kill my family," Rowan said, and tried, oh, he tried, not to add blame to his tone.

It wasn't Mack's fault his father was a monster.

Mack's face went white. "That's impossible. He was home all morning. We had breakfast together, talked about ranch business—"

"When did you last see him?" Saxon interrupted.

"Around eleven. Said he had meetings in town." Mack's voice grew smaller as understanding dawned. "I've been working the south pasture all day."

Rowan drew in a breath. Stared at Mack's truck.

Alden had maybe a thirty-minute head start. In the right vehicle, Rowan could catch him before he reached the county line.

"Rowan." Sierra's voice, soft.

He stilled. No. He wasn't going to leave her. Or Huck. Sheesh—what kind of person was he that he'd even consider—

"Rowan Wallace." Sierra's voice.

He looked down at her. She'd pulled off the oxygen mask, her eyes clear and focused despite everything she'd been through. "Go get him."

He blinked. Shook his head. "No—I'm not leaving you."

"Jackson's here. Mike's here. We're safe." Her voice grew stronger. "But if you don't stop him now, he'll disappear. And then we *won't* be safe, will we?"

Rowan swallowed. Looked at Saxon, who stood, hands on his hips, breathing hard. He gave him a shrug, a look. "She's not wrong."

Sierra reached for his hand, her fingers wrapping around his with surprising strength. Her dark eyes held his, steady and sure.

"Go get him, Hammer."

She should feel grateful. Relieved.

Instead, someone had scooped out Sierra's insides, turned her hollow. Smoke still saturated her hair, turning it greasy, and every time she closed her eyes, she saw flames.

Saw Huck, tied to a chair, bruised, terrified.

Saw Rowan in a fist fight, or diving out of the window of his burning house.

So yeah, she just wanted to go home and get in her bed. Thankfully, Bailey had Huck, was feeding him junk food from the cafeteria, and frankly, Sierra couldn't leave the hospital without talking to Morrie.

He might help her make sense of all this.

The crutches rubbed against her palms as she maneuvered through the doorway of room 314 at Renegade Mercy General

Hospital. Three hours had passed since Rowan pulled her from the burning house. Two hours of X-rays and breathing treatments and doctors poking at her scraped knees and twisted ankle.

And one hour since Rowan had finally left her side and headed out on a manhunt. Martinelli made him take backup, but the look on her man's face suggested they might just get in the way.

She didn't know how she felt about that.

But she had a different mission.

Walt Morrison lay propped against white pillows, his weathered face pale against the crisp hospital linens. IV lines snaked from his arms to bags hanging on metal poles, and the steady beep of monitors filled the room with electronic reassurance. His eyes opened as she settled into the visitor's chair, the oxygen cannula under his nose turning his voice thin.

"Sierra." His words came out raspy. "You okay? What happened?"

"Long story. But I'm fine." She positioned her crutches against the bedside table. "How are you feeling?"

"Like someone used me for target practice." Morrie attempted a smile that didn't quite reach his eyes. "But breathing. Thanks to that man of yours finding me."

"Rowan's not—" Sierra stopped herself. "He's not exactly mine."

"Please."

She smiled. "Fine, yes."

"I could see it from the first day he walked onto the ranch." Morrie's eyes sharpened despite the pain medication. "Man looks at you the way a drowning person looks at the shore."

Heat crept up Sierra's neck. "We're complicated."

"Most worthwhile things are." Morrie shifted against his pillows, wincing at the movement. "Sierra, I need to tell you some things. About your grandfather. About what really happened."

The monitor beeps seemed to accelerate. "What do you mean?"

"I mean, I don't think Elway died in any ATV accident." Morrie's voice dropped to barely above a whisper. "I saw Alden Jenkins talking to him the day before he died. Saw them having words near the south pasture."

Sierra's chest tightened. "What kind of words?"

"Heated ones. I think he threatened you. Maybe even Huck." Morrie's jaw clenched, and the monitors registered his rising blood pressure. "Your grandfather suspected Rousseau, but he began to believe Alden was involved too. The land deals, the intimidation, all of it."

"So Alden killed him?" Probably Morrie didn't need to know what Alden had done to her and Huck, given the beeping of his heart monitor.

"Elway got sick that night. Real sick, real fast. Same symptoms we've been seeing in the cattle." Morrie's eyes fixed on hers. "I think Alden poisoned him with whatever he's been putting in the water supply."

She knew it—really knew it, in the bottom of her soul, but it didn't make hearing it easier.

"Why didn't you tell me this before?"

"Because Elway made me promise to keep you and Huck safe, not to get you involved in whatever he was investigating." Morrie's hand found hers. "Made me swear I'd watch over you both if anything happened to him." Morrie squeezed her fingers gently. "He was building a case, Sierra. Had documentation, photographs, financial records. He believed the Shadow Syndicate was behind it all."

"The papers in his safe." Sierra's voice came out as a whisper. "I found them. I told Detective Martinelli about them."

"Good. He always said you had steel in your spine, just like your grandmother."

The door opened, and Mike entered carrying a coffee cup. His rumpled suit looked like he'd slept in it, and dark circles shadowed his eyes.

"Morrie." Martinelli nodded to the man in the bed. "How are you feeling?"

"Like I've been shot, but grateful to be vertical." Morrie's tone held wry humor despite his condition. "Sierra been telling you about what Elway found?"

"She has. And it correlates with what we're discovering about Jenkins's operation as well as Rousseau's involvement." Martinelli pulled up another chair, setting his coffee on the bedside table. "Sierra, I need to ask you some more questions about the evidence your grandfather collected."

"Of course."

"You said he had maps showing targeted properties. Were there any other ranches marked besides the ones we already know about?"

Sierra closed her eyes, trying to remember the documents she'd found. "The St. Claire place south of town. The Hendrick spread. The old Kowalski ranch that sold last year."

"All of them have significant lithium deposits," Martinelli said. "And all of them were approached by Rocky Mountain Land Development before the harassment started."

Morrie's mouth tightened. "It's my fault I got shot."

"What?" Sierra frowned at him.

"I found more tracks, by the river, near where our water supply got fiddled with, and started to follow them. I saw a man in the distance—didn't get a good look at him, but my guess is that he got a good look at me. Shot me off my horse. I broke my radio in the fall—and then . . . the next thing I remember was waking up here."

"That's not your fault," Sierra said, standing up.

"Yeah, it was. I was on Jenkins land."

A nurse appeared in the doorway—a middle-aged woman with kind eyes and efficient movements.

"I'm sorry, but the party is over. Mr. Morrison needs to rest," she said, checking his heart rate monitor tape.

"We'll go," Martinelli said, standing and gathering his folder. "Morrie, thank you for the information. We'll need a formal statement when you're feeling stronger."

"I'll be here." Morrie's voice was getting weaker as the pain medication pulled him toward sleep. "Sierra, you take care of yourself. And Huck."

Sierra leaned forward and kissed Morrie's forehead. "Thank you. For everything. For watching over us all these years."

Not alone.

In the hallway, FBI Agent Quinn Morley stood talking quietly with another agent near the nurses' station. Sierra had met her on the way in. Pretty, with black hair and dark eyes, she wore dress pants and a white shirt. When she saw Martinelli approach, she excused herself and walked over.

"Detective. Ms. Blackwood," Quinn said. "How are you feeling?"

"Like I've been through an episode of Shadrach, Meshach, and Abednego."

Quinn raised an eyebrow. "We're going to need your full statement about the kidnapping and what the perpetrators said to you." She took out her phone. "Anything you can remember about their conversations, their plans, their associates."

Associates? "Like Tank, the guy who hit my son? And Billy, who wanted to just shoot me? Or how about Alden Jenkins, my son's sort of grandfather who tried to burn him alive? Those perpetrators?"

Quinn held up a hand. "I understand this is personal—"

"This isn't just personal. This is . . . it's . . ." She stared at her. And then . . . "Justice." She stepped back. "Rowan's justice. Finally. If Jenkins hadn't come after him, we'd never know that . . ." She looked at Mike. "The land belongs to Rowan. All of the Jenkins land. It's his."

Mike nodded. "That makes terrible sense."

She turned back to Quinn. "Alden Jenkins wanted me to sign

papers transferring the ranch to him. Said he'd kill Huck if I didn't." Sierra's voice steadied as she recounted the events. "He knew about the lithium deposits under our property. Said the ranch was sitting on top of something valuable."

"Okay." Quinn put away her cell phone. "Ms. Blackwood, I want you to know that we take these threats very seriously. We'll have agents monitoring the situation until all perpetrators are in custody."

"There you go with the perpetrators again. Alden Jenkins is behind this. Find him. *He's* the perpetrator."

"Yes. What happened to you and your son was just the latest in a long pattern of intimidation and violence. But it's not just him. There are others behind this."

"The Shadow Syndicate," Sierra said.

Quinn frowned.

"It was in my grandfather's notes."

"I'll get a copy for your office," Mike said to Quinn.

Sierra looked at Mike. "I need to get Huck."

The elevator arrived with a soft chime, and they rode down in silence, Mike shifting weirdly. Finally, "For the record, Rowan is a good man."

She glanced over at him. And then gave a small laugh. "What is that—your approval?"

He lifted a shoulder. Looked away. "Maybe?"

"Thanks, bro."

He swallowed. "Now, that hurt."

She laughed and Mike smiled.

His phone rang as soon as he exited the elevator. "Martinelli."

Sierra couldn't help herself. She paused, listening. He nodded. "When?"

She stopped at the concern on his face. Frowned.

"Keep trying." He hung up.

"What? And remember, I know when you're lying."

His mouth tightened. "Rowan's phone went dark."

She stared at him. "I thought you said you were sending backup."

"We did—we went to the mayor's office, but no one was there. And Alden's phone has fallen off the grid too."

She stared at him. "You don't know where they are."

"Could mean anything," Mike said. "He might have turned off his phone to avoid detection."

"Or Alden found him," Sierra said quietly.

"We have BOLOs out," Mike said. "State police, federal agents, local search and rescue. If they're out there, we'll find them."

Not if Rowan didn't want them to. "We need to get home," she said finally.

"I'll drive you. And stay until Rowan gets back," Mike offered. "It's the least I can do."

"Thank you."

She picked up Huck from the cafeteria and got a hug from Bailey. "Call me if you need anything," Bailey said.

The automatic doors opened, and the cool evening air washed over them.

Somewhere out there in the darkness, Rowan had morphed into the previous version of himself.

She—they—needed that version tonight. Right now.

But . . . *Rowan, please come home.*

The words carried on the mountain wind, a prayer and a promise wrapped together. She would wait. She would hope. She would believe in the man she loved and the future they could build together.

But first, Hammer had to survive the night.

FIFTEEN

NO NEED FOR THIS TO GET CRAZY. ROWAN gripped the steering wheel tighter as he navigated the winding road toward the Jenkins place, his knuckles white against the worn leather. He just wanted to talk. That was all. Have a conversation between two adults about attempted murder and decades of lies.

Talk. Right.

Maybe with some hurt added—no. He cut off that thought before it could take root. He wasn't Alden.

The empty clip in his Glock should probably concern him more, but Rowan had brought down Alden Jenkins once before with nothing but his fists—and tonight, that might feel more satisfying anyway.

The stopover in the mayor's office had turned out to be a dead end. And frankly, he wasn't interested in letting Martinelli's backup have first crack at Alden anyway, so yeah, he'd gotten lucky.

And then, just in case, he'd turned off his phone. Taken out the SIM card. No need for company.

He pulled into the circular driveway of the Jenkins house, gravel crunching under his truck tires as amber light spilled from the windows of the log home.

Rowan cut the engine and climbed out, his boots hitting the ground with purpose. The front door opened before he reached the porch steps, and Catherine Jenkins appeared in the doorway, wearing a cream cashmere cardigan over dark slacks. Her graying hair hung loose around her shoulders instead of its usual neat bun, and mascara streaked her cheeks in dark trails.

"Rowan." Her voice cracked on his name. "I heard about the fire. About Sierra and Huck. Are they—"

"They're safe." Rowan's tone cut through her question. "Where's Alden?"

Catherine's hands twisted together, her wedding ring catching the porch light. "He's not here. He left hours ago, right after—" She stopped, pressing her lips together.

"Right after what?"

"After Detective Martinelli called looking for him." Catherine stepped back from the doorway, her shoulders hunching inward. "Rowan, he's never acted like this before. He was pacing, making phone calls, throwing things. He broke my grandmother's vase."

Rowan studied her face, noting the genuine fear in her eyes. "You don't know him like I do."

Something flickered across Catherine's expression—a shadow of recognition, maybe. "Or maybe you do."

She drew in a shaky breath. "He was never like that with me. But I heard about . . . about how he was with you. Dolly and others. I never . . . I couldn't . . ." She sighed. "Your mother was a good soul. I knew her from church—a number of years older than me, but . . . Rowan. Please don't hurt him."

He stared at her. Her hand moved to her throat, fingers finding a pearl necklace.

"Where would he go?" Rowan said quietly.

"He has another office," she said softly. "He keeps files there. Important papers. He said he had to—" She pressed her hands to her mouth, cutting off whatever she'd been about to reveal. "Promise me you won't hurt him."

"He tried to burn my son and my . . . the woman I love alive." He barely stopped himself from yelling. Took a breath. Held up his hand. "Please tell me where he is . . ."

"Hammer."

He looked up. Mack stood on the stairs. He looked wrecked, almost—

"Did you get into a fight?" Rowan said, his voice almost a whisper. Mack wore a bruise on his face.

Catherine looked at him. "Mack—"

"Yes." Mack's voice cracked. "He was here when I came home, and I confronted him." He came to the bottom of the stairs.

Only then did Rowan see the finger bruises on his neck. "He tried to strangle you."

"He was angry."

"Shut up! Do you *hear yourself?*"

Mack held up a hand. "I'm fine."

"You're *traumatized.*" He looked at Catherine. "You both are. Don't you get it? You live in fear of being hurt—physically, emotionally—and that's not okay. It's *never* okay. Because people who can't control their emotions damage other people." He raked a hand through his hair. Blew out a breath. "Listen. Okay. I won't . . . I won't hurt him."

Sheesh, that felt weird to say. But the words settled in, grounded him. "But I do need to bring him to justice."

Mack had sat down on the stairs. Put his face in his hands. "I can't believe he's done all this. I thought he'd changed. Thought he was trying to make up for how he treated you."

Rowan sighed.

Mack looked up at him, his voice hollow. "But maybe I just

wanted to believe it so badly that I ignored the signs. The late-night meetings, the phone calls he didn't want me to hear, the way he'd get angry whenever Rowan's name came up."

"He was threatened by Rowan," Catherine said. "Even I knew that."

Because Rowan could take everything from him. The thought drilled into him, through him.

Alden was a monster because he was scared.

It still didn't excuse his behavior.

"I should have known." Mack buried his face in his hands. "I should have seen what he was doing."

"You were a kid when I left," Rowan said. "You had every right to hope your father had become a better man."

"But he hasn't." Mack lifted his head, looked at Rowan. "He's been killing people. Terrorizing families. And I've been living in his house, eating at his table, believing his lies."

Rowan stared at his brother. Betrayal. How he hated it.

Mack got up. "I know where his office is. He took me there this week. He's a consultant. I'll go with you."

"No. You won't." He met Mack's eyes. "This is not for you, Mack. This is between me and . . . Alden."

Mack seemed a little undone, but he swallowed and nodded. "I'll send you a pin." He pulled out his phone.

Aw, that meant he'd have to turn his phone on. "Thanks."

Rowan turned back toward his truck, but Catherine's voice stopped him.

"Rowan, wait." When he looked back, she was gripping the doorframe like it was the only thing keeping her upright. "Be careful. Whatever he's done, whatever this is about—he's desperate. And desperate men do terrible things."

"I know *exactly* what desperate men do," Rowan said. "I've been one."

The drive to downtown Renegade took fifteen minutes through

empty streets, the downtown district a mix of restored brick buildings and modern glass structures that housed law offices and investment firms.

Most of the buildings stood dark now, their windows reflecting the streetlights.

Rowan pulled into the three-story parking garage attached to the Renegade Commerce Center, his truck tires squealing slightly on the polished concrete as he climbed to the third level. The structure was nearly empty.

The Commerce Center itself rose five stories, made of steel and glass. During business hours, it housed accounting firms, real-estate agencies, and the kinds of consulting companies that helped small towns navigate growth and development. Tonight, security lights illuminated the main entrance, but the interior lay dark except for the red glow of exit signs.

Rowan parked in a corner spot and climbed out. The security system on the Commerce Center was standard corporate fare—key-card access, motion sensors, cameras at the entrances. Rowan moved around to the building's north side, where a maintenance door provided access to the loading dock. The lock was industrial grade but not military, and his tactical knife made short work of the deadbolt mechanism.

The interior stairwell smelled of cleaning supplies and fresh paint. Emergency lighting cast everything in a red glow, turning the neutral colors of the walls and railings into something more ominous. Rowan climbed past the first floor—medical offices and insurance agencies—and the second floor—lawyers and accountants. According to his brother's text, Alden Jenkins maintained his private consulting office on the third floor.

Rowan's phone buzzed against his ribs. Saxon's name appeared on the screen. He stood in the stairwell and swiped it open.

"Where are you?" Saxon.

"Where do you think?"

"That's not an answer, Hammer. After what happened tonight, you don't go dark on me."

"I'm fine."

"You should have waited for me to get stitched up." Saxon's tone shifted to the voice he'd used during ops briefings. "Listen, I can track you if I need to. Your phone's GPS is active, and I'm looking at it right now. You're at the Commerce Center."

Rowan paused on the third-floor landing. The hallway beyond the stairwell door stretched into darkness, lit only by the red exit signs and the faint glow from the windows at either end. "Then you know where to find me if this goes sideways."

"Rowan—"

"Third floor, northeast corner suite. Jenkins Municipal Consulting." Rowan's hand found the door handle. "Give me thirty minutes."

"Don't do anything stupid."

"Wouldn't dream of it."

The hallway, in the darkness, with only the exit signs for illumination, felt like a tomb.

Rowan moved past door after door—Sterling & Associates, Mountain West Development, Pioneer Realty Group. At the northeast corner, brass letters spelled out *Jenkins Municipal Consulting* beside a door of frosted glass that revealed lights burning in the office beyond.

Bingo.

Rowan reached for the door handle, then stopped.

He's desperate. And desperate men do terrible things.

Not a plea, but a warning, maybe.

He turned the handle, stepped into the reception area, and hit the deck.

The muzzle flash lit up the space like lightning, and the bullet meant for his heart only creased his upper arm.

Rowan rolled behind a leather sofa as another shot splintered the doorframe where his head had been. "Hey, *Dad*. We need to talk."

"Too late, kid." Alden's voice came from somewhere deeper in the office suite, probably from behind his massive oak desk. "You always were too stubborn to know when to walk away."

Blood seeped through Rowan's shirt where the bullet had scored his bicep. Didn't even feel it. "I'm not here to hurt you. I just want to talk."

Really. Because if Saxon had him lit up on GPS, so did the police. This didn't have to end with either of them in a body bag.

Another shot punched through the sofa's leather upholstery, sending stuffing floating through the air. Alden was moving.

"You should be grateful I took you and your mother in." Alden's voice had shifted to the left, probably near the windows. "I took care of you."

Now he was trying to egg Rowan on. Deep breath. No one gets hurt . . .

Rowan belly-crawled toward the reception desk, staying low as glass shattered somewhere behind him. "Is that what you call breaking a kid's ribs?"

He popped up from behind the desk, spotting Alden's silhouette against the window.

There you are.

He picked up a heavy glass paperweight and hurled it with deadly accuracy. It struck the window beside Alden's head, spider-webbing the glass and sending the older man scrambling for new cover.

"You were mouthy. No respect."

Rowan moved deeper into the office, using the maze of furniture and equipment to stay hidden. "So that's your excuse? Only cowards beat up on their kids."

"Coward?" Alden's laugh held no humor. "It took sacrifice and courage to build what I have."

"You mean what *I* have."

"No, son. That land is mine. You died. The deed has my name."

"I don't care about the land—"

"It belongs to me! Your dad promised *me* that land!"

Rowan froze. "What—"

"Your father is the liar here. He stole billions from me—or tried to."

"What are you talking about?" Rowan crawled over, behind a desk.

"Lithium deposits. Billions of dollars' worth, sitting right under that old house, that land. *My* land."

Rowan spotted him moving through the reflection of the front window. *You can run, but you can't hide, Buttercup.*

"We had a plan, him and me. We were friends. He had mineral surveys done, geological reports—he just needed the money to start mining. That's where I came in—we were *partners*!"

Rowan stilled. "No—that's not right—"

"And then he died. Stupid man."

Died. Wait. The pieces clicked into place with sickening clarity. "That's why you married my mom. Not for love. For the land."

"Your father cut me out. He never signed the partnership."

Rowan stilled.

Another shot rang out, this one aimed at the front glass.

It shattered, a waterfall of lethal shards. Rowan ducked behind a table.

"And then he died. And left you and your mom on all that land."

Rowan's voice came out deadly quiet. "How long did you wait? A week? A month?"

"She needed help. You both did. She was scared, alone, didn't know how she'd keep the ranch running." Alden seemed to believe his own righteousness. "I provided stability. Protection. A future for her and her son."

"You provided a nightmare." Rowan spotted movement near

the corner office and adjusted his position. "And you terrorized me so I would leave. Never come back."

"It worked."

Oh wow. It *had*.

Not today. Not anymore.

Rowan eased around a filing cabinet, getting closer to Alden's voice. "So what's next?"

A shot pinged the filing cabinet. How was he seeing him—

Oh. Cameras peered down at him in corners. The man probably had him on his phone, monitoring his movement.

Rowan picked up a stapler and took out the camera staring at him.

"Next is self-defense. The mayor defending himself against his crazy stepson, who possesses lethal skills. Probable cause, honest threat to life and limb. And not to mention him going a little crazy after watching his woman and child die."

He'd shimmied across the floor, rolled, spotted Alden squatting next to his desk.

The guy had a clear shot to the door, the hall, the stairway, with too much clutter between Rowan and the space to catch up.

If he didn't trip him up, Alden would get away.

He dove under a desk and spotted it—a long extension cord. He unplugged it and dragged it to himself.

Might work.

"Yeah, that sounds about right. All except the last part—Sierra and Huck are alive."

Silence.

"Shame. This is getting messy."

Breathe. Rowan made a loop, coiled it up, tried it out.

The throw fell short of the intended stapler, but with a little more wrist . . .

Alden stood up and pointed the gun. Probably to pin him down and make a run for it.

Now or never.

Rowan stood, swung the coil, once, twice, the shot pinging past him—

And threw.

Alden caught the loop and laughed, wrapping his wrist around the length. "What kind of stupid are you?"

This kind.

Rowan yanked, hard, and the movement caught Alden, threw him off-balance, tangled him into the desk enough for Rowan to charge. Alden stumbled forward and his shot went wild as Rowan tackled him around the waist.

Rowan drove them both into the windows that overlooked downtown Renegade.

The glass held, but the impact slammed the breath from Alden's lungs. Rowan grabbed his wrist and hammered it, once, twice against the glass. The pistol skittered across the floor.

Rowan kneed him, then sent his fist into the man's face.

Blood erupted in his destroyed nose.

It only incensed Alden. He slammed his fist into Rowan's gut, but yeah, not a problem. Tried it again, and Rowan grabbed him around the throat with one hand, deflected his arm with the other.

"You destroyed my family," Rowan snarled, pinning Alden against the window. "You terrorized my mother. You tried to *murder* my son."

"I made you strong," Alden gasped, clawing at Rowan's hand. "Everything you are, you owe to *me*."

"I owe you nothing."

Rowan's other hand found Alden's throat, and—oh, ending it would be so easy. One squeeze. One final payment for twenty years of debt.

"And what about Mack?" Alden wheezed. "What happens to my son when you murder his father?"

The words hit Rowan like cold water. Mack.

His half brother, who'd grown up believing Alden was a good man. Who'd defended him, protected him, loved him despite everything.

I won't hurt him. The promise he'd made.

Oops. Maybe he should amend that to . . . *I won't kill him.*

But even that . . . Because Alden's pale-blue eyes held no remorse, no recognition of the lives he'd destroyed. Only calculation, even now looking for an angle to exploit.

Rowan's grip tightened.

"Hammer." Saxon's voice cut through the red haze. "Breathe."

Rowan didn't turn, didn't release his hold on Alden's throat, but felt Saxon's presence as he came into the room—calm, steady, the voice of reason in a situation that had spiraled, yes, beyond his control.

"Does he deserve it?" Saxon asked quietly.

"Yes."

"But that's not your job." Saxon's footsteps moved closer. "Don't let your emotions win. This isn't a military op. You kill him and you destroy your future, and he wins."

Rowan's hands shook with the effort of restraint. Alden's face had turned gray, his hands losing their power.

"This is not your destiny," Saxon continued. "This is not what you were made for. Don't let anger win. Don't let it get a foothold and destroy everything you've found."

Sierra. Huck. The family he'd thought he'd lost forever. The future they could build together if he didn't throw it away on revenge.

Rowan released Alden's throat and stepped back, his chest heaving. Alden collapsed against the window, gasping for air.

"Smart choice," Saxon said, pulling flex-cuffs from his tactical belt. He swept Alden's feet out from under him, and the man slammed to the floor. He secured Alden's hands behind his back with practiced efficiency.

"When did you become so well-equipped for civilian law enforcement?" Rowan was still shaking.

"Three YouTube videos and a correspondence course." He hauled Alden to his feet. "Like I said, I'm very dedicated to my continuing education."

The sound of sirens rose from the street below.

"That would be Detective Martinelli's backup units that you ditched."

"Yeah, well, we needed to have a private conversation. You okay?"

"Scars are cool. Chicks dig 'em."

Rowan grinned as red and blue lights painted the windows in alternating patterns. A few moments later, the elevator dinged.

Rowan held up his hands, no gun, as SWAT poured in.

"You're destroying everything your father built," Alden snarled as Saxon handed him over to police custody.

Rowan met his stepfather's gaze one final time, seeing not the monster who'd haunted his childhood but a broken man whose greed had poisoned everything he touched.

"Actually," Rowan said quietly, "I'm saving it."

Sierra had spent ten years learning not to wait for ghosts, but tonight she sat on her grandfather's porch doing exactly that.

Here she was again. Waiting. Just like she'd waited for letters that never came, phone calls that never happened, promises that got buried in foreign soil. Except this time, she knew he was alive—somewhere out there, hunting the man who'd tried to destroy them.

But alive didn't mean safe. And safe didn't mean coming home.

Especially when Mike had left to answer a call downtown, something about Rowan and Alden and . . .

Please, Rowan. Come home.

She should go inside, get some sleep, stop acting like some tragic heroine in a romance novel. But what if he needed to see a light in the window? What if he needed to know someone was waiting? What if this time, waiting was actually an act of faith instead of foolishness?

The October night wrapped around her like an old, worn blanket, with the scent of woodsmoke drifting from distant chimneys. Stars blazed overhead in the clear mountain air, the Milky Way stretching across the darkness in a river of light. The porch light cast a warm golden circle around her, pushing back the shadows but not the silence.

Sierra pulled the quilt tighter around her shoulders—the one with the blue-and-white wedding ring pattern her grandmother had stitched forty years ago. The wooden porch swing creaked softly as she shifted her weight, the sound mixing with the distant lowing of cattle and the whisper of wind through the cottonwoods.

Her phone sat silent in her lap. No calls from Saxon. No updates from Mike. No word from Rowan since he'd disappeared into the night with murder in his eyes and justice on his mind.

The grandfather clock in the hallway chimed eleven times, each note echoing through the house like a countdown. How long did it take to confront a monster? How long to end a nightmare that had haunted him for years?

Her eyelids grew heavy despite her resolve to stay awake. The adrenaline from the kidnapping and fire was finally wearing off, leaving behind bone-deep exhaustion that made thinking coherent thoughts feel like swimming through honey.

Maybe she could close her eyes for just a moment . . .

My precious daughter.

The voice came from everywhere and nowhere, warm as summer sunshine and familiar as her own heartbeat. Sierra's eyes fluttered open, but the porch looked exactly the same—golden porch light, empty driveway, star-filled sky. Yet the presence beside her felt as real as the wooden swing beneath her.

"Grandpa?" Her voice came out small, uncertain.

You're not alone. The words settled over her like a blessing, carrying the scent of pipe tobacco and Old Spice aftershave that had always meant safety. *You've never been alone.*

Tears slipped down her cheeks as the familiar presence grew stronger, more comforting. "I'm scared. What if he doesn't come back? What if I lose him again?"

Yet I am always with you; you hold me by my right hand. You guide me with your counsel, and afterward you will take me into glory.

The psalm flowed over her, not in Grandpa's voice but somehow through it, as if he was simply the messenger for words that came from somewhere infinitely larger and more loving.

Whom have I in heaven but you? And earth has nothing I desire besides you. My flesh and my heart may fail, but God is the strength of my heart and my portion forever.

Yes. Peace flooded through Sierra's chest, washing away the terrible clench of her heart.

I love you, my precious daughter.

The words sank into her bones. Not just loved—cherished. Valued. Held close by hands that would never let go, never abandon, never fail.

Sierra's breathing deepened as peace settled upon her. *I trust You, Lord.*

The quilt rose and fell with her steady rhythm while stars wheeled overhead and the mountains stood sentinel in the darkness.

The sound of tires on gravel pulled her from sleep. She blinked awake to headlights sweeping across the yard as a truck pulled into the driveway. Sierra's heart hammered as she recognized the vehicle—Rowan's Ford, dented and dusty but unmistakably his.

The engine died. A door slammed. Boots crunched across gravel.

Rowan stepped into the porch light, and Sierra's breath caught in her throat. Blood stained his shirt and ran down his arm, dark patches that spoke of violence and pain. His face was streaked with dirt and exhaustion, his dark hair disheveled from whatever battle he'd fought.

But his eyes—his eyes found hers with the desperate hope, and a sort of peace.

He'd defeated the monster.

And maybe not just the one that lived next door.

"Sierra." Her name came out rough, broken, like he'd been holding his breath since he left and could finally exhale.

She launched herself off the swing and into his arms, the quilt falling forgotten to the porch floor. His embrace lifted her off her feet, spinning her around as if he needed to convince himself she was real, solid, here.

When he set her down, his hands framed her face. "It's over."

"You're bleeding." Sierra's fingers found the tear in his shirt sleeve where blood had dried in dark streaks.

"It's nothing." He caught her hands, stilling their worried exploration. "A scratch."

"Don't lie to me. Please."

"Fine. Alden shot at me. Bullet grazed my arm." Rowan's thumb traced her cheekbone. "But I'm here. I'm whole. And he's in custody."

"You caught him?"

"Saxon helped. Stopped me from doing something we'd both regret." Rowan's eyes grew distant for a moment. "Turns out he married my mother to get control of the land."

"The mineral deposits."

"Lithium. Billions of dollars' worth, sitting under our ranch." Rowan's mouth twisted. "He's been quietly sabotaging landowners and buying up land under shell corporations and fake names for years. Saxon did some digging—Alden Jenkins is on the board of Meridian Holdings. And one of the anonymous investors in Rocky Mountain Land Development."

Sierra pressed her forehead against his chest, breathing in the scent of smoke and sweat and the indefinable something that was purely him. "It's over?"

"It's over." His arms tightened around her. "Detective Martinelli has enough evidence to put him away for life."

"And us?" The question slipped out before she could stop it. "What about us?"

Rowan pulled back to look at her, his blue eyes serious. "I love you, Sierra. I've loved you since we were kids, and I'll love you when we're both old and gray and sitting on this same porch, watching our grandchildren play in the yard."

"Our grandchildren?" Laughter bubbled up from her chest, bright and breathless. "Aren't we getting a little ahead of ourselves?"

"Maybe. But I've wasted ten years, and I don't want to waste any more time pretending I can live without you." His voice dropped to a whisper. "Marry me."

The words hung in the October air between them, simple and profound and everything she'd dreamed of hearing since she was eighteen years old.

"Rowan—"

He silenced her with a kiss that tasted like promises and homecoming and forever. His mouth moved over hers with desperate hunger. Sierra melted against him, her hands fisting in his shirt as he backed her against the porch post. His hand tangled in her hair as she arched against him.

Oh, he could make her lose herself again.

Happily.

Forever.

"We should go inside," Sierra whispered when they finally broke apart. "You need food, a shower, medical attention for that arm."

"I need you." His voice was rough with want and exhaustion.

"Inside." She took his hand, leading him toward the front door. "Where it's warm and private and Huck won't wake up to find us making out on the porch."

He laughed. "You do know that someday he's going to find out that . . ."

"What?"

"Well, that I'm staying. And that he'll probably end up with a brother or sister."

He had come into the house and now put his hands on her hips. She hung her arms around his neck. Met his eyes.

Oh, she had words inside her. Invitation.

And his gaze in hers contained a hunger that made her breath catch.

"But . . ." he said softly, "I want to do this right. All of it. The proposal, the wedding, the life we build together."

"What are you saying?"

"I'm saying soon. Very soon, I'm not going to stand in this hallway." He pulled her close enough that she could feel the heat radiating from his body. "But tonight, I'm not the renegade who sneaks you into the barn and leaves you with a broken heart. That man's gone."

"Tamed?"

He raised an eyebrow. "Don't get crazy. But maybe a little." His voice gentled. "I want us to have everything we should have had ten years ago. So, we're going to do this right."

"Rowan—"

He kissed her forehead, gentle and reverent. "Good night, sweetheart."

Before she could protest, he put her away from him and headed down the hallway.

"What about your medical attention?"

"Go to bed, S." He stood at his doorway. "Now."

She laughed, and the guest room door closed.

In a moment, the shower turned on.

Sierra headed upstairs, pressing her hands to her flushed cheeks. Ten years of waiting, and now he wanted to court her properly. She should be touched by his restraint, his desire to do things right.

Instead, she was pretty sure she was going to die of anticipation.

The bulldozer's rumble pulled Sierra from the deepest sleep she'd had in months. Sunlight streamed through her bedroom windows, painting everything in golden warmth that spoke of a perfect October morning. The sound of voices carried from the yard, mixing with the distant lowing of cattle and what sounded like construction equipment.

Sierra grabbed her robe and padded to the window, pushing back the cream curtains to peer down at her yard.

Her breath caught.

The entire front yard teemed with people. A bulldozer was methodically clearing away the charred remains of her barn while trucks delivered stacks of lumber and building supplies. Men in work clothes moved with purpose, some operating equipment while others sorted materials.

What looked like blueprints spread across sawhorses.

And there, in the middle of it all, stood Rowan. And Huck.

Her son held a dog biscuit and now crouched and balanced it on Bandit's nose while the Jack Russell terrier sat perfectly still, his whole body quivering with the effort of restraint.

Huck held up a hand, as if to say *Stay*.

Bandit held his position.

Then Huck stood and snapped his fingers.

The dog flipped the biscuit into the air and caught it with perfect precision, tail wagging triumphantly. Huck whooped and threw his arms around Bandit's neck while Rowan's laughter rang out across the construction chaos.

Her heart, oh, her heart.

She just. Couldn't. Breathe.

This. This was joy.

She threw on jeans and a flannel shirt, pulling her hair into a ponytail as she hurried downstairs. The kitchen smelled like coffee and bacon, and she could see Bailey through the window, manning a folding table loaded with food while other women organized what looked like enough breakfast to feed an army.

"Well, good morning, sunshine." Saxon appeared in her kitchen doorway, holding a steaming mug. "Sleep well? It's nearly nine a.m."

"What is all this?" Sierra gestured toward the window where the organized chaos continued.

"Community barn raising. Old-fashioned tradition." Saxon's eyes shone. "Your boyfriend has some serious organizational skills. Had this whole operation planned and coordinated before you woke up."

"How is that possible?"

"He's been up since five, making calls and arranging deliveries." Saxon took a sip of coffee. "Turns out when you save a town from a criminal conspiracy, people are pretty eager to help with construction projects. Even on a Sunday."

Sierra stepped onto the back porch. She recognized faces from church, from the rodeo, from years of living in a small community where everyone knew everyone else's business.

Dolly directed the food station with military efficiency, her graying hair covered by a bandanna as she kept coffee flowing and plates full. Bailey waved from behind a table loaded with egg sandwiches and homemade cookies.

Mike stood at a cement mixer, with a shovel.

And there was Mack, working alongside other young men to frame what would become the new barn's foundation. His presence here, helping rebuild, spoke of healing that went deeper than construction.

"Mom!" Huck's voice cut through the morning air as he spotted her on the porch. He bounded over with Bandit at his heels, both of them radiating excitement.

"Look at all these people! They're building us a new barn!" Huck's words tumbled over each other in his rush to share the morning's wonders.

"I see that." Sierra ruffled his hair, her throat tight with emotion. "Pretty amazing, isn't it?"

"The best. And Dad says maybe we can build a bigger stall for Jasper, and maybe get another horse, and maybe—"

"Maybe you should let your mom have some coffee before planning the entire ranch expansion," Rowan's voice interrupted, warm with amusement.

Sierra looked up to find him approaching, sawdust in his hair and a satisfied smile on his face. He looked completely at home directing the organized chaos, every inch the natural leader who could coordinate complex operations and make them look effortless.

Of course he was. He was still Hammer, former Delta Force operator, somewhere under all that cowboy.

"Morning, beautiful." He leaned down to kiss her cheek, the casual intimacy of the gesture turning her warm to her bones.

"You did all this?" Sierra gestured toward the bustling activity.

"We did this." Rowan's hand found the small of her back, steering her toward the porch railing, where they could survey the work. "Amazing what people will do when they're grateful."

"But how—"

"Actually, I started it a few days ago. The blueprints are from that barn at the Collins place—and I got Bobby St. Claire to clear the permitting, and Raol Martinez hooked me up with the lumber. Saxon talked Dolly into the food, and Bailey showed up to help. Apparently she, um, knew some secrets?" He raised an eyebrow.

Oops.

He grinned. "Turns out Mike Martinelli knows every contractor in three counties, and Bailey has the phone numbers of every ranch family between here and Denver." Rowan's eyes crinkled with satisfaction. "Plus, Saxon has surprising logistic skills for a private investigator."

"I heard that," Saxon called from across the yard. "And I'm going to need more coffee if we're going to keep this pace up."

"There's a whole pot in the kitchen," Sierra called back.

"Already tried it. It's not strong enough. I need the industrial-grade stuff Dolly makes."

She laughed, then turned to him. "How are we affording this? I haven't gotten my insurance check yet."

"Babe. Have you not heard? I'm rich." He grinned.

Then, Rowan perched a hand over her head. "I figure we needed to get started on that barn if we are going to make any more of those."

His gaze shifted meaningfully toward Huck, who was demonstrating Bandit's trick to a group of appreciative teenagers.

Sierra's pulse quickened at the implication. "More of . . . ?"

"Children. Lots of them. Running around this ranch, learning to ride and rope and carry on the family traditions." Rowan's voice dropped to a whisper. "What do you think?"

"I think there are better places than the barn for making children."

"Me too." His mouth moved closer to hers, close enough that she could feel his breath against her lips. "You still haven't said yes."

Oh. She put a hand on his chest. "Yes, Rowan Sean Wallace. I'll marry you."

"Attagirl," he growled and leaned in.

"I still need coffee!" Saxon's voice cut through the moment. "Real coffee! The kind that can wake the dead!"

"And I'm going to need you to back off," Rowan called without taking his eyes off Sierra.

But Sierra was laughing, the sound bright and free as it carried across the yard. She put her hand on Rowan's amazing, perfect chest and pushed him away.

"I'll make a fresh pot," Sierra called to Saxon. "Dolly style."

"Good!" Saxon called. "I have a feeling this is going to be a long day."

Sierra headed for the kitchen, but paused at the door to look back at the scene unfolding in her yard.

Rowan was crouched beside Huck again, both of them laughing as Bandit performed his trick for an audience of construction workers.

Mack hammered nails with steady precision while Mike scooped out cement. Dolly organized food with the efficiency of someone who'd been feeding crowds her entire life.

Her ranch. Her community. Her family.

Sierra wasn't alone anymore. She never had been, really—she'd just been too scared to believe it.

She had her men—both of them, the boy she'd raised and the renegade man who'd come home to claim them both.

The love that surrounded her wasn't fragile or temporary.

And outside her window, the sky stretched out over the city of Renegade, bright and wide with possibility.

THANK YOU!

Thank you so much for reading *Renegade*. We hope you enjoyed the story. If you did, would you be willing to do us a favor and leave a review? It doesn't have to be long—just a few words to help other readers know what they're getting. (But no spoilers! We don't want to wreck the fun!) Thank you again for reading!

We'd love to hear from you- not only about this story, but about any characters or stories you'd like to read in the future. Contact us at www.sunrisepublishing.com/contact.

Don't miss what happens next with the Heroes of Renegade in *Warrior*!

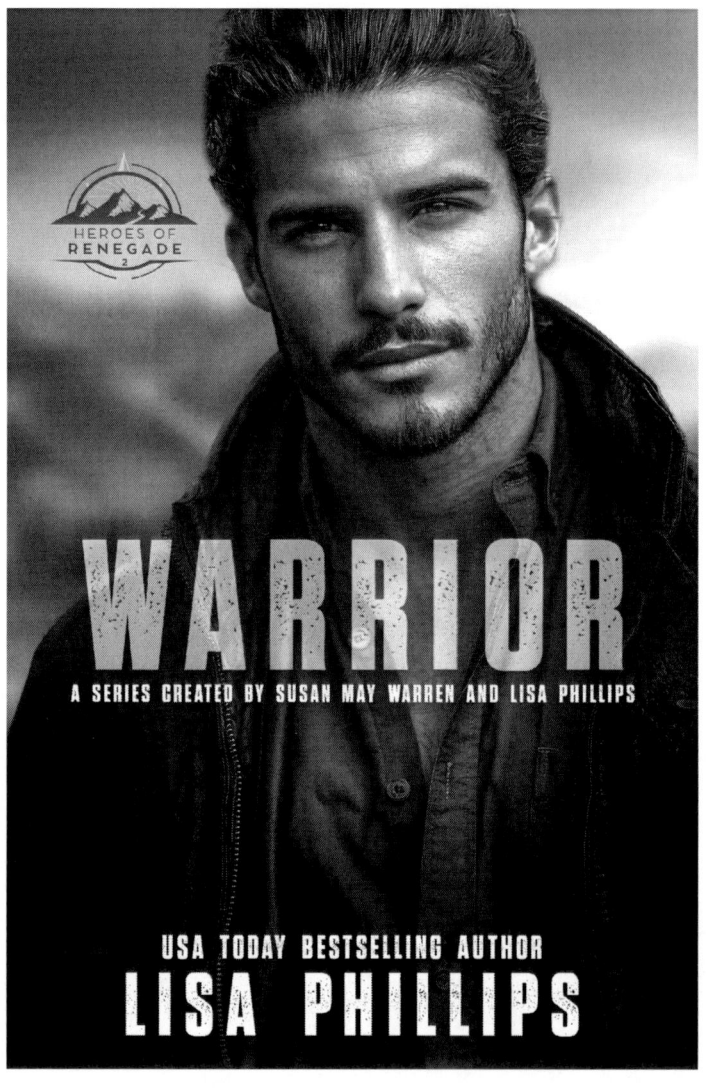

Some rescues require more than medical training. Some battles are worth the risk.

The last person Dr. Kira Yassan expects to walk back into her life is the soldier whose life she saved in a war zone three years ago.

She came to Renegade, Colorado to disappear—to work her ER shifts and forget the classified missions that nearly destroyed her soul. But when US Marshals drag her into a witness protection case, every carefully built wall comes crashing down.

Private investigator Luca Saxon thought the mysterious doctor who patched him up in Syria was just a beautiful memory. Now she's standing in front of him, and the chemistry that burned between them in that refugee camp hasn't dimmed. But someone wants their witness dead, and keeping Kira safe might cost him everything.

When cartel enforcers storm the hospital and prison riots explode across town, ther's nowhere left to run.

Their witness is Francisco Abalos—former cartel kingpin with secrets that could topple governments. The shadow syndicate controlling Renegade wants him silenced. And Kira's medical expertise makes her the perfect target.

From midnight shootouts to explosive prison breaks, Luca and Kira race against time to expose a conspiracy that reaches into the highest levels of their small town. But as buried secrets surface and old enemies emerge, they must decide: Can love survive when trust becomes a weapon?

ONE

Northern Syria

LUCA SAXON HAD BEEN BORN IN THIS DIRT. IT stood to reason he was going to die here as well.

His back hit the ground, and he rolled. Sand and dust coated everything. He coughed against the wave of grit but was unable to hear it over the sound of his ears ringing. Someone pulled him up roughly, lifting him by his vest to his feet.

The bearded face of his sergeant swam in front of him. Luca watched Hammer's lips form the words *not today*.

Luca could barely breathe, but he coughed out the words, repeating them back to his team leader. "Not today."

Hammer slapped the back of his shoulder, and they were on the move, weaving through rows of white tents while the oppressive July sun beat down on them. Away from the tent that was in flames and what remained of the camp stove, nothing but charred debris now. All thanks to a member of an ISIS sleeper cell working in this forsaken part of the world.

A woman hurried past them in a black niqab, completely covered except for the slit of her eyes. Clinging to her hand was a little boy who couldn't be more than six years old. Both of them needed a full meal and a peaceful night of sleep—neither of which were commodities that could be easily obtained in the back alleys of this refugee camp.

The comms earbud in one ear hummed to life. "Trigger One, this is Trigger Three. I have visual."

Sweet. Kane, a member of their team and one of Saxon's best friends, had the suspect in sight. But this was far from over. They needed to get their hands on Namir Hassan Al-Hijazi, fleeing through the camp up ahead, before the ISIS terror cell members that remained after last night's raid caught him first. Namir needed to be in prison for what he'd done, betraying those Marines for such a deadly cause. And while he was at least partially responsible for the death of six US soldiers, he had also stolen sensitive information that was now on a flash drive in his pocket.

Not only could they not lose Namir, but they also couldn't afford to lose the information he carried.

Running full speed ahead of Saxon, Hammer called on the radio. "Trigger Three, give me his twenty. Over."

Kane responded, "Three rows west of the medical tent."

Saxon could see the Red Cross flag flying high in the center of the refugee camp and made a beeline toward it, catching up to Hammer so they were almost side by side. His buddy glanced over and grinned, as if this was just your average footrace through a war-torn country.

Up ahead, in the direction they were going, gunshots rang out. Someone screamed. Answering gunfire sounded across the open air.

"We've got company," Elias said over the radio. The fourth man of their team, Redding, wasn't someone Saxon would have called a friend. The guy was too edgy for his taste. But the US Army had seen fit to put them together on a team. Considering how well he liked Hammer and Kane, Saxon wasn't going to complain about one team member.

Hammer raced around the corner of the next tent, almost colliding with an armed insurgent. The two faced off against each other for a second before the other man slammed into the Delta Force team leader. They hit the ground in a cloud of dust.

Another man stepped between two tents about twenty feet up the row.

Saxon lifted his rifle and squeezed the trigger for a split second. But it was too late. The man's gun fired, and the bullet slammed into the left side of Saxon's arm. Tearing through flesh with heat and pain.

He cried out, almost going down, but managed to keep his wits about him. He aimed again with the rifle and squeezed off another grouping of shots. His left arm hung loose by his side, trickling blood down to his elbow.

The man collapsed to the ground in a pool of regret and bad choices.

Saxon turned to Hammer. The sergeant was on his feet now, blood running from a cut on his temple, his gun aimed at the man on the ground. The insurgent looked at Saxon, fully aware of what was about to happen.

He said the word *brother* in Arabic. More of a question than anything else.

"I'm not your brother," Saxon replied in the same language, turning away so he could go and help Kane and Elias.

The shot exploded behind him, and a second later, Hammer caught up. "You need to get that arm looked at."

Saxon wouldn't have said he did, except that now Hammer pointed it out, the whole thing started to throb. "Let's secure Namir and I'll put some cream on it or something."

Hammer snorted. "I will make it an order."

"Did you get a picture of that guy?" They were supposed to photograph everyone they killed. With most of them being high-value targets, the higher-ups always wanted proof when a target was taken out.

"I recognized him from the briefing. Last year the guy blew up a home for orphans about a hundred miles east of here."

Up ahead, the gunfire had eased off. Which could mean good or bad things for Kane.

"This is a lot of fuss just for a flash drive." Saxon checked around the next corner. The opening of the tent flapped in the nonexistent breeze. The scent of curry spices hung in the air with a current of charred wood and the smell of too many bodies packed together with poor hygiene conditions.

His head swam, the heat beading drops of sweat across his forehead. He lifted a hand and swiped at his skin.

The world seemed to shift around him. Blood coated his fingers where it had dripped all the way down from the outside of his arm. He moved his fingers on that hand against one another, rubbing his thumb across his fingertips. Smearing the blood.

Hammer grabbed his elbow. "Easy."

Kane's voice came over the radio. "Package secure."

"Meet us at the medical tent. Saxon needs a bandage." Hammer's arm snaked around his waist, and his buddy walked him under the flap of the tent. A long room flanked with medical beds on either side. Equipment seemed too sparse in here, except where crates had been stacked in one corner.

He didn't need a hospital.

"Just put . . ." The name of the bandage eluded him. Saxon couldn't string two thoughts together. "The thing on it. Let's go."

They had something with them that would go over his wound and stop the bleeding. At least long enough so they could get back to the rendezvous point and get picked up. There was a packet of it in the right thigh pocket of his cargos. He reached down and patted it.

Hammer grunted. "And I went to the trouble of bringing you all the way to the finest hospital in Syria."

A woman in a white lab coat over blue scrubs came over, her hair covered with a blue scarf. She had dark eyes that were like huge midnight pools trying to suck him under the surface. He tried to blink or look away, but she drew him. She said something, but he couldn't make out the words that seemed to swim around him.

Hammer walked to the bed she indicated and dumped Saxon down on his back.

He hissed out a breath between clenched teeth and tried to focus on the woman, because she was the best-looking thing in this place. Like a single flower in a garden that was nothing but neglected shrubs and trampled bushes. One of those plants that only bloomed at night.

Hammer leaned over him. "You're going to wanna stop talking, buddy."

Great. Whatever he'd been thinking just now, he'd apparently been saying it out loud as well. The doctor lady tapped a syringe, then stuck the needle into the outside of his arm.

Saxon hissed out another breath.

She patted his chest. "Just a few minutes and you'll be good to go."

He couldn't look away. "Does it cost extra for the express service?"

She smiled at him, and so many things in his life seemed to fall into place. "Only because you showed up in the middle of a malaria outbreak and I need to get back to treating patients. Not because you're the only Americans in the place." She spoke with a crisp British accent that made him want to ask her what her favorite kind of tea was.

A commotion over by the entrance to the tent drew his attention.

He could feel her begin to irrigate the wound on the outside of his arm. *Ouch.*

He attempted to pay more attention to Kane and Elias striding down the center aisle of the hospital tent with dark looks on their faces, coming over to where Hammer stood at the end of the bed.

Elias had dirt smeared across his forehead and the side of his head, and Kane had grazes on the knuckles of his left hand.

"Tell me, Doc . . ." Kane clasped Saxon's hand and pushed something small and made of hard plastic between their palms. When Kane pulled his hand away, Saxon closed his fingers around the flash drive. "Are you going to be able to reattach his brain?"

Saxon snorted. "Even if she doesn't, I'll still be smarter than you."

Behind Kane, Elias and Hammer spoke in low tones too quiet for him to hear. Saxon slipped the flash drive into his pants pocket.

The doctor said, "If you're going to demand the express service, it requires minimal questions."

Kane stared at the woman like he'd fallen in love. Saxon cleared his throat, and Kane looked down at him.

"Understood." Kane replied to the woman's comment, but Saxon knew it was meant for him. As usual, they were on the same page.

Saxon wasn't here to find the love of his life. But if she was going to show up suddenly, he wouldn't argue.

Saxon said, "Get lost."

Kane grinned. "Don't worry, you'll live. After all, only the good die young." He turned and wandered back to the huddle of Hammer and Elias. Whatever had happened with Namir, it seemed they had the flash drive but not the man himself. Had he escaped?

Saxon didn't like the sound of that, with members of the terror cells still scouring the refugee camp, looking for all of them. The bad guys were trying to take out Namir before the Delta Force team could grab the guy and drag both him and his information out of here.

"I won't bother asking if you're US military." The doctor's dark eyebrows drew together, all her attention on the stitches she was putting in the outside of his arm. "Or what you're doing here."

"Good call. I'm Luca." Saxon studied her Middle Eastern features and the casual adherence to cultural strictures. "British?"

She nodded. "Born in Iran, raised in England. Harvard Medical School, then straight to the Red Cross. I'm Kira Yassan."

Nice to meet you sounded so lame. "That's an impressive résumé."

"You haven't even seen what I can do with phyllo pastry." She looked up for a second and winked at him.

Saxon pretty much fell in love right at that moment.

Hammer wandered over and said, "We're going to do a quick sweep. Try to find him." He squeezed Saxon's shoulder. "We'll be back in less than twenty minutes."

When Hammer got that look in his eye, there was no point arguing with him.

"Understood."

They were leaving the flash drive in his safekeeping and giving it one more shot to locate Namir. Saxon didn't have any choice but to comply—at least, not until Dr. Kira Yassan finished stitching him up.

He glanced at her, about to say something corny like *Do you come here often?* Figure out how to maybe email her or something later. Get to know each other and see what happened after.

Except, when did that ever develop into something solid for a guy like him?

She snipped the edge of the thread with a pair of scissors. "Stitches are all done. I'm going to cover it with a bandage."

He glanced at the front entrance to the tent, but his teammates had already left without him.

"The drug that I put in that syringe is going to knock you out for a couple of minutes." She taped down the bandage. "I'm surprised you're still awake. But you'll be all set to go just as soon as you wake up."

Saxon started to argue, but everything around him sucked down into darkness, and he passed out.

———————

Dr. Kira Yassan watched Luca's eyes roll back in his head. It really was easier this way. Apart from the fact that he seemed like a nice guy and he might actually be attracted to her, it was best that he passed out. Attraction wasn't something that happened often in her world.

Actually, maybe that made this whole situation worse.

She glanced around to make sure no one else on the medical staff team was watching, then reached over and pulled out the flash drive that she'd seen him tuck into his pocket. The one his friend passed to him. The reason they were here, most likely, given how he'd safeguarded it.

She'd known what she had to do the moment she saw it. There would be just enough time before he woke up and his teammates returned. She needed to make a copy of the flash drive on her computer and then return the storage device to his pocket.

Kira ducked into the back, where a tall curtain that hung from a frame covered the area in the rear of the tent from view of the main room. Back here, it was occasionally necessary to perform surgery on a patient or deliver a baby. That or a hundred other things that occurred when people lived in such close proximity in horrible conditions.

Maybe she was growing jaded.

Kira sat on the stool and scooted up to her laptop, inserting the flash drive into the port on the side. Passing along whatever was on this storage device had to earn her some credit with the government. After the high-value target the Brits had been after had passed away on her operating table, they hadn't been entirely pleased with losing their shot at intelligence. Whatever the Americans were after with this thing, it had to be valuable enough for them to risk their lives to obtain it and the person who'd been carrying it.

She tapped her foot on the groundsheet tarp under her sneaker while the files transferred. Didn't look at the framed photo of her at age nine with her parents on holiday in Egypt. She'd been so excited to see the pyramids, and in the months before they went, she'd read everything she could get her hands on about pharaohs.

In the end, it was the last time they'd ever had fun together as a family.

She leaned back on the stool and looked out at the soldier. He really was a good-looking guy. Middle Eastern like her, but she'd guess from his features that he was Syrian. How a man like him ended up in the US Army—or whatever branch of the American military he was in—she couldn't even fathom. So many who lived here would consider that a betrayal of all they stood for.

Luca Saxon.

He'd been self-assured enough that she knew he didn't consider the life he lived as a betrayal of anything. More likely, Luca was one of those hero types who thought every mission was to right all the wrongs in the world and restore the balance of justice.

As if that was how the world worked.

Still, she had to admit that, without people like him, the world would be a pretty sorry place.

"Dr. Yassan?" Simon, one of their nurses who was originally from Australia, stuck his head around the curtain.

Kira tried to pretend he hadn't startled her out of her skin. "What is it?"

"Dr. Chen is bringing in a family. All of them have fevers and nausea."

"I'll be right there." She checked the file transfer and saw it was complete, copied the files to a password-protected drive that only belonged to her, and attached everything to an email she left in her draft folder.

Kira pulled out the flash drive, then tucked it into her pocket, leaving the surgical area and stepping back into the main room. Luca was still unconscious, this soldier with his ropey arms and thick chest. Dark hair that was short and fell over his forehead in a way that begged her to brush it back and made her wonder what it would look like long and in need of cutting.

As if her life would ever be conducive to a relationship. But then, that was the entire point of being here. Because it was as far from the person she had been in the Western world as she could get. Out here in the forgotten places of the world, giving all her sweat and tears to people that no one else seemed to care about.

She pretended to adjust his bandage, then wandered around the bed so she would be close to his pocket in order to return the flash drive. She glanced around again, ensuring no one was watching her, and slipped the flash drive back into the folds of his dark cargos.

His hand whipped up and grasped her wrist. Those strong fingers squeezed the fine bones in her hand. "Who do you work for?"

She loosened her grip on the flash drive, moving her hand away from his pocket. He didn't let go of her wrist. Those dark eyes of his bored into her. She wanted to tell him everything. Just open her mouth and unburden her soul on someone—anyone. But he wouldn't understand.

"Answer the question."

"I'm not your enemy." She forced the words from her mouth, trying to figure out how to explain this without incriminating herself.

His dark gaze assessed her, just a hint of betrayal in his eyes. And why would that be? They didn't even know each other. They wouldn't ever see each other again.

"Saxon!" Someone called out from by the entrance.

The other three men on his team rushed into the tent, moving fast. The one in front with the light-brown beard covering the bottom half of his face came first. The leader of this team. "Gotta go, we have incoming."

The man's gaze swept across Saxon holding her wrist.

A second later, she had been released. Saxon sat up on the bed and swung his boots onto the floor. She wanted to step forward, help him steady himself as he stood. He'd lost a lot of blood and hadn't eaten anything. But instead of supporting him, she folded her arms across her chest. She had what she wanted, and now it was time for him to leave.

Outside the front entrance of the tent, gunfire sounded in quick succession.

All four of the men shifted, a deadly intention overwhelming their body language.

"We can't get out that way," one of the men said. "They'll kill us before we even step into the light."

Kira cleared her throat. "You can leave out the back, if you want."

Her patient turned to her. "And walk right into unfriendly fire?"

"I told you I wasn't your enemy." She lifted her hands, palms up, and then let them fall back to her sides. "I'm just a doctor."

Saxon's gaze narrowed, the skin around his eyes contracting. "You can't expect me to believe that."

"I don't think you have time for anything else." Kira lifted her chin.

The team leader tugged on Saxon's good arm. "Let's go."

He clearly didn't want to, but he complied with the instruction from his boss. The group of four men moved to the rear of the tent, where they would find the back exit. He didn't even look back. None of them did.

A second after they disappeared behind the curtain, two men

strode into the medical tent. Rifles across their bodies and sweat-soaked hair on their foreheads. She knew the type. Had seen them in the shadows every day since she got here. The kind of men who showed up when danger happened and capitalized on the suffering of others.

She crossed to the center aisle and stood in their path, her palms raised as she had done with Saxon. But this time Kira was certain her life was in danger. She used the language her father had taught her, speaking in their native Arabic. "This is a place of healing. You are not welcome here."

The man on the right, the older of the two, though not by much, replied in the same language, "We go where we please. The will of God Almighty will be done in this place, as it will be done everywhere in the coming days."

Now there was a terrifying thought. Was this all about some impending attack? She would have to ask her contact at MI6 if they'd heard anything.

"What do you want?" She needed to delay them as long as possible, giving that American team as much of a head start as possible. "You cannot steal our supplies. There are people here in need."

"We do not want the kind of hope you offer, that only weak people are willing to accept. Our cause is just. We will kill the infidels who invade our country."

And they'd do it caring nothing for the people in their way. Innocents they viewed as nothing but collateral damage.

"There haven't been any of those people in here." She shook her head, playing the dumb female they considered her to be—or someone with too much to lose if she spoke the truth.

But what did she have to lose? Everything she valued was on her person. There was nothing for her anywhere else in the world other than here.

The thought struck her with something a lot like grief. But it was the loss of something she'd never had.

A dream she had long since given up on.

"I have patients coming in who need to be treated. You both need to leave." She squared her shoulders and lifted her chin.

The older of the two muttered something that would have made her gasp if she wasn't already on high alert. She couldn't give away that she was anything more than a doctor in a war-torn country.

He crossed the space between them in a second and brought his gun down on her temple. She swung her arm up to block the blow, but it was far too late to do anything about it. Pain exploded in her skull, and she started to collapse.

A gunshot went off inside the tent, so loud it sounded like fireworks. The pain felt like it was fracturing her head, but she couldn't get up.

The man who struck her fell to the ground, his lifeless eyes staring at her from where he had slumped. His friend turned and didn't even take one step before more bullets slammed into his back. He tripped and landed on the ground.

Someone in the tent started screaming, the sound far too close to her splitting head.

Kira was rolled to her back. She tried to focus on the person over her and managed to discern Simon's features. Saxon knelt on the other side of her. Both of them stared at her with similar expressions on their faces.

"That looks bad." Saxon glanced at Simon.

The nurse palpated the edges of the wound on her forehead. Kira screamed at the pain that whipped around inside her head. "It's bad," Simon said. "And our X-ray machine is on the fritz. I'll have to call for a medevac chopper to take her to the hospital."

She felt moisture run from the corners of her eyes.

"Sax, we have to go. There's a change of plans." The other man came over, his face swimming into view. "That was a brave thing you did."

"More like stupid."

"Sometimes those two things look the same." The team leader grasped the collar of Saxon's bulletproof vest and tugged. "Come on. Time to go."

"Not until I know she's going to be okay." He was tugged all the way to his feet, whether he liked it or not.

The team leader said, "Right now, we have to go save someone else's life. Someone who doesn't have a medevac chopper coming for her."

Saxon knelt again quickly. "I'm sorry you got hurt."

Kira tried to think past the pain.

Strong fingers squeezed her hand, and then he was gone.

ACKNOWLEDGMENTS

My heart is so full knowing you've experienced Rowan and Sierra's story! From burning barns to midnight rescues, watching our wounded warrior and fierce rancher find love in the midst of danger has been such a joy to write.

We have more thrilling books coming to wrap up this adventure-packed series! We're just getting started with The Brave: Heroes of Renegade series, and I know you'll love each of these amazing books!

If you found yourself holding your breath through Rowan and Sierra's journey from heartbreak to healing, would you consider sharing your thoughts in a review? Even a tiny note helps other readers discover their story (though maybe keep those sneaky mayor surprises our little secret!).

I'm blessed beyond measure by my amazing team. To my brilliant editors, Lindsay Harrel and Kristyn Fortner—you always know exactly how to make these adventures sparkle and shine.

Special thanks to my incredible co-creator and lead author of this series, Lisa Phillips—your vision and partnership have made this world come alive in ways I never imagined possible!

A huge hug to my incredible Marketing Director Rel Mollet—you're like a magical organizing fairy who keeps everything running smoothly. I honestly don't know what I'd do without your amazing attention to detail!

Big love to Sarah Erredge for creating such gorgeous, exciting covers, and to Tari Faris for making the insides just as beautiful.

Katie Donovan, you're a proofreading superhero, especially when deadlines are breathing down our necks!

To my dear readers—you make all of this possible. Thank you for bringing these adventures into your hearts and homes. I'd love to hear your thoughts at susan@sunrisepublishing.com

USA Today bestselling, RITA, Christy, and Carol award-winning novelist Susan May Warren is the author of over 100 novels with nearly 2 million books sold, most of them contemporary romance with a touch of suspense. One of her strongest selling series has been the Deep Haven series, a collection of books set in Northern Minnesota, off the shore of Lake Superior.

Visit her at www.susanmaywarren.com.

With books translated into eight languages, many of her novels have been ECPA and CBA bestsellers, were chosen as Top Picks by Romantic Times, and have won the RWA's Inspirational Reader's Choice contest and the American Christian Fiction Writers Book of the Year award. She's a three-time RITA finalist and an eight-time Christy finalist.

Publishers Weekly has written of her books, "Warren lays bare her characters' human frailties, including fear, grief, and resentment, as openly as she details their virtues of love, devotion, and resiliency. She has crafted an engaging tale of romance, rivalry, and the power of forgiveness." Library Journal adds, "Warren's characters are well-developed and she knows how to create a first rate contemporary romance..."

Susan is also a nationally acclaimed writing coach, teaching at conferences around the nation, and winner of the 2009 American Christian Fiction Writers Mentor of the Year award. She loves to help people launch their writing careers. She is the founder of www.MyBookTherapy.com and www.learnhowtowriteanovel. com, a writing website that helps authors get published and stay published. She is also the author of the popular writing method The Story Equation.

Find excerpts, reviews, and a printable list of her novels at www. susanmaywarren.com and connect with her on social media.

HEROES OF RENEGADE

Another epic series created by

SUSAN MAY WARREN
and LISA PHILLIPS

SUNRISE PUBLISHING

We solve the problem of what to read next.

LAST CHANCE
FIRE AND RESCUE

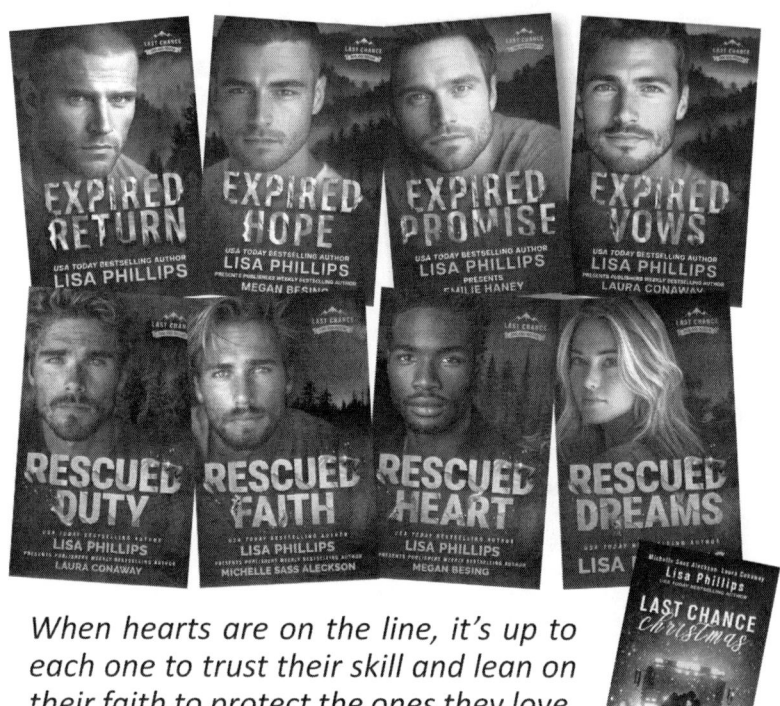

When hearts are on the line, it's up to each one to trust their skill and lean on their faith to protect the ones they love. Before it all goes down in flames.

USA Today Bestselling Author
LISA PHILLIPS

with **LAURA CONAWAY**, **MEGAN BESING** and **MICHELLE SASS ALECKSON**

We solve the problem of what to read next.

WE THINK YOU'LL ALSO LOVE...

Infiltrating a dangerous militia to save her troubled brother, Jamie Winters finds herself kidnapped. Only Logan Crawford, the man she once broke, can rescue her—but he demands a promise in return. As they navigate peril in the Alaskan wilderness, their unresolved feelings spark a chance for love and redemption.

Burning Hearts by Lisa Phillips

Stunt double Vienna Foxcroft's stunt team are the only ones she trusts. Then in walks Sergeant Crew Gatlin and his tough-as-nails military dog, Havoc. When an attack on a film set sends them fleeing into the streets of Turkey, Vienna must face the demons of her past or be devoured by them. And Crew and Havoc will be tested like never before.

Havoc by Ronie Kendig

When an attempt is made on Grey Parker's life and dead bodies begin piling up, suddenly bodyguard Christina Sherman is tasked with keeping both a soldier and his dog safe... and with them, the secrets that could stop a terrorist attack.

Driving Force by Lynette Eason and Kate Angelo

SUNRISE PUBLISHING

We solve the problem of what to read next.

SUNRISE PUBLISHING

**WHERE EVERY STORY IS A FRIEND,
AND EVERY CHAPTER IS A NEW JOURNEY...**

Subscribe to our newsletter for a free book, the latest news, weekly giveaways, exclusive author interviews, and more!

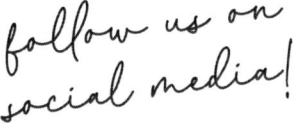 follow us on social media!

 @sunrisemediagroup

 @sunrisepublish

 @sunrisepublishing

Manufactured by Amazon.ca
Acheson, AB

33669438R00192